HAWK'S BREW

HAWK'S BREW

Viking Saga, Book 2

GARY DOC NELSON

Waterside Productions

Printed in the United States of America

First Printing, 2021

ISBN-13: 978-1-951805-94-4 print edition
ISBN-13: 978-1-951805-95-1 ebook edition

Waterside Productions
2055 Oxford Ave
Cardiff, CA 92007
www.waterside.com

*For my friend and mentor, the real Dr. Charlie Tobin,
who set me on the right path.*

TABLE OF CONTENTS

PROLOGUE

THE BEGINNING
935 AD

Three longboats rowed west, around the toe of land to the north. Each side of the lead ship had twenty-five oars, half of them manned by two men. The two following, each had twenty oars on both sides. Somewhat faster than their leader they were single stroked, but with extra men in the hold, sitting below the rowing thwarts. At a signal from the lead boat, they came along side and the captain of each climbed on the larger vessel.

They were dressed the same, long woolen tunics with seal skin boots with wrappings around wool leggings. On their shoulders, extending to their waste were cloaks of animal fur, one of wolf, one of sewn pelts of artic fox. The leader who welcomed them preferred wolverine as it never froze, no matter how low the temperature, or the ferocity of the wind. All three wore beards, with various strains of blond and red mixing in perfusion. The only thing that distinguished them from each other was their shoulder covering. In all other aspects they were identical. So much so that in a hall, having discarded their cloaks, their own men could not tell them apart.

They were triplets, indistinguishable in all aspects, size, strength, and courage, and inseparable since their birth, a birth that had caused their mother's death. They grew up until they were eleven in an isolated village, three wet nurses giving them nourishment without regard to which child they suckled. The village, small and isolated, offered no other children their age to play with. Their father was conflicted, both proud of his three-male offspring, yet blaming them for the death of his wife. He resolved his dilemma by providing for them, retaining the three women, and at the age of three, sending one of his men to the village to instruct them in manly arts. At age eleven, he brought them to his own stead and soon wished he had not.

The boys were strange. They could speak the Nordic tongue, but when they conversed with each other they used their own language. Most times though, they would not even speak. They would just look at each other and get up at the same time, or nod, as if they had spoken out loud. Each had an affinity for a specific skill. One, Kjell, was becoming a fine sailor, seemingly one with the small boat that he sailed in the bay. Another, Jan, could sail as well, but always had an eye toward the horizon with an affinity of knowing what weather was in the offering. The third, Jarl, whom the father suspected had been the first born, spent more time learning weapons, and asking the older warriors about battles, his questions penetrating and insightful. The other boys looked up to Jarl as their leader, following his actions with a unity of purpose. The three had quickly dominated the other children, even older boys by providing a united front. The nurse maids had done their job well and each was large for his age, looking to take on the strength of their father. At twelve he took them a-Viking raiding south across the inland sea. Seven years later they had their own longboat. A year after that they had two, but rather than raid independently, they always operated in concert.

Standing in the stern, the longboat rising and falling in the swell of the rising tide, they discussed the final preparations of their attack. It was a conflict that they had not wanted, but now felt was inevitable. Despite their successes in the past year, the three had been shunned by other Vikings, unable to join the fleets which were raiding to the south or across the North Sea to the island of the Angles. They had sent a messenger to the chief of this land, asking for a meeting to resolve whatever the dispute was, but the request was not answered, and the messenger had not returned.

Jarl had decided to beach their ships on a small rocky spit and march inland to the chief's sted rather than row the two kilometers up the small inlet. Kjell had a fear that the banks of the inlet would provide for an ambush by archers and would not allow for the turning around of their craft if a quick withdraw was necessary. They knew the chief, Redhand, was powerful, able to call at least twenty longboats to his leadership, but his men were widespread, and it was their hope to strike quickly before help could arrive.

As they moved across the rocky, boulder strewn landscape and moved into the rich cultivated ground that fronted the Redhand's sted, a group of armed men appeared from the village nestled in the hollow at the end of the inlet. Jarl noted that the numbers were equal to his own band, but the quality of the weapons and armor were not. With a silent command to his brothers they moved at a run toward Redhand's Warriors.

Only a few weapons had clashed when a grey bearded giant with fine armor stepped forward and yelled, "Stop" with a voice so deep and powerful that both sides hesitated. Jarl quickly bellowed, "Falkhand hold!" Only a few clashes of sword, axe and shield followed and those quickly fell quiet as well.

Kjell, in his covering of artic fox watched as the giant chief took two more steps forward and called.

"Jarl Falkhand, I would speak with you," the giant held his sword level with the ground in the palms of both hands.

Kjell moved to the right, Jan to the left as Jarl stepped forward. "I am Falkhand."

An uneasy truce was quickly agreed, and Kjell stood to the side as chairs were hurried from the adjacent longhouse. After Redhand and Jarl were seated, Redhand asked, "Why have you attacked me. I have ever been on good terms with your father."

"You and other Vikings have shunned us for last raiding season and this. You've killed our messenger who was sent to you to ask why. An attack by you and others was expected," said Jarl, his tone calm but accusing.

"I've not killed your messenger. He is in my home," Redhand jerked his head toward the longhouse that had produced the chairs. "I never planned to attack you. You really have no idea of why you are scorned by all?" Redhand shook his great head in disbelief.

"Two seasons ago did you not raid with the chief, Bloodaxe?"

"We did. We had two ships. We joined his eight. It was successful."

Kjell had been captain of the second boat that raid, and Jan had been with him. What Jarl said was true. It was successful.

"Not so for Bloodaxe," said Redhand. "He lost many men and gained little. It 's said that you betrayed him. left him to perish."

"That is a lie. Before we attacked the village, he had selected, we could see that they were prepared and had many men to repel our landing. There were too many men to have come from that small town. I realized that they must have brought the entire defenses from the larger settlement to the north. I spoke to Bloodaxe, telling him this. We could row there faster than the defenders could travel by land, but Bloodaxe is a stupid brute. He would not listen. He had eight ships, I had two. We left him to his folly and attacked the northern town. It was empty of men and rich in plunder. If he lost men, it is his fault not mine."

"This is not what the skald's sing in their saga," said Redhand leaning forward

"What saga?"

"You really don't know! You have never heard it told. Of course, you wouldn't. No skald would risk his life singing it to you or your brothers."

Kjell heard the quiet sound of muffled weapons and turned as one with his brothers. Between their men and the sea were advancing an equal number of warriors as protected Redhand's sted, but these were fully armed most with mail and shield. Kjell and his men turned toward the new threat.

"Ease Falkhand. I have no desire to fight you or your men, but only a fool would not ensure peace at a council," yelled Redhand

"If that is true," answered Jarl, realizing that a fight would no longer be in his favor, "then I ask you to bring a skald who can sing me this false saga."

"That will offer no problem," said Redhand, motioning a man from the third rank behind him to the front. "It's not a long saga."

The skald began nervously, but after a few sentences, his deep resonate voice caught the cadence of the tale and seeing no reaction from either Falkhand or his men, his confidence grew. He sang about Bloodaxe's heroics and fighting prowess, and of the Falkhand's treachery and their use of black magic to conjure up more enemy to face Bloodaxe's men. At the end, Jarl stood, his body rigid. The skald backed quickly away through the ranks of warriors.

"I misspoke about Bloodaxe. He is a stupid brut who lies and would lay the blame on others for his own stupidity. He was warned before the raid, both of the danger and that I was leaving."

Kjell saw the movement behind Jarl and immediately thought "*To your back!*" The words filled Jarl's head. He couldn't tell which of his brother had sent the warning, but he moved to the side, drawing his sword and swinging it over his head to the spot he had just been standing. Behind him a youth was trying to stop his axe from the path that seconds before would have hit Jarl Falkhand. The axe slammed down onto the chair as Jarl's sword took the boy's hand at the wrist, slicing cleanly through it. The hand, still gripping the axe that would have taken Jarl's life fell to the grass of the meadow as the boy was grabbed by Kjell and two of Redhand's warriors.

"*Thank you, brother,*" thought Jarl, as his breathing again slowed. He did not re-sheath his sword but turned toward Redhand, who he now realized had also shouted a warning.

"That is not my doing," said Redhand. "I am never foresworn. You'll not be harmed here."

Falkhand was loth to show fear in front of the old chief, particularly as he was surrounded by his warriors. He nodded and slid his sword back in the scabbard. However, a group of Kjell's men circled around him, facing the rear ranks from where the youth had come. "I have been told that of you, which is why I sent my man to ask for a counsel."

"He came, but a delegation from Bloodaxe came three days before, asking for my boats to join him in this year's raids, and also warning me that an attack from you was eminent. That was a moon ago. Your man told me that if he did not return that you will consider me of the same mind as the others that believe the saga. Your man was right. Bloodaxe was wrong. What would you have of me?"

"The saga explains much. It worries me that so many believe the lie," said Jarl. "I would ask two things of you?"

"What are they?"

"I would ask your advice on how to deal with this saga. How to get the other tribes to trust us again?"

Red Hand laughed, a deep roar of a laugh moving up through his chest and throat, crinkling his eyes, spitting saliva into the air in front of him. "To think we almost came to blows. I have been thinking on that very thing since I first heard the saga and considered the nature of the man at its source. You and your brothers have a good names. All that have sailed with you praise your ability and your trustfulness. However, they also all suspect dark magic in your success.'

'The saga has two messages: that you deceived and broke your oath to Bloodaxe. This most that know you or Bloodaxe do not believe. The second part about black magic is the more dangerous element. Even watching your response here today, I am inclined to believe it. How did you know the youth was about to kill you?"

"My brother warned me. It was not black magic." Kjell listened, wondering how much that Jarl would disclose of their gift. "We are brothers born together," continued Jarl. "Our mother died during our birth and our father left us alone with our nurses. Growing up we developed our own language that only we use. It's not magic, it is just the circumstance of our birth. The same is true of our luck. Kjell has great ways with ships, Jan has great weather luck and with crops I have a knack for battle. All these are things that other Vikings have, but we use them together, and it is perceived as magic." Jarl kept from the older chief that they each could speak to each other's minds. It was something that even their father had not known, only suspected.

"As to my advice, I offer a simple solution," said Redhand. "One that I recognized when your messenger first arrived. You must separate, at least until you each have your own separate reputation. I suggest that one of you go south and join the Danes under my banner. Another I will keep with me as my second in command. You Jarl Falkhand, I would have you stay at your lands. I will assist you in raiding south and will pay you each year for securing our lands from the east when I go a Viking with your brother. Soon the talk will be of Bloodaxe's deceit and your luck. Everyone wants to sail with luck. What is your second request?"

Kjell thought that he would be satisfied if he were the one to sail with Redhand. Not only would it allow him to raid but it would put him close to Bloodaxe and their revenge. He wondered what Jarl's second request of Redhand would be."

"If I am to stay at my sted, I would have the boy I have hurt today. I would teach him how to fight and sail. I would help him become whole again."

"Granted, but you get more than you bargained. The boy is my daughter, Gun."

IRELAND

CHAPTER ONE

Donegal, Ireland – March 2003

The wind blew cold over the dune, pressing the sea grass flat against the sand. Patrick Keohane stood without feeling its chill, aware only of its power. He tried to anticipate the gusts that affected his balance, using whatever primordial instinct is left in humans to become one with the elements.

He could see his target moving almost two hundred meters away. He would get only one shot. He squinted against the wind. Voices of children playing at the seashore just out of sight threatened to intrude on his singleness of purpose, as he forced himself to concentrate: the shot, the wind, his target. He relaxed his fingers, taking a deep breath, exhaling, forcing his heartbeat to slow. The wind picked up, then just as abruptly abated. His ears heard the lull, the break in the wind's intensity, before his skin felt the slacking. He had been thwarted for months, but now, just now, he had the opportunity to end his frustration.

He forced his right hand to relax, his fingers lightly touching the grip. Slowly he brought the club back, hesitating a second before swinging it downward. He struck the ball cleanly, compressing and then propelling the small white sphere toward the green nestled between the dunes in the distance. Keohane watched the flight of the ball. He had started it well to the right of the green, relying on the wind to push it back over the fairway and toward the flag. At first, momentum overcame the elements, but as gravity pulled the ball toward earth and air resistance slowed its flight, it moved left, guided by the irresistible power of the wind.

The ball landed ten yards in front of the green, bouncing hard with the over-spin imparted by both player and wind, coming to rest less than two meters from the hole.

"Nice shot," shouted Mia Keohane as she turned to address her own ball.

Her drive, given the twenty-five-meter benefit of the forward tees, landed fifteen meters in front of her husband's. Mia took less time to judge wind and distance than Patrick; one waggle, a quick look at the flagstick, and she swung. Her shot, being of lower trajectory, was not affected by the wind to the same degree as her husband's. It stayed on line, bouncing hard on the apron and rolling past the pin just off the back of the green.

"Nice shot, Mum!" A young boy ran over the dune that separated the eighteenth fairway from the beach hard on the Atlantic Ocean. His red cheeks attested to both his level of activity and the sharpness of the wind.

"Thanks, Bri. You want to play in?"

"No thanks, Mum. I'll get the flag for you, though."

Without waiting for a reply, he ran toward the green, jumping the small burn that fronted it rather than using the plank bridge. The boy was a perfect composite of his mother and father. His hair was not as red as Patrick's nor as blond as his mother's, but his eyes, which were sky blue, and his strong, slender build belonged to both parents. A few months short of his thirteenth birthday, he was starting to develop the square, muscular shoulders that were so striking in his father.

"How ya playing, Dad?" he asked, approaching his father, who was marking his ball on the green.

"You shouldn't have quit when you did, Brian. I birdied two of the last four holes. If I sink this one, I beat your mother."

"Wow! Good luck. It looks like it breaks a little to the right to me."

Patrick Keohane was not used to being in this position. He maintained a seven handicap at the Murvagh Club, the longest course in Europe, but only once or twice a year was he able to best his wife, Mia. She had come to Donegal in northwest Ireland as a member of the Swedish Women's Amateur Team to play in the Irish Women's Amateur Championship fifteen years before. They had met and fallen in love.

After the tournament Keohane had followed Mia to Sweden, leaving the Harp and Hawk, his small family brewery, in the hands of his brew master. It took a month to convince her that she would be happier as his wife than following the trail of the women's fledgling professional circuit. One year after their wedding, Brian, their only child, had been born.

The brewery gave them a comfortable income, allowing Mia to travel to various amateur championships in Ireland, Britain, and even the Continent. It was a good life, with love deep and true. Still, he loved to beat her at golf, and that was especially true today, with Brian tagging along.

"Hold the flag, please," Mia said to her son from the back of the green. "I want to see if I can lengthen out that putt of your father's by making this."

She chipped, and the crisp sound of her seven-iron contacting the ball signaled a well-played shot. The ball traveled two meters in the air, landing on the back edge of the green and rolling straight and true toward the hole.

Patrick watched as the ball slowed, curling right as its pace slackened. Brian took the flagstick from the cup as the ball neared, lifting it but not moving himself out of the way. The ball caught the edge of the cup, horseshoeing around before coming to rest less than ten centimeters from its edge.

"I believe you were really trying to make it," said Patrick, as his wife walked across the green and nudged the ball into the hole. "Just for that I'm really going to try to make mine."

He stroked his ball, the putter flowing smoothly down the chosen line. The ball slowed as it approached the cup, pausing momentarily on the left edge before falling into the hole.

"Great round, dear," said Mia, giving him a hug and a kiss.

"Thanks. I owe it all to my caddie." He tousled Brian's hair as the boy tried to duck.

"Aw, Da."

"Tell you what. This victory—well deserved victory, I might add—calls for a celebration. Let's go to the Seascape House for dinner. I have to stop by the brewery to check on today's orders, but after that we can eat. What do you say?"

"It's a grand idea. Maybe I should let you win more often." Mia smiled at him.

The Harp and Hawk Brewery was a ten-minute drive from the course, five minutes on a single-lane road and another five north on the N15 road to Donegal. It had been founded by Patrick's ancestor, Donovan Keohane, over three hundred years before, following William of Orange's victory over James II in the Jacobite rising of 1691. At its founding the brewery was intended to free the men of Donegal from the necessity of drinking beer from the Protestant counties to the east, but its success was assured four years later with the Flight of the Wild Geese. Donovan rightly guessed that as the bulk of the Irish army traveled to the Continent, they would miss their familiar strong Irish brew. He bought two light cargo ships and redesigned the brewery's label to display a proud hawk sitting on an Irish harp, long the instrument that had led Irish troops into battles.

As they neared the brewery, Brian stuck his head into the front seat and asked, "Can I get an ice cream to celebrate your great round, Da?"

"You're pushing it a bit, don't you think, Bri?" Patrick responded with a laugh.

Mia reached over and gave her husband's thigh a squeeze. "It was a good round, and he did pack your bag for at least three holes." A mischievous smile curled the corners of her mouth.

"How is it that it costs me when you play well, and it costs me when I play well? Tell you what, Brian, you can buy some chocolates at Haney's, but don't eat them. Bring them to the Seascape for dessert." Patrick pulled the car over to the left shoulder and handed a five euro note to his son in the back seat.

"One scoop of ice cream won't spoil my appetite, Da."

"All right. Just one. Then come straight to the Seascape and don't eat the chocolates."

The boy grabbed the money and practically flew out of the car as it slowed, running across the stone bridge toward Haney's Sweet Shop.

The Harp and Hawk occupied a large two-story stone building on the eastern edge of the town of Donegal. It was only distinguished from similar buildings by the large chimney attached to its northern end. Two tall wooden gates fronted the street. The weathered, almost neglected appearance of the outside stood in contrast to the state-of-the-art equipment and clean interior within the gates. Patrick had somehow kept the image of a handmade Irish family brew while increasing both the quality and production of the beer. Guinness would be surprised by how many cases of Harp and Hawk were sold each year. In fact, so would the government, as Patrick Keohane, like his ancestor Donovan, was adept at evading taxes and their collection agents.

Patrick pulled up in front of the large arched door and stopped the car. "You might as well come in. It will probably take a few minutes to review the orders."

"All right," agreed Mia. "It's been a couple of weeks since I've heard one of Cathal Magee's tall tales."

"Now don't get him going. He has enough to do break-ing in those two nephews of his."

As they got out of the car, three men watched from inside a dark van parked across the street. All three were dressed in black. The large man in the back moved across the bench seat, looking at the driver, as did the front pas-senger. As the door to Keohane's car opened, the driver pulled a black woolen mask down over his hooked nose. "Well, here it is now, lads."

The three stepped out onto the street just as Mia and Patrick reached the small door cut into the larger gate. At forty meters there would be no missing their targets. The sound of automatic gunfire echoed off the sides of the building. Each gunman concentrated on a specific target. The driver rushed directly toward Patrick, his automatic weapon spraying out death in front of him. The second assassin concentrated on Mia, while the third poured round after round into the car. In seconds the carnage was complete. The bodies of Patrick and Mia Keohane lay inert, riddled with bullet holes, against the splintered gate of the brewery.

Inside the building, a small, wiry old man heard the sound of gunfire. He stopped setting the timer on the fermentation vat, cocking his good ear toward the street. As the echoes slowly diminished, he heard a van start and then pull away, not with a screeching of tires but casually, the sound of the engine unhurried. He wiped his hands on the rag he kept in his back pocket and went to the front door. Hearing nothing, he opened it. The limp and lifeless form of Patrick Keohane fell across the high step of the door, dripping blood onto the floor of the warehouse.

"Oh, my dear and merciful God," whispered Cathal Magee, sticking his head out of the opening, where he saw Mia Keohane lying on the street against the building. He quickly jerked his head back in, placing Patrick's lifeless arm outside the door, which he then closed and locked. "Liam!" he shouted. "Bring an empty beer case up to the office right now."

The old man sprang up the stairs to the office, heading straight for the computer, where he backed up the contents of the hard disk onto a flash drive.

"Put this and all the files in the lower two drawers of that cabinet into the crate," he instructed his nephew, throwing him the flash drive and the keys to an old black fireproof file cabinet.

Without checking to see if his orders were being carried out, Magee systematically accessed file after file, deleting them one after another. Then he scanned the contents of the screen in front of him again. Satisfied, he dumped all the deleted files and turned the computer off.

"Got 'em all?" the old man asked, looking at Liam for the first time since he had entered the room.

"Yes, Cal. All in the bottom two drawers."

Cathal Magee looked at the contents cramming the box and nodded. "Close that up and put it in the back of the truck with the load of beer. Drive it to the parking lot behind the woolens shop at the square, lock it up, and go home. You left before the shooting. Understand?"

"Yes, Cal. Who was shot?"

"Both Pat and Mia. Go."

As Liam left, Magee looked at the computer. "I hope this is what you would have wanted for Brian. God bless you."

The old man took a deep breath and reached for the phone. "Minahen, please." He waited, listening to a number of clicks as the connection was made. "Minahen, is that you? This is Cal Magee at the Harp and Hawk. There's been a shooting … Patrick Keohane and his wife … No. I have not seen the lad, but I haven't been outside. I've not seen the likes since the Troubles. I'm sure they're dead …. I'm not about to go outside. I came up to phone you first. No, I'm here alone. I won't touch anything. Hurry."

The old man set the phone down gently and looked around the room. Below him he could hear the sound of the large gate doors close and lock as the delivery truck pulled away from the building. He slowly crossed the room, removing the key from the file cabinet, leaving it unlocked after placing some papers from the drawers above into them. "My dear merciful God. What is this all about?"

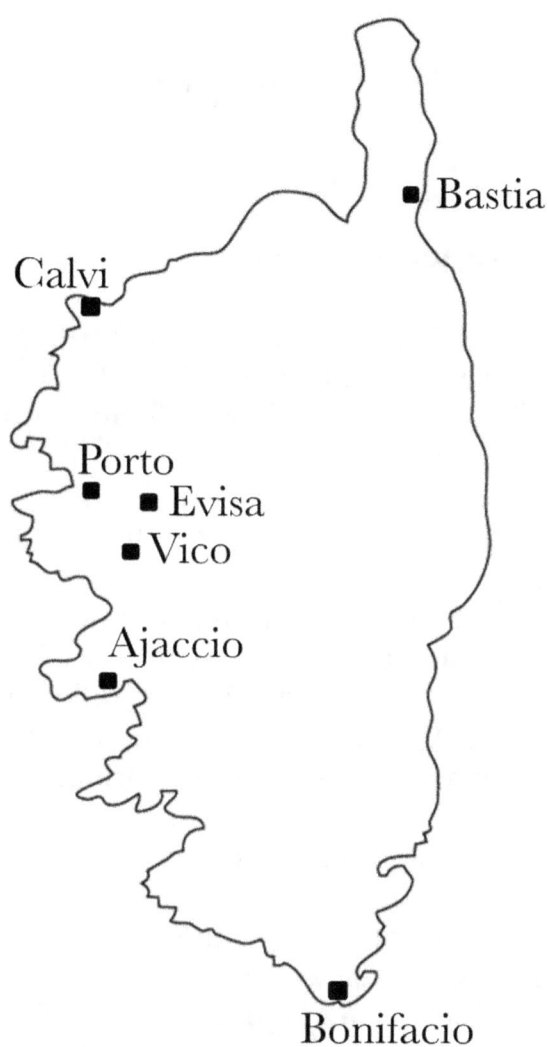

Bastia

Calvi

Porto

Evisa

Vico

Ajaccio

Bonifacio

CORSICA

CHAPTER TWO

The Mediterranean — 1941

Egel Falconi both praised and cursed the darkness. A meticulous seaman, he finished his last entry in the ship's log, dating it 17 November 1941, and knowing that what he wrote was a lie.

There was no distinction between the sky and the water of the Mediterranean. Except for the occasional flash of phosphorescence and the rocking of the boat, he might have lost all orientation. Still, he knew that it was out there, just off the starboard bow: the island of Corsica, the island of his birth. When he left as a young man after World War I, he'd thought he would never return, certainly not under such dire circumstances.

With the rise of Hitler and the Nazi conquests in Europe, Egel Falconi had at first felt smug. It was obvious to all except Roosevelt that the Nazis would not be satisfied until they had all of Europe under their power. France would fall, or more likely whimper, into submission, and with it, Corsica. Falconi had felt safe in America. His fishing business and land holdings in Sausalito, just across the Golden Gate from San Francisco, provided him the insulation of both money and distance from the turmoil raging in Europe. But slowly his feelings had changed. He had immigrated to America because he'd suspected that the solutions imposed after the First World War would lead to another war, and the dangers on Corsica threatened the continuation of his line. In the six years since he had left the island, he had prospered financially but had not been fortunate enough to fall in love. He was the last of the Falconi line and the thought weighed heavily on him as he made the decision to return.

Corsica was not a major theater in the war and did not get the news coverage that was lavished on Paris, North Africa, or even Sicily. It was hard for Egel Falconi to glean much information from the newspapers, but every once in a while, there was a mention of Resistance fighters on the island, thwarting the Nazi occupation troops. Usually it was part of a longer article on the exiled French general Charles de Gaulle, who seemed to take personal credit for every bullet fired at a Nazi on French soil.

The Italians and the Nazis were not very effective at combating the freedom fighters in the Resistance on the mainland. On a small island, however, with modern weapons, they were much more so. The Corsican Resistance was under tremendous pressure. In California, relief for his own safety turned to concern for the friends Falconi had left on the island, principally the Guibega clan, who had served the Falconi for generations. Concern turned to uneasiness and finally to fear that if he did not return to help them in this fight, he would be betraying an ancient trust. Finally, he could not live with the feeling that the Guibega needed him and he was not there to help, so in October of 1941, he left his fishing business in Sausalito in the shadow of the Golden Gate Bridge, giving control to one of his captains, and secretly slipped out of the country.

It took Egel almost a month to arrive in Spain. Gold coins, the only currency he had brought with him from America, were a good enough introduction for him to procure a small fishing boat and supplies. A week after he arrived in Spain, on a night he had picked for its nearing new moon and overcast sky, he sailed. Now, somewhere off the southwest corner of Corsica, he cursed his choice of this night.

The boat was ideal, just large enough to take the unpredictable winds and choppy waves of the Mediterranean but small enough for one man to sail. It was also in a deplorable state of repair, seaworthy but sloppy in its upkeep. Falconi would not have been seen in it back in Sausalito, and he hoped that he would not be seen in it now. Being careful to shield the light, he carefully packed a small waterproof knapsack, placing the rest of the gold coins among the rough clothes of a Corsican peasant. Using his mouth, he blew up a small latex observation balloon and stuffed it inside, along with an eight-inch fisherman's knife, securing the waterproof flap over the contents. It would float. He momentarily wished he had been able to obtain a handgun, but it had been impossible without risking detection even before he left Spain. Once he contacted the Guibega, it would be of no matter; still, for the next few hours, it would have been reassuring to have one.

Flicking off the light, Egel returned to the rail, letting his eyes adjust again to the darkness. A break in the clouds allowed the little starlight to outline the rocky, mountainous coast of Corsica. According to his reckoning, he was just north of the port of Ajaccio. At least that was what he hoped. If he was off by even one degree of latitude, he could end up on the northern tip of Sardinia or on the almost inaccessible coastline of Corsica, south of Porto.

Falconi looked again, seeing the white caps of breaking surf just before the clouds closed. He judged the shore to be less than a mile away. Tightening the line on the jib, he lashed the tiller tight on a course that would take him directly to shore. Then, from its mount on the side of the cabin he removed a short-handled fire axe and went back down into the shallow cabin. He could hear the slap of the waves against the hull as the boat fought the current on its new course. He stripped off his clothes, leaving only his shorts, and applied a thick layer of black grease over his legs, torso, and head. The grease felt cold on his skin, but Egel knew it would help him retain heat as well as camouflage him from prying eyes once he was ashore. Hefting the fire axe, he swung at the lapstrake construction of the sides of the hull. The grease caused the axe to twist in his hands as it hit, and he swore, finding himself already reverting to the Corsican dialect of his youth.

A rag provided an improved grip as Egel swung again at the hull just below the waterline. On the fifth swing, water squirted through. On the seventh, it flowed in great gulps. Switching to the port side, he duplicated his efforts until he was sure that no matter which way the boat listed, it would sink. He found his knapsack floating on the floor of the cabin. He was about to toss the axe aside when a second thought stopped him. Grabbing the knapsack, he lashed the axe to it, testing it in the water that was rapidly filling the cabin to see if it was still buoyant. It bobbed lower but still above the surface. Satisfied, he hefted it and climbed out of the cabin. At the stern he re-lashed the tiller, now heading the sinking craft west, away from the shore. He did not want, even by chance, for the boat to provide evidence of his arrival on the island.

Egel tied a lanyard through both shoulder straps of the pack and the other end tightly around his right ankle. Holding the knapsack in his arms, he jumped off the stern into the waters of the Mediterranean and started swimming toward Corsica.

Approaching from the sea without the benefit of a deck to stand on, Falconi was unable to determine whether the waves broke on a stretch of beach or directly on rocky cliffs. He had only the sound of the crashing waves to guide him, and that sound told him he was in trouble. Offshore the current had been southwesterly, but close in, waves pushed him directly toward the coast. To his right the breakers appeared to crest further inland, increasing the possibility of a small bay or inlet with a beach but at the same time offering no chance for recovery if he guessed wrong.

Towing his knapsack behind him, Egel struck out to the south, struggling to stay just outside the line of breakers. He was getting tired. It had been many years since he had swum such a distance, and the endurance he remembered no longer occupied his still well-muscled frame. As he passed the point, entering what he had perceived as a small inlet, he spotted the now visible waves just to the north crashing on a rocky cliff face. His decision not to go straight ashore had been a good one; now he just hoped the alternate direction would also prove the correct choice. Falconi was moving fast, faster than he would have liked, toward the shore. Even from his present position just outside the line of cresting surf, he could not detect the slope of a beach. He hoped the fact that the waves sounded muffled, rather than crashing against cliffs, meant that the beach he could not see was indeed there.

Falconi crested the wave, propelling down its slope as it broke toward the shore. He could feel his ankle where the line attached to his knapsack acting as a sea anchor. For a split second he could see the wave ahead of him break on a narrow, rocky beach that sloped quickly up to cliffs some ten meters beyond. He tried to bring his feet down, both to slow his speed and to protect himself from the rocky bottom. His right leg would not cooperate. Loss of strength and the buoyancy of the sack made it impossible;

Falconi felt his left foot strike a rock, throwing him off balance. A second wave struck him in the back, pushing the knapsack ahead of him toward shore. Falconi's right leg was pulled out from under him as the sack preceded him the last ten meters. He tumbled over, striking his back against a submerged boulder, his left knee receiving the same abuse. Rolling in a tucked position onto the small rocks that lined the shore, he clutched at anything that would slow his retreat back to sea. Again the knapsack pulled against his leg, this time working to drag him back to the surf. He held the line, pulling it hand over hand from the foam, and crawled up the rocks toward safety.

Above on the cliff, a lone German sentry looked down from his observation post. He could barely make out the man who had washed ashore. At first, he had thought him a clump of seaweed, but then he saw him pull an object from the surf, his movements giving him away more than his shape. It was too far, and there was not enough light to attempt a shot. Besides, his superiors would want to question this one—a man who would risk his life swimming ashore at this forsaken inlet.

He brought his small handheld radio to his lips. "Patrol boat Z-32, patrol boat Z-32, come in."

"Patrol boat Z-32. What is it, shore watch?"

"Corporal Gunnar Heinz, sir, at observation point H-10. Repeat, Corporal Heinz at observation point H-10. A man has just swum ashore on the inlet just south of my position."

"Jawohl. How many?"

"Just one that I can see, but he has brought some sort of object with him."

"Is there any sign of a submarine or boat?"

"No."

"We are only three minutes from your position. Keep him under surveillance. Over and out."

"Jawohl," repeated Corporal Heinz, neglecting to depress his send button. As if he would let a sure promotion to sergeant slip away in the dark. He lifted his rifle and started towards the head of the only trail that led up from the beach.

❧   ❧   ❧

Shannon Airport – July 2003

"I know you want to expand the import business, but beer? Why beer?"

Suzanne's touch entered Mats Falconi's subconscious like a knife. There was no chance to resist, to remain in his dream. The fragile thread was lost, leaving Mats awake.

The flight from Orley, just outside Paris, to the Shannon airport took two hours. For Mats Falconi it was too much time; for his bride of six months, Suzanne, it was not enough. The trip to Ireland had interrupted the celebration of her twenty-ninth birthday. She had managed a party at the Bibliothèque National with the staff that had worked with her on the cache of thirteenth-century manuscripts now known as the Bougainville Library. She and Mats had also had a wonderful dinner with her parents in which Mats had given her a beautiful gold Montalvo bracelet watch, but she had planned at least two more parties that the trip to Ireland had not allowed.

"How long was I asleep?" asked Mats.

"You just nodded your head a few seconds ago. I'm sorry. I tried to raise your seat up. I should have let you rest."

"It's not that. I just had a dream about my father."

Mats saw the concern on Suzanne's face, her dark hair framing her blue eyes and the sharp angle of her jaw. If it were possible, at that moment Mats fell even more deeply in love.

In the previous year, Mats had dreamt rarely. When he did, his dreams were normal—sometimes weird and disconnected, but nevertheless, ordinary dreams. When on rare occasions he dreamed of his ancestors, the true dreams of Falconi's "Gift," they were of the thirteenth century, dreams he had already had, varying only in the addition of small details. None of the Gift dreams seemed to relate to events in the present. Now this—a dream of his father, Egel Falconi, in a time before he was born. Was it because he was also arriving on an island? Mats didn't know. He only felt that it had been powerful, real, experienced through the eyes and mind of his father.

"Your father? What was it about?" asked Suzanne.

"His return to Corsica during World War II. I didn't finish the dream, but I know one thing for sure. It had the substance of a true account." Mats felt his wedding ring, which bore the crest of the Falconi: two crossed battle axes on a shield. "I don't know why I had it, but I am sure it will prove to be important."

Before he could speculate further, the pilot announced their descent into Shannon.

"We've satisfied the demand for the wines we now import," Mats said as they walked down the collapsible hallway from the plane to the terminal. "Demand for them will grow, but slowly. Beer is the logical addition, but we have to find a niche. French beer is out of the question. We would be laughed out of town if we tried to create a market for it. All the good Swiss, Dutch, and German brands have distribution contracts. That leaves breweries in England and Ireland, and I think Irish beer has a better chance of being a success, at least in the San Francisco Bay Area."

"But why non-alcoholic beer?"

"Not necessarily only non-alcoholic. I'd like a regular lager as well, but I've watched the tallies of beer sold at the Sea Hawk for the last year. Ten percent of the beer we serve is non-alcoholic, and most of it is imported. If I can find an Irish brewery small enough to be exclusive to our distribution company and large enough to produce enough to fill our demand, I can create a market. If I find the right beer, I know I can sell it."

"I don't doubt your instincts, Mats," said Suzanne as they entered the main terminal. "Just your reasons, and this focus on money. We don't need the money. Your restaurant is doing well. My salary at the Bibliothèque National has increased since we uncovered Bougainville's Library. The wine import business has grown and is now making a substantial profit as well. Besides, you've hardly touched your father's treasure. How much more do we need?"

It had been almost three years since Mats had met Suzanne in that turbulent period after the death of his father, a random victim in a drug war. Three years since he had first traveled to Corsica, finding Nando Guibega waiting for him with accounts of his family's history and the discovery of his Gift. Two years since they had become lovers. It was true that Suzanne's academic standing had progressed greatly with her discovery and administration of the cache of thirteenth-century man-uscripts. It was also true that his restaurant in Marin County, the Sea Hawk, provided him with more than enough funds as well as the free time to travel back and forth to France.

"Suzanne, I thought you might want to resign your position at the Bibliothèque National now that the trans-lation and cataloging of the library is complete. You have set up the traveling exhibit, duplicated the originals for the discovery site, and preserved the originals. How much more can you do?"

"Quit my position at the Bibliothèque? How can you be serious? What would I do?"

"It would allow you to spend more time at home in Sausalito, or in France, whichever you would like. It's important to have a stable home when raising a family."

Suzanne stopped short, forcing Mats to turn and meet her eyes. "A family?"

It was the only subject they hadn't covered in their two years together. They had talked around the topic but never had a serious discussion. She had hoped that he would one day want children, but she loved him too much to force her own desires upon their relationship.

"Yes, a family. We've been married almost a year now. Wouldn't you like to have a child?"

Suzanne answered by reaching up and kissing him tenderly on the lips, letting the kiss linger in an unmistakable affirmation of her answer.

"Mon chéri," she whispered in his ear. In her mind she was already decorating a nursery.

"I'll take that as a yes." He grinned.

"Oh Mats, I love you more each day. I won't say another word about your fixation on adding beer to our line."

"I just hope the man who is meeting us at Shannon is as knowledgeable as he sounded on the phone," said Mats, swinging Suzanne back toward the main greeting area. "He says he knows every brewery in Ireland."

The appearance of the man dressed in a brown tweed jacket, holding a sign printed with "MR. FALCONI," gave little reason to inspire confidence. His pants were rumpled, his shirt stretched tight over a stomach that protruded from a body with no other signs of fat. A cap was perched lightly on a head crowned with uncombed graying hair. He held the sign with two hands over his head, as his height could be no more than five feet, two inches.

Suzanne looked at Mats, whispering, "Oh God, this is your expert on Irish breweries?"

"So it would seem," answered Mats.

Mats saw the little man smile as he lowered his sign. He had noticed their looks of concern along with the recognition.

"Mr. Falconi?" he asked, walking toward Mats.

"Yes," said Mats, extending his hand. "Mr. Tobin, I take it?"

"Charlie Tobin, sure 'tis me," came the reply, almost sung in an Irish lilt. "Have you baggage to pick up?"

"No, we only brought two carry-ons. Mr. Tobin, this is my wife, Suzanne."

"Glad to make your acquaintance, ma'am. Here, let me take that bag for you. There's a pub just down this ramp. We can stop and have a beer while I go over the breweries that I think fit your needs. There are a number within a few hours' drive from here."

The little man led the way, bouncing rather than walking.

"Really, Mats?" whispered Suzanne in Mats' ear, taking his arm as the Irishman moved ahead with her bag.

"Let's give him a chance. He was recommended by a friend in Sausalito who has spent a lot of time in Ireland."

The airport bar had tried to emulate the look and feel of an old Irish pub, but it had missed. It was the type of place you could only find in an airport—any airport. Still, it offered semi-private seating along the walls in three-sided booths, and it was there that Tobin led them, depositing Suzanne's bag on a chair at a nearby table.

"Three beers, darlin'," Tobin called in his musical voice as the waitress approached. "A Murphy's, a Dugan's, and a Cork Cream. Oh, and you might as well bring me a Bushmills chaser." He turned to Mats. "No reason you shouldn't start learning about what you are thinking of buying, now, is there?"

"I like your style, Mr. Tobin," said Mats, meaning it. He had seen the intelligence in the man's eyes as he'd appraised his employer and his wife before sliding into the booth.

"Charlie. Call me Charlie, Mr. Falconi—and I yours."

Falconi looked at Tobin, peeling off his rumpled camouflage. There was nothing condescending in Mats' manner, just an intelligence that recognized the good and discarded the frills and showmanship of the impish Irishman.

"These two are medium-sized family-owned concerns that might be receptive to making an exclusive label for you." Tobin pushed two glasses and the bottles of Murphy's and Dugan's toward Mats. "Cork Cream is a cooperative owned by the workers. They might be harder to deal with since everything is done by committee."

Mats tasted one, then the other, passing the glasses to Suzanne, who also sipped the golden liquid before placing the glasses back on the table. Only the Cork Cream held any promise. The others tasted watered down despite their raw alcoholic content.

"Not exactly what I had in mind," said Mats, pushing the bottle of Cork Cream slowly toward Tobin, who took what was left in the glass and drained it before answering Mats.

"You've got good taste as well as bein' a good judge of character—mine, that is. Cork is the best of the three, but no matter. I have six other places lined up for you to visit. We'll just cross Dugan's and Murphy's off the list."

The little man stood as he downed the shot of whiskey. "Shall we be off? We can knock off two or three breweries before I deposit you at your hotel."

It took only minutes to rent their car, Tobin explaining that he had been dropped off by a cousin with the thought that it would be easier to drive with Mats and Suzanne.

As it turned out, Charlie Tobin did have connections. He was greeted with a handshake at first brewery they visited. Smith's brewed ale and was not interested in changing their process in order to produce a non-alcoholic beer. The second, family-run but owned by Budweiser, produced a lager but was already running at almost full capacity. The manager was less than friendly and the beer second rate.

"Have you considered talking to Guinness?" Tobin inquired after the second rebuke. He sensed his job was going to be more difficult than he'd assumed. Falconi was all business—not some American wanting to re-discover his Irishness. They were on their way to the third brewery, which was near the hotel they had booked at Rosses Point.

"Guinness wouldn't be interested. Not only are they too big for what I have in mind, but they already have Kaliber, and a distribution system of their own."

"Dugan's is just up the road on your right. It's the smallest of the three you will have seen so far and not as popular. Good chance to do some business there."

"Maybe, but I did not like their product at all at the airport. Let's give it a pass."

Tobin dropped them off at the Ballincar House Hotel. Mats could tell the little man was impressed that his charges were staying at the most expensive place in County Sligo. The day had begun with much to recommend it but had turned out disappointing. Not all was lost, however; Tobin had shown extensive knowledge, even if none of their stops had proven productive. He had another three labels to visit the following day. But after he and Tobin had gone over these three, two of which were local craft beers, Mats anticipated the next day would hardly prove better than the first.

After showering, Mats and Suzanne went downstairs to the dining area. Eight tables were set up for dinner, four of them already occupied. Mats selected one near the window, holding a chair for Suzanne as she sat down. The waitress nodded a welcome as she passed by with an armful of dishes destined for another table. "Be right with you," she said with a smile.

Unlike most of her American counterparts, this Irish waitress was true to her word, returning immediately with two menus and the same cheery smile. "Hope you enjoy your stay at Ballincar House. The fish of the day is salmon stuffed with shrimp. Would you like to see the wine list?"

Mats looked at Suzanne, receiving her answer. "We'll have two of the salmon. What kind of beer do you have?"

"We have Dugan's, Murphy's, and Harp and Hawk."

"Harp and Hawk?"

"It's a local beer, a lager. It's my favorite."

"We'll have two, please."

As good as the salmon was, it was the beer that impressed Mats the most. It was a rich, thick-foamed lager with a great taste and a kick that had to come from an alcohol content greater than seven percent. They would ask Mr. Charlie Tobin about Harp and Hawk the following day.

"The Harp and Hawk? Of course I know it." Mats watched the little Irishman rise up on his toes. "I know all the Irish breweries." Tobin looked like he had slept in his clothes.

"Good, then tell me about this one."

"It's small, about an hour north of here in Donegal. It's been around for centuries, family-owned, makes a good lager and once a year, for about a month around November, a thick brown ale as well."

"Let's visit it next. Can you arrange a meeting? The taste, even the label, is exactly what I'm looking for."

"Oh, I can phone ahead all right, but it won't do any good."

"Why not?"

"Because it has stopped production. That's why."

"Stopped production? Why? Isn't it popular?"

"Oh, it's very popular. Very patriotic to drink Harp and Hawk. It probably dents Guinness sales in Galway, Sligo, and Donegal Counties."

"Then why did they stop brewing?"

"Death in the owner's family. It's up for sale."

"Make the phone call. I'll talk to the broker, the agent, even the brew master. I would like to see the physical plant, see how it compares with those we saw yesterday."

Tobin moved away and used his cell phone. It took about five minutes, but he was back with a smile on his face.

"The brewery number has been disconnected, but a friend tells me there's a man left on the premises who used to be the brew master."

Mats still was not sure if Tobin really did have connections or if he was the world's greatest huckster, but whatever the reason, fifteen minutes later they were on their way to Donegal.

"I couldn't get anyone on the phone. Like I said, they stopped brewing. The beer is still being sold, though, or at least it was up to a week ago." Tobin drove, which suited Mats, as he was unaccustomed to driving on the left side of the road and the roads were none too wide, often bordered by stone walls. Sitting in the front left, several times he found himself putting his right foot down to the floorboards, looking for the brake.

At a point where the border of Northern Ireland pressed toward the Atlantic coastline, leaving only a four-mile corridor separating Donegal County from Sligo County, Charlie Tobin crossed himself and cursed in a whisper, looking toward the east.

Donegal was a small city even by Irish standards, with less than eight thousand permanent residents. Tobin announced the town square, which Mats noticed was a triangle, as they rode through. He had no problem finding the brewery, needing only one U-turn. They found the door in the main loading gate half open. Mats hesitated as he got out of the car. The building was obviously old, its stone foundation chest high, the rest of it timber filled with stucco. It had a look of permanence and respectability, the smell of fermentation barely discernible and the inside seemingly deserted.

As they approached the entrance, Mats noticed a row of bright splinters in the dark aged oak of the loading gate, marring the thick planking.

As they stepped through the door, Mats yelled, "Hello!"

He was answered by an abrupt voice from the second floor of the building. "Whatcha want?"

"To talk about the brewery."

An old man appeared at the top of a flight of stairs. Descending while smoothing his hair back with his hand, the man introduced himself as the brew master, Cathal Magee. Standing behind him was a much younger man whom he referred to only as "me sister's son."

As opposed to the aged feeling of the outside, the interior looked modern and functional, filled with stainless steel vats and piping. Tobin took over as the man reached the floor and approached them, explaining that Mr. Falconi was interested in seeing the plant.

"No reason not to," said Magee. "It's not like I'm doing much else here now, is it?"

Magee took Mats' party through the facilities, concluding in the upstairs offices and his own living quarters. Mats asked a few questions as they progressed on the tour, mostly limited to production and the time it had taken to set up the machinery from brewing lager to ale and then back again. Magee answered everything with a knowledgeable confidence that comes when a person knows his job and has known it long enough to feel comfortable in the role. The more he explained, and the more questions were asked, the more the two felt comfortable with each other. There was no unsolicited information offered, but when Magee did explain either a piece of machinery or a process, Mats knew he was getting accurate information. The directness of the questions and the succinctness of the answers slowly built a trust between the two men.

"Could you make a non-alcoholic beer without modifying the plant?" Mats had seen more positive signs as he was shown around by this old man than he had at all the other breweries combined. Mats' experience with old Nando Guibega on Corsica had taught him to hold no prejudice as to age. Magee was obviously clear-thinking and knowledgeable.

"Now why would you want to go and do something like that?" Magee's manner suddenly became suspicious again. "Did Grady at the solicitor's office send you here?"

Tobin saw his chance to gain control of the exchange. "I talked to no solicitor. It was John Herlihy who told me I could find you still here at the plant. Mr. Falconi is interested in regular lager as well as non-alcoholic beer."

"I was just wondering if it could be done," answered Mats, smiling at the expression of disbelief on the old man's face.

"Herlihy, huh. He might have told me."

"The brewery's phone has been disconnected, and he didn't have a number for you when I called, but it was little more than an hour ago," said Tobin with a smile.

"Sorry for being a little touchy. I never know what Grady and his bunch will drop on me next," said Magee, shaking his head. "We keep the beer at eight percent, always, and the ale a smidge above eleven. What would anyone want with a beer that had no alcohol? Has all that three-percent American piss affected your brain?"

As Magee said this, all harshness was removed from the remark by a mischievous glint in his eye and a smile that cracked the parchment of skin at the corners of his mouth. He liked this American. In many ways, he reminded him of Patrick Keohane. He was a man who asked questions with intelligence and forethought. He had a sense of humor and the wisdom to put up with Magee's smart remarks without reacting.

"Actually, Mr. Keohane—he was the owner—looked into it some six months ago. Read up on it, that is. He didn't actually brew the piss for real," Magee lied, salvaging some pride from the fact that while Patrick Keohane had learned about the process, Magee as brew master did not have to confess to committing such a heinous act.

Mats stood silent, looking at the old man, and then, prompting a reply to his still unanswered question, he raised his right hand, palm up, curling his fingers toward him, a sign that he wanted more information.

"Oh, we could do it, all right." Magee sighed as if he had lost a battle in admitting this. "We even have the equipment on order. At least, I don't think it has been canceled, but I don't know for sure. The solicitors think the workers should be the last to know what's going on. They are great ones for stopping production and putting fifteen fine young men out of work so they can make a fee for starting it back up again."

"You have equipment on order?"

"Well, the truth of the matter is that Mr. Keohane ordered it before he died. Against my advice, mind you— ordering the equipment, that is, not getting himself dead."

"Yes, Mr. Tobin told me there had been a recent death," Mats said, gesturing toward Tobin, who had been skulking behind them during the tour of the plant. "Tell me about the non-alcoholic process?"

"Well now, there are two ways to get non-alcoholic beer. One is to make regular beer and filter or boil out the alcohol. This at least leaves you with the alcohol, which is as good a drinking mix as you could want. The second way is to brew the beer from the start without alcohol. That's tough, since any fermentation process produces the stuff. Mr. Keohane had been working with a Swedish biochemist, a relative of his wife's, on a form of bacteria that ferments the barley and hops without producing alcohol. It's been tried before but never successfully; never produced a good brew. The machinery that's on order is special holding vats for the rejuvenation of the bacteria and yeast as well as a filtering device to remove any that stay in the liquid."

"Then Mr. Keohane thought he could produce a good beer with this method, enough to spend money on equipment?"

"Mr. Keohane didn't *think* he could do it. He knew!" Magee finally admitted.

"How did he know?"

"Because we did it in that little workshop I showed you earlier. The one behind the main vats. Two small batches, you know. Just testing the bacteria and yeast combination.

The equipment on order was to be able to produce it in quantity while not stopping production on the real stuff. It was all very hush-hush. All the boys working the tests runs were sworn to secrecy. I guess it's not important anymore."

"You're telling me that he produced a non-alcoholic beer with a new process already? How did it compare to the regular Harp and Hawk?"

"Didn't hold a candle to our regular lager. Oh, it tasted the same. In fact, we put it in bottles with the same label and people couldn't tell the difference, but it had no kick. You could drink the stuff bottle after bottle. You still had to piss a stream, but you were standing at the end of the night when you did. It was like taking out a nun on a date. No matter how pretty she looked and how nice she smelled, the potential for fun did not improve as the night wore on. Terrible stuff, it was."

"You mentioned a biochemist, a Swede. How would I get in touch with him?"

"Oh, I imagine I could find his name and address, but would it do any good?"

"Why? Do the solicitors have control of the patent and process as well?"

"They have the records. Control, I don't know. Mr. Keohane patented the process and the bacteria strain before he died. Guess it's part of the business or his estate. Don't know which."

"Where would I find more information on the patent?"

"Ah then, you would have to talk to the solicitors for that, wouldn't you?"

Mat looked at the brew master, wondering if he should bring up the deaths of the owners. He decided he would have to ask at some point, so now was as good a time as any. He took a deep breath. "I understand the owner and his wife were killed. Mr. Tobin heard that they were shot— that it sounded like an assassination. Were the Keohanes mixed up in anything that would cause another owner a problem?"

Magee looked hard at Mats before answering. "Let me give you a little history of the Harp and Hawk. Donovan Keohane, the founder, started brewing beer here over three hundred years ago. It became patriotic to drink Harp and Hawk. The beer was superior, and the label gave credence to the republican tendencies of the Keohanes. Donovan started sending it to France to quench the thirst of the Wild Geese."

"Who were the Wild Geese?" asked Suzanne.

"You bein' French should know," said Magee, reprovingly. "In October 1691, the Irish boys in the Jacobite Irish army went to France to serve in the Continental Army. They were called Wild Geese. They took their thirst for Harp and Hawk with them."

"Even if he had paid taxes and import duties, Donovan Keohane would have gotten to be well off; but without them, he grew rich. He bought land made available by the penal laws that crippled the Irish woolen industry, planting hops and grain for his brewery and leaving the families on the land to use it as their own once his allotment of grain was fulfilled. He was a landlord, but unlike the British, he gave the tenants a sense of belonging, and with it came a fierce loyalty to the Keohane clan. Partly because of this loyalty, partly because of the thirst of the Irish, and partly because the Keohane family produced few offspring, the brewery prospered and has been passed down from father to son until it fell to Patrick Keohane. There has never been any violence associated with the brewery or the Keohanes. Patrick had no dealings with the IRA. He wasn't political at all. He was Catholic, of course. I can't see politics being involved with his murder, and I don't see why it would fall on anyone that would buy the brewery, if that's what you're asking."

"Why were they murdered, then?" asked Mats. "Did they or the brewery have enemies?"

"I've worked here since I was a lad," said Magee, shaking his head. "I tell you; I just don't know. I spend nights trying to think of reasons. There just is nothing."

He was killed for some reason, both he and his wife — violently, from what Tobin has said, thought Mats. *With both murdered, it speaks of either passion or a vendetta. I shouldn't push Magee too far about this until we know more about it.*

"Well, thank you, Mr. Magee, for the tour and the information. Do you know if there have been any offers on the brewery?"

"I'll tell you what I know, Mr. Falconi, which isn't much. I haven't been told much since the Keohanes' deaths. There have been no offers that I know of, and if the damned solicitors don't wise up, there won't be anything left to make an offer on. You can't expect the crew to stay around forever. Without any production or profits, Guinness or some other company will come and pick it off for spare change. They'll keep the label and the profits, let the quality slip, and underpay the workers. What would the poor lad need with a fair sale price, anyway?"

"What poor lad are you talking about, Mr. Magee?"

"Ah, that would be young Brian, the Keohanes' only child."

"One more question, if you don't mind. Would you stay on as brew master if the place were sold?"

"Well now, that depends, doesn't it, on who's doing the buying."

It took only five minutes to find the solicitor's office on the north side of the triangular town square and arrange a meeting.

"Mr. Grady, this is Mats Falconi, my client, who is here from America, and his wife, Suzanne. Mr. Falconi is interested in the present disposition of the old Harp and Hawk brewery. We breezed past the place on our way over here."

Mats smiled. He could see that Charlie Tobin now sensed there was money to be made somewhere in the transaction. Tobin had asked for a flat fee for his service, but he had left open the possibility of a further commission based on what deals were struck. Mats could see the little Irishman was re-thinking his compensation in terms of a finder's fee on the sale of a property.

Gavan Grady was tall and thin, completely bald on top, with dark hair forming a sharp contrast as it grew thickly above his ears and neck. He wore half-glasses, looking over them as they perched on his long, straight nose. "The Harp and Hawk. I'm afraid we are still working on the legalities on that one."

"It's common knowledge that you have stopped brewing out there," prompted Tobin.

"Yes, that's true. We did not want to incur any more expenses than necessary until we decided who was to have the ultimate financial responsibility for the property."

"Is that why you sold off the beer stock?" asked Tobin. "To pay your fees?"

"We have incurred expenses," snapped Grady.

"And the two trucks?" asked Suzanne, sweetly, as if she had no concept of business.

Grady was about to answer, but Tobin waved him off.

"If my client were to tender an offer, what would be your stance?" asked Tobin, receiving a sharp look from Mats.

"I would listen to it."

"Nothing else? Who else would have to decide to sell, and for what amount?"

"Just the partners of this firm. Did you want to bid on the brewery, Mr. Falconi?" asked Grady, looking directly at Mats.

"What I really want to know is the asking price," answered Mats.

"It's not that simple. There is an heir, but he is not of legal age. We at Grady, Duffy, and Walsh have been given custody of the lad until relatives can be located. Mr. Keohane had no kin except for the boy, but we are attempting to find relatives of his wife in Sweden. That in itself has presented a problem. Mrs. Keohane was also an only child and both of her parents are deceased."

"Where is the boy now?" asked Mats.

"That is also a problem. A boy of thirteen is not the easiest to place. But we did find him a temporary foster home with Widow O'Dwyer in Killybegs, a few miles down the coast."

"Did you consider keeping the brewery in production, using Magee and his workers?" asked Tobin, trying to keep control of the meeting.

Grady looked at Tobin over his glasses and down his nose. "Magee? Of course not. The whole bunch of them are incompetent. I don't know why Mr. Keohane kept them on the payroll. They couldn't even help us find the invoices and delivery documents."

"I understand," said Mats, "but I would still like for you to name a price. At some point the estate will have to be settled, so it won't be work wasted. I would appreciate the effort and be happy to pay an appropriate fee, even if I don't tender a bid."

"I will talk to my partners and discuss the matter. Perhaps we should start thinking of the disposition of the property." At the mention of a fee, Gavan Grady had smiled for the first time. It was a thin, unpleasant smile.

CHAPTER THREE

Charlie Tobin's recommendation of a bed and breakfast on the outskirts of Donegal was a good one. It was run by an enchanting lady by the name of Maureen O'Toole who let out three rooms and happened to have two still vacant when Tobin phoned.

"Let's have an early dinner," said Mats. "We can discuss how best to deal with Mr. Grady."

"The Seascape restaurant has a fine reputation," said Tobin quickly, sensing a free meal as well as a few free drinks and keeping to himself that it was the most expensive restaurant in Donegal County.

The Seascape was just northwest of Donegal on the coast road to Dunkineely. Perched on a slope, fast against the small inlet of Inver Bay, the restaurant had a view that earned it its name. Inside was the bar that the airport lounge had tried unsuccessfully to emulate. The dining area, like the lounge, appeared to have evolved from generations of good fellowship rather than from intent. Wooden tables, each with its own view of the bay, were set against the windows.

"Tobin's the name," announced the guide to a woman standing at a small table next to the dining area. "Here with Mr. and Mrs. Falconi, party of three."

"Would it be possible to have a beer at the table?" asked Mats. "It would be terrible to waste the sunset."

"Of course." The hostess picked up three menus and led them to a table in the corner of the room that allowed them a view of not only Donegal Bay but also the small harbor directly below them. "I think you will find the salmon and trout especially good today—that is, if you like fish. Now what about those refreshments?" asked the waitress as she laid down menus in front of them.

Mats ordered a Harp and Hawk, Suzanne a glass of white wine, and Tobin his usual beer and Bushmills. "What do you think the asking price will be, Mr. Tobin?" asked Mats.

"It depends on what's left. After meeting Mr. Gavan Grady, I suspect they've sold off anything useful and used the money to pay their fees for the sale. If that's the case, then they are only selling the brewery, building, machinery, and name. I would guess that all of it put together is going to be about five hundred thousand euros. Grady will ask for more, knowing his type. Did you plan on taking my fee out of their side, or will you take care of it yourself?" Tobin looked transparently unhappy at the prospect of Grady paying his finder's fee.

"Why, Mr. Tobin, why should that matter?" asked Mats with a smile.

"Charlie. Call me Charlie. I've dealt with slick Willies like him before. Now Mats, you are a fair and honest man. I could tell as soon as you walked off the plane. But Grady would stick it to his own mother."

"What do you think of the discrepancy between what Cathal Magee told us and what Mr. Grady seemed to know?" asked Suzanne.

"I think Magee has as little use for solicitors as I do. Magee wouldn't tell Grady if the sun was out. If you want straight information about sales or the running of the place, it's Magee you'll be wanting to ask."

"Then there's a chance Grady is making a price based on figures that are low. How could Magee have hidden the figures from Grady?" asked Mats.

"Grady's type never gets their hands dirty. They just go over figures. Find out how and where he got the figures and you'll probably find that either Magee supplied them or had his hands on them before Grady did."

"Could you work with Magee, Charlie?" asked Suzanne.

"Sure, and it would be easy. I have a brother just like him. You want me to work with him to get the real figures?"

"No, I think Mats can do that," answered Suzanne. "I was thinking about after we buy the brewery, if we buy it." She added, in French, to Mats, "You'll need an Irishman who knows both the territory and how to sell and do the things the Keohanes did."

Mats watched with amusement as Charlie Tobin gazed wide-eyed at Suzanne. He had watched Suzanne follow Falconi around, like a good wife, for two days – a beautiful Frenchie. She had said little, leaving all the decisions to her husband. Now she had taken control. Mats could see Tobin thinking back over the last day and a half, trying to come up with anything he might have said or done to offend this woman who had just acquired new importance.

"What did you say, Mrs. Falconi?"

Suzanne switched back to English. "I'm sorry, Mr. Tobin. Sometimes I speak French without thinking. Mr. Magee seems more than competent as a brew master, but we will need someone to supervise sales and distribution. Could you handle the paperwork part, Mr. Tobin?"

"Sure, that I could." Tobin hoped neither would ask if he had ever had similar responsibilities. It was true that he had held many jobs in the brewing business, starting as a flunky on the bottling line. But he had never held a position higher than salesman.

"Are you ready to order?" They looked up to see a waitress standing next to the table.

As Suzanne and Tobin ordered, Mats looked out the window, watching the gray surf break against the rocky coast. Fishing boats that were impossibly small by California standards had been winched up onto a stone dock. Sloping away from the restaurant was a footpath that followed the edge of the cliff down to the water, a broken stone fence crossing it halfway down the incline.

Mats stared out the window, vaguely aware of what Tobin was saying. A young boy sat on the stone wall, idly throwing rocks into the water. As Mats watched, the boy turned and looked directly at the restaurant. His eyes seemed to focus on Mats, and even at this distance, their stark blue color was visible below a shock of strawberry blond hair. As Mats returned the boy's stare, the sea behind the boy seemed to grow colder, grayer, the shore slowly shifting from lush green slopes to land strewn with boulders and sparse grass.

"Sir?" Mats' attention was pulled from the boy by the waitress, who had finished with his companions.

"Who is that boy?" asked Mats, pointing toward the window.

"What boy do you mean, sir?"

"The boy by the … " Mats stopped midsentence. As his gaze followed the waitress's, he saw no one, just the broken wall with the bay behind.

"Five hundred and fifty thousand Euros," said Grady, passing a slim file over his desk to Mats. "As you can see, that includes quite a lot—the building, the new Swedish vat order that was already paid for, distribution contracts, and all inventories."

"Thank you for putting this together for me, Mr. Grady," said Mats, thumbing through the documents. It had been two days since Mats had first entered the solicitor's office and asked about the price. During that time, Mats had had three talks with Cathal Magee, slowly learning the true numbers of sales and production. Tobin had been right. Mats was glad to see that the two men appeared not only to be cut from the same cloth but to genuinely like each other. Magee had confirmed Tobin's guess that the lawyers had sold off anything not physically attached to the brewery.

At the front door of the brewery, Magee showed Mats the splintered boards and the blood-stained macadam, recounting the murders with emotion that only the truth could evoke.

"Why?" Mats asked, and Magee had stumbled with his answer. "I just don't know. There's often craziness living so close to Northern Ireland. The Keohanes had never disguised their Republican bias but they were not connected with the IRA, at least not recently." In the end, Magee just looked at Mats in silence with upturned hands, seeming truly old for the first time since Mats had met him.

Mats fingered the holes in the doorway. "You say an automatic weapon was used?"

"Minahen thinks there were three guns involved," answered Magee.

Mats looked again at the stained doorway and a great sadness overwhelmed him, as if the murder of these two people had been a personal loss to himself. He'd been asked by Grady to visit the plant only with one of the firm's attorneys present, a request he had ignored. Now, looking at the remains of the carnage, he couldn't escape the feeling that he was being observed.

"Look behind me," he said softly to Suzanne. "Is anyone watching us?"

"No. There isn't anyone on the street except a young boy and he is walking in the opposite direction."

"What is the color of his hair? Can you see?"

"Blond. No, maybe red."

Mats spun around but caught only a momentary glimpse of the boy as he turned the corner two blocks away.

"Five hundred and fifty euros," said Mats, retreating from his thoughts and handing the file to Tobin. "It is more than I expected to pay for a business that appears to have had a net profit of only two hundred and forty thousand pounds last year."

Tobin thumbed through the file, obviously pleased that his estimate of Grady's asking price had been on the money. "And, you've already sold off all the beer and the grain and hops as well."

"The price, I think you will find, is well justified." Grady smoothed his sleeve with his hand. "We calculated it using two methods, as you will see in the report: once by the profits, and again as strictly a real estate transaction based on comparable rent and cost of equipment. The price quoted reflects the real estate method, which is the higher of the two."

"Mr. Grady," said Tobin with mild skepticism, looking at the file one last time before handing it back to Mats. Mats had dictated the strategy for the session and had decided that Tobin would be the hard nose, pointing out the negatives, while Mats would play the unassuming American buyer. "Old Magee, over at the brewery," continued Tobin, obviously relishing his role, "told me you took possession of over six hundred cases of Harp and Hawk. I only see two hundred cases on the inventory."

"Yes, well now, Magee is a total incompetent. If he were not living in the building rent free, he wouldn't be able to find his way to work. We probably shouldn't have kept him on as caretaker when we closed the place down. It's true that we did sell off some inventory to cover the costs of probate and of fostering the boy. I don't know where Magee came up with the six hundred cases."

"I also don't see anything that protects Mr. Falconi's right to exclusive use of the brand name or the license to brew." Tobin turned to Mats and explained, "Without those, you could end up with just a building and machinery while Guinness sells Harp and Hawk and this one gets a fat commission from both sales."

"Look here, Mr. Tobin, I have tried to accommodate Mr. Falconi. We have presented him with a price. I take offense at your suggestions. If we have left some things out in haste, then that is open for discussion, not accusations. You will find that everything is done to the letter of the law by this firm. I shouldn't tell you this, but we have had two other inquiries about the brewery, one from a very large company whose name I can't mention, but it has been mentioned here today."

"That's hardly the whole truth, Mr. Falconi," snapped Tobin, relishing his role of baiting Grady. "I'm told they contacted Guinness, but when the details of the murders of the previous owner and his wife came out, Guinness wasn't interested. Too much risk, not enough profit. They passed."

"Mr. Tobin!" Grady stood up behind his desk, pointing a finger at Charlie Tobin, who sat with a smug expression on his face, his hands clasped below his belly.

"Gentlemen," said Mats before Grady could voice the disdain he clearly felt for Tobin. "Suzanne, would you please take Mr. Tobin out for lunch? I think it would be more productive if Mr. Grady and I spoke alone for a few minutes. I will meet you later at Mrs. O'Toole's."

Tobin got up and followed Suzanne. At the door he turned, unable to resist a parting shot. "Don't you be signing anything till I look at it for you, Mr. Falconi." He moved out of the office, Grady assisting in his exit by closing the door with more than his usual firmness.

"I am sorry, Mr. Falconi. He is a most disagreeable man. How long have you known him?"

"Only four days."

"Did you check his credentials?"

"No, he was referred. Gavan, let's forget about Tobin for a moment. Some of the points he makes are valid, but better not discussed in a room full of people."

Grady walked to the chair that had been occupied by Suzanne, lifting it so that it faced Mats. "I have explained the sale of the stock. It is gone, no longer part of the sale. As far as the trademark, it was just an oversight that a stroke of a pen will correct. I take it you are interested in the property?"

"Yes," said Mats, "with a couple adjustments that I'm sure could be worked out. May I ask what your firm's percentage of the sale is?"

"Certainly. It is the standard probate fee of ten percent."

"I was thinking of a sale price of, say, four hundred thousand Euros. That would free up working capital while we produce the inventory that has been depleted." Mats held his hand out to stop Grady from rising in hostility. "I'm aware that what I propose costs your firm ten thousand Euros in commission. To compensate, let's say I award you, personally, a finder's fee of twenty-five thousand Euros. That's a net profit of fifteen thousand. I'll take it out of Tobin's end for almost messing up the deal."

"That sounds like a fair and equitable compromise, Mr. Falconi. I will have to speak to my partners, of course."

"Of course," Mats agreed. "Just a few other things, Mr. Grady. I would like placed in the sales document the points Tobin mentioned and also a clause giving me ownership of any patents, yeast cultures, or bacteria that are unique to the Harp and Hawk process or that were developed by Keohane, the previous owner."

"That should be no problem," said Grady, making notes in his yellow pad.

"Well then, please draw up the papers. I will be needing a temporary residence when we conclude the sale—one we could lease for a year, perhaps with an option to buy. If you happen to hear of one, please let me know."

"The Keohanes had a nice three-bedroom farmhouse just twenty kilometers west of Donegal, toward Dunkineely. We could arrange a lease, for an additional consideration, of course."

"I don't know about that. I would have to ask my wife. She might have reservations about living in the dead couple's home. We can give it a look, though."

Mats stood to leave, reaching out to shake Grady's hand. At the door, he turned. "The heir, the boy...I would like to speak to him before we conclude the deal."

"You could if I knew where he was," replied Grady. "He ran away from Widow O'Dwyer's three days ago."

Mats picked up Suzanne at O'Toole's and drove like a tourist along the north side of Donegal Bay. Grady had given him directions along with a set of keys to the Keohane farm. Eventually Mats came to two stone columns flanking a cobbled road leading to the two-story farmhouse. The construction was old, perhaps hundreds of years old, but a new two-car stone garage and a modern slate roof told of recent updates. Roses grew in profusion up the driveway and in front of the house. Behind the building, Mats could see a small stone jetty thrusting a stubby finger into the bay.

Mats had accepted the keys to the Keohane farm mostly out of curiosity. He doubted that either he or Suzanne would be comfortable in a house of a couple so recently murdered, especially if they bought the Harp and Hawk. Suzanne was particularly aware and concerned about the circumstances. She walked through the rooms without touching the furniture or walls. The interior was light and cheerful, however, and gradually she found herself affected by the warmth and comfort of the house and furnishings. They both sensed there were no unfriendly ghosts in this place, only fond memories of happy, loving times. In the tearoom just off a modern kitchen, Suzanne finally sat down.

"I don't know what I expected to find, but this is a wonderful spot," said Mats, standing behind her and rubbing her shoulders.

"It is, but I still wouldn't want to live here, Mats," said Suzanne. "There is too much of a sense of the previous owners. We would never be able to forget the way they died."

Mats' eyes scanned Donegal Bay in the late afternoon sun, first looking east toward the Atlantic, then south along the narrow spit of land that formed St. John's Point. Coming up the trail from the jetty was the red-haired boy. Over his shoulder was a fishing pole, and on his hip rode a large wicker creel. Mats moved to the back door, finding it unlocked.

"Brian Keohane? I'm Mats Falconi," said Mats, extending his hand as the boy reached the back door.

"I know." The boy climbed past Mats without shaking hands and headed up the four stone steps to the kitchen without slowing. Inside he turned on the oven, then went to the sink. Opening a drawer, he took out a knife and expertly gutted two small salmon. "When I saw you drive up, I thought I'd better catch another fish. Would you like to join me for dinner?"

Suzanne's mouth dropped open and she looked at Mats. It was the same boy Mats had asked her about at the brewery, she realized—or at least, he had the same color hair. He was red-cheeked from his climb from the water, and his ice-blue eyes dominated his young face.

Receiving a nod from Suzanne, Mats responded. "Thank you, Brian. We would be happy to accept."

Mats watched the boy prepare the meal. He cut three potatoes in thin slices, sautéing them in butter over the burner. He placed the fish on a steel platter surrounded by potatoes and shoved it into the oven. Snapping some green beans into a pot, he turned. "It won't be as fancy as the Seascape, but it'll be fresher, no doubt."

Both Mats and Suzanne were speechless as the young man cleaned the counter with a few efficient swipes of a towel. They followed him as he moved to the table and sat down.

"Are you going to buy the brewery?"

"I haven't made up my mind yet, Brian, but if I can work things out, I probably will. I'm sure you know that Mr. Grady has been looking for you since you ran away from Widow O'Dwyer's?"

"I haven't been that hard to find now, have I?"

"I guess not. If you had your way, what would you do with the house and brewery, Brian?"

"You should buy the brewery. They won't let me run it. You trust Cathal Magee and that's good. My father did, as do I. He will produce good beer for you as well as make you a profit. The house I would like to keep. It's been in my family for generations, and I would like to keep it so."

"How do you know that we trust Magee? Have you been talking to him?"

"Of course. Why do you think he told you the real production figures?"

While Mats looked at the boy, Suzanne reached across the small table, offering her hand. "I'm Suzanne. It's nice to meet you, Brian."

"You're French?" asked Brian, shaking her hand and for the first time allowing the curiosity of a thirteen-year-old to show.

"Yes, I am. Mats is American."

"I'm glad to meet you both," said the boy. "I think dinner is ready. Salmon takes almost no time to cook."

Grady had disconnected the house phone and the cell reception was nonexistent, so Mats had to drive two kilometers, almost to Dunkineely, before gaining enough bars to be able to call Tobin to tell him they were staying the night at the Keohane house. After parking his car in front of the garage, he found Suzanne and Brian playing chess in front of a cheerful fire.

"Brian made up our beds, Mats. At least he allowed me to do the dishes."

"Would you like another cup of tea, Mr. Falconi?" asked the boy, looking up from the board.

"No thank you, Brian, but I would like to ask you some questions about the Harp and Hawk when you are through."

After six moves Brian realized that Suzanne was an accomplished player and that he was going to lose. Lifting his eyes from the board, he smiled at Suzanne. "Shall we call it a draw and play again later?"

Suzanne merely smiled and began rearranging the pieces for another game.

Whether it was the caffeine in the tea, or the puzzle posed by a thirteen-year-old Irish boy with the maturity of an adult, Mats had a hard time falling asleep. When he finally did, it was a fitful, tossing, uneasy sleep that promised to leave him exhausted in the morning. His thoughts were as disjointed as his rest, like a nervous man switching stations on a radio. Finally, after midnight, he fell into a deep sleep and dreamed ...

Corsica—1941

Egel Falconi shook himself like a dog, spraying the salt water of the Mediterranean from his body. Once he was reasonably dry, he opened his knapsack and gently cut the balloon that had given it buoyancy. Placing a rock inside the balloon, he threw it into the surf. Then he removed his wet shorts, replacing them with the rough corduroy pants of a Corsican farmer. He put on a long-sleeved shirt and a double-breasted wool vest before placing the wet shorts in the bag. Then he stopped, took the shorts back out, filled the pockets with rocks, and threw them after the discarded balloon. He wouldn't need them, and if he were to be stopped, wet shorts would be hard to explain. He smiled at his thought process. It felt good to be back on Corsica.

Falconi untied the short-handled fire axe before slinging the knapsack onto his shoulder and starting up the trail. His plan was simple: traveling at night, he would walk inland until he crossed the coastal road, which he would then follow to Falcon's Roost. Around that ruin he would find the Guibega. With them, he would make the Germans pay a dear rent for their occupation.

The trail was steep and Falconi, already half spent from the swim, was breathing heavily after the first hundred meters. He stopped to catch his breath, looking back down at the beach to make sure the fishing vessel had not somehow survived a watery grave. He saw no signs of the boat, but he could hear the throb of a diesel engine in the darkness, a sound that was coming closer. Listening for only a moment, he renewed his climb. On the coast, especially in this narrow defile leading from the sea, he was vulnerable. Once inland he would be invisible, just another Corsican.

Falconi was almost at the top of the trail, the sides of the canyon quickly converging, when he heard the static of a radio. He stopped, waiting for a darker cloud to obscure his movements. Silently, he pulled himself up onto a boulder that flanked the trail. On his thick black rubber-soled shoes, he moved from boulder to boulder, paralleling the trail some ten meters away.

Corporal Gunnar Heinz sat hidden behind a large rock at the head of the trail. He cursed his forgetfulness in not having shut off the incoming messages. Fortunately, the man from the beach could only be halfway up the trail, still out of hearing range. The last message he had received told him that the patrol boat was landing a party of men that would follow the man up the trail, forcing him into Gunnar's trap. All he had to do was wait. Once he had his captive, fat chance he would turn him over to the navy. He would walk the bastard all the way back to Ajaccio before he would do that. If the man resisted, he would shoot him in the leg and carry him back himself.

Training his rifle on the path, he leaned back against the cold stone of the boulder and waited.

Falconi scanned the area in front of him but it was impossible to pick out anything except the large shapes of boulders. He had not heard the hiss of the radio again and after five minutes of climbing over the rugged terrain that bordered the trail, he had lost his orientation as to the direction of the sound. Falconi reviewed his options and they were few. He knew that someone was waiting for him, someone with a radio who was most likely hostile. He could only hope that this person was alone. A coastal watch would certainly not assign more than two men to this lonely, unlikely landing site. If there was only one, it was possible he could be overlooked. If there were more than one man, the odds of successfully slipping by or surviving a fight decreased considerably. Once day broke, he would have trouble hiding from a well-organized search party.

Cautiously, he inched back down to the trail. Visibility was only fifteen feet. He slid off the boulder to the sandy path and stopped. Looking up, he could discern the crest above the boulders only as a slightly less dense blackness. The shallow, muffled sound of fabric scuffing against rock turned his attention back down the trail. He peered into the darkness and slowly, the outline of a man's boots and legs became apparent. He had rejoined the trail only three meters from where his adversary lay in wait.

Falconi had started to move away when he heard the cries of men on the beach. If there was any doubt as to their nationality, it was dispelled when he heard their officer's orders.

Egel saw the feet of the trail watcher shift, the vague shape of a rifle barrel barely discernible. He could no longer expect to move away undetected. His decision was made for him by the pursuit from the beach. Falconi took two quick steps around the rock and swung the axe in a compact, powerful arc. The pointed end of the weapon, designed to break down doors and walls, did the same to the chest cavity of Corporal Gunnar Heinz, piercing his heart before deflecting off the boulder at his back.

Falconi looked at the man, whose mouth was open in a noiseless scream, his blood still pulsing from the wound in his chest. He quickly slipped the rifle off the man's shoulder, removing the radio and depositing it into his own backpack. Then, reaching down, he hoisted the dead sentry, lifting him up and over the boulder that had provided the backstop for his deathblow. As the man crumpled out of sight, Falconi picked up his sack, moving quickly up the trail at a trot.

It took him less than an hour to find the road, his navigation having been better than he had hoped. The cove at which he had landed was no more than fifteen kilometers north of Ajaccio and once he had gained the road, less than five from Falcon's Roost. Falconi made good time, the landmarks of his youth coming back to him. Driven by a sense of urgency that had grown in him since leaving Spain, he left the road, moving quickly up the steep incline to the ruin of stone that centuries before had housed Falconi's ancestors in a small but well-protected stone keep.

The ruin was dark, no movement evident inside its broken walls. Egel Falconi had not seen it in over six years. Still, its solidity gave him comfort. At the top of the grade, he stopped. He could sense someone nearby.

"Put up your hands, now!" The voice was a woman's, coming from just inside the ruin. The metallic click of a trigger mechanism underscored the importance of obeying. Falconi raised his hands, wondering how the woman could tell if he had complied, so dark was the night.

"Who are you?"

"I am a Guibega," answered Egel in the musical Corsican dialect of his youth.

"You are no Guibega." There was strength of conviction in the accusation. "Answer truthfully or die."

"You are right. I am not a Guibega. I am Egel Falconi." Falconi spoke into the darkness.

"If you are Falconi, who will vouch for you?"

"He is a Guibega. Nando Guibega."

"It is true, then, what Nando tells me." Falconi heard the soft words from the darkness.

"What is Nando to you?" asked Egel.

"I am Teresa Guibega. Nando is my uncle." The young woman stepped out of the shadows. In her black dress, she was almost invisible until Egel made out her shape outlined against the gray stone of the ruin.

"I know your uncle. He is younger than I by four years. We were friends. I need to speak to him. Is he near?"

"He is near, but you cannot speak to him. Three days ago the Germans picked him up, along with six others. He is being kept in a barbed wire enclosure on the Rue Fesch."

"What did they arrest him for?"

"The Germans need no reason. The Resistance gives them trouble, so they pick up our men."

"What will they do to him?"

"They take their prisoners off the island. We are not told where."

Falconi took the young woman by the arm, moving close to see the look in her eyes and seeing her pride through her tears.

"He is going to try to escape, just before dawn. I am afraid."

"Your uncle is a remarkable man. If he is trying to escape, he will be successful." Falconi's words were meant to reassure the girl, but they had little effect.

"We had a woman who worked in the Musée Fesch, next to the prison. She could hear my uncle's voice and bring us messages. It was she who brought us word that he would try to escape, but before she could relay the particulars of the plan, she too was arrested by the Nazis. We think she has been tortured."

"How long will it take us to get to the prison?" asked Falconi, now as worried as Nando's Teresa for the man's safety.

"About thirty minutes. It is ten kilometers, but I have my uncle's motorcycle. The Germans have patrols and roadblocks, but if we take the back roads over Mount Salario, we will avoid them."

The genetic trait that accounted for the Gift was not as prominent in Egel as it had been in his father. The dreams of ancestors had come to Egel only infrequently, much to his father's disappointment. In fact, Egel's only truly vivid dream had occurred when he was a young man, just before he had decided to leave Corsica for America. It had told him of Jarl Falkhand, a leader of the Varangian Guard in Constantinople, and the circumstances that had forced him to flee that city. The warning had been clear; it was the main reason that Egel Falconi had left Corsica for America. Now he had returned, and his life was in the hands of this young woman.

Egel Falconi had not ridden a motorcycle since he was a boy. Now, riding behind Teresa Guibega, both the fear and the exhilaration came back to him. She drove without headlights, leaning into turns before he could even make out the change in the road's direction. Holding tightly to her slim waist, he could anticipate the movements of the bike much better than by using his eyes. Minutes passed, and he came to trust her skill. He could feel the muscles of her legs and back willing the bike to overcome the unseen ruts and potholes in the road. He could feel the rifle and axe move along with his pack, the straps tightening first over one shoulder and then the other as they rounded barely visible curves. They were climbing; he knew by the laboring of the engine rather than by any visible clue.

"We are only five kilometers from the Palais Fesch." It was the first time Teresa had spoken since they had climbed on the motorcycle. "We must be quiet from this point on."

She crested a hill with a burst of speed and turned off the engine. They rolled down the hill without losing speed, the only sound coming from the squeak of the suspension. The road became better surfaced as they continued down toward the lights of Ajaccio, the noise from the springs less frequent.

Buildings became numerous, the small houses of the poor gradually replaced by larger dwellings. Teresa pulled into a courtyard, which Falconi immediately recognized as the Alta Mira, a restaurant that had been owned by his family prior to his leaving Corsica. The vines of bougainvillea had grown in his absence but the building, with its arches leading to the balcony, were unchanged and unforgettable.

"We'll walk from here. The rifles must be left as well." Teresa moved to a bench, lifting its seat board to expose a storage area. Falconi handed the girl the guns and was about to hand her his pack as well when he hesitated.

"We will need a reason to say we are out if we are stopped," he said, emptying the contents of his pack into the seat chest. Moving to a stack of fruitwood along the side wall, he flattened his pack, piling stick after stick over it. When the stack was two feet high, he stopped and fastened the load with the ties on his pack. On top of everything he fastened his axe. Shouldering the pack with its load of firewood, he started down the steep street to the main section of town.

At first, Falconi was content to let Teresa lead him through the labyrinth of curved streets, but as they neared their destination, he called her to his side. "If we are stopped, I am your uncle, Egel Guibega. We have been gathering wood to the south and are on our way to the restaurant." He took her hand and they walked openly down the center of the street.

Sounds of German coming from around the corner stopped Falconi. He understood only a little German, but everyone knew the meaning of the words "Dum kopf." This was not a confrontation Falconi wanted if it could be avoided.

"Can we get around this intersection?" he whispered to Teresa.

"Yes, there is an alley that goes around this building, but we will still have to cross the street."

Falconi followed the girl in the improving light of pre-dawn. She led him through an alley so narrow that the sticks on his pack scraped the walls. At the end the alley turned to the right, widening slightly before exiting on the street a block up from the Germans.

"We have to get to the alley across the street." Teresa pointed at a dark slit between two buildings. "It leads to the prison enclosure."

Falconi slowly stuck his head out from the protection of the alley. He could see the Germans clearly. There were three of them working on a Citroën delivery van parked at the curb, or rather, two of them were working while an officer stood apart, admonishing them from the curb to be careful. Egel could only see the back of the man in charge. He was of above average height with blond hair worn short under an officer's cap. His shoulders were broad, but it was not the man's physical presence that caught Egel's attention most; it was the harsh, abusive tone of the orders he barked at his men. The German punctuated his remarks with thrusts of a stick strapped to his left hand. It was not a swagger stick like many of the British officers carried instead of a sidearm; it was much thicker. It was made of a dark stained wood, long but almost thick enough to be termed a club. On his hip, opposite his right hand, hung a Luger.

Falconi watched them, hoping for an opportunity to cross the street. One of the Germans placed what looked like sticks of explosives under the van while the other, a sergeant, wired something under the hood. Falconi watched, confused as to their purpose. The man beneath the vehicle finally indicated that he was finished and passed the end of a wire up through the engine compartment to the sergeant. Egel watched as the officer backed several steps away while the sergeant wired the last connection and gingerly lowered the hood.

The two enlisted men wiped the sweat from their foreheads before putting on their uniform jackets. Egel saw the sergeant move to the side of the officer and mimic the turning of a key.

"Kaboom! It's ready, Lieutenant."

The officer nodded, looking anxious to be away from the booby-trapped van. As soon as his men had replaced their tools in the carrying sack, he led them down the street and away from Falconi and Teresa. Falconi, giving less thought to what he had observed than to the fact that their way was now clear, lifted his load and moved across the street with Teresa close behind.

The enclosure was no more than a square that had been ringed inside its perimeter with a double fence of barbed wire. Inside were open-ended lean-tos providing partial cover for better than one hundred men. There were only two guards at the entrance and one who patrolled the exterior perimeter every hour.

When the patrol had passed, Falconi took a fagot from his pack and threw it over the fence. It landed on one of the tents. Someone stirred. "Who is it?"

"I would speak with Nando. Is he awake?"

"What makes you think I sleep?" came the low, guttural reply from an adjacent tent.

"Nando, it is Egel. I am with your niece. She says you will escape?"

"Egel! I have prayed for your return. Yes, tonight. When the bells ring at the Church of St. John the Baptist, a car will be driven through the wire from the north on the Boulevard du Roi Jérôme."

"And after you are out of the enclosure, how do you avoid recapture?"

"It has been taken care of, Egel. Take Teresa away from here. I will meet you at the Roost this evening at dusk."

"You have not answered me, Nando. How will you avoid the Germans?"

"A van, a black Citroën, has been left for us one block from here. It will provide transportation. Now take Teresa and go!"

Egel was about to warn Nando of the booby trap, but the patrol guard could be heard running toward his position, alerted by the sound of their conversation. Both he and Teresa melted back into the darkness of the alley.

CHAPTER FOUR

Dunkineely, July 2003

In Mats' dream, Egel Falconi, his father, jerked his head violently as Nando told him the details of the escape plan. So real was his shock that Mats, lying asleep, involuntarily emulated the movement. It woke him, leaving him disoriented in the strange bedroom of the Keohane house. Suzanne turned beneath the sheets, disturbed by his movement but not awakened by it.

Gently, Mats swung his feet to the floor and raised himself to a standing position. He had had trouble getting to sleep and now his heart was pounding. Moving to the window, he checked the time on his wristwatch by the cool silver moonlight streaming through the light curtains. Two-thirty; he felt the pulse just above the watch band. His heart was still responding to the adrenaline rush it had received in his dream.

He took a deep breath, forcing himself to calm down by looking over the moonlit landscape to the Bay of Donegal. This was the second time in a week that he had dreamt of his father. The first time, he'd put it aside as probably caused by the discussion with Suzanne of having a child, of passing on the Falconi line to another generation. But this dream was different. It had a message. It was real, and without question, Mats knew that it was true. He also knew that it had some connection to the present.

When Suzanne's and his own life had been in danger in the south of France two years ago, Mats had come to trust the dreams. Those dreams had had the same authentic quality, the same cadence in their telling as did these.

A metallic click drew his attention. Looking through the window at the barn-like garage, he saw two figures, little more than shadows in the moonlight, moving around his rental car. The hood was already raised. One man moved to the front, bending so that only his legs remained visible from beneath the hood. The other, his back to Mats, was handing the first man items from what looked like a canvas athletic bag. They worked quickly; no sooner had a hand reached out from the engine compartment than something was placed in it and immediately withdrawn. The man beside the car kept casting his eyes nervously toward the house.

Mats moved back behind the curtain, parting it enough so that one eye could clearly see the scene below. At first the shadows made it difficult to make out anything very distinctly, but then he saw the man holding the canvas bag straighten, turning again toward the window. Mats stiffened. The man was wearing a ski mask, but the stretched dark wool did little to hide the profile of the hideously hooked nose beneath it.

The man under the hood pulled back and stood. Even at this distance, Mats could see his quick nod. He slowly lowered the hood with two hands, closing it with a firm push from his palms. Mats heard the same muffled metallic click.

Mats stayed by the window, fearing to move lest the two men were still watching from the shadows. Five minutes passed and he heard a car start in the distance. Only then did he dare to move back to the bed, slipping under the covers without waking Suzanne. Thoughts raced through his mind. If he'd had difficulty finding sleep before, now it was impossible. He knew what he would find under the hood, but why had it been put there? Who were these men and why were they trying to kill him?

Mats was not sure that he had slept. He knew some time had passed since he'd watched the two men rig his car, and much of it had been spent turning from side to side beneath the sheets. Still, there were stretches that he couldn't account for. If he had slept, it had made no impression on either his body or his brain. He was ragged as he slipped out from his spoon position next to Suzanne and quietly stepped down the stairs. He was worried that Suzanne or Brian would try to start the car. There was little sense to it but still he worried.

Dawn was breaking as he crept silently into the kitchen. He found a bottle of freeze-dried coffee crystals stashed among the tea containers and started a pot of water boiling on the stove. Long fingers of dark gray clouds caught the first rays of the rising sun, accentuating their darkness against the lightening sky. There would be rain later in the day.

Keohane's house was built in the Irish tradition. It had a main room which contained the front door, a fireplace, and tables and chairs. On each end was a door leading to bedrooms. One, the larger of the two, had a fireplace which, in the frugal Irish custom, shared the same chimney as the one in the main room. The exterior walls were over a foot thick. Originally there had been a sleeping loft but at some point, probably in this century, the house had been modified. A second story had been added to provide not only a master bedroom but also inside plumbing and facilities. The larger of the downstairs bedrooms had been expanded toward the back of the house, providing room for the present modern kitchen and tearoom. The addition mimicked the original construction, and Mats was sure that it was capable of withstanding the worst the Atlantic could throw at it.

The hot water was just dissolving the coffee crystals when Brian appeared. He had changed both his trousers and sweater from the previous evening. Somehow, he looked smaller, more vulnerable. His parents had been murdered only three months before. He had been shuttled off to a foster home away from his familiar surroundings by a solicitor who had only his own interests at heart. Still, the previous evening he had seemed very grown up and in control. This morning in the early light, his hair still ruffled from sleep, Brian looked more like the thirteen-year-old boy that he was. Looking at Brian this way, before he had had time to put up his emotional defenses, Mats felt deep compassion for the tragedy the boy had suffered and the pain and uncertainty he must be enduring.

"Water's hot, Brian. Can I make you a cup of coffee or tea?"

"I'll get it, thank you. What time is it?"

Mats glanced at his watch. "It's a quarter to six."

"Is Suzanne up?"

"No. I had trouble sleeping."

"So did I. What are your plans today?"

"I think I'll see if we can get a flight back to France."

"I thought you were going to buy Dad's brewery."

"Things have changed. I think that whoever buys the Harp and Hawk is in for big trouble. I don't want to risk Suzanne's safety, or mine for that matter."

Brian moved to the table, his hands cupped around his mug of tea. He looked at Mats with piercing blue eyes, the same eyes that had made such an impression on Mats when he had first seen them outside the Seascape Restaurant. Mats held eye contact until he finally had to turn away.

He had made the decision to leave Ireland just hours before in his restless half-sleep. The brewery spelled danger; it had already killed Brian's parents, and if they started the car in the driveway, it would kill them as well. The Falconi were brave, but their bravery always had a purpose: it protected and avenged their own. They did not go looking for trouble, and the Harp and Hawk was clearly trouble. A business deal was not worth risking one's life.

"You had a dream, didn't you?" the boy asked suddenly.

Mats' eyes shot back, meeting Brian's with almost physical force. "Yes," he answered slowly, trying to gauge the intent in Brian's question. Brian was the only snag in his decision to walk away from the deal and leave Ireland. Brian was special: an adult in a boy's body. More important, Mats liked him, and so did Suzanne. To leave him to the mercy of Gavan Grady seemed almost unthinkable.

"It warned you of something, didn't it?"

"Yes," Mats answered, again slowly, drawing the word out as if he were asking a question.

"Heed the warning," said Brian, sitting down but still looking intently at Mats. "I didn't tell you this last night, but my father had a dream the night before he was murdered. It was one of the dreams he called the 'Knack.' It was a warning. That's why he took the day off and went golfing. I was supposed to be in school, but Mum wrote me a note. After we finished, he drove by the brewery to close up. That's when they were gunned down. Did your dream warn you about buying the Harp and Hawk?"

"No. It was about my father during the war. He was in Corsica fighting the Nazis and saw a van booby-trapped with explosives. It was so real it woke me up. I thought I heard a noise in the yard. I didn't want to wake Suzanne, so I got out of bed to look out the window and saw two men with ski masks at work on our car. The hood was up. I don't think they were checking the oil."

"What are you going to do?"

"Well, I'm not going to start the car. I'll phone the agency and tell them the car wouldn't start. It's better that whoever did this thinks that we were just dumb lucky. I don't want them to know we are on to them. By the time they figure it out, we'll be back in France. I'll phone Grady from France and tell him we are no longer interested." Mats hesitated. "Brian, do you have dreams like your father did?"

"No. Dad said I was a little young yet. He told me he started getting them when he was courting Mom. He used to tell me stories about them, great battles and sea voyages. I liked them, but I always thought they had a bit of blarney in them." Brian looked up at Mats. "Did you have your dreams when you were my age?"

"No. At least I don't think I did. My father used to tell me bedtime stories. Sometimes I would be dreaming, but I'd wake up and my father would still be sitting there in the dark, telling a story. I didn't have any like the one last night until two years ago when I first went to Corsica. Even then, I really only had them when I was in danger. I thought my family was the only one that had such dreams. We call them our 'Gift.'"

"All the men in my family have had the 'Knack.' At least that's what Dad told me. Does your father still have them?"

"My father is dead. He was gunned down by a drug dealer just over two years ago." Mats looked seriously at the boy. "Brian, having these dreams … it's a unique ability. It is not normal. So it's important not to let others know that we have them. How was it that you came to ask me about them?"

"You have the look...the same as my dad had after a dream. It was very distinctive. Dad looked scared, or maybe haunted. His eyes were nervous."

"That reminds me of something, Brian. You might also get hurt here in Donegal. I don't think I have to tell you that Mr. Grady does not have your best interests at heart in settling your father's estate. He was willing to cut you out of a hundred thousand pounds for a fifteen-thousand-pound bribe."

"Mr. Grady sent me to Mrs. O'Toole when I asked to see the books," Brian said.

"I like you, Brian, and so does Suzanne. Do you want to come with us until it's safe here? We have a house in France, but we live mostly in America. You could even go to school in California until the business is sold and things calm down here."

"I'd like to visit America."

"Good. I'll have Mr. Tobin recommend an attorney to help you with the necessary papers and a passport."

Brian smiled, but he was clearly longing to return to an earlier topic. "Mats...when you dream, are you in someone else's body?"

"Yes. It's like I'm looking through the eyes of one of my ancestors but using my own brain to think. When they speak, I don't know what they are going to say until the words come out. It's weird, especially when I know that what I'm seeing happened for real. Why?"

"Because I wasn't entirely truthful with you. Last night I had my first dream. It was all mixed up and confusing, but it was different from any dream I've ever had. I was in the body of a grownup and I was in a boat. We kept sailing toward some port, but we never got there. There was some important reason, but when I woke up I couldn't remember what it was."

"Was there a warning?" Mats watched the young boy.

Brian was staring down at his teacup, but he finally looked up, confusion in his eyes. "I can't remember. But when I woke up, I was afraid. That's when I heard you come down the stairs."

"Well, well, aren't you two up early!"

Mats turned quickly. He had been so intent on Brian's story that he hadn't heard Suzanne coming down the stairs.

Suzanne's tone changed as she noticed the look on Mats' face. "What's wrong?" she asked.

"Both Brian and I had dreams last night. It was Brian's first. He has the Gift."

"Oh God. Is there trouble?"

"Yes. I'll make more coffee. We'd better talk about it."

Mats gently placed the battery cable on top of the explosives and closed the hood of the car. It would be impossible for anyone to start the car or to miss the bomb once they opened the bonnet. "Okay. That's done. We'd better start walking to Dunkineely."

"Why don't we just take the skiff? We could be in Donegal before the car gets here," said Brian, glancing toward the water.

Mats had not seen any sign of a boat, but he still felt stupid for asking. "You have a boat?"

"And how might you be thinking I was getting back and forth from Donegal?" asked Brian, a mischievous smile cracking the right side of his mouth.

It was the first time since they had met the previous evening that either Mats or Suzanne had seen the thirteen-year-old relax a little. Suzanne threw her arm around the boy and gave him a hug and Mats laughed out loud.

Brian led the way down the path to the jetty. Hollowed out into the cliff was a shelter for a small boat. Two parallel stone tracks with their tops angled toward each other ran from the weather break at an angle of twenty degrees into the water. Sitting on them, lashed securely to iron rings pounded into the cliff face, was a small skiff.

When his father was still alive, Mats had spent hours each day on the Sausalito docks. His father had taught him to love the sea and also to respect her. He had taught Mats how to take care of a boat, and now, looking at the way Brian had left this one, he was impressed. All the gear and lines were properly stowed. The sail was still rigged but lashed tightly against the beam.

Without hesitating, Brian grabbed a large tin bucket with a long-handled brush from deep in the enclosure and started slopping black grease onto the stone ways. He untied the mooring lines and began turning a small hand winch, loosening the rope attached to the bow. When there was about three feet of slack, he moved behind the boat and gave it a shove.

Mats marveled at the boy's efficiency as the boat slid over the horizontal portion of the way and down the incline toward the water. When gravity took over, Brian returned to the winch and lowered the boat into the water. Mats was first into the boat, offering Suzanne a hand in her descent. Brian was right behind her, pushing the boat away from the rocky shore as he stepped in.

The boat was about eighteen feet long and had a single stout mast that held a gaff-rigged sail. Brian unhooked the line still attached to the winch, tying it off on a small buoy. This arrangement had been well thought out and Brian had obviously used it many times. The boy turned around to start raising the sail only to find that Mats had already done the chore and was in the process of lowering the center board. The rudder had already been removed from under the thwarts and placed over the stern.

With Brian at the tiller, the sail caught the wind, propelling the boat out of the cover afforded by the small inlet and into the waters of Donegal Bay. With his arm bent over the tiller, the boy showed the same confidence that Mats felt when he sailed—at peace with the sea and with the vessel that allowed him to survive on it.

Mats felt the boat change direction slightly toward the nearing port, closing his eyes against the sting of the salt spray. The wind that whipped through his jacket seemed colder, harsher than it had been minutes before. Behind his closed lids, familiar figures were coming into focus. Knowing what was happening, Mats gave in to his dream...

When Mats opened his eyes, they viewed a different shore. The coast of Donegal County had been somewhat rocky, but still green and hospitable. This landing before him was anything but hospitable. It was stark gray, made of slabs of sharp-edged rock. The land above, without the benefit of topsoil, was devoid of vegetation. Already drawn up on the steep incline were two longboats with their crews camped beside them. The third longboat— the one he was on—was just off the shore, a gentle swell softly rocking the boat.

Mats recognized this scene. Two years before, this had been a dream within a dream. He had needed to learn the origin of the Gift and had dreamt of his ancestor, Baron Falconi. In his dream, the Baron had also dreamt—of three Viking brothers and their battle with Eric Redhand, a Viking chief. His head turned toward the sound of a voice. The words were strange, yet he found that he understood them.

The North Sea—943 AD

"Our men await our decision, brother." The man who addressed Mats was large, with reddish blond hair that grew long from under a conical metal helmet.

"There is no decision to make. They will leave us if we do not heed Eric Redhand's counsel. They know as well as we do that it would be folly to choose to be shunned by all Vikings save our kin."

Mats turned to face the second of the speakers, a perfect copy of the first but for a wolf-skin cloak that draped his shoulders. Two years of absence from Mats' dreams had not changed the brothers' appearance or manner. Without looking, Mats knew that he was seeing them through the eyes of their triplet brother, Jarl.

"You are right, Kjell. Redhand has offered us a way out. If we sail away together, all Vikings will become our enemies, thanks to Bloodaxe's lies. Because we know each other's thoughts, they think we have dark magic. But if we separate, we will still have our men and our luck."

"One thing, brother," said the first, putting a hand on Jarl's arm. "We should not give up anything that is ours. Our longboats stay under our command, our stead remains ours by rights, and all that belongs to the Falkhand should remain ours."

"Jan is also right," said Jarl. "It is agreed that we will follow Eric Redhand's plan and serve under different kings. We must now agree on who will go where."

"I would stay with Redhand," said the triplet named Kjell. "I have the best weather luck of us three. Redhand speaks of raids on the Isle of the Mists, the Isle of Avalon. He will prize my luck the most."

"And you, Jan?" asked Jarl. "Which bearing would you take?"

"If Kjell is to stay with Redhand, then I would offer protection by joining the Danes to the south. My men would welcome the warm weather and the plunder of the southern rivers. What would you do, Jarl?"

"I will return to our stead. I will take with me Redhand's daughter, as I have promised. You will always be on my mind. I will avenge you if the alliances made here prove false."

"As will I," swore Kjell.

"And I," added Jan. "And I will have the greatest chance of making Bloodaxe wish he had never thought to discredit us."

The three identical men stepped toward one another, each grabbing the others' wrists. They tightened their grip, as if to stop the flow of blood through the triangle of bone and muscle. Their vows were true. They would protect each other and keep what was theirs.

"Oarsmen! Man the oars and take us back to shore. The Falkhand do not wish to keep Eric Redhand waiting."

As the sleek craft made its way toward the shore, Jan turned to Kjell. "You surprise me, brother. I thought you would want the warm climate and the Frankish women."

"Ah, but that would take me farther from Bloodaxe, wouldn't it? If I get a chance, his skald will compose Bloodaxe's dirge for his next saga."

"I thought that might have been your reason," said Jarl, and all three brothers laughed into the freshening wind.

"Mats!" Suzanne yelled as the boat narrowly missed the breakwater and continued under full sail into the harbor at Donegal.

Mats shook his head. It took several seconds to realize that he was no longer dreaming; time had passed, enough to reach the harbor at Donegal. They were still several hundred meters from the stone pier, but they were moving far too fast for the close confines and crowded conditions of the harbor. Without waiting for Brian's order, Mats dropped the rigging, furling the sail as it fell to the thwarts. Leaving the jib in position, he turned to Brian, still standing at the tiller.

"Brian, Brian!"

The boy was staring transfixed at some point halfway up the stone wall protecting Donegal Castle from the harbor. At Mats' cry he twitched, blinking before lowering his gaze. As Mats had done seconds before, he shook his head, trying to clear his mind to react to the new input. He swung the tiller to port, pointing the bow immediately toward starboard. The boat slipped under the stern of a large ocean-going fishing boat, which momentarily robbed the jib of its wind.

Suzanne breathed deeply as their boat slid gently against a stone pier and stopped. Mats jumped ashore with a line. Once it was fastened, he reached down for Suzanne. Brian was already stowing the rudder and raising the center board. His were practiced movements. He would leave his ship the way he found it, ready for its next trip. Mats reached down, offering a hand to the boy, and their eyes met with the touch of their hands.

"You had another dream?" asked Mats.

"Yes, but this one was clearer. How did you know?"

"I had one too," answered Mats. "Let's find someplace where we can talk." He started walking up the stone pier.

Brian led Mats and Suzanne to a small sweet roll shop in the triangular area that served as Donegal's town "square." The pastries were fresh and delicious, the coffee strong and hot. They sat a table close to the back of the shop. Mats described his dream, explaining to Brian that it was not the first time he had dreamt of the Viking triplets. He had learned, years earlier, that they were the origin of the Gift. Something in their birth, their genetic similarity, had made it possible for them to hear each other's thoughts without speaking.

"One thing is certain," said Mats, after recounting his dream. "Those three brothers are our ancestors. By accident of their birth, they had the original 'Gift.' Sometimes you hear of identical twins being able to understand each other intuitively, but this must have been something more powerful. Their abilities have become diluted over the centuries in us. I could sense you watching me at the Seascape, but I can't read your thoughts. We both have the ability to dream, though. I saw that the triplets made a pact not to give up any of their possessions in their alliance with Eric Redhand. But I'm not sure how this information applies to me. I don't own the Harp and Hawk yet."

"I might have the answer," said Brian. "I had the same exact dream as you. I also experienced the action through the eyes of a grown Viking. There was a great difference, however. You tell of seeing the brothers Jan and Kjell through the eyes of Jarl. In my dream, I made the decision to stay with Redhand. I was seeing through Kjell's eyes."

Mats understood. How simple. Given the boy's dream, he could see the pieces falling into place. He had known almost from the beginning of his own dreams that they were accounts of real events of the past, which somehow he was able to experience through the eyes of his ancestors. Both times he had dreamt of the three Viking brothers, he had done so through the perspective of Jarl. Up till now, he had thought this was because Jarl was the leader, or so it seemed. Now Brian had experienced the same event from the past but from the perspective of another brother. Kjell was Brian's linear ancestor. Jarl, then, had started the Falconi line that led to Mats. He and Brian were related. The tie lay twelve hundred years in the past, but they were related.

"Then the warning not to let go of any of their holdings was directed at you, Brian, not me."

"But that must have happened a thousand years ago."

"Longer than that, but we are still kin, and we share an ability passed on by those three brothers. The message is clear. We should keep the house and the brewery in the family, despite the risk."

"If you do, then you better figure out who stands to benefit or be hurt from the sale of the Harp and Hawk." Suzanne had remained quiet while Mats and Brian recounted their dreams, but now she spoke up. Brian was the missing piece in her own puzzle. She shared the Gift, but not nearly as powerfully as either Brian or Mats. Until now, there had been no explanation for it. Now she would be surprised if she were not the descendant of the third brother, Jan. The Vikings who raided France had settled and become Normans, occupying lands that her parents still farmed. Her lineage would be more diffuse than Mats' or Brian's. The Falconi and Keohanes had been island people, which increased the chance that their blood lines were purer than those on the Continent. Now, through fate or design, they had been brought together. Her feelings for the boy they had met less than twenty-four hours ago attested to that.

Mats phoned Tobin and told him where they were, then punched in another number.

"Hello, Hertz Rental Car? Yes, I have a car that won't start…"

CHAPTER FIVE

"So, now, who would be wanting to blow you to ribbons?" asked Constable Robert Minahen. He was a large, imposing man, and his size was emphasized by the small dining area in which he was questioning Mats and Suzanne. The rental agency had sent someone to pick up their car and the bomb had been discovered.

"Mr. Minahen, we didn't even expect to spend the night."

"Someone knew you were there." Minahen slid a large beefy hand across the table, flipping his palm up as if to physically receive the answer.

"Mr. Grady gave us the key and the directions, but I don't think he expected us to spend the night. The only other person was Charlie Tobin."

"Ah yes, Mr. Charlie Tobin, your Irish business consultant with no references to speak of. I will be talking with him next. And how is it you know Mr. Grady?"

"We're negotiating for the purchase of the Harp and Hawk. I think we will have an agreement within a day or two."

"Have you ever done business in Ireland before?"

"No. We've never even been to Ireland before."

"Have you ever had any dealings with the Irish Republican Army, the IRA, or spoken against them?" Minahen shifted his bulk and leaned toward Mats. His forehead was impossibly broad, framed by short-cropped, sandy blond hair.

"To my knowledge, I have never even met a member of the IRA."

"Nor probably would you have known it if you had," said the policeman. "Well then, why would someone want to kill you?"

"I was hoping you could answer that for me, Constable. I have no idea."

"Well, if it is the IRA, I'd be thinking of leaving County Donegal if I were you. It's said they holiday here, and I couldn't say that's a lie. In the meantime, I'll be leaving a man with you, sort of to look after things till you can arrange for airline tickets."

"So, your solution is to get us out of the country, not catch the men who tried to kill me?"

"Undoubtedly the easier of the two," Minahen answered truthfully. "I don't want another murder investigation on my desk."

"What about the boy?" asked Mats.

"I'll be taking the young runaway with me. He has some serious answers to give. For one, we don't know that he wasn't the one who wired the car."

Mats could see the panic rising in Suzanne's eyes. "Mr. Minahen, I can vouch for the boy. He was planning to ride back to town with us. He was in the car when it didn't start," Mats lied.

Minahen grunted as if he'd been punched. "There's still the runaway charge. Mr. Grady, being the boy's solicitor and his legal guardian, will have something to say, I'm sure."

Mats suddenly glimpsed the possibility of a solution. "Mr. Minahen, the boy does not like Mr. Grady. On the way back here, he talked about obtaining another lawyer. I think he called him a barrister."

"What is the difference between a solicitor and a barrister?" asked Suzanne.

"A solicitor does all the legal contracts and paperwork out of court; a barrister argues cases in front of the bench. You're sure the boy said a barrister?"

"That's what he said. He seems content to stay with us and show us around," added Mats. "He might not even be a runaway. We found him living in his own house. I'll get him a room here where he'll get three square meals a day. Let him stay with us until we conclude the sale. I'm sure Mr. Grady would approve."

"You plan on staying in Ireland then?" Minahen's great bushy eyebrows rose halfway up his massive forehead.

"Yes, at least until the sale is complete and we hire men to run the brewery."

Minahen pushed his bulk back from the table. "I'll have to talk to Mr. Grady. Meanwhile, I'll ask the lad a few questions."

"Minahen checked out Tobin," said Gavan Grady as soon as Mats answered the phone. "He's nowhere near qualified to negotiate this transaction for you, Mr. Falconi. He's had some jobs in the beer business, but they've mainly been as a hired hand or salesman. Are you sure you want him to sit in on the meeting?" Grady's voice came silky smooth over the phone, as if the cell had been oiled.

"I signed an agreement with him early on," said Mats. "It would be more trouble getting rid of him than keeping him on."

"I'm just trying to save you money, Mr. Falconi. If it's his agreement you're worried about, I'm sure I can break it for you at no charge."

"I appreciate the offer, Mr. Grady, but I think I'll just let it ride. I'll try to keep him from being so belligerent. We'll see you at your office at three."

"Belligerent! I would have said incompetent and obnoxious. But then, I'm Irish and would always prefer to use two words when one might do. I'll see you at three. Goodbye."

Con O'Shields, the guard left by Minahen, drove them to the office of Grady, Duffy, and Walsh in the police van. While Mats, Suzanne, and Tobin finalized the sale with Grady, Brian and O'Shields went shopping for chocolates and champagne.

Mats had faxed the final documents to John Powers, a solicitor who was a friend of Tobin's. The lawyer worked in Cork for Apple Computers of Europe but was happy to pay off an old debt to Charlie Tobin by looking over the final sale papers. He found that they were generally well drawn and had only one suggestion as to procedure, should transfer of funds take longer than the five working days stipulated. Grady saw no problem in redoing the clause and had the revised package waiting for Mats when they arrived.

Despite Mats' previous approval, Tobin made much of reading the entire package. Fortunately, the section stipulating his finder's fee was close to the front, so the process did not take as long as it might have.

"It doesn't look like anything tricky has been slipped in, Mr. Falconi," Tobin announced, glaring across the desk at Grady. "But it doesn't hurt to check, now, does it?"

"Mr. Tobin, I thank you for your attention to the paperwork, but that will be enough now." Mats looked at the small Irishman, who had a twinkle in his eye, having been unable to resist one last dig at Grady.

Mats signed three sets of documents, returning them to Grady for his signature. The entire transaction had taken less than twenty minutes, fifteen of which were taken up by Tobin's posturing.

"Welcome to the Donegal business community," said Grady, rising from his side of the desk and extending his hand toward Mats. "I don't have to tell you how important the brewery is to Donegal. After the Magee woolen mills, it is probably the most identifiable of all our products."

"I hope to keep it so," said Mats, shaking Grady's hand. "Thank you again for expediting this transaction. There is one other piece of business I would like you to arrange. Brian Keohane wants to retain ownership of his parents' house. He has no concept of the inheritance tax aspect or the probate fees due your office. Could you compile the costs for the transfer of the title to the boy? You can deduct the fees and taxes from what he has coming from the brewery sale."

"Yes, I can do that. The boy will have to sign some papers, of course."

"Thanks again, Mr. Grady." Mats stood and followed Tobin and Suzanne from the office.

Cathal Magee popped the cork on the fifth bottle of champagne. Magee and Tobin had done the lion's share of damage to the bubbly, but Suzanne had helped. The rest of the party was drinking Harp and Hawk with the exception of Brian, who was on a sugar high with Coca-Cola.

They had arrived at the brewery within minutes of signing the papers. Magee had called all of the previous workers and their wives or girlfriends, inviting them to the party celebrating the re-opening of the brewery. The women had brought cakes and cookies along with freshly baked bread and cheese. Magee had even coughed up a case of useless non-alcoholic beer, proudly offering a chilled bottle to his new boss.

Mats was encouraged by the feeling of camaraderie and good will shown by the group. He made sure that everyone met Charlie Tobin and Suzanne. Most of the men were related to Magee, who became more and more eloquent in describing their family relationships as the champagne flowed.

Before the party got too far along, Mats asked for everyone's attention. Brian Keohane, Mats told them, would be a full partner in the ownership of the brewery with Suzanne and himself. With a sense of the dramatic, he pulled out a paper that had been faxed to him by John Powers. It spelled out the terms of the gift of thirty-three percent of the firm to the son of the previous owner.

Then Mats spelled out how the Harp and Hawk would be run. Cathal Magee would remain brew master. He would have complete control of production and quality as well as of the hiring of all brewery personnel except for the salesmen and the drivers. These would be under the direction of Tobin, who would be in charge of all distribution, pricing, and procurement of supplies and raw materials. The two of them would mediate any gray areas and report to Mats should any disputes develop.

"I want this to remain a family business," said Mats to the assembled workers. "I have only two rules. One, answer to yourself, have I given an honest day's work? Two, anyone caught stealing or cheating me will be fired. There will be no recourse. If you see anyone stealing or cheating and don't tell me, then you will also be fired. I will be away a great deal of the time. I will have to trust things to be run fairly in my absence, just like in a family. Loyalty must be earned. I expect it from each and every person in this room, and I will make sure that I deserve it."

"To the Great Boss!" said old Magee, his glass already half empty.

"To the Great Boss!" echoed the gathering.

"Like family." Mats repeated the words out loud as if to hear them better over the din of the party still going on downstairs. The small office was the first door off the staircase, separated by only a wall from Cathal Magee's apartment. Mats surveyed the seat of his brewing empire and repeated the words for a third time.

Like family… The words struck a chord, but he could not readily bring their significance to mind. Magee and Tobin were to join him in five minutes. Until then, he could close his eyes and try to remember…

❧   ❧   ❧

Corsica, November 1941

"Nando will come for the van," said Egel Falconi. "He'll probably have a number of men with him. I will intercept them, but when the explosion doesn't occur, the Germans will be after them. We'll need a place to hide or another way for them to escape."

"I'll leave the motorcycle," said Teressa. "The Alta Mira has places to hide that the Germans will never find. The food and a spillage of pepper stops the dogs. Can you find your way back?"

"Of course," said Falconi, smiling to add assurance to the young girl. "Things have changed, but I grew up here. You take the motorcycle. Only one person can use it, and we will have many to rescue."

Falconi watched the girl move silently away, pushing the bike. She had left her uncle's safety in his hands without question. Centuries of mutual trust between Falconi and Guibega had brought him back to Corsica, and that same trust dictated her complete obedience.

The Germans had planned this escape for some reason. It would be well watched, the escape route covered. It was up to him to discover their motives and foil their plans.

An old man with a great bundle of sticks walked with a limp down the Rue Fesch. On a normal day, he would be stopped and interrogated for being out before curfew ended. Certainly, his burden of hardwood would be confiscated for the stoves of the officers. This day, however, he was allowed to pass.

The sentry looked at the old man making his way painfully toward him, then at his watch. According to his commandant, in less than two minutes there would be a prison break. A car would crash the barbed wire gate of the enclosure. He had been instructed to shoot wildly, only aiming to kill if he himself was threatened.

The sentry looked up from his watch. The old man was directly in front of the gate when the bells of the church announced the end of curfew. As the bells pealed, the sound of an engine, tortured past its red line, broke the peace of the morning and the serenity of the bells. The car, a stout wooden table lashed to its front bumper, hurled down the street toward the enclosure. The driver was shielded, wooden planks covering both the windshield and side windows, allowing only small viewing portals.

The old man looked up in terror as the vehicle bore down on him. He stumbled as he tried to escape certain death under the wheels of the car. The sentry could not help but smile at the irony of the punishment about to be meted out to the stupid peasant for breaking curfew. At the last second, the old man lurched out of the way of the car as it struck the first of the wire gates. The car traveled past him, slowing, but carrying enough momentum to knock one side of the inner gate from its hinges.

The sentry saw the old man narrowly escape death, his burden of sticks flying in a lazy arc toward the platform where he stood. The sentry recoiled as sticks from the old man's pack struck him around the head and shoulders. Instinctively, his arm went up to protect his eyes. As the wood clattered at his feet, he lowered his hands, bringing his rifle with them. When he looked up, the old man was standing next to him, an axe in his hand. The sentry swung his gun around, alert to the danger. This was not in the commandant's briefing. The rifle never came to bear on its target. The axe shattered his right knee and continued in its arc upward, striking him squarely under the chin.

Slowly, the German's brain stopped sending signals to muscles that no longer acted with purpose. Falconi stripped the man's gun and ammunition from him, as well as his radio. Only then did he turn to watch the first of the prisoners start to push the car away from the breach in the gate. The driver was trying to get out the door, held closed by the wire it had pushed aside.

As Falconi pulled the dead sentry across the street into a darkened alcove, a group of five men, acting in unison, pushed against the front of the car. As the gate was cleared of the vehicle, the driver joined the five prisoners at the front of a surge of men dressed in prison gray, pressing through onto the Rue Fesch.

As the six men moved in a group past the alcove, Falconi stepped back out into the morning light. He straightened his German uniform, adjusting the strap of his rifle to cover the blood on the collar, and strode purposefully toward the Citadel.

Just out of sight of the enclosure, Falconi came upon a barricade manned by twenty German soldiers. The few prisoners who had tried to escape in this direction lay bleeding on the street in front of the barrier. Falconi ducked into a crouch, running with short, choppy strides as he passed among the withering bodies of wounded prisoners. Falconi's blond hair and tall, thin frame complemented the disguise provided by the sentry's uniform. Passing quickly through the first rank of infantry, he stopped only when he reached the rear fender of a staff car. There he doubled over and began retching.

Two officers watched his retreat. One moved, walking with measured strides up behind him. The officer remaining at the barricade was recognizable as the one who had booby-trapped the van.

"Achtung! Achtung!"

Falconi retched one last time, his stomach clenching with the dry flow of air from his lungs, then slowly straightened. As he rose, he wiped the corner of his mouth with the back of his hand.

"Have they escaped?" the German asked. The soldier's orders were to stay hidden for ten minutes after the break. He was to kill or capture any prisoners who came through his position but not to pursue those traveling in different directions. After ten minutes he was to make a thorough sweep of the area and secure the stockade again, sealing off any prisoners who had remained inside.

"I said, have they escaped?"

The officer said no more as Falconi's knife entered his chest just below his ribs, traveling upward and piercing his heart. The man started to fall but Falconi moved quickly to his side, supporting him as if they were looking into the car. Luck was with him; the keys were in the ignition.

Falconi opened the rear door and placed the officer in an upright position on the rear seat. So far, all the soldiers were maintaining their positions. The lieutenant from the booby-trapped van was looking attentively across the barricade in the direction of the stockade.

Falconi started the car with the first throw of the ignition. "German efficiency," he thought as he moved forward slowly. Then he accelerated, releasing the clutch and stepping on the gas. The car bumped, rather than rolled, onto the uneven Corsican street. A cry of alarm was raised as Falconi sped past the corner and down the Rue Fesch. He heard several shots from behind and felt the impact of at least one bullet strike the car. He hoped his timing was right.

The car turned the last corner and skidded to a stop at the street where the deadly van was parked. Egel Falconi, dressed in the uniform of a German soldier, with the dead officer now slumped and bleeding across the back seat, looked frantically for Nando. He reached up and took his hat off, still searching the street for his friend. Then he realized that although he had spoken with Nando, he had not seen him in years. He might not recognize his old friend, and since he was dressed in a German uniform, Nando would have the same problem. Four men came running around the corner.

"Stop! The van is a trap. A bomb is inside. Where is Nando?" Egel shouted in the Corsican dialect.

"Are you the one he told us about?"

"Yes. Where is Nando?"

"He and the driver of the car are in the yellow house down the block. We are to take the van."

"Climb in this car. Don't go near the van."

The men immediately dove into the car, staying out of sight while propping the officer up again.

"Nando!" shouted Falconi. Above him, shutters banged open on the second story of a building.

"Signor Falconi, we will be right down."

Falconi looked in the rearview mirror as the door to the building flew open and a man rushed out, followed by Nando, considerably older than Egel remembered him but still possessing the strength and dignity that had made him so remarkable in their youth.

"Prop the German up and lie down flat, out of sight. The van was wired with explosives," instructed Falconi as Nando entered the back seat.

"It is too crowded. I will make my own way home," said the other man, and he ran back into the building.

Nando leapt out of the back seat and followed the man into the house. A minute later he returned, shutting the door behind him, and climbed back into the staff car.

"Go!" said Nando as he closed rear door.

Falconi followed the streets that Teresa had taken, somehow avoiding German roadblocks and patrols. When he reached the smaller houses that denoted the poorer district of Ajaccio, he stopped.

"I dare not take the car into open country. Can you make it to the Alta Mira?"

"Yes, signore," said Nando, speaking for the group.

"Good. Leave me one man in case things are not as I remember."

"I will stay with you," said Nando.

"No. We must not be caught together. Leave me a Guibega, if possible."

"Mario, stay with the signore," ordered Nando. A small, wiry man with the strong, gnarled hands of a blacksmith nodded in response.

"Meet me at the Roost. Tomorrow at 5 AM."

"Yes, signore," said Nando, answering the command. Then he and the other men were off among the baked white walls of the small houses that surrounded them.

"Do you know this area?" Egel asked the remaining Guibega.

"Si, Signor Falconi."

"How do you know my name? Did Nando tell you?"

"No, signore. Who else would risk his life for the Guibega? Who else would Nando obey without question?"

"All right, but never use my name again. Let's go."

"Turn right at the next corner, signore. I have a cousin who lives near here in an area the Germans still can't patrol for fear of death."

Falconi spent the day in a loft of a small house just a few blocks from a roadblock that was visible from a small louvered window. Below him, Mario's cousin stripped the car of anything that could be carried by hand. Mario and his cousin seemed skilled at the labor, so much so that Falconi would remember not to park his own vehicle in this part of town after the war.

Falconi stirred any time there was activity at the German roadblock, but for the most part, he slept. He had been awake for almost thirty-six hours, sailed a boat into German-occupied waters, swum a mile to shore, walked seven kilometers, and killed three men. The heat rose inside the house but Falconi didn't notice. He slept more soundly than he had when he was safe in bed in California.

Dressed again in the shirt and wool trousers of a Corsican farmer, and with Mario wearing similar borrowed clothing, Falconi left his hiding place at midnight. They walked cross-country for five kilometers before joining the road.

"Mario, take me to Falcon's Roost."

Three hours later, Falconi and Mario arrived at the Roost. They had only had to hide once, briefly, to avoid a German patrol. Egel had been to the Roost just once since returning to Corsica, and that just the previous evening, but already he thought of it as his. He sent Mario back to his own house, six kilometers further on, and then climbed the steep incline to the stone ruin.

"Signore?"

The voice was Nando's.

"Yes, my friend."

From out of the shadows of the building came Nando Guibega and his niece. First the man, then the girl, embraced Falconi, holding him tight against their chests for long seconds before relinquishing their hold. With Nando he could almost feel the years of separation melt away, as if physical contact was erasing the years they had missed. When they finally pulled apart and Teresa replaced her uncle, Falconi was aware of a different sensation. His mind raced back to the motorcycle ride to Ajaccio, the slimness of the girl's waist and the strength of her arms and legs as she melded to the steel of the bike. As she lingered against him, he had the distinct feeling that the embrace became sensual, her body heat rising, the tips of her breasts becoming hard against his stomach. When she released him, she did so with her head lowered, unwilling to look him in the eye. Then she straightened, raising her head and eyes, her proud expression visible even in the dim light of the gathering morning.

"Thank you for my uncle's life, Signor Falconi."

"The Guibega and the Falconi have always helped each other. Nando, tell me everything that happened from the time I first spoke to you before the break until the time I picked you up."

"You knew that the car would break the gate. There were six of us who were to use the van means of escape."

"The six who left the stockade together?"

"Yes, signore. Five Guibega and Pino, the driver of the crash car. Pino had arranged for the van. It was he who was leading us to the street where it was parked."

"Were all of you to escape in the van?"

"That was the original plan, but when we got near the street, Pino said I should change out of the prison clothes. We could hide in the cellar of the house. The others would take the van."

"Is he a Guibega?"

"No. Pino was his last name—Louis Pino. He would have killed four Guibega. I killed him when he ran back into the house. My wire is quiet."

"The Resistance has clearly been infiltrated. He probably hoped to gain further access for his German masters by appearing to rescue you. One thing is certain: we will find out nothing with your garrote around his neck."

"I would have found out who gave him his orders," hissed Teresa.

"There was no time," said Nando with a shake of his head.

"The men who escaped with you, they are to hide in the mountains and stay away from their homes. Their families are to act as if they are dead. We must organize a group made up only of Guibega. No one outside our clan can know what we plan, or that it is we who fight the Germans."

"Signore, what of the Resistance?" asked Nando.

"As I said, it has been infiltrated. Act as if you belong to it, as before. But the Guibega will be a force unto themselves, as they have been through the centuries."

"Pino asked your name on the way from the prison. I told him that you were from the mountains, and I knew only your code name."

"And what was that?"

"I told him you were called Maquis, the rock-rose of Corsica."

"Maquis, a shrub that is almost impossible to uproot. You have given me a fine name, my friend."

❧ ❧ ❧

Donegal, Ireland, August 2003

Mats heard the knock on the office door but was unable to respond. When it came again, he felt the walls of the room replace the darkness of a Corsican hillside.

"Come in," he managed, his voice uncertain, the language of the dream still intruding on his thoughts.

Cathal Magee and Charlie Tobin entered. Each held a fresh bottle of champagne. Even with all they had drunk before, neither showed signs of drunkenness.

"Like family," said Mats, pointing his finger first at Magee and then at Tobin. "There's someone who wants to harm the Harp and Hawk and its owners. They succeeded when they murdered the Keohanes. It's now our business to make sure they don't have any more success. Family ties are easy to check and unlikely to be broken. I want you to recruit exclusively from your own families. If someone isn't as well trained as another worker, train him. If he can't handle the job, then find someone who will. Pay top wage but tie it to performance. There is to be no talk about the risk."

"You won't stop talk. Talk is the Irish way." Magee smiled at the thought of trying to stop what had been the main topic of conversation in Donegal in the past three months.

"What about the workmen who were here before?" asked Tobin. "Those who are not part of our families?"

"Keep them. Watch them at all times but treat them like family unless they prove themselves undeserving. I will be out of the country for a few days. I want the new equipment set up and working as soon as it arrives. Tobin, I want you to go with Magee to the suppliers of hops and grain. Get to know these people. Learn how Keohane hid the real production figures, for he had to hide the pro-curement amounts as well. Have the materials delivered so that we can begin production at least on a small scale as soon as Cathal gets the plant up and running. Magee, I want the boy guarded day and night by at least two of your nephews. You know how to pick them. I'll see you again near the week's end."

Mats stood, signaling the end of the meeting. In unison, the two men raised their glasses in a toast.

"Long live the Great Boss," said Tobin.

"And may he cast a long shadow," added Magee.

CHAPTER SIX

The young man pushed himself away from his computer screen, the chair scraping on the tile floor before sliding to a stop against the edge of the rug that differentiated the living area from his workstation. He looked again at the screen, smiling to himself as he passed his right hand through his already thinning, wispy blond hair. He nudged his gold wire-rimmed glasses back up his nose and smiled again.

The work was good. It had taken Lars Bjursten only a fraction of the previous time to reconstruct the formulas and procedures. The concept was the important thing. Once the concept was known, there were several ways to arrive at the solution, enough at least to bypass patent laws.

He looked again at the computer screen, black formulas racing across the gray dot background on the Mac PowerBook Pro he had brought back from Ireland with him. The program would run for another fifteen minutes, perhaps as long as twenty.

He stood, unbending his two-meter frame from the hunched posture he had adopted while at work. Again he passed his hand through his hair, rubbing his scalp rather than straightening the few strands still growing from his widow's peak. "*Widow's peak*!" Bjursten thought. "What a strange name for loss of hair in an unmarried man just turned twenty-nine." He walked stiffly toward the window, the overcast scene making it impossible to estimate the time. The stiffness in his joints told him he had been at the computer for hours.

He looked at his watch. It told him what his senses could not: it was four P.M. He had been at work since nine that morning. No wonder he now felt hunger working on his conscious mind. But food would have to wait until the program was finished. There would be just enough time to take a shower. Then he would reward himself with a good German meal of sauerkraut and schnitzel, maybe even a few beers. Once his employer had accepted his work, he would be out of this drab, uninteresting apartment in this drab, uninteresting town.

"PING!" The sound announced that the formula program had finished its calculations. Bjursten moved to his workstation and pressed the command to print. He watched as the first page came out filled with writing interspersed with formulas, dropping onto the holding tray. Then he straightened and headed for the bathroom.

The shower felt good. He enjoyed them and sometimes took two a day. Dressed, he sat down again at the computer and took a small flash drive from the plastic storage case sitting next to it. He saved the file and removed the drive from the machine. Labeling the copy "Harp and Hawk," he placed it in an envelope. Then he copied part of the folder—the revised and modified formula—onto another flash drive, labeling it in German "Rohde."

The hard copy of the shorter, modified formula was eight pages long. The young man folded it carefully, placing it in a large envelope along with the Rohde flash drive. Then he went to the phone and dialed a number from memory.

"Hello, it is Lars. I have finished." He listened for a few seconds and then added, "Tonight then. At eight. At my apartment. Please bring the rest of my fee."

Bjursten went back to the computer. Opening a new document, he wrote a letter of explanation of what to do with the drive and saved it. As an afterthought, he typed "Love, Lars" at the end of the page. Printing it, he placed it in the envelope with the Harp and Hawk formulas and drive, quickly scribbling an address. He stamped it with the efficiency of a man in a hurry. Then, shutting down the computer, he tucked the envelope into his back pocket and headed toward the door.

Mats and Suzanne landed at Stockholm under clear blue skies. The flight from Shannon had allowed them to watch the patchy clouds that approached Ireland from the Atlantic meld into a solid gray cover over Scotland, only breaking up again as they hit the fjords of Norway. The moisture that made it past the fjords and the steep mountains that backed them to the east broke into spaces of blue as they passed over Sweden.

It took them an hour to arrive at the address that Cathal Magee had provided them for the biochemist, Lars Bjursten. Phone calls from Ireland had gone unanswered. Mats had two reasons for wanting to find the man. First, although Magee remembered the process and how to maintain the yeast and bacteria culture for the non-alcoholic top-fermenting brew, he could not find any written or computerized mention of the patent protection. Second, Mats hoped that Lars, being some sort of relative of Brian's mother, could help clear up the muddled custody circumstances Brian Keohane found himself in.

The address was in a fashionable part of Stockholm, away from the center of town but still close enough to feature fifteen-story apartment complexes. The door was opened by a tall, thin woman. Her gray hair and eye-glasses suggested to Mats that she was in her early fifties.

"Hello. Is this the Bjursten residence?"

"Yes." The woman looked at Mats and Suzanne with suspicion.

"My name is Mats Falconi. This is my wife, Suzanne."

A man, slightly taller than the woman, came to the door and stood behind her but did not speak. "What do you want?" asked the woman.

"Lars Bjursten did some work for my brewery in Ireland. I was told that he was a relative of the wife of the man who previously owned the business. This was the address he gave us. Does Lars live here?"

"Yes, but he is not in at the moment."

Mats sensed the woman's reluctance to speak. "When will he be home?"

"It's hard to say. I am Lars' mother. We are just straightening up a few things for him before he returns."

Mats looked past the woman. The man had stepped closer, as if to provide support. The pictures that hung on the wall to their right were family portraits, with the man and woman in the center of a small group of young adults and a smaller group of children. A chair behind them had a lace headrest cover. It did not look like the furnishings of a young bachelor.

"I need to speak to Lars. It's important." Mats smiled. He was impressed that almost every Swede spoke English, most with a clipped British schoolboy accent. Lars Bjursten's mother was no exception.

"Would you please come in?" The woman and her husband stepped aside in unison, showing the way to a spacious living room that was partially visible from the doorway. "Would you like some coffee? I will try to get in touch with Lars and see when he will be home."

"A cup of coffee would be nice, but not if it is any bother," said Suzanne.

The man whom both Mats and Suzanne assumed was Lars' father turned and spoke for the first time. "It will be no bother. I will see to it while you get in touch with Lars," he said to his wife.

Lar's mother nodded and left the living room, passing down a short hall to a room where she closed the door behind her.

Lars Bjursten was putting on his coat when his cell phone sounded, the tone specific to his mother. He almost let it ring, annoyed by the intrusion on what was to be a personal celebration of achievement. But knowing that he would only make his mother wonder why he didn't pick up, and surely she would call every half hour until he did, probably spoiling the dinner he was now coveting, he took the call.

"Lars?"

"Mother!" He was glad he had decided to answer the call. "How nice to hear from you. How is Father?"

"He is fine. I am calling because an American is in our living room looking for you. He says it is important, and that it has to do with the Irish brewery job you took last year. Do you want to talk to him?"

"What is his name?"

"Mats Falconi. He says he just bought the brewery."

"Just bought the Harp and Hawk? Did you tell him I was in Germany?"

"Of course not. I thought at first he was from the housing bureau."

"Would you give him your phone?"

Mrs. Bjursten walked back into the living room and handed her phone to Mats. "I have Lars on the line for you, Mr. Falconi."

"We had two choices," Mats said to Suzanne as he lugged her suitcase back through the airport, which they had left only hours before. "We could wait until Lars gets back to Sweden in two or three days, or we could meet him in Frankfurt. I'm as anxious as you to get back to France, so we go to Frankfurt."

"I understand, Mats. It's just that Frankfurt is so … so depressing."

Lars Bjursten whistled as he took the steps to his apartment two at a time. There were five floors, enough to make him feel he was exercising by not using the elevator.

The meal had been more than satisfying. He preferred a quiet place to eat, one with cool jazz, not the loud music of a German beer hall. Still, the schnitzel had been great and the beer strong. Within the hour, he would turn over his calculations and receive enough money to last the rest of the year. Even better, it had been promised in cash. He could take it back home and avoid the Swedish income tax.

The call from his mother had unsettled him, though. She was upset, he could tell, but for the wrong reason. She had thought the American was from the housing bureau and checking on his place of residence. The apartment had been assigned to him while he worked on a government research project more than three years ago. His academic credentials merited him special treatment, thus the prime location and generous size of the place. The job had lasted only a year, but he still had the apartment, or rather, his parents still had it. He had switched with them, their small two-room pension being more suited to his lifestyle.

Falconi was an American, not a housing representative, but the news he had relayed of Patrick Keohane's death was shocking. Mia Keohane had been his second cousin, and like most athletes who gain national stature, she had been a legend in their family. Lars had been honored to help her husband with his special project, flattered that the Keohanes even knew of him and his biochemical laurels.

The solution to the problem had come to him over a period of six months and was, if he was not too humble to say it, brilliant. They had patented it, but with Keohane dead, Falconi said they could not find any reference to it at the brewery. That hardly surprised Lars. The name of the process would not be recognizable to a layman. Even another biochemist would have to know the application before realizing its worth. He had given Falconi the patent number and the names of the countries in which they had filed, but the American had still wanted to meet with him in person. Lars suspected that Falconi wanted to make sure his process was secure legally. It was. Keohane's patent, and his own backdoor method which he had intentionally left out of Rohde's computations, that would effectively block the German from any exclusivity.

His key turned in the door and he entered the darkened apartment. The computer screen glowed in the corner of the room. It was odd. He thought he had closed it before he left. Lars flicked on the light and was immediately grabbed from behind. Strong arms pinned his to his sides, lifting him to the center of the rug, where an armchair had been placed. Only after his arms and legs had been tied to the chair and his mouth gagged did his assailants show themselves.

Lars recognized only one of the two men, Bernd, the blond square-shouldered assistant of Herr Dieter Rohde, his employer. The other man was younger but bigger, both in height and weight. His eyes were the only small thing about him: tiny, close set, and watery blue. Lars had seen such eyes before in his own homeland, and they were the eyes of the hockey bully—the enforcer who was kept on the national teams to inflict pain and punishment on opposing stars. Those eyes sent a chill through Lars' immobilized body.

Wide cloth straps fastened by Velcro held Lars' arms and legs to the chair. When his panic subsided, Lars recognized them as arm bands used by tennis players and golfers who had elbow or wrist problems. He was not an athlete, but he found himself thinking that if the straps were as effective for sports as they were for holding him against the chair, then he could understand their popularity. He tested them only briefly, the futility of getting loose with two strong men in front of the chair to which he was bound quickly apparent. The man with the squinty eyes, as if sensing his thoughts, curled the corner of his lip in an expression that would never pass for a smile and reached for Lars' wrist, checking the tightness of the strap. As he drew his hand back, Lars fell deeper into fear. Both men were wearing thin rubber gloves.

"Ah, Herr Bjursten, please forgive our precautions." The voice came from behind him, from the entrance to his bedroom. "You will understand when I tell you what we have learned. I only want to ask you a few questions."

With slow, casual steps, Herr Dieter Rohde came into view. The man was old, but Lars could not guess his age by his face. His skin was drawn like parchment, tight over bones that pressed for release. His lips moved when he spoke but with an economy of motion, using his tongue and teeth to form sounds rather than his lips. Lars had never seen him change expression—not smile, not frown. He suspected that Rohde had received a face lift or skin grafts, but despite the tautness of his face and lack of expression, there were no signs of an operation.

"If you promise not to make noise, I will have Bernd remove the cover from your mouth."

Dieter Rohde stood in front of Lars as the gag was removed from his mouth. The old man was bent, not at the waist but at the height of his shoulder blades. His posture still managed to appear erect, however, and his impassive face gave him a seriousness that chilled Lars.

"Now then, Herr Bjursten, these print-outs that Bernd found at your computer. They are the only copies of the process and formulas?"

Bjursten nodded.

"Good. And the computer? Bernd could not find the file."

"It's in Word, in a folder titled Myform. The file is named for you, Rohde."

Bernd moved to the computer screen and clicked the mouse twice. "Jawohl, here it is."

"Good." Herr Rohde rocked up on his toes as if trying to regain the height that the bend in his spine had taken from him. "Have you made any other copies?"

"No," Bjursten lied, shaking his head to prevent his eyes from giving him away. "I just finished the figures, just before I phoned you. It's all there."

"The Irish brewery, they also have the formulas?"

"No, sir. They have only one method and it is for top-fermenting beer, crude compared to the work I did for you." Bjursten nodded his head toward the sheath that Herr Rohde's assistant still held in his hand.

"But they have the method, nonetheless?"

"Yes. Herr Rohde, why have you tied me up? You knew that before you hired me. I will freely give you any information that you ask for. If it is a question of money—"

"Just one last question," Rohde interrupted. "The owner of the Irish brewery has died. There is a new owner. I believe the owner you worked for was named Keohane? I understand that you were related to him. Is that not true?"

Tied up and helpless, Lars had thought he couldn't feel more afraid. Herr Rohde's question accomplished the impossible, however. He had not mentioned either the name Harp and Hawk or the name of Patrick Keohane to the German. Mats Falconi had informed him of Keohane's violent death just two hours previously. Now Rohde used the past tense in naming him. Bjursten looked at the old man and carefully measured his answer.

"I am not related to Keohane, except by marriage. My second Cousin Mia is his wife. She is Swedish." Lars was careful not to indicate that he knew she was dead.

"Well, as I said, that was the last question. Bernd, have you finished with the computer?"

"Ja, Herr Rohde." Bernd tapped the laptop, and the file that contained the formulas disappeared into the fat trash can at the bottom of the screen. Another tap and it was purged from the computer's memory.

"You know what to do then." Rohde moved to the couch on the other side of the living room, watching his men carefully, as if he was the director of a play in dress rehearsal. Lars watched too, fascinated, as the thug with the squinty eyes went to the end table and opened a wide briefcase. He took out a small battery and a full bottle of schnapps. Flipping the battery to Bernd, he went to the pantry and returned with a glass, which he put on the computer table and added a splash of the liquor.

"Herr Rohde would like to buy you a drink," he said in a deep, rasping voice. "I hope you like schnapps."

The man grabbed Lars by the neck, just under the angle of the jaw, pinching his massive thumb and fingers into the muscles just below the ear. Lars felt his mouth open and fill with burning alcohol. He tried to spit it out, but the man, anticipating this reaction, put a hand tightly over his mouth while at the same time pinching his nostrils.

Lars coughed as the liquor burned its way down his esophagus into his stomach. He started to protest, but the man's strong hands repeated the procedure, with the same results as before. A third time and the bottle was half empty.

Bernd had pulled a chair under the fire alarm fixed to the ceiling in the apartment's short hallway. He pressed the test button and got a short burst of noise. Twisting off the cover, he replaced the battery with the one from his briefcase. Pushing again, the test button gave no alarm. Jumping down from his perch, he brought the chair back to the table.

Lars was confused. They had replaced his gag. Rohde obviously wanted him drunk, probably to get him to tell them more about the formulas. He could feel the booze warm his stomach and flush the skin on his face. *It'll take a lot more than half a liter of schnapps to make me spill anything I want to keep secret,* he thought smugly, the alcohol prompting him to a certain bravado, at least in his mind.

The squinty-eyed thug returned to the case and took out a pair of pliers and something that looked like a small dark bag. He waved the object in front of Lars' nose. "How do you like your rats? Electrified? Hahaha!"

Lars now recognized the object as a brown rat. He watched in fascination as the thug knelt beside the computer, unplugging it from the wall and dropping the rat, took the pliers and began taking small snips from the insulation on the power cord. "Took me two days to grind this cutter to the shape of a rat's incisors," he said to Lars.

When he had snipped through to bare wire, the man stopped, opened the rat's mouth in much the same way he had done to Lars minutes before, and dropped a few of the shreds of wire insulation down the rodent's throat. Then he placed the plug in the wall socket. "Ready, Herr Rohde," the thug announced, getting up from his work.

"Thank you, Karl," said Rohde, using the thug's name for the first time. From the briefcase he removed a foot-long piece of wood, the end wrapped in a ball of undyed yarn. Its shaft was carved with odd shapes and figures.

Lars watched, the alcohol making thought difficult, as Rohde walked from the table and stood in front of him. He was not afraid of the stick the man carried. It was tipped in yarn and too slender to make an effective weapon. Still, the man looked sinister, his tight skin stretched over his teeth in a slight opening of his lips that could have been a smile but was more like a sneer.

The man with the pliers carried the glass of alcohol to the old man, who dipped the end of the stick into the glass until the fluid was blotted dry. With a flourish, Bernd took a large clear plastic bag from the briefcase, snapping it downward, opening it to its fullest. Karl reached into his pocket and took out a lighter, igniting the yarn on the end of the stick. Herr Rohde turned the stick on a downward cant, allowing the flames to feed upon themselves and the wooden shaft, feeding on the unevenness of the carved inscriptions. Bernd held the open end of the bag over the flames. The hot air rose, slowly, then with more force, filling the bag.

The smoke was noxious. What little escaped the bag smelled like burnt hair. The bag was now hovering above the flame, held completely aloft by the hot, swirling smoke inside. When the smoke started to curl out the bottom of the bag, Rohde nodded to Bernd.

Lars suddenly understood. Bernd lifted the bag, its top almost touching the ceiling, and brought it down over his head. He tried to plead with Rohde, but the gag muffled his voice. Through the clear plastic of the bag, he helplessly watched Rohde, who kept the flame filling the bag that covered him from the shoulders up.

"There are two reasons you must die, Herr Bjursten," said Rohde, turning the burning brand under Lars' chin. "First, I don't want you doing for someone else what you have just done for me. The process you have developed for non-alcoholic beer is worth a fortune. It is much too valuable for a small Irish brewery. The second reason you will never know, as it is much more personal."

Lars tried not to breathe but he had exhausted his air supply. His lungs were repelled by the heavy smoke, now coming as much from the wood as the yarn. He coughed, then coughed again, as his lungs filled with smoke. He tried to tip the chair over, but Bernd's companion held it steady. His eyes watered. He gasped again as he felt one of the men fasten the edge of the bag tightly around his neck. The bag slowly compressed around his head, but he was unable to bite it, being barely on the edge of consciousness. Lars Bjursten's last thought was *"Damn Germans!"* He tried unsuccessfully to take one last breath, the plastic sucking into his nostrils.

A minute passed, then two, and Rohde gave his instruction. "Finish your jobs."

Well drilled in their work, Bernd and Karl moved swiftly. Bernd removed the bag and the straps one by one. Then he lifted the chair and Bjursten to a position in front of the computer. Checking again for any forgotten restraints, he carefully lowered the dead man's head onto the computer keyboard. Karl wrapped Bjursten's lifeless hand around the glass, then splashed alcohol on the rug directly below the plug as well as on the drapes. The glass he laid on its side, empty on the computer table. When the bottle was almost empty, he replaced it next to the Mac.

The three men nodded to each other as Rohde handed the still burning stick to the squint-eyed Karl. The thug lit the alcohol-soaked carpet and drapes. The flames seemed reluctant to start, barely flickering despite the continued application of the torch. Then they took, racing up the drapes and along the floor.

Karl handed the brand back to Rohde after extinguishing it by rolling it with his foot against the carpet. Rohde dropped it into the plastic bag along with the restraints and the battery, checking each item off in his mind. Handing the bag to Bernd, he turned and headed for the door.

As the three men left the apartment, smoke was already filling the front room. Rohde closed the door, then locked it, being careful not to touch the knob. "There," he muttered under his breath. "The task is done."

Rohde turned toward the stairway, hesitating only long enough to drop the key into the plastic bag that Bernd held open for him.

CHAPTER SEVEN

The taxi dropped Mats and Suzanne off half a block away from the apartment building, three fire engines blocking any nearer access. Mats paid the fare with euros he had exchanged at the airport. His wallet was starting to annoy him, fat with residual bills from the U.S., Euros from Ireland, and now Swedish Krona.

They walked the last two hundred meters to the building's entrance. Firemen were in the process of recoiling long sections of hose, folding them into exact lengths along an aluminum carrier. A few sat, sweat-stained, with their helmets in their laps, watching their fellows perform the labor of cleaning up. Mats nodded at them as he came to a yellow plastic ribbon barrier stretched around the front of Lars Bjursten's address.

"Do you live in this building?" The question came from a policeman in unmistakable, demanding German.

"Nein," answered Suzanne. "We are here to meet a business associate. He lives here." Her German was perfect, although the softer dialect of the south. There was no hint of the French accent that still existed in her English speech. The policeman took her for a German.

"What is his name?" the officer demanded.

"Lars Bjursten. He is a Swede."

"Which floor does he live on?"

Suzanne took a slip of paper from Mats' hand, on which he had written Bjursten's address and phone number.

"His number is 532," Suzanne said, consulting the note before looking up and smiling at the policeman.

The man did not return the smile. Instead he raised the yellow tape with one hand for them to pass under and said, "I am Lieutenant Kurt Schiller. Come with me."

It was three hours before Mats and Suzanne were free to go. Only fifteen minutes had been necessary to establish that they had just arrived by SAS from Sweden. Their story was easy to check, with too many people involved to be fabricated. Bjursten's parents, the phone call from Sweden, the baggage slips and boarding passes from their flight—all evidence spoke of the truth.

In bits and pieces, Mats was informed by Suzanne that there had been a fire. Bjursten's room had been the focal point, but it had spread to two other apartments. They had found a dead man in unit 532. Although a formal identification had not yet been made, all signs indicated it was Lars Bjursten.

The police questioned them singly, Mats interrogated by Lieutenant Schiller, who spoke perfect, though accented, English. The more they were questioned, the more Mats realized that the police suspected Bjursten had been drinking. Finally, Schiller took them both aside.

"Herr Falconi, I ran your name through Interpol. Wonderful things, computers, for storing all sorts of unrelated information. I also spoke with a Parisian inspector, Medau. He said you were always honest with him in his investigation two years ago and that he would trust you implicitly. He warned me that you seem to attract violence but that you and your wife are good guys." Schiller pursed his lips, as if he was trying to make up his mind about something. "Inspector Medau said to ask you if you are still carrying a sword."

"Medau's little joke. You must have made a good impression on him if he mentioned it. As far as I know, you are the first person to hear of the sword."

"We police have our little cliques. Medau is known as one of the best investigators in France. Kurt Schiller has a similar reputation in Germany. What about the sword?"

"A year ago, a drug lord named Colletti had already murdered three men and was about to kill me with a shotgun. The only weapon I had was an antique sword that had been in my family for centuries. I disarmed him with it."

"I can see why Medau didn't want that to get out. It would have been a circus. His secret is safe with me. You are free to leave Germany, but I must be able to reach you should we need more information. Bjursten's death was probably an accident, but I must make sure. It is very unusual for a fire to kill only one person in an apartment building. Fires don't usually behave with such German efficiency." The Lieutenant allowed himself a small smile. "Let me drive you to the station."

On the Continent, few methods of transportation are as convenient, efficient, or comfortable as the train, and few cities are as beautiful to see at sunrise as Paris. Mats had ticketed a first-class sleeping compartment, expensive but very much needed after their three-country journey of the previous day. The change of time from Ireland to Frankfurt helped to ensure their early rising. They boarded the train just before midnight.; the trip would take a little under six hours. Now, looking out on the suburbs of the French capital, the morning sun cast long shadows, painting everything it hit in hues of red and gold.

Despite their fatigue, they had made love the previous evening, the rhythm of the train providing cadence to their movements. The cramped quarters lent excitement rather than difficulty to their desires.

"It will be close to an hour before we reach the station," said Mats. "You freshen up if you want. I'm going to try and sneak a few more minutes of sleep."

"I hope I didn't tire you out last night," said Suzanne with a glint in her eye that promised she might be inclined to try again if the answer was no.

Mats smiled back at her, not giving an answer other than his arms open in welcome. Even now, after knowing her for a year and a half, he could not resist the sight of her naked body. "*Magnificent,*" he thought as she came toward him, weaving slightly to the swaying of the coach.

Fifteen minutes later, Suzanne slid out of bed and returned to the window as Mats pulled the covers over his head. Within seconds, his breathing pattern changed, and Suzanne knew he was asleep...

⚜ ⚜ ⚜

Corsica, November 1941

"I must reacquaint myself with the land," said Egel Falconi. "I must see all the places that are safe for the Guibega and known only to them."

"I will show them to you," said Nando.

"No. You already have a job, my friend. You must contact all the Guibega and tell them that they are to confide in no one outside the family. We will form a small but effective unit. The members who are still not outlawed, go to them as well. Urge them to keep their jobs, maintain normal activity. It is best the Germans don't figure out that it is just one family harassing them, rather than the whole Resistance. Mario will be my guide."

"There is no need for Mario. I will guide you, signore." Teresa looked at Egel with the same resolve she had shown the evening before, when her uncle had still been a captive of the Germans.

The sun was just rising, streaking the stones of the ruin known as Falcon's Roost with the red light of dawn. Mats looked at Nando, who gave a nod of approval to his niece's suggestion.

They spent five hours in discussion, Nando providing concise answers to Falconi's questions about German strength, deployment, and tactics. As Nando spoke, Falconi found that he could picture the land, drawn from childhood memories. Teresa spoke only twice. Both times she showed that she was much like Nando, giving succinct information with an economy of words.

By morning's first light, Falconi had formulated a basic plan. The Germans were too numerous and well-armed to confront directly. Moreover, there was an unlimited supply of them, as opposed to the number of Guibegas. Egel did not want to lose even one member of the clan he had come to Corsica to protect.

Egel turned back to Teresa. "This is my plan. If we cannot match the number of Germans, perhaps we can make them less effective. By attacking and sabotaging their equipment, we reduce their mobility. We force them to provide guards in greater numbers, effectively taking men away from other duties. When we have them spread thin, we go after their patrols, always with a mind to attack their officers. It is unlikely that the Germans will increase their numbers on the island while their equipment and soldiers become less effective. They have stretched themselves thin over Europe."

"We will need safe places to gather in numbers near the targets," added Teresa, catching on quickly.

"Well, then, let's go. We'll meet back here at midnight, three nights from now."

Falconi and Teresa rode in spurts, cresting each rise and turn in the road with caution, looking ahead before committing themselves to any open stretch. After five kilometers, Teresa stopped, pulling the motorcycle around a boulder and hiding it from view.

"This meadow has always been special for your family," said Teresa, as she led Egel Falconi down a narrow trail that followed a dry wash toward the Gulf of Sagone to the west. "Uncle told me that your ancestors are buried here."

Falconi did not need to be told. He had left Corsica in order to avoid becoming the last of the Falconi. Now, in this meadow carved between boulders at the base of a rock cliff, he was struck by the realization that he was just that.

"We will not use this place to gather. This place was shown to me by my father. We did not realize it was known to the Guibega. It will remain our secret place." Falconi looked at the ground at the base of the cliff and nodded toward the narrow inlet from which they had come. "Find another place from which we can ambush the Germans."

They had started back down the trail, heading toward the road, Falconi leading Teresa, when they heard the drone of an engine. There was no place to hide on the trail; there was a bare wash on one side, a sheer wall of rock on the other. The sound of the Messerschmitt's engine became louder, turning into a wail as it dove on them.

Teresa pushed Falconi flat against a small outcropping of rocks, pressing herself as a shield against his back as the first bullets struck the trail behind them.

"Come!" she ordered as the plane arched back into the sky above them. Holding his hand, she pulled him along the trail until she found a small hollow between large boulders less than twenty meters from the road. They could be seen from directly overhead, but the likelihood of another pass of bullets finding them was almost nil.

The niche in which they hid would have been adequate for one. With two, both trying to keep as low as possible, it was cramped. Falconi, having been pushed in first, found himself occupying the space below Teresa, whose knees were against his hips, her breast firmly pressed against his cheek.

"Lie still!" hissed Teresa as he tried to move, partly to remove a bulge of rock that was pressing into his shin and partly to assuage his embarrassment at the thoughts racing through his mind each time she took a breath. "They will not look for us much longer."

As if on cue, the plane could be heard gaining altitude and moving away. Teresa kept pressed against Falconi until the engine was only a whisper, and then she slowly shifted her weight to the rocks that had provided their safety. She stood on the boulder, her legs spread for support, and reached down, helping him to stand.

"Quickly. The pilot will radio our location to a patrol. Help me with the motorcycle."

They headed north, Teresa urging the small one-cylinder engine to its maximum capacity. After seven minutes of hard driving, they came to a small clearing on the right side of the road. Slowing, she left the road, following a barely discernible path until they came to the apex of the small canyon. Teresa pulled under an outcropping of rock.

"Take a branch and cover our tracks from the road," she said as she dismounted.

As Falconi returned, he saw the rear wheel of the motorcycle disappear over a waist-high rock. He gave the small area in front of the boulder a few careful sweeps, lifting up some grass that had been bent over by the wheels, and then followed Teresa over the boulder. From the clearing, it appeared as if the boulder was close against the cliff, but it was an illusion. A small trail about a meter wide existed, running about three meters before it disappeared into the shadow of the cliff. Falconi could see the tracks of the motorcycle as they turned into the darkness of the shade and were lost from sight. He used the branch again along the narrow corridor until he was satisfied that no trace of their passing remained.

The shadows deepened as he squatted in a depression that lengthened into a tunnel before widening into a small cave. The cave, though only roughly five meters in diameter, was still spacious due to its almost vertical walls, which extended up ten full meters before narrowing in a gothic arch. Only the back wall angled in toward the living space and only marginally, providing space for several shelves that had been cut into its stony outcroppings. Teresa was kneeling beside the motorcycle, unpacking the provisions and bedrolls that Mario Guibega had given them.

"The Germans always follow the same plan," she said, without looking around. "If we are not on a road or at work, they assume we are Resistance and fire on us. Then they dispatch motor units with dogs to search us out. At first we hid in the caves, but their dogs often tracked us. There are many places we can no longer use, especially around Ajaccio. That is why I drove as far as I did before turning off the road."

She tossed a bedroll to Falconi and watched him catch it with one hand, swinging it to his hip with the grace of an athlete. She met his eyes momentarily with a fixed gaze of her own before turning back toward the food and utensils she had piled next to the motorcycle. She moved the few items further against the rear wall, hiding her face while she tried to sort out her feelings for the man standing behind her.

Teresa had never looked away from any man before. She was a Guibega, the only living relative of Nando Guibega. She was as secure in her self-worth as any man and more intelligent than most. Why was it, then, that she had turned away, reluctant to look him in the eye? Was it fear that he might read the feelings that were forming behind her own?

Teresa had grown up with Nando's stories about Egel's father and his son, the last of the Falconi line. Nando, being only four years older than she, was more like a brother than an uncle. He had passed on to her, as his father had to him, the legacy of the Guibega clan's service to the Falconi.

Two nights before, at the Roost, she had been suspicious of Falconi. It was not until he had named Nando that had she accepted who he was: Egel Falconi, the hero of her uncle's tales. As he spoke, and as she had told him of her uncle's captivity, the difference between her perception and the reality of the man merged. She thought of Nando as old, only because he had raised her when her mother and father died. She had been eight, Nando had taken over her upbringing, his parents trusting him totally even at that young age.

On the motorcycle, driving toward Ajaccio that first night, she had felt Falconi's strength, felt the way he quickly accustomed himself to her driving, leaning into turn after turn as if anticipating her movements. She was also aware that his hands were exploring her, not like a teenaged boy would do, but as a warrior, appraising her strength as she drove through the darkness.

On the drive to the cave, he had held tightly to her waist, but the feeling was different from the previous evening. His hands no longer changed pressure as they moved into corners. It was as if he was afraid of moving them, afraid of what reaction it would elicit from her. Damn, she thought, I might as well paint a sign on my chest: SIXTEEN-YEAR-OLD VIRGIN, NO EXPERIENCE, NO CONTROL. He was eight years older than she, experienced, from America, not some rural village.

The thought that she was a virgin, and what it might mean to the man behind her, sent a shiver through her body. Again, her pulse quickened, and she could feel blood rush to her face and groin. This cave was known only to the Guibega. At least, no Guibega had ever encountered a person outside the family in it, nor had any trace of other occupation been noted. The Guibega always laid a stick, seemingly haphazardly, across the spent hearth when they left a place. If it was moved, the next Guibega would know and be cautious. It was a custom they had passed on through generations, even centuries. This custom, along with many others, had enabled the Guibega not only to survive but to prosper as the fighting arm of the Falconi.

"Foolish girl!" Teresa thought, busying herself with the supplies. "He has had the love of many women."

Feeling him watching her, she slowly turned toward Falconi. He stood in the same spot, still cradling the bedroll under his arm. She felt an urge to avert her gaze again but fought it, raising her chin proudly instead.

"Can you read my feelings as well as my thoughts?" she asked, almost in defiance.

"No. I can only guess your feelings from your expressions and body language. I sensed your embarrassment back by the meadow, then nothing. You are like a beacon, stronger than even your uncle. It was as if you were reaching out to me."

Teresa stood in shock, confused, not knowing what to say or do next. Her hands came up to her waist, held open as if trying to catch some thought that had spilled unvoiced from her heart, damning her inexperience, damning her naiveté in even thinking of love.

Falconi sensed her turmoil. This young woman was so mature, so strong in body and will, hardened by the German occupation of her island at a time when she should have been courted by half the eligible young men on Corsica. He stepped toward her. He wanted to tell her that he had been aroused by her touch, that he had felt drawn to her from the first time he had heard her voice from the shadows of the Roost, that he had known he was in love with her even before they had rescued her uncle. He wanted to tell it all, but he stopped at the thought of her age.

She took his hand, looking up at him, seeing an unsureness, a vulnerability, that few others had seen in this man. Raising herself on her toes, she placed her hands on his cheeks, drawing his mouth to her lips.

His kiss was gentle, lighter than the force she was using to pull his face to hers. His lips, soft, parted only slightly as hers moved back and forth over them. He neither responded to her kiss with increasing passion nor separated from its contact. Teresa had acted on the basis of instinct. Now she felt her own insecurity rising, afraid Falconi's passion did not equal her own. She slowly lowered herself, the difference in their heights making her feel even more like a child and started to turn away.

"Teresa." His voice stopped her. It was the first time he had used her name. The sound came from deep in his throat, husky, as if the word required great effort to say. His arms came up, holding hers, preventing her from moving further.

"Teresa." Again her name. There was a question in his tone.

She looked up into his eyes, blue, piercing to her soul. She saw her own fear mirrored in his eyes and knew that instinct had not deceived her. She smiled up at him, wanting to remember every line, every angle of his face. She moved closer to him, pressing herself against his chest. She could hear the beat of his heart as his arms encircled her, sliding from her shoulders to the small of her back. She gripped his waist, feeling him harden against her. Fear again prevailed, this time not fear of letting her emotions show, but fear of the unknown. She moved one hand up his back, separating only enough to raise her face again to his.

This time he met her kiss with full, deep passion, his lips pressed against hers, sending an increasing awareness to every part of her body. Finally, they parted. Bending slightly, he swept her off the ground, whirling her around, cradled in his arms. It was a celebration of unbounded joy. Around and around he whirled, finally stopping only to kiss her again.

When he lowered her to the floor, her hands slid over his erect manhood. As if her touch hurt, he stepped back. Teresa could sense a moral struggle, conviction and judgment working against his passion.

"Signor Falconi," she said, stepping back. Without waiting for a response, her hand flew to the top button of her shirt, quickly slipping it through its hole. When she had undone the fourth button, she stopped and slowly opened the shirt, pulling slowly at the material with her right hand until her breast was completely uncovered.

His eyes told her that his passion was again in control. She wanted this man. And at this time and place, he wanted her. Teresa was not about to risk the possibility of rational thought taking him from her.

"Signor Falconi," she said again as she brought his hand up to touch her breast. She felt his fingers move lovingly to the soft hardness at its tip, lightly touching, exploring. When she could stand it no longer, she pulled its twin from the still partially buttoned shirt that it might share in the delight.

In the dim reflected light, she moved away from him, quickly spreading the bed rolls over the floor of the cave. "Signor Falconi," she said, taking his hand and sitting at his feet. "I do not know much about making love. Please help me, for I want you more than anything else in my life."

It was near dawn when they awoke. Falconi had taken her offered gift slowly and gently. Teresa had such passion, such pent-up desires, such a lust to learn the secret pleasures, that he had found himself fighting to maintain his self-control. He slowed the paces of his advances by speaking to her in whispers, explaining what he was doing and what she could do to complement his movements, speaking to her as he had to no other woman in his life. There was no embarrassment either in his teaching or in her questions, and when the moment finally came, her desire and excitement masked the initial pain. Except for a single gasp that escaped her lips, she gave only signs of pleasure.

Falconi's pleasure had been supreme as well. He had not known such lovemaking could exist, that such a woman could exist. The afternoon passed, filled with questions Teresa had for Falconi, often followed by another embrace so that she might test her understanding.

They slept, having exhausted their bodies' reserves, until hunger awoke them. When they first entered the cave, Falconi had felt its coolness as a welcome relief from the hot Corsican sun. As they made love, their body heat had made the temperature even more agreeable. Now, even clinging to each other, it was becoming uncomfortably cold. He tried to reach across her body to lift the cover of the bed roll over her sleeping form, but his movement, as he had feared it might, awoke her.

Teresa looked up at him and smiled. She stole a glance at the entrance of the cave. "What time is it?"

"Just after eight," he answered, looking at his watch.

"Fine guide I am," she said, springing to her feet. "Earlier I could have cooked you a meal, but now the light from the fire would illuminate the entrance."

Without turning she started to dress, looking only fleetingly at the blood that covered part of her leg. "Pack up the bedrolls," she ordered as she replaced the food items in the backpack and tied it to the motorcycle. Before he had finished, she had begun pushing the bike toward the cave's opening. Egel hurried to her side with the bedding in time to be handed the handlebars and told to wait.

Teresa ducked through the mouth of the cave and out into the flat light of the early evening. In minutes she appeared again.

"It's safe. A motorized division could have set up camp outside while we were making love and I wouldn't have heard it." She smiled, the truth of the remark not causing her embarrassment.

She moved quickly past him to the unused hearth and repositioned a small stick to the opposite side of the large one that haphazardly crossed the cold ashes. Then she moved back to Falconi, stopping to kiss him on the mouth before taking the handlebars again.

"Please help with the rear wheel. I don't seem to feel as strong as when we arrived." She shot another smile over her shoulder and Egel Falconi knew in the dim light of the cave that he was helplessly and forever in love.

"Where are we going?" he asked as they drove north, away from the cave.

"The winery you gave the Guibega when you left Corsica is just up ahead. We can spend the night there. Paulo Guibega will make up for my blunder in not feeding you earlier."

"Teresa!" he yelled into her ear over the staccato of the motor's single cylinder. "It would be best if no one knew that we were lovers. The Germans might target you. They might capture and torture you to get at me."

A peal of laughter burst from Teresa as she turned onto a dirt road that led into a small, narrow valley. "Egel Falconi, my love. You might keep our relationship from the Germans and even from the French, but you will never keep it from the Guibega. Ours is a small family. They will only need to look at me to know that I am now a woman, and a woman in love."

Again, her laughter floated back to him, musical, almost keeping beat with the engine. He squeezed her around the waist, then impulsively reached up and touched her breast, feeling her immediate response.

"Be careful or you might not get to eat at all tonight," she laughed. "Here we are now."

Teresa pulled up in front of a stone house. As the motorcycle sputtered to a stop, the door opened. Light from inside momentarily blinded Falconi, causing him to turn his head away...

Paris, Fall 2003

"We're here."

Suzanne's voice and the light in his eyes tore Mats from his sleep. He tried to re-establish the scene, wanting to learn more about his father, but it was too late. Only the sleeping compartment, Suzanne, and the view of Paris flying by the window remained.

"Another dream?" Suzanne asked, concerned.

"Yes."

"Mats, what's wrong? You look like you've seen a ghost."

"I have, in a way. I'm learning things about my father that he kept secret for some reason. Things even Nando has not told me."

"It'll take an hour for you to arrange the line of money transfer at the bank," said Suzanne holding his hand as the train eased to a halt. "I'll phone Jennette and let her know our schedule. When we get on the train to Marseille, you can tell me about the dream."

Chapter Eight

Nando was waiting for them on the platform as they got off the train at Marseille. Suzanne had phoned Jennette Guibega at the Alta Mira and told her that Mats wanted to see the old man as soon as they arrived on Corsica.

"*Better to do more than expected, rather than less,*" thought Nando as the train pulled to a stop at the platform in front of him. "Signor Falconi!" His voice rang out, still full, though cracked and crusty with age. "Signor Falconi!" he shouted again, waving his hand unnecessarily across the barrier railing.

Mats waved back, only a little surprised to see the old man. As they passed through the gate, their bags were taken by Nando's strong, gnarled hands.

"I have a taxi waiting, signore," said Nando as he moved with a smoothness that belied his years. Hardly breaking stride, he threw their bags into the back of the cab.

"I suppose you have arranged for transportation to Corsica as well?" asked Mats, taking the back seat next to Suzanne.

"Yes, signore. I thought you would have missed the Mediterranean after such a long absence. I took the liberty of booking the ferry."

"First I want to ask you some questions about the war. When does the ferry leave?"

"We have almost two hours, signore. There is a fine café run by a civilized Corsican family near the dock. Fantastic calamari. We can talk there."

The Café Island was on the first floor of a brick building across the street from the ferry terminal. Nando was recognized as soon as they entered and ushered to a table next to a shutter framed window looking out at the sea. A waiter appeared, notepad and pencil in hand, before Nando had finished sliding his chair to the table.

"Vichyssoise, some calamari fritti, a pitcher of sangria, and don't bother us," said Nando, reflecting on Mats' serious demeanor.

Mats had thought long and hard during the train ride as to how to ask Nando about his niece. The old man had been a friend of his father's and now was his own. He would trust him with his life. Yet never during the two years they had known each other had he mentioned Teressa. There was bound to be a reason, either private or privileged, for his not telling Mats. Now Mats had to invade that privacy.

"Nando, I do not ask you this lightly. I have had dreams of my father in the past week, only this time, I cannot figure out the warning. You are also in my dreams, as is your niece. I did not know you had a niece."

Nando stared at Mats as if he had been hit between the eyes. No sound came from him. After a minute Mats was about to ask again but was stopped by Suzanne's hand reaching across the table and grasping his. He looked at Suzanne, then back at the old man, and saw why Suzanne had stopped him. A single tear had left the corner of Nando's eye and was cascading over the creases that had long since ceased to be mere wrinkles. As it dropped off his cheek Nando blinked, releasing more tears.

Nando's eyes went down to his hands and the silence remained. Then he looked up at Mats. "Regalo, the Gift. It is such a wonderful thing. Sometimes I forget that it can remind one of the bad times as well as the good. Your dream was correct. I called her Little Esa. She used to follow me around when I was a boy. She became like a daughter to me."

"I would like to tell you of my dreams and see if you can help with their interpretation. Then you can tell me about her, if it is important."

"It can wait, Mats," said Suzanne, her voice choked with emotion.

"Thank you, Signora Falconi. It is all right. But first let me have a glass of sangria and give you news that may be significant. After you phoned from Paris, Jennette received two calls from Ireland. The first was from Signor Cathal Magee, who says he runs a brewery for you. He said that you gave him Jennette's number in case he wasn't able to connect with you."

"My cell was without battery for half a day while I was in Germany and on the train. What did he say?"

"That he had found the patents and also that a Mrs. Bjursten had called from Sweden and thanked you for your kindness in phoning her after the German police informed her of her son's death. She said that she had just this afternoon received some computer disks from her son with the brewery's name on them. She is sure he meant them for you, so she is sending them to Ireland before the authorities start rummaging through her son's papers."

"Her son died tragically in a fire while we were on our way to see him in Germany. I think my last dream might be connected to his death, and if it is, then he was murdered. You said there were two calls...what was the second about?"

"Signor Magee called again. He phoned just before I got on the plane. One of your beer trucks was shot returning to the brewery. A man named Tobin was hit."

"Oh God! Is he dead?"

"I don't know, signore. Perhaps Jennette does, but she did not tell me. We did not have much time. There is one other thing. A boy got on the phone after Magee. Jennette liked him. He said to tell you that he had had another one."

"Brian? He said he had another one?"

"That was his name. Brian. Curse my old man's brain for not remembering."

"Why didn't you tell me this immediately?" Mats' eyes bored into Nando's.

Nando seemed to recover from the grief that the mention of his niece had brought upon him. He straightened in his chair. "Signore. The most important thing to a Guibega is his relationship to the Falconi. My first duty is to make sure that that relationship is maintained. I had to find out what you needed. I did not want to be the one to breach the faith."

"Still, you should have told us about the shooting immediately. We now have to change our plans and return to Ireland. We could have gone straight to the airport. We might have been on a flight by now. How does not telling me first serve our relationship?" Mats bit off the words harshly, regretting them almost as they came out of his mouth.

"The relationship is still served," said Nando, a smile curling the corner of his mouth. "You could not have been on a flight, as the first one is not due to depart for Ireland for another hour-and-a-half. I took the liberty of reserving you two seats. It is only ten minutes to the airport and the taxi is still downstairs, so there is at least time to enjoy a good meal before you depart."

Mats looked at the old man in wonder. Nando had anticipated Mats' reaction, serving both the Guibega and the Falconi in the process. Only the mention of his Teresa had taken him by surprise. Mats was reluctant to mention her again, but he still had to probe the reality surrounding his dream.

The food was set down on the table in front of them, the waiter leaving as quickly as he had come.

"I would still like to hear about your niece's relationship to my father, Nando."

"My Teresa," whispered the old man. "There is much to tell. I fear it will take more time than we have available before your plane leaves."

Mats saw the honesty in the old man's eyes. He would not shirk his responsibility, no matter how painful it was. "Old friend, I wish I did not have to raise ghosts and painful memories, but I suspect it will serve the living. I'd like you to come to Ireland as soon as possible. You must tell me of Teresa, and you must meet a young Irish boy."

Liam Magee was waiting for them at the Shannon Airport. Mats was glad to have a driver for the trip to Donegal. It seemed that all they had done for the last forty-eight hours was travel, and he was tired. He sat in the left-hand passenger's seat, letting Suzanne spread out in the rear.

Liam filled him in on the details that Jennette had not been able to provide. Three armed men in ski masks had stepped in front of a delivery van driven by Charlie Tobin just three blocks from the brewery. They had fired a dozen rounds into the tires and the back, one of them passing through Tobin's shoulder. The impact had knocked Tobin out of the cab onto the pavement, but while the men had sprayed the cab, including the passenger's seat, they had not fired at him again.

Mats listened to the account with his eyes closed, his body swaying with the curves of the road. He was relieved to hear that Tobin was already out of the hospital and talking about work, although he would be unable to drive for a month.

"What was he driving a truck for, anyway?" Mats asked as an afterthought. "He hasn't assigned himself a route in addition to all his other duties, has he?"

"No, though I think he would like to," answered Liam with a laugh. "He's hired two Tobin boys for that. Says they know the back door to every pub in Ireland, and I'm not about to dispute it. He'd just borrowed the van to pick up young Brian."

Mats' eyes flew open.

"Was he in the truck?"

"No. Tobin had gone over to pick the lad up at the dock but the boy refused the lift. He had a line of fish he wanted to drop off in town and thought it would be easier to do on foot, what with the usual talk about the catching of them and all. It was on the way back that the truck was fired on."

"And what does your uncle think of it?"

"He and Tobin had a long talk as soon as Tobin was able. Whatever they think, they are waiting to tell you first. The only thing they told us was always to walk home in twos. Oh, I'm supposed to tell you that Minahen wants to see you as soon as you return to Ireland."

"Take us to the Seascape," said Mats, taking out his phone, explaining to Suzanne. "I want Cathal and Tobin to bring Brian to the restaurant."

They were an odd group that huddled around one of the larger tables next to the window. The main dinner crowd had already left the dining area, many of them stopping at the lounge, where a fine tenor voice could be heard singing softly over the strumming of a guitar.

"So that's all you can tell me about the shooting? Three men step out from behind a hedge with ski masks on. One is tall and thin. They start blasting away. You fall out, but they leave you be and just shoot the shit out of the cab."

"That's it. None of them spoke a word. I thought I had bought it." Tobin sighed deeply before downing the rest of his beer.

"It would appear to me that it is the IRA repaying some debt, or some Orangemen retaliating against a brewery that has long been a patriotic symbol of Irish resistance," said Mats

"It's not the IRA, and it's not the Northern Irish either."

Mats turned to his left to look at Cathal Magee straight on.

"You sound sure, Cathal," said Mats.

"I am. It was not the IRA."

"Minahen seems to think so," said Tobin

"For Minahen it's easy to blame the IRA. Politics take the police out of it, but it wasn't the IRA."

"Could you be mistaken? The weapons, the masks, even the explosives and ambushes are all IRA trademarks," said Mats.

"Mr. Falconi, could I show you something outside?" Magee stood up and moved toward the entrance without looking to see if Mats was following.

"The IRA exists because people protect it," said Magee as the door closed behind them. "Another reason is that most people really don't know who the boys are. An IRA chief could live next door to you and you would probably never even suspect it. It allows for a normal life, both while active and after retirement. It's protection, an insurance policy. So, what I am about to tell you is something most of my nephews don't know, and those who do would not tell you."

"I'm the IRA in Donegal. Not actively, not for some twenty years now, but I am still IRA. Fifty-five years ago, I was the chief intelligence officer for County Donegal. I am not told much anymore, and I certainly don't advise the new breed or approve of some of their tactics. Nor do I agree with them about the killing of innocents with their indiscriminate bombs. But still, when I ask a question, the boys answer it straight. I asked about the murder of the Keohanes. Not only was it not IRA, but they promised to let me know if they found out anything that would lead me to the murderers. So far, they have come up as empty as Minahen. We are checking the guns and explosives, as they might be easier to identify than the men."

"Cathal, did Patrick Keohane know that you were IRA?" asked Mats.

"Yes. That is one of the reasons I got the job. Patrick's father was my immediate superior. He retired at the same time I did, when the bombs became accepted policy, when the training started to come from the Russians in Libya."

Pride was evident in the way that Magee stood straight, looking at Mats. He had the look of a man who had the sure knowledge that he had done the best he could.

"Well, then, Cathal, since it wasn't the IRA and you don't think it was the Protestants, let's go inside and try to figure out who the bad guys are." Mats placed his hand on the old man's shoulder and opened the door.

"It's not the IRA, and probably not the Prods," Mats announced as he and Magee sat back down at the table.

Tobin let out a low whistle as he looked at Magee. The significance of Falconi's statement was obvious.

"Okay, it isn't an IRA, Prod squabble. It isn't some crazy, because there are three of them and a crazy would act alone. What do we have left? Could it be another brewery? Had the Harp and Hawk cut into anyone's business?" Frustration showed in Tobin's voice.

"We have three men. They have to have identities. They have to have names. Cathal is tracing their guns and ammunition. We have a motive that eludes us. If we can figure it out, we will probably know the murderers as well." Mats looked up as he saw the waitress approaching. "It might be a good idea to pass on the word that the Orangemen are responsible. We might have more luck if whoever it is thinks we are barking up the wrong tree, and it sure won't hurt business in the south. In the meantime, let's think about the other brewery angle."

The dinner came and with it a stop to their conversation. After eating, they picked up a second car and Mats drove Suzanne and Brian to the farmhouse.

As soon as they were inside the warm comfort of the large front room, Brian turned to Mats. "I had another dream. It might be important. It might even bear on what was discussed before dinner."

"Tell me about it. Suzanne can see to the fire."

Brian looked at the large fireplace, relinquishing the chore with reluctance until he noticed the smile on Suzanne's face.

"Okay. I was out fishing on the bay the day the truck was shot up. I had set my lines and sat down in the stern. I had the dream. I don't know how long I dreamt, but it must have been hours. When I awoke, it was afternoon and I had three fish on the lines."

"You said the dream could be important. Why is that Brian?"

"Because it warned me. I was to be driven back to meet Mr. Magee in the truck. Mr. Tobin came to pick me up at the dock. I didn't tell him about the dream. I just made an excuse to walk instead of going with him as planned."

Mats looked at Brian until, feeling Suzanne's eyes on him, he turned. She had stopped laying the fire and was staring at Brian, the realization of the significance of his words coming to her at the same time as to Mats.

"Brian, that means the ambush of the truck and the spraying of the passenger's seat was meant for you. The bomb that we thought was for us was placed because you were with us. It makes sense now. Whoever killed your parents is after you as well. Tell me your dream. I will tell you about mine when Nando arrives."

"Who is Nando?" asked Brian.

"A friend, a Corsican whose family has been friends of the Falconi for hundreds of years. He might have the key to unlocking my dream. Now tell me of yours."

Brian looked at them and then out through the window at the bay. "It was as before. The same sea raiders. I saw through the eyes of the brother called Kjell. We were in a large hall. There were large boards carved like sea serpents that ran the length of the sides of the room. Only men were allowed between them. The chief they called Redhand sat at a table at the head of the room. It was a council of captains and Redhand was giving them instructions on the upcoming raid."

Mats and Suzanne listened as Brian stared out the window and slowly unfolded his dream as a narrative seen through his own eyes.

The North Sea—944 AD

"Our eleven boats will be joined by six from the south under the command of Bloodaxe," said Redhand from his perch. Food was passed to him from the rear by women; one handed him a horn of mead.

"Kjell Falkhand, come here." Redhand motioned with the hand that held the horn. "I would talk to my captain."

Kjell moved to the front of the hall, vaulting the head table filled with food and drink to settle on the bench next to the Viking king.

"Falkhand, this raid will be different. I want to leave men there to make a permanent base. I am tired of fighting for the same piece of land every year. I can't do this without the additional men and longboats of Bloodaxe."

"You have explained all that. I have agreed."

"Yes, you have agreed to go, but I fear that you see it as an opportunity to take revenge on Bloodaxe for the lies he spread about you and your brothers. The saga his skald wrote is still sung, the lies still as potent as two years ago when they forced you and your brother to part ways."

"It's true. If Bloodaxe passes within my sword's arc, it would give me pleasure to end his days."

"That must not happen. Not only do I need his support, but I'll not have Viking killing Viking under my command. If that should happen, I would have trouble attracting other chieftains to my banner. I want your oath that you will not kill Bloodaxe."

Redhand had drunk with his captains for over six hours while laying out his plan for the raid. Now, speaking softly to his most capable captain, he showed no sign of drunkenness.

"I will promise this, Redhand, I, Kjell Falkhand, will not take revenge on Bloodaxe during this summer's raid. I will honor my pledge to you."

"Good. But remember this, Kjell Falkhand. If you break your oath, you will again become an outcast."

Brian stopped his account of the dream, as if suddenly remembering that Mats and Suzanne were in the house with him. The fire was now burning brightly, its warmth taking the chill from the room.

"Something happened on my boat. Maybe a fish struck. It woke me for a few seconds. When I shut my eyes again, the dream had changed. The Viking fleet was in the protection of a small, rocky harbor. I remember seeing the sun rise over the water and knew that the harbor and the small town it served were on the east coast. The sun rose to the north; winter was near. There was a fight."

Brian looked into the flames of the fire, slipping away from the present again. His voice became older as he continued to recall his dream.

Kjell traveled the length of the longboat, inspecting every package, every lashing of the baggage. Stowed away was their share of the plunder that had come to them over the past four months. Redhand had been right. By capturing the coastal village in force, they had come to an uneasy truce with both the inhabitants and the surrounding villages. To keep the peace, they had sailed several days in either direction to plunder, leaving the immediate area untouched after its initial conquest.

"Kjell Falkhand, may I come aboard?" Even Redhand, the Viking chief, recognized the authority that a captain had over his own vessel.

"Welcome, Redhand." Kjell slapped the man's palm as he moved easily over the gunwale.

"Falkhand, I wish you would reconsider. I wish you and at least one longboat of your men would stay with the three of mine that will winter here. I would leave you in charge, and cede you a vast holding in land, enough to make you a chief."

"I would take your offer if it were my own choice, but my men have voted to return to winter at their own steads."

A shout of excitement from the beach made both men look for the source. Two of the remaining three longboats under the control of Olaf Bloodaxe had shoved off from the shore. The vessels sat deep in the water, like Kjell's, filled with items plundered from the castles and monasteries of the island. A lone longboat, Bloodaxe's own, remained on the beach. Its crew shouted encouragement and insults at their comrades already pulling toward open water.

Bloodaxe stood with his men but did not join in their shouts of joy and farewell. His hands were on his hips, his fur jerkin covering his chest and protruding stomach, as he gazed past his boats to the open sea. Slowly he turned, and even from this distance, his eyes locked with Falkhand's.

The months on Avalon had not been easy for Kjell. He had promised Redhand that he would not instigate violence or seek revenge while on the island. It had been a credit to the leadership of Redhand that Kjell had been able to keep his pledge. In all of their sorties, Kjell had been kept separated from the boats of Bloodaxe by the tactics of the chief. Sometimes Kjell was left to guard their camp, but they were always separated.

Kjell had not changed his opinion of the southern chief. Bloodaxe was stupid. He had no sense of tactics or diplomacy. He was a brute, vicious in battle, using his viciousness to hide his stupidity. Now, looking across the water at the man, Kjell knew that someday one of them would die by the hand of the other.

Kjell had only one boat that was entirely his own. It was crewed by the men who had been with him since he and his brothers had left their fjord to go a-Viking while they were still in their teens. They were more than a match for Bloodaxe's men, but with six longboats, his numbers were too great. But two weeks ago, three of Bloodaxe's longboats had departed, leaving three behind, including Bloodaxe's personal ship, to follow when the rest broke camp. Now only Bloodaxe's longboat remained of his fleet of six.

Redhand's plan was to leave three boats and eighty fighting men to hold the camp until they returned next spring. Establishing a base on the island had proven even more successful than he had anticipated. The Vikings on this trip would return rich men.

"Bloodaxe had men to spare. Some would have volunteered to stay," said Kjell, scanning Bloodaxe's great boat as it was eased into the water. He noticed with a Viking's attention to detail that it did not sink deep in the water, no extra weight of supplies or plunder crowding the storage area amidships. His treasure had been sent back on his previous boats.

"I do not need more men. Eighty is more than enough to hold our position. What I need is a leader. I have not discussed my plans with the other captains. Next year this settlement will provide a staging area for another permanent camp one day's sail to the south. For that I need a man I can trust."

"Next year I will be able to talk to the men of staying before we leave home. I agree with you that the land here is rich and ripe for the taking. We could easily rule the coastal area."

"With your share of the riches, build another dragon ship to add to the one you are now having built. That would give you three vessels. Word of your battle luck and the promise of more treasure next year will fill your ships with men."

"You have advised my family well, Redhand, first in the matter of Bloodaxe's saga and now this. I will take your advice and return with you next year with two long ships and a knarr.

"I will still need Bloodaxe," said Redhand, following Kjell's stare across the water to where Bloodaxe was standing while his men checked the oars and rigging of his dragon ship. "I hold you to your pledge not to kill him. I have seen how he has goaded you. With him I can do nothing. He acts before he thinks, if he thinks at all. You I can trust to understand the consequences of your deeds. If you kill him, I will ban you from future raids. The story of black magic will again spread. Until I have a string of settlements, filled not only with our men but also with our women, I will not condone his death. You will have your revenge, but not until then."

"I understand. You are my chief." Kjell again held his hand out to be slapped by Redhand.

Two hours after his two ships left, Bloodaxe bade his farewells to Redhand and boarded his great vessel. Within an hour he had rowed out to sea and out of sight of the camp.

Kjell Falkhand drew a deep breath as the great boat pulled around the promontory. Once it was gone, he turned back to the readiness of his own vessel. Whenever Bloodaxe was near, there was a tension, a promise of violence.

"We leave within the hour," Kjell announced. They would still be able to sail five hours before dark.

The wind was light, the seas moderate, as Falkhand piloted his boat toward his homeland to the north. He stood in the stern; his arm hung over the steering oar. His men pulled at the water, happy to be homeward bound, their shares ensuring prosperity for another year.

Kjell looked at the scattered white clouds above, watching for any indication of a change of wind that would allow him to lift his sail and reduce the burden of his men.

"Do not sail!" The command came as a harsh whisper, almost as if the wind were speaking to him. Kjell's senses sharpened as he cocked his head, straining to pick up more.

"Do not sail! Return to shore, to Redhand!"

The thought was so quiet—almost in his subconscious—that he was not sure if he should trust the message.

"Brother?" He used the Gift to try to answer in kind to the warning. He received nothing in return. Still, his heart rate had increased, and all his senses were raw in expectation.

"Brother!" he thought again, trying to span his thoughts across the open sea. He understood the warning and was about to change course when in front of him, scarcely two leagues distant, he saw Bloodaxe's dragon ship, rising and falling in the swell.

Kjell watched as the oars on the resting ship surged into motion, a splash of white foam visible along the length of the vessel. He watched as the square sail with Bloodaxe's crest was raised mid-ships. What little wind there was came almost directly off his own ship's bow, aiding Bloodaxe but working against his own way.

Kjell remembered the trim of Bloodaxe's ship as it had left the settlement, high in the water, not laden with supplies or booty. It was the trim of a ship set for fighting, light on its keel, ready for quick response to the steering oar. He remembered the extra men who crewed the great ship. It was now clear. Bloodaxe had delayed his departure so as to just precede Kjell's own. It was a trap. Bloodaxe's great ship was faster than his own, especially with extra oarsmen and no cargo, but the sea was clear and wide. Still, Kjell was confident that he could outsail or outwit Bloodaxe. He had luck and confidence in his own skill.

Kjell chose to heed his brother's advice. He might win a sea battle with Bloodaxe, but he would lose the support of his chief and be banned from alliances that had made him rich. Kjell had no illusions that Redhand would not carry out his threat just because Bloodaxe had instigated the attack.

Kjell swung the stern around as he issued the order to ready the sail. His men were still fresh; with the help of the sail, they would keep ahead of their pursuers until they reached the settlement. The sail raised quickly, only two men on the middle thwarts attending to it as the others pulled hard at Kjell's urging. At their oars, his men could now see the shape of Bloodaxe's ship as it crested one swell after another. Only one man cried out, "Death to Bloodaxe!" But Kjell could tell from the general murmuring and half-spoken grunts that the entire crew would relish the opportunity.

He looked back over his shoulder at the other ship. It had closed half the distance. They would still make the settlement. Bloodaxe had laid his trap stupidly. It had been easy to intercept him close to the settlement, but in clear weather, this also gave Kjell the opportunity for retreat.

Then, off the port bow, Kjell saw another sail closing on them from the east. There would be still another, he was sure. He scanned ahead, looking for the boat that would be stationed to cut off his retreat to the settlement. Bloodaxe was stupid in many things, but in this, the trap had been well planned. The three ships converged on him. The warning that came with the Gift had been correct. He should have heeded it immediately. He would die, but he would die like a Viking. His men would get their wish. He swung the steering oar again hard to larboard. If they were to die, they would die fighting Bloodaxe himself.

Chapter Nine

The phone rang harshly, interrupting the fabric of Brian's story. Mats immediately regretted having had Grady reconnect the phone. He answered on the second ring, but the moment had been lost. Brian had stopped speaking and was moving toward the fireplace.

"Hello," Mats said into the mouthpiece, irritation barely disguised in his tone.

"Mr. Falconi? It's Cathal here."

"Yes, Cathal. Is something wrong?"

"No. I'm sorry to bother you so late, but I have something I thought you would like to know right away."

"What is it?" asked Mats, the impatience in his voice giving way to concern.

"I told you that I was checking on the guns and ammunition. I sent some of the bullets to Dublin to a professor who teaches Gaelic here in the summer. He knows a ballistics expert at Trinity, one who wouldn't mind doing a favor for the right people. When I got home there was a message to phone him, which I did."

"So, you have a lead on the bullets?"

"Not exactly. They came from a Russian-made AK-47, but that's not what he found so strange. He also examined the bullet I took from the door of the brewery. He had thought it was odd, but that it might have been something that was picked up from striking the wood. When the second batch arrived, the ones I got from the truck, he realized his mistake."

"What mistake?"

"Well, most military ammunition is hard-nosed. It's designed to go right through a target as cleanly as possible. It will take a man out but not make a mess of things. These bullets had been dummied. The noses had been drilled hollow. When they hit a target, they spread and splatter things to kingdom come."

"So the bullets on the street have been modified."

"I'm sorry, Mr. Falconi. It's an Irish thing, the telling of a story, that is. What makes it strange is that they had then been filled with a wedge of wood."

"Wood?"

"Yes. When the second bunch had the same configuration, our expert knew the wood hadn't come from the door and he was on to something weird."

"Wood was shoved into the tip of the bullet? What's the advantage of wood? Did your expert say?"

"That's the other weird thing. There's no advantage, no reason. Wood, especially hardwood, is too dense to allow the maximum flattening of the bullet as it strikes. In other words, it might as well be a solid bullet. He had never seen anything like it."

"He was sure the bullets from both attacks were doctored in the same way. There was no chance that you mixed the two samples?"

"No. I sent the first bunch before the truck was shot up."

"Then for sure we are dealing with the same group of men. Why would they take pains to wear ski masks, then leave a signature like that?"

"Sure I don't know, Mr. Falconi. I just thought that you would want to know about it right away."

"You did right, Cathal. You said hardwood. Did your expert tell you what kind of wood it was?"

"He did. That was the first thing he asked, what type of wood was the brewery door. I had to check. It's pine. He said that was strange because the first bullet had traces of bog oak and ash."

"The things were stuffed with two types of wood?"

"Yes, sir."

"Any ideas?"

"Not a one. Tobin's at a loss as well."

"Okay. Don't tell anyone else. This is our little secret. Has Minahen said anything to you about the bullets?"

"Not a thing. But then, that one doesn't talk to his mother unless he wants a second serving."

"Okay, I'll see you at the brewery tomorrow at eleven. Please have Tobin there as well. Goodnight, Cathal, and thank you for the information."

Mats hung up the receiver and turned back to the fireplace, where both Brian and Suzanne were looking at him with apprehension, the telephone call having heightened the tension they already felt from Brian's account of his dream.

"It was Cathal. The bullets that were used at both the brewery and the van were hollowed out and filled with wood, a mixture of bog oak and ash. Does that strike a bell with either of you?"

Both Suzanne and the boy shook their heads in response. Mats could see from his half-lidded eyes that Brian was at the end of his endurance. His shoulders slumped into the upholstery of the chair and his head hung, jerking erect at intervals. Mats had hoped to hear the rest of the dream, but it would have to wait until Brian had had some sleep.

"Is there more to your dream, Brian?" he asked.

"Yes," replied the boy without enthusiasm.

"Let's wait till tomorrow to hear the rest. Maybe even until Nando Guibega gets here. I still have to tell him of my dream of his niece. He might shed some light on yours as well."

That night, with Brian sleeping soundly below, Mats and Suzanne made love. The imprint of his father's depth of feeling for Teresa resulted in a sustained passion that left both their bodies as exhausted as their minds.

They awoke to brilliant sunlight streaming in through the light curtains covering the window. Below they could hear the sound of pans moving on the stovetop. The smell of frying sausage confirmed that Brian was already up.

"The family down the road keeps some fine-laying hens," said Brian as they came down the stairs. "Have a seat. It'll be done in a minute."

Brian, in the manner of thirteen-year-old boys, looked as if he had grown an inch overnight. Gone was the fatigue that had covered him like a shroud the evening before. The fire was lit, taking the morning chill from the inside of the house as the sun warmed the outside. Mats watched as Brian slid two perfect eggs onto each of the three plates already containing square-cut fried potatoes and large homemade sausages.

"Da always wanted a good day to start with a good breakfast," said Brian, sliding into his seat. "We took turns doing the cooking. Whoever cooked let the others do the dishes. I figure you're no longer guests, so you have some work to do after we eat."

Mats looked back over the boy's shoulder at the kitchen and saw that almost all of the mess had already been taken care of while the food was cooking. The pots and utensils were stacked, drying on the sideboard, and only the skillet that had fried the eggs was still in the sink.

"You'll never get fat in an Irish house eating that slowly," said Brian, pointing his fork at their plates.

Mats chuckled and dug his fork into his potatoes. "I want to meet with Constable Minahen as well as Grady today. Nando could also be arriving. The sooner we unravel what the dreams are telling us, the sooner we will be out of danger."

"I was thinking about the bullets being filled with wood," said Brian, pushing his already empty plate away. "Granddad was killed with a Hurley stick, a caman. It was made of ash and bog oak. It's an unusual blend of woods—not the ash but the oak. I thought it was odd the way Dad told us about it, as if he was as disgusted with the type of wood as with the killing itself."

"How did it happen?" asked Mats.

"I don't really know. I was really small. I can't even remember Granddad now. Dad told me about it when I was ten. It was during the World Cup matches. Ireland had qualified a team. They say there wasn't a voice that wasn't hoarse or a head that didn't ache in all of Ireland the next day. The Prime Minister declared a legal holiday, not that anyone was busting to get to work anyway. That morning they found Granddad, his head caved in and his hand tight around the hurling stick that had killed him."

"Was he killed here in Donegal?"

"No, it was south of here, at Rosses Point."

Mats was almost certain that the men wouldn't try to rig his car again, but it didn't stop him from laying a small piece of string across the corner of the hood and the lower part of the driver's door. If someone tampered with the vehicle, he would know about it. He used the phone to set up his appointments, then left for Donegal town with Suzanne beside him and Brian in the back seat.

"It's probably better if I talk to Minahen alone," he said as he pulled up alongside one of the triangular edges of Donegal's town "square."

The station was hardly more than a hole in the wall of a building next to an Irish sweater outlet. Inside it consisted of an entry room with two desks and seating for five. At the far end, behind the larger of the two desks, was a door that stood open to reveal another made of thick bars.

Mats was shown into Minahen's private office and told to wait by the desk sergeant, who sported a name tag reading "Edward O'Deaver." He waited almost ten minutes before O'Deaver got up and unlocked the barred door behind him. Mats saw the massive head of Minahen move out of the shadows, followed by another man. The sergeant gestured toward the room where Mats was waiting before walking the third man to the front door.

"Mr. Falconi, what can I do for you?" asked Minahen as he entered his office, closing the door behind him.

"Thanks for seeing me. I just had a couple of questions concerning the murder of the Keohanes as well as the shooting up of my truck."

"I'll answer what I can, but the cases you speak of are still under investigation. There are some facts that I can't reveal."

Mats looked at Minahen as he slumped, round-shouldered, over his desk. He remembered reading somewhere that a policeman on duty should try never to smile; it just didn't fit the job. Minahen's face lent truth to that opinion. His smile was out of place on his large square face. It was supposed to show friendliness and willingness to help, but instead it looked to Mats like insincerity and an attempt to hide a shrewdness that the man didn't want exposed.

"When I bought the Harp and Hawk, I of course knew about the Keohanes. I didn't think it would affect the running of the brewery in the future. Then you discovered the bomb in my car, and now my truck has been shot up. I am frightened for myself, for my wife, and for the workers at the brewery. I bought the place to make beer, not get myself killed. I'm thinking of shutting it down until you find out who is doing this and why."

"That would be a shame. It's still the best brew Ireland has to offer. Not only that but it's the only brewery in Donegal, a treasure so to speak. I think it is unnecessary to shut it down."

"Have you learned something I should know about?" asked Mats.

"Let's just say I have found enough to know that whoever it is, they aren't interested in killing you or stopping production at the brewery."

"How can you say that? The bomb, the attack on the truck?"

"The bomb was little more than a firecracker. It would have blown the hinges off the bonnet and done little else. The road service man did not know what he was looking at and exaggerated its importance. We dismantled it. It looked like it might have been in place for weeks, long before you rented the car."

Mats remembered the coil of wire from the starter motor and the large bundle of explosives and was glad he had kept quiet about seeing the men place it. Minahen was lying.

"What about the ambush of the truck?"

"Your truck was just in the wrong place at the wrong time. Nothing more. It was driving by Mersk's shipping office just as three holdup men were trying to make their getaway. From what your man said, they could have killed him, but they didn't, just shot up the truck. Probably just to stop him from following."

"What about the weapons, the bullets?" asked Mats. He wasn't sure what he'd been expecting from Minahen, but it hadn't been a cover-up.

"What about them?"

"Were they the same type as the ones that killed the Keohanes? Was there anything special about them?"

"Both were from automatic weapons. Nothing special. Nothing that we could trace."

Mats got up and extended his hand. He was afraid of staying any longer, afraid that his emotions would give him away. "I'll feel a lot safer when you get these people behind bars."

"You can be sure that we're working on it, Mr. Falconi. I'll call you if anything breaks." They shook hands and Minahen watched Mats turn and start toward the door.

Mats stopped when he reached the door. "Who was the man you were with just before you came in here?" he asked. "I've only been in Ireland a couple weeks, but I thought I knew him. He isn't one of my workers, is he?"

"Naw, he's Gavan Grady's brother, Ian. He just ran over some legal papers."

"Thanks. I would have felt stupid if he was one of my own men and I didn't recognize him," said Mats. "And thanks for the other information as well. I feel more comfortable knowing what is going on." Mats meant it more than Minahen could suspect.

Mats' meeting with Grady lasted less than five minutes. The lawyer had warned him on the phone that he had a very heavy schedule but could give Mats a few minutes between meetings.

"Thanks for seeing me this morning, Mr. Grady," said Mats, sitting in the chair in front of the desk. "I'm just trying to decide if it is safe for me and my wife to operate the Harp and Hawk."

"I would think that you are quite safe," offered Grady, considerable relief in his voice. "Constable Minahen told me just the other day that he felt the two shootings were completely unrelated, probably different individuals."

"Yeah," said Mats, a warning flashing through his mind. "He told me that as well. Oh, by the way, I saw your brother at the police station a little while ago. Is he a lawyer too?"

"My brother, Ian?" asked Grady, clearly taken off guard. "No, he has his own business. Sometimes he helps me, but he has no training in the law."

"Oh. When I first saw him, I thought he looked familiar. I thought he was one of the workers at the brewery. I guess he just reminded me of you. Thanks again for squeezing me in," said Mats, getting up and moving toward the door.

"How did it go?" asked Suzanne as Mats rejoined them outside the building.

"Interesting, very interesting. Minahen and Grady might be in cahoots. He gave me the same line as Minahen, almost word for word."

"My dad didn't like Grady, and he always told me to stay away from Mr. Minahen and the police station," said Brian. "I thought it was just to make sure I behaved and didn't get into any trouble, but now I wonder if there was more to it."

"Let's run it by Cathal when we get to the Harp and Hawk," said Mats, turning down the street. "It's such a nice day. Let's walk."

"I didn't know where to get in touch with you except at Grady's," said Magee, "and I didn't think you would want me to leave a message with that snake in the grass. You had already left the house when we got the call that your friend from Corsica was coming into Shannon at noon. Tobin thought it best if someone was there to meet him and bring him directly back here."

"He was right," said Mats, clapping Magee on the shoulder. "I wanted to run some things by you two. It would be good if Nando could hear them too. We'll wait till they get here. Meanwhile, see if Maureen O'Toole has room for Nando. I'll take care of the bill."

Mats spent the next four hours going over the production figures with Magee. He was impressed at how fast the old man had gotten the brewery back to full production. No non-alcoholic runs had been made yet, but the machinery was now in place and ready to function. Magee wanted to wait until the production of Harp and Hawk was sufficient not only to fill the pent-up demand but also to get a couple hundred cases in reserve.

"I know a lot of extra hours have been worked to get this place going again so fast," Mats told Magee. "I want you to make sure the workers put in for overtime."

Mats could tell the old Irishman was blowing him off and was about to blast him for it when they heard the honk of Tobin's car outside the main doors. Brian and Suzanne, happy to be doing anything after the long wait, rushed to open the doors. As soon as Tobin stopped the car, Suzanne moved forward, leaned through the open window, and kissed Nando on the cheek. She helped him out of the car, the old man stiff, the inactivity of sitting during the drive from Shannon making him look frail and uncertain on his feet.

"Did you have any trouble finding him?" asked Mats as Tobin pushed himself out from behind the steering wheel.

"Nah. He had two flight attendants helping him all the way through departure. They found me," said Tobin, shaking his head in amazement. "I don't know how he did it, but he even got a case of red wine through with his luggage."

Suzanne smiled and gave the old Corsican a hug, which he acknowledged with a wink.

"Up to your old tricks," she said affectionately.

"They were very kind to an old man," said Nando, showing upturned hands. "It is good to see you again, Signor Falconi."

"It is good to see you again too, old friend," Mats answered.

"Now, is a guest supposed to die of thirst before he is offered any hospitality?"

"Nando Guibega, this is Cathal Magee, our brew master. He will take care of your thirst and probably the better part of that case of wine you brought with you," said Mats, introducing the two men.

The two old men shook hands, facing each other squarely. They were almost mirror images of each other, both small and wiry, hardened by a lifetime of physical labor, but their eyes were the feature that was most alike. Both Nando and Magee squinted through a mass of wrinkles, but there was truth and a sharpness of intellect in their eyes.

"Aye, I'll take care of that thirst for you, then show you around the place," said Magee, placing his hand on Nando's shoulder and guiding him toward a refrigerator that stood under the staircase to the upper floor.

Suzanne looked at Mats and received a nod accompanied by a smile. There would be no trouble with the heads of the Guibega and Magee clans becoming friends.

"We never kept the stuff cold until an American bought the place," said Magee in mock disgust as he and Nando returned with a six-pack and some glasses. The men drank beer while Brian, after being introduced to Nando, fixed tea for Suzanne and himself. They were well into their second round before Mats finished telling of the bomb that had been placed in his car. Magee and Brian related the murder of the Keohanes, and Mats was again astounded by the young boy's calmness and acceptance of the loss of his parents.

Nando sat still during the telling, sipping his beer, not asking questions or offering comments. Not until the mention of the two types of wood that had been used to fill the dummy heads of the bullets did he show any clear sign of interest.

"Oak and ash—are you sure?" he asked, raising an eyebrow.

"Yes, we are. That's what makes Constable Minahen's insistence that there was nothing remarkable about the bullets so incomprehensible," answered Mats.

It took Mats half of another beer to explain what Minahen had said and how Grady had told him the same thing.

"I can't understand why Minahen would tell you that," said Magee. "But then, I never could figure that bugger out."

"What do you mean, Cathal?" asked Suzanne.

"Well, the man has done some strange things in his time. Fifteen years ago, he was the best goalie in Ireland. He could have played on the World Cup team, for sure. Instead he gives up football and becomes a policeman. Gives up a hundred thousand pounds for playing a few games in order to make six thousand a year as a rookie Garda."

"Strange or not, the man is lying, and that much we know," said Tobin.

"And what about Grady?" asked Mats.

"What's to trust in that weasel?" answered Tobin. "Obviously he and Minahen are tight. They both know what they're telling you is a lie."

"I agree," said Mats. "Cathal, what can you tell me about Grady's brother?"

"Ian? He's stranger than Minahen," answered Magee. "He's smart. Made fantastic marks reading for the University. We all thought he'd be at Trinity. Had a scholarship offered, if I remember correctly. Then out of the blue, he leaves school and buys a back-break little rock farm way out on Fairies Point. Stays to himself mostly. Why do you ask about him?"

"I saw him today with Minahen. Looked serious, but when I asked Minahen about it, he just said he was delivering some papers from his brother."

"From his brother? Young Ian Grady went to school with Minahen. They were best chums. Ian quit school at the same time Minahen quit football."

"Liam!" Magee yelled across the brewery floor at his nephew, who was the last of the workers still there. "Liam, you know Ian Grady, don't you?"

The young man who had become his foreman walked toward the group. "We went to school together, but that was fourteen or fifteen years ago. What's he done now?"

"Nothing that we know of. What's he like?" asked Mats.

"Smart bugger he was, but weird. Always talking about magic, the little people and such. I haven't had much to do with him since he left school." Liam waited for another question.

"Ask around for me, will you, lad?" said Magee. "Let me know what he's been doing, how he earns a living, who his friends are … that sort of thing."

"In my dream—" began Brian, only to be stopped midsentence by Mats' hand coming down on his arm. If Magee noticed the pause, he didn't show it. Nando, on the other hand, looked up with more interest than he had shown since the mention of the wood in the bullet tips.

"Nando, you must be tired. Let's get you some food. Then we'll take you to Mrs. O'Toole's."

Nando hesitated. "There was an English soldier, a medic in Corsica during the war, named Grady. He saved the life of a German officer and then disappeared. I would very much like to speak to him if he's still alive."

CHAPTER TEN

"How is it the boy has the Gift?" asked Nando as soon as they were alone in the farmhouse.

"He is a distant relative of the Falconi," answered Mats. "His family has had the Gift for generations. They call it the Knack."

Nando looked through the open door to the kitchen, where Brian and Suzanne were preparing dinner. "He has the dreams?"

"Yes. I will ask him to share his dream with you later. Now, while they're busy, I'll tell you about my dream of your niece. I am sure that it's meant to be a warning, but this time I cannot fathom how they relate to recent events."

Nando only nodded, knowing he would have to tell his own secret, one he had lived with for fifty years.

When they had first met, over two years ago, Nando had sketched for Mats the significance of Egel Falconi's return to Nazi-occupied Corsica, but he had left out the details. Now, it was Mats who filled them in, starting with his father's rescue of Nando from the German detention camp. As Mats supplied detail after detail, he could see from Nando's expression that the events were true. He stopped short of describing the details of the passion between his father and the old man's niece, saying only that they first became lovers in the cave. Here he stopped his story, seeing the mixture of pain and pride in Nando's face.

"So, you see, old friend, I can't decipher the warning. I need you to tell me the significance of what is being shown to me."

"I should have known that the story would eventually be given to you," said Nando, wiping a tear from his eye as he looked at Mats. "It is good that it happened while I am still alive so that I will not die carrying this weight.

"Only seldom has there been a union between a Falconi man and a woman of the Guibega clan. In ancient times there could not be, because the Falconi, being noble, married only noble women, usually from Normandy or Sicily. Over the last two hundred years, occasionally a Falconi daughter would marry a Guibega man, but never the other way around. My own mother was born of such a union. The children of such a couple were often gifted—never as much as the Falconis—but more so than other Guibegas. I have always thought that my position of leadership in the clan was a direct result of my being the first grandson of my Falconi grandmother. She taught me about the Gift early in my childhood. I grew up at her side.

"I knew that my Teresa and your father were lovers. Every Guibega who saw them together knew, but they never let on. It was the war and we had more than one traitor in the Resistance. That is why your father insisted that we secretly break off as a fighting unit from the Resistance. He thought that Teresa could be used against him if it was ever discovered that she was the lover of the 'Maquis.' That was your father's code name."

"Yes, I know," said Mats, not wanting to break the thread of the story Nando was weaving.

"I could see they were meant for each other. I was so proud of her, my Teresa. I should have known that it would end poorly. I should have insisted that I be his guide, that I be the one to take the risks. But my Teresa, she was so proud to be a part of your father's mission, so happy to be in love. Once it happened, I could never have separated them."

"What happened to your niece?" asked Mats, fearing that he already knew the answer.

"For a year and a half after they met, she acted as your father's lieutenant. Just as warfare had changed for the Germans with the use of aircraft, so did it change for the Guibega. Never were more than five Guibega to be found together except at the moment of attack. If they had jobs, they kept them. If they lived at home, they continued to do so. The Guibega disrupted the Germans rather than confronting them. We set Hun Traps, wire pulled taut across a road, until the Germans were afraid to ride their motorcycles at high speed or after dark. It took two men to set the trap, one to signal when to pull the wire taut and one to tie off its end. Both were gone before the Germans hit it.

"Did you know that the word 'sabotage' comes from the French workers in the beginning of the Industrial Revolution who threw sabots into moving machinery to wreck it? It is one of the few French words I like the sound of. Sabotage was our weapon.

"One of the women doing clerical work for the Germans would make a mistake that would end with misplaced supplies or send troops on a longer route to their destination. Nothing major, nothing that couldn't be blamed on stupidity, an honest mistake made by a less than perfect race.

"The German reprisals were brutal. The Resistance fighters they captured were tortured during interrogation. Some they shot. Some they sent off the island. Always they tried to find out who 'Maquis' was and how they might trap him. Only the Guibega knew the answer to this question, and they were never captured, as they only fought with the regular Resistance when it would arouse suspicion if they did not. Your father taught us well. Strength came from vanishing, not holding ground that would soon be reclaimed. All of it was coordinated through Teresa until the Allies landed on September 20, 1943.

"Most of the time, your father stayed in the storage shack at the winery, but sometimes he washed dishes at the Alta Mira and slept in the kitchen. Only once did he let the Guibega fight directly against the Germans. We killed fewer than three hundred soldiers, but we tied thousands of them up looking at their rear instead of for the Allies."

"But what about your niece?"

"I told you when we first met on Corsica that your father saved the Guibega, that only one of our clan died after he arrived. It was Teresa who paid that price," said Nando, tears pressing from the corners of his eyes. "The German that the corpsman, Grady, saved murdered her."

"But how?" asked Mats. Before Nando could answer, a hand was laid softly on his shoulder. Mats followed Nando's eyes, turning to see Suzanne standing at his shoulder. He did not know how long she had been standing there or how much of Nando's tale she had heard. It was fully apparent from the set of the old man's jaw that he would not finish his story with Suzanne present. It was for Mats' ears only.

"Dinner is ready," Suzanne said softly, understanding the intimacy of the conversation she was interrupting.

The dinner was fish, North Sea haddock, served with noodles and chard. Suzanne had added thin slices of tomato and capers to the noodles, covering them with a delicate cream sauce. The chard and fish had been Brian's contribution. He had added small bits of bacon and sprinkled vinegar over the greens.

As Mats watched Nando eat, he was reminded of his friend's age. Nando ate like an old man, as if the effort was not worth it for the little nourishment he needed. Mats ate slowly, too, trying to keep pace with the old Corsican as he picked first at the fish and then at the greens. Eventually the rich flavor of the meal won out and most of Nando's food had been eaten.

Brian excused himself from the table while Nando was still eating and started a fire. Suzanne went next, clearing the dishes as the two men finished.

"Listen to Brian's dream first," said Mats in Corsican, when they were left alone. "I only need to know if you see any warning. Brian's dreams did not come until last month, after his parents' deaths. His father had told him, though, that dreams were part of the Knack. His dreams are different from mine only in that they deal with his ancestor and his line. Other than that, they are the same. One has already saved his life. He was supposed to be in the van that was shot up. His dream told him of an ancient ambush, and he heeded the warning. Our lines separated long ago, before the Falconi settled on Corsica, perhaps many hundreds of years before. Yet, he is of my blood."

"I might have something to tell you about the men who shot the boy's parents," Nando said finally, in a voice cracked more with emotion than age. "I take it that neither Magee nor Tobin has the Gift? Is there no one Brian can confide in as you confide in the Guibega?"

"Evidently not," answered Mats, looking over at the boy, who now had the fire roaring.

Nando stood up and moved toward the fire. The aroma of wood and peat filled his nostrils as he took the armchair nearest the flames. "Signor Falconi tells me to regard you as his son," said Nando to the boy, reverting back to English. "My family has dreams too, but they are unlike yours. They are not as powerful. They come only rarely and are only remembered history, not warnings. When a Guibega dreams, we send for our keeper of histories and he writes it down. I am told you don't have the support of a family such as mine."

"Well, not exactly," said Brian. "The Magees have worked for us for centuries, and fought with us, always on the same side, but they don't have the Knack. My father told me that before the Magees, there was another family, but they were wiped out a couple hundred years ago. I don't know anything else about them."

"Brian had a dream of a Viking," said Mats, bringing a chair from the dining table to the living room. "A Viking captain who was attacked at sea by another Viking chief. He had received a warning from his brother using the Gift. Because of his dream, Brian didn't go with Tobin when the van was shot up.

"I stopped you at the Harp and Hawk," continued Mats, pulling his chair closer to the fire and looking at Brian, "because the Gift should not be mentioned or discussed with anyone outside our family. It's our protection. It's saved my life and now it has saved yours."

"Please finish telling your dream to us," Suzanne requested softly.

Brian looked at Mats, receiving a nod of assent before he started.

"I stopped when Kjell—he was my ancestor," Brian explained to Nando. "Was trying to sail back to the safety of the camp. He was surrounded by three of his enemy's ships. Was that where I stopped?" asked Brian, again looking at Mats.

Mats nodded. "You said that Kjell feared it was hopeless, but he would at least take Bloodaxe with him."

Brian settled deeper in his chair. After a slight pause, he continued his story.

❧ ❧ ❧

The North Sea—946 AD

Kjell knew that the greatest danger was from Bloodaxe's dragon ship. It was the largest of all the ships and held no cargo, only extra warriors. He didn't want to waste the lives of his men on the two ships that blocked his return to the settlement.

"I come, my brother!"

This time the message rang clearly in Kjell's mind. He scanned the horizon and detected the top of a sail. Above it waved the long thin blue banner of the Falkhand.

"There are three ships attacking me," Gifted Kjell, concentrating on the sail that was fast closing the distance between them. *"The one to the south is laden with treasure and minimal crew. Attack it, my brother, and you'll draw the second to you out of greed. Bloodaxe lies to the north in his great dragon ship. I'll attack him before he knows of your presence. He laid his trap well, but overconfidence will be his death."*

"Prepare to come about!" Kjell threw the steering oar hard to starboard. "Down sail."

As they came about, the sail caught the small headwind that was now aiding Bloodaxe and stopped Kjell's boat in the water.

"Step the mast," ordered Kjell from the stern platform.

Vikings were used to obeying orders immediately and without question when in battle, but even so, the men taking down the sail turned and looked at their leader. The mast was fastened into the deck by friction and wood wedges that held it tight against the center thwart. Under normal circumstances it was never taken down.

"Step the mast now!" Kjell again bellowed. "When it is down, lay it fore and aft between the oarsmen."

This time the command was heeded. Butt ends of battle axes drove the wedges from their position around the base of the mast.

The distance from Bloodaxe's great ship was now less than half a league. Even at that range, it was apparent that Bloodaxe's higher rails, gave them the advantage of looking down into the bowels of Falkhand's ship. Kjell sensed no fear from his men. They had suffered the insults of Bloodaxe's men as much as their captain had. Now Kjell had ordered them to battle. It was like being permitted to scratch an itch that had been out of reach. They moved with power and purpose toward the great dragon ship.

Even with his cargo, Kjell could outmaneuver the larger vessel, but that would only allow Bloodaxe's archers to pick them off. Not only did Bloodaxe have height on his side, but he had extra men who could shoot while others rowed. Kjell's men would have to do one or the other. While he could keep away from Bloodaxe, he would not be able to outrun him either downwind or under oar. Trying to ram would fail for the same reason. Bloodaxe had almost double the men that his own ship carried.

Growing up on their bay, Kjell and his brothers had often carried out mock sea battles. Then it was whose skiff would be overturned or who would take a dunking that determined the winner. When brothers fight, there are no dirty tricks, no rules that can't be broken. Their father often watched them play their war games. Later, in the evening, he would go over with them those tactics that had been wise and those that had been useless. He always gave reasons for both his praise and his condemnation of their actions.

Now, when death rather than a dunking faced the loser, Kjell remembered a trick that Jan had used on Jarl. It had not worked, and their father had explained why. Kjell had thought hard about his father's explanation, and although he had never said so, had thought he was mistaken. Jan had failed to overturn Jarl, but the failure was not in the plan. It was in not thinking out the tactic to its conclusion. In the years that had passed, Kjell had not had the opportunity to test his theory in battle. The only sea engagements he had fought had been against the small fat cargo vessels that skirted the coast. No trick had been necessary until now, and now the lives of his crew depended on it. The key was knowing the weakness of the opponent and his vessel.

"Vikings, hear me!" Kjell shouted to his men. There was still time before the two ships came within range of bow and arrow. He gave them his plan. Every man in his crew was a freeman, each pledged to him by their own free choice. Each knew Kjell's battle luck was unmatched by any other captain. They looked at each other and then back at Kjell, standing at the tiller, and laughed. They were laughing at their acceptance of the audacity of the plan and because they were sure, as was Kjell, that with a little luck, it would work.

Kjell's longboat had, alongside the inside of each gunwale, a bench that ran from bow to stern. It was here the Vikings sat on their sea chests when rowing. Under foot, running across the width of the ship, was decking, providing a level footing against the rolling of the sea. Under the decking, water and supplies, plus any cargo, were normally stored. But on this trip so much plunder had been taken that it was piled high between the rowers' benches as well.

Kjell's plan relied on his understanding of Bloodaxe's behavior. Kjell had observed his foe in several battles. At sea as well as on land, Bloodaxe depended on brute strength rather than careful thought. He tended to wait until the numbers were strongly in his favor and then attack without finesse. It would be the same today.

Both crews pulled at their oars, closing the distance. Kjell relied on Bloodaxe to hold his archers, keeping them armed with sword and axe instead. It worked. At less than fifty yards, Kjell shouted an order to his starboard oarsmen.

"ONE, TWO, THREE."

The men gave three giant strokes, closing the distance almost to the point where their oars could touch. Then they stood, sliding their oars across the boat, even though there was no chance of hitting the other vessel.

Bloodaxe laughed as Falkhand's boat turned toward him. His own vessel was superior in every way. He had twice the men and they were his best warriors. Falkhand was doing nothing but hastening his own doom.

Bloodaxe scanned the sea behind the approaching longboat of Falkhand. His other vessels would follow their prey, closing the trap even tighter. Bloodaxe hoped they would not arrive too quickly. He wanted Falkhand's head on his own spike.

"May Odin damn them!" Bloodaxe muttered under his breath as he spotted the blue banner of Jan Falkhand in the distance, engaging his other two vessels. "Vikings, take arms for boarding! Ready the grappling irons!" The boats continued directly toward each other.

"NOW!" shouted Kjell, leaning on the tiller, forcing his boat to pass alongside, twenty feet to starboard of Bloodaxe's dragon ship.

Kjell's men, on the side nearest the other ship, immediately stood, grabbing the mast in brawny, calloused hands, lifting it high above their heads. They heaved it on the count of three, before Bloodaxe could react, before he could issue the command to ship oars.

Bloodaxe had been anticipating grappling the smaller ship, then boarding it. By avoiding the fight, the other vessel would only delay the outcome, not change it. Too late he saw the true purpose in Falkhand's maneuver. He was still trying to form the command to ship oars when the mast crashed down on the sixteen oars suspended through the oar ports.

The timber that had served as the mast was heavy. It landed on the oars halfway between the water and the ship. Most of the oars cracked. Three at the stern did not crack but became hopelessly tangled in the loose rigging of the mast. One was pulled away from the hands of the oarsmen, unbroken but useless as it floated away from the great boat.

"Retrieve the mast," shouted Kjell to his sternmost oarsman. The man stood, throwing a grappling hook into the rigging as it floated by. His snag held. Immediately, he started pulling the tangle of mast, line, and oars toward him even as the rest of the men pulled away from the disabled great ship. As the timber came alongside, others lent a hand, and in seconds the mast was again on the deck.

Kjell had struck at the only vulnerable point of the larger vessel—its maneuverability. Viking ships carried spare oars, but not as many as were broken. Kjell knew that he must strike again and quickly, before Bloodaxe could regain his composure.

"Olaf, Lars, go to the bow. Hold the small end of the mast just above the water, an oar's length out from our ship. The rest of you, fix shields over the backs of the oarsmen. This time we can expect Bloodaxe's archers to be ready."

Kjell again leaned on the tiller, turning back toward the disabled dragon ship. Even with only eight oars on each side, his longboat slid through the water with increasing speed. Shields were quickly hung from the necks of the rowers, protecting their backs from the arrows that were sure to come.

"Have swords at the ready. Cut any grappling irons quickly." Kjell scanned his crew as they bore down on Bloodaxe, who had already transferred some of his oars from the other side and was starting to make way. Kjell's path would take him just astern of the larger vessel if it did not turn.

"Thrust the ram at his stern and his steering rudder!" yelled Kjell.

Again, his men gave three powerful strokes, adding momentum to the thrust given the mast by those standing mid-ships. The top of the mast slid cleanly through the slate-gray water of the channel until it hit the wood of Bloodaxe's stern. The great ship listed, and Kjell's men were thrown backward by the impact. The base of the mast swiveled off the figurehead of Kjell's longboat, hitting several of his men before it twisted overboard. The violence of the collision created confusion on both vessels.

Kjell, holding onto his own steering oar to keep from being knocked overboard, shouted commands to his crew. "Make way! Make way now!" He knew they were most vulnerable under the stern of Bloodaxe's ship.

The first arrow came, and with it the first scream from his crew. One of his men lay across his oar, an arrow through his neck. Another lay unconscious, blood streaming from a deep gash on his head where the mast had struck him. One of the men who had thrust the mast pushed the stricken Viking aside and took his oar. His example was followed by another. Another volley of arrows hit their boat. This time they were thick, but the distance was increasing and the aim more difficult. A grappling iron hit the side, bouncing off harmlessly into the sea. Another caught the rail but Kjell himself severed its line with a vicious swipe of his sword.

Twenty strokes took their boat out of range of Bloodaxe's archers but not of his curses. Kjell laughed out loud at the oaths Bloodaxe shouted at Odin, Kjell, his men, and the gods in general. Thirty more strokes and his longboat was at speed, moving swiftly away from the disabled vessel.

"My brother," thought Kjell, using the Gift. *"Can you hold until I get there?"*

"Hold? You'd better hurry if you want there to be anyone left to fight," came the reply.

Jan's bravado did not match the scene that Kjell saw before him. Jan's longboat was trapped between the two ships belonging to Bloodaxe. His men were fighting on both sides, holding their own but in a poor tactical position.

Kjell slid up against the nearest of Bloodaxe's vessels. It had the greatest number of warriors and was pressing his brother the most. Grappling irons held the two ships fast as Kjell's leapt over the gunwale, attacking Bloodaxe's men from the rear.

Jan had almost completely taken over the treasure ship by the time Bloodaxe's second boat had joined the fight. With the arrival of the second ship, the five or six men remaining on Bloodaxe's treasure ship fought like tigers. Now with the arrival of Kjell, they laid down their weapons. Soon the men on Bloodaxe's second vessel, facing warriors front and back, had done the same.

"Take their weapons, their oars, and their sails. Place them in my ship," commanded Jan. "Then tie a line between the empty treasure ship and our stern."

Both brothers watched as the orders were carried out. Four archers stood on the afterdeck of each boat and made sure that there was no treachery as Bloodaxe's men surrendered their weapons. When they were secure, Kjell yelled, "You Vikings fought bravely and well this day. I will return your oars and sails to you after I have killed Bloodaxe."

"Are you up for another fight, brother?" thought Kjell teasingly, as he looked across the short expanse of water that separated him from Jan's longboat. Jarl had towed the crewless treasure ship half a mile away from Bloodaxe's second vessel before dropping the line, letting the ship drift up one swell and down another.

"Just like you used to do at the stead," sent back Jan. *"You show up just in time for dessert. Now I guess you will want a share of the booty."*

"When Bloodaxe is dead, I will have earned it. It was your trick that I used to disable his vessel."

"What trick?" asked Jan.

"Remember when you tried to break Jarl's oar by throwing your own at it? Father was wrong. The tactic wasn't faulty. The oar just wasn't heavy enough for the task."

"I notice that you have no mast. I was wondering if you planned to row all the way home." Jan laughed out loud and Kjell joined him.

The crews looked at their leaders. It was no coincidence that the brothers had laughed together, as if they were sharing the same joke across the expanse of water. Those who had sailed with the Falkhands back when all three of them were together were not surprised. The others, who had only heard of the special gifts of the brothers, looked to the older hands for reassurance. If magic was being used, it was good to have it on their side.

They were nearing Bloodaxe's disabled dragon ship, still out of bowshot but closing fast on the point where they would be vulnerable.

"Shall we grapple at the same time on either side?" asked Jan. It was the usual tactic when two boats were attacking a single one.

"It would be better if I grapple and you stay behind my ship and shoot arrows to keep them away from the rail."

"Better yet, you grapple on his starboard side and I will rain arrows on him from his port side," added Jan. *"That way the men who use their shields to protect themselves from you will be open to my shafts."*

"Do it!" Kjell nodded as he turned his boat to port, away from the parallel track of his brother.

Kjell sailed directly to the side of the rudderless dragon ship. Men on bow and stern, crouching behind the wall of shields, threw grappling irons high over their heads. They came down on the deck of Bloodaxe's ship and were immediately pulled taut. Soon five stout lines held the boats in a death embrace.

Kjell commanded his men to feint a rush to board the larger vessel but stop short of leaving their own boat. The quiet tone of his voice was picked up and relayed from man to man, unheard by Bloodaxe's warriors. Whatever else they did, they were to keep covered behind bulkhead or shield.

"Now shoot, my brother!"

"Now!" Kjell shouted, watching his men move forward en masse, as if to storm the larger ship. As he expected, Bloodaxe's men raised their shields and brandished their weapons over the side in response to the fierce war cries of his men. As his men stopped, banging swords and axes against their shields, the arrows from Jan's archers hit home. Most found the deck of Bloodaxe's boat, but some sailed in an arc over it and hit the shields of Kjell's crew. One of Kjell's men was hit in the shoulder. Kjell watched without emotion as the man broke the arrow in half and pulled it through his own flesh before resuming his feint and withdraw orders.

The second volley was less effective. Fewer of Bloodaxe's men were hit, but the confusion that it caused was greater. The defenders of the great dragon ship did not know which way to direct their defenses. On one side, Kjell's men were about to board, their war cries drowning out Bloodaxe's orders. On the other side came death from the archers of the second boat. The third volley delivered the results Kjell had been waiting for. Now almost all shields were facing Jan's attack.

"Now, Vikings, attack!" screamed Kjell. *"Now, brother, grapple while we hold their attention. Hurry."*

Kjell did not hesitate. He leapt to the rail, pulling himself over the body of a defender before another could fill the gap. Once on Bloodaxe's ship he was attacked by two men, both with swords. Over their shoulders Kjell could see that nearly all of Bloodaxe's men were facing the attack from his boat. They were two deep at some points, too many of them to gain the rail at one time. Those of Kjell's crew who had gained the deck were hard pressed.

Kjell tried to fight back toward the rail. It was the duty of the first men to create the opportunity for more men to board. It was the duty of the defenders to prevent it, and they were doing it well. One swordsman maintained a position between Kjell and the backs of the men at the rail, while another attacked him, looking for a weakness in his defense.

"Hurry, brother," Gifted Kjell, knowing that the thought was unnecessary. Jan would know that the conditions were murderous for his brother's crew and would not delay his own attack.

Kjell got his reply, not in the manner of the Gift, but in a battle cry that came from a dozen of Jan's warriors as they leapt to Bloodaxe's deck over the unprotected side.

As Bloodaxe's men turned to meet the new threat, Kjell's men gained the deck in ever increasing numbers. One of Kjell's opponents had to defend himself from a new quarter, leaving only the other man to face him. The axe in Kjell's hand felt light, as if it had no substance. Only the splintering of the man's shield under his blows gave

Kjell a sense of the power behind it. The man backed up until he was up against the railing, Kjell having moved so close that only the axe was an effective weapon. Kjell was about to deliver a maiming blow to the man's exposed legs when a sword thrust from Jan made it unnecessary. The warrior fell dead at Kjell's feet.

No thanks were spoken, but the two men looked into each other's eyes before turning to the remainder of Bloodaxe's defenders. Less than a minute after Jan's crew stormed the deck, Bloodaxe's men were surrounded in the center of the ship. Over a dozen had died, spilling their blood over the deck where others now fought. Then one of the defenders yelled "Truce!" and threw his weapon at the foot of Kjell's man. The first was followed by another and then quickly another. Only the very brave or the very frightened fought on.

"Hold, Vikings! Listen to me!" Bloodaxe stood at the bow of his great ship, looking at what was left of his crew. His axe was red with blood and sweat streamed from under the gray metal of his helmet. "Listen to me."

Those who were still fighting stopped, turning toward the Viking chief. As they turned, those nearest to Bloodaxe moved away from him.

"Who has not heard the saga of the Falkhand brothers? " screamed Bloodaxe. "How they use black magic on both their opponents and their own crews? Magic, magic that will enslave you and cost you your soul if you surrender!"

"Ha, you stupid oaf." Jan strode forward, standing in the middle of the deck. "There was no magic. There was luck—luck that had me carrying Christian priests north from the land of the Franks, luck that I chose an inn where six drunken men bragged of your trap: your own men! Men you had sent home early to unload their cargo. These men talked freely of your plan to kill Kjell and take his share of plunder. It was easy to wait for your arrival."

"The only magic here must be protecting you. It would explain how such a dumb brute has stayed alive as long as you have." Kjell walked through the group until he stood directly in front of Bloodaxe. "You wanted a fight." Kjell held his hands with shield and axe parallel to the deck. "Well, have one with me."

"Aargh!" screamed Bloodaxe as he swung his battle axe in a high arc over his head.

Kjell anticipated the blow even before it began. The axe, unlike the sword, was lethal only for eight inches of its length but made up for its deficiency by the fact that it could not be parried. The stoutest Viking shield could not withstand a direct blow. The best defense was to deflect the blow by holding the shield at such an angle as to make the axe head glance off of it. Against an opponent with a sword, the shield could be held with its full diameter offering protection. Against an axe, the angle of deflection was so acute that it effectively narrowed the useful width of the shield to inches.

Kjell gauged the path of the axe perfectly. It tried to bite into his shield but instead was deflected toward the deck, sparking as it notched one of the inlaid brads. Kjell moved to the right and started to wield his own axe, but Bloodaxe was so strong that he was able to stop his own weapon before it was buried in the decking. Bloodaxe parried Kjell's blow with his shield, staggering backward from the force of the impact. As Kjell stepped forward to deliver another strike, Bloodaxe recovered and, holding his shield high to take the blow aimed at his head, swung his own weapon parallel to the deck at Kjell's hip.

Kjell was unprepared for the maneuver. The axe was the perfect weapon for a brute such as Bloodaxe, and he was skilled in its use. Kjell changed the direction of his own axe, knowing its metal head provided the only defense against Bloodaxe's blow. The axes struck each other with a sound like a squat, ugly bell ringing. The note was off key, as if the harmony of the impact had been lost before it could reach their ears. Kjell's hand stung with the vibration, his weapon jarred from his grip by the momentum of Bloodaxe's blow.

Bloodaxe stood to his full height, still several inches shorter than the crouched form of Kjell Falkhand, and he laughed. Kjell knew he could parry blows, but without a weapon of his own, the outcome was already decided.

"Brother, move back to the mast. Use it as your shield." Jan's thoughts came to Kjell's mind, their clarity heightened by the intensity of the fight. At the same time, he heard a clunk of metal into wood and knew that he would find an axe waiting for him in the mast.

Bloodaxe struck again, another horizontal swing, harder to deflect than an overhead blow. Kjell moved back, avoiding contact altogether, then pushed forward, shield against shield, against the bulk of Bloodaxe.

"Ha, Falkhand! You die, and then your brother," shouted Bloodaxe, surprised but unaffected by the shove.

Kjell again moved backward, trying to sense the position of the mast behind him.

"Two steps behind you and one to your right, brother," came the instruction.

Again, Kjell moved backward, the first step cautious. The second was a quick jump, as Kjell tried to keep the cadence of his movements uneven. The mast came into his peripheral vision as he set himself for Bloodaxe's next blow. He could not see the axe that he knew was sticking into the wood of the timber, out of sight of Bloodaxe's approach as well, but he knew it was there.

Bloodaxe rotated the head of his axe first around one ear, then the other, gaining momentum from its weight, trying to confuse Kjell as to exactly which angle his next blow would come from. He walked forward toward his unarmed opponent, knowing that he was in no danger, knowing that Falkhand could not continue to avoid his blows. Much like a cat plays with a lizard, Bloodaxe feinted first in one direction and then the other, a smile that had no mirth in it set in his thick mouth.

Kjell moved to his right, placing the base of the mast between himself and Bloodaxe. Bloodaxe was clearly annoyed by the obstruction that the mast caused. He was tiring of the game and wanted to conserve as much energy as possible for the other brother. He swung a blow along the right side of the mast, aiming at Falkhand's left shoulder.

Kjell had hoped Bloodaxe would put more energy into the blow. As the axe passed beyond the mast, he knew that only then would he have the advantage of surprise. Moving to the right, avoiding Bloodaxe's blow, Kjell grasped the handle of Jan's axe, still stuck in the mast, swinging it in a compact arc around the other side of the mast. The quickness of execution and the tightness of the arc prevented Kjell from putting full power behind the blow. Still, the blade struck Bloodaxe squarely in the neck, just above the shoulder. Kjell knew that even without his full strength behind it, it was a killing blow. He felt the bones of the vertebrae stop the progress of the blade, saw the spurt of blood from the severed carotid artery, but still Bloodaxe did not fall. He stumbled slightly as he swung his own axe upward, then downward toward Kjell, whose shield was trapped by the mast much as Bloodaxe's own weapon had been seconds before. Kjell could not avoid the blow; he could only move enough to minimize the damage. Then, as the axe neared Kjell, the nerves that held its handle in the grasp of Bloodaxe's hand suddenly realized that they had been severed. The axe flew across the deck, striking one of Bloodaxe's warriors at the start of its second rotation. Both men, Bloodaxe and his warrior, fell to the deck, dead.

"The killing is over. Viking should not fight Viking!" Jan Falkhand stepped forward into the middle of Bloodaxe's remaining crew. "This death could not be avoided. It was written on Odin's list two years ago with the insult by Bloodaxe's skald." He looked at the faces of the warriors, one by one, trying to sense if he should expect further violence. He saw only shock and resignation that their leader had been bested with an axe.

"Vikings, lay down your weapons. You will have a ship and provisions to return home. You will also have a share in the booty. You have the word of a Viking, the word of Jan Falkhand."

"*And then, brother,*" Jan added, using the Gift. "We must plan the future."

Chapter Eleven

As Brian came to the end of the recounting of his dream, he shifted in his seat, his eyes refocusing on the group in front of him, noticing the fire had grown low during the telling of his story.

"Oh," said the young boy as he got up and moved to the open hearth, looking at the bed of coals. "Have I been talking that long?"

"It's been over an hour," said Suzanne, noticing the rasp in Brian's voice. "I'll make you some tea and honey."

"What do you make of it?" Mats asked Nando.

The old man watched the boy intently as he arranged new logs on the fire. He turned to Mats.

"Signor Falconi, you once told me you thought your dreams were bedtime stories that your father had told you," said Nando, his eyes narrowing with concentration.

"Yes, the first batch of dreams I had when I arrived in France two years ago—I thought I was just my remembering my father's stories."

"What about before, when you were a child?" asked Nando.

"I don't remember much about my early dreams. Why?"

"I am guessing," said the old man, as Suzanne came back to the front room with four steaming cups. She handed Brian and Nando the sweetened cups and gave Mats one with milk. Placing the serving tray on the dining table, Suzanne sat back down next to Brian. "Our family's oral histories tell me that the Falconi usually do not start dreaming of the past until they approach manhood," said Nando. "I didn't know, until you told me, that you experience the dreams through the eyes of an ancestor."

When Mats had first realized that his dreams had the substance of truth, that they pertained in a very real way to real events, he had kept the knowledge from Nando. But two years of friendship with the Guibega clan had taught him to trust and rely on the old man. Mats had had Brian tell Nando of his dream without reservation.

"But do you see any correlation between our dreams and any of the things that are happening now?" asked Mats.

"Maybe, signore," was the slow reply.

"In Brian's dream, Kjell wasn't even in Ireland," interjected Suzanne.

"I think there is more to the story...more to his dream," said Nando, looking at the boy. "There was something Magee said about the bullets. During the war on Corsica, there was an English medic who used the same woods, ash and oak, to save a soldier. If your dreams tell you of that, it might be what ties these dreams together."

Suzanne looked at the clock on the mantle of the fireplace and said, "That can wait until tomorrow. I'm tired and Brian is also. We could all use some sleep."

The next morning, Mats heard the phone ringing downstairs in the living area. It rang only twice before Brian picked it up. Mats could not make out the exchange, but after a few garbled phrases, he heard footsteps running up the stairs and a quiet knock.

"Mats, are you up? You have a long-distance phone call."

"I'll be right there," said Mats, swinging his feet to the floor.

"Who is it?" Suzanne asked sleepily.

"I don't know." Mats groped his way down the stairs, trying to clear his head.

The voice on the other end said, "Herr Falconi. This is Lieutenant Kurt Schiller. I hope I didn't wake you. I could not get you on your cell, but the manager of the brewery said that you might be at this number."

"No problem, Lieutenant. I should have been up by now anyway. What can I do for you?"

"Just a few questions. I want to make sure that I understood you and your wife correctly. You said that when you talked to Mr. Bjursten from Sweden, and he did not sound like he had been drinking. Is that correct?"

"That's right. Of course, I had never talked to him before, so I don't know what he sounded like normally, but his mother talked to him too. You could ask her if he sounded drunk. I am almost certain he wasn't." Mats shifted the receiver as Brian handed him a cup of hot coffee.

"We have. We also checked at the beer hall where he had dinner after you phoned and he only had one beer and no hard liquor there," said Schiller.

"Is something wrong?"

"You could say so," replied Schiller. "Mr. Falconi, could the work Herr Bjursten did for the Harp and Hawk in any way be connected with his death?"

"I don't know," answered Mats truthfully. "I told you I bought the brewery after Bjursten had finished his work. He had been working on a new process for making a non-alcoholic beer using the traditional Irish top-fermenting method. I never met the man. Something that might connect, though, is that I bought the brewery from an estate.

The owners, a husband and wife, were murdered. The wife was Bjursten's second cousin."

"Three murders in the same family and you didn't think it was important to tell me of the first two?"

"Murder? I thought the fire was an accident," said Mats.

"Herr Falconi, the previous owners—how did they die?"

"They were shot to death with automatic weapons."

Even over the phone Mats could hear the sigh.

"I believe you are being truthful with me, Herr Falconi, so I'll tell you that I now believe Bjursten was murdered. I'll also confess that I'm alone in my division in believing this."

"If I left out one piece of information that proved important, maybe I left out others," Mats said sincerely. "What makes you think it was murder?"

"The first thing that caused me to wonder was the alcohol. He had lots of it in his stomach, but his blood alcohol was only 0.07. That is enough to lose his driver's license but not enough to make a grown man pass out. He would have to have drunk about half a liter in a very short period of time. This from a man who had nursed a single beer while he ate wiener schnitzel. Then came the lab report on the cause of death. He died from smoke inhalation and asphyxiation."

"Isn't that what you would expect with a fire victim?" asked Mats.

"Yes, exactly. But you know what I said about German efficiency. Well, our pathologist is a good example of it. He continued to test to find out what kind of material the smoke came from. Sometimes there are toxic plastics and paints in these apartments, but it turns out the smoke in Bjursten's lungs came from wood."

"I don't follow your meaning, Lieutenant."

"I'm sorry. I forget that you never saw Bjursten's apartment. It was a very modern apartment. There was no wood."

"Lieutenant," said Mats, already knowing the answer, yet still fearing it. "Did the pathologist mention what type of wood it was?"

"He did that study, yes."

"Was it oak and ash?"

"Yes," answered Schiller after a pause. "How did you know?"

"It has to do with the murder of the Keohanes."

"Herr Falconi, I would like you to return to Frankfurt. I could file papers, but I think you would like these murders solved as much as I would."

"You don't have to serve me. I have plans today. Will tomorrow be all right?"

"That will be fine. Give my office a call saying what flight you are on, and I will have you picked up at the airport. Now that my suspicions are founded, I can start a thorough investigation. Who handled the murder investigation in Ireland?"

"It's still going on," said Mats. "They haven't found the men responsible. Lieutenant Schiller, please don't contact the Irish police until after we talk. When I see you in person, you will understand. It is ... something like the use of a sword."

"Ja, if Medau trusted you on that one, so will I. See you tomorrow."

"Yes, sir," said Mats and hung up the phone.

The coffee had cooled. Mats did not notice until after he'd swallowed a gulp while still looking at the receiver.

"Is something the matter?" asked Suzanne as she came down the stairs. Nando joined them from the bedroom he shared with Brian on the ground floor.

"It seems it wasn't an accident that took Bjursten's life. He had drunk a lot of alcohol before the fire, but it hadn't even had time to make it into his bloodstream. They found that he died, as they suspected, of smoke inhalation. But when they analyzed the smoke, they found that it was wood smoke, and Bjursten's apartment contained no wood. They must have a crackerjack forensic lab, because they could even tell the type of wood smoke that killed him."

"Oak and ash?" asked Suzanne.

"Signor Falconi," said the old man. "It was a German who killed my niece was saved by the English medic, Grady. He used the skin of a tree to cover his burns. It was a cure that I had never heard of before, nor have I heard of it being used since."

"What is going on?" asked Mats, addressing all of them and no one in particular. "Last night I was sure it was Brian they were after. Now a biochemist is killed after working on a new brewing process, and he's killed by the same bizarre combination of wood that killed Brian's parents and his grandfather."

"But if it is connected with the Harp and Hawk, why should Brian be in danger?" asked Suzanne. "He doesn't own it anymore."

"I would still keep a very close watch on this boy," said Nando, reaching over and squeezing the boy's shoulder.

Early the next morning, Liam Magee picked up Mats, Suzanne, and Brian and drove them west on R263, a road named the Wild Atlantic Way. The designation rather than the name amused Mats; that the narrow two-lane road would have a number seemed ludicrous.

"Why do they call this Fairies Point?" Mats asked Liam, who was driving with Mats in the left passenger seat. Nando and Suzanne were squished in the back seat with Brian.

"I don't know for sure, but it's always been called that," answered Liam. "The small mountain over there is supposed to be the home of nine dwarfs. They are from a famous Irish folk tale. The whole of the area is filled with legends of fairies, little people, and banshees."

"Have you ever seen any of these strange creatures?" asked Suzanne from the back seat.

"Not personally, Mrs. Falconi, but I wouldn't be betting against their being here. This is a strange piece of land. Things disappear here, and so do people. Vanish without a trace." Liam pointed to the west. "That over there, that's what you asked about—Ian Grady's farm."

Mats looked in the direction in which Liam had pointed and saw a small white-washed farmhouse with a circular addition to its far end. Behind it was an area that must have been nearly a hundred acres, enclosed by a stone wall before giving way to a hedge some eight feet high. Sheep and goats grazed inside the stone enclosure.

"What does he farm?" asked Nando.

"Used to grow barley. The Harp and Hawk even bought from the previous owner, but Ian only cut it for two years after he bought the place. After that he just let it go to seed."

The car crested a small rise and started down a gradual incline toward the water to the north of the point some two miles away.

"What's that group of buildings ahead?" asked Mats.

"That's Gleann Cholm Cille," answered Brian, using the old Gaelic. "It's an ancient place with roots going back far before Christ. There is a museum there. Not much inside but lots of old stuff around. Da said they guessed wrong on a lot of the history."

Looking back, Mats saw Brian shiver.

"Would you mind showing it to us?"

Brian gripped his arms across his chest. "If you want."

It was, as Brian said, more of an outdoor museum than an indoor one. There were three ancient dolmen, two stones set into the earth with a third set across them like a miniature Stonehenge. An old Irish woman walked with them, giving a history of the structures and of the area itself. She led them through a path which meandered through the woods to the third dolmen, shorter than the other two, almost a bench. They could hear waves breaking in the narrow inlet and smell the salt in the air. Every now and then Mats would catch Brian shaking his head, but not once did he correct their guide. When they finally moved back to the car, he looked relieved.

"You didn't have much to say in there, Brian," said Suzanne as the last door closed. "Are you all right?"

"Sure I am," answered Brian in a soft voice. "It's just that I feel strange in that place. Dad once told me it would be unusual if I didn't."

They took the same road back across Fairies Point, driving slowly past the Grady farm, the choice made easy as it was the only way back from Gleann Cholm Cille.

"Over there." Liam pointed at a group of low jagged mountains as he drove. "The mountains are said to be the home of the nine dwarfs. They come out long past sunset, in the dead of night. They play music as sweet as the world has ever heard. Humans who hear their harps and see their procession are able to solve the great mysteries of life."

It was just past two in the afternoon when Liam parked the car in front of the Harp and Hawk. Cathal Magee came out of the building.

"I hope you don't expect a full day's wages after going off for the better part of the day?" said Cathal to Liam, a twinkle in his eye. "It's enough that your brothers and I had to work through lunch doing double duty while you were sliding."

"I thought you worked through lunch every day, Cathal? Or is it that you take two lunch hours?" asked Mats, grinning.

"Two lunches, two lunches it is. Maybe I shouldn't be telling you of the package that arrived from Sweden," whined Magee, in mock indignation.

"I have to be getting inside now, Mr. Falconi," said Liam. "If it's true that Cathal's been doing my work, there will be a terrible mess to clean up. The empty bottles and all." Liam turned from the car, passing Cathal, whom he hit lightly on the shoulder as he went inside.

"I don't know how you can expect me to run this place at a profit with you rousting my workers like this," said Magee.

"Why, I expect you to work through lunch," answered Mats.

Magee was forced to smile, caught in his own trap and out-blarneyed by a man who wasn't even Irish. "Oh, the shame of it all," he moaned, half meaning it.

"What package?" asked Mats, ignoring Magee's pique and the giggling coming from Brian and Suzanne. With all that had happened before, he worried that it might be a bomb.

"It's up in your office. It's from Mrs. Bjursten. Just some papers and a flash drive."

"You opened it?" asked Mats.

"I did. Before I realized it was addressed to you, of course," said Cathal with a wave of his arm. "I happened to slip the drive into the computer, egh, before I read the address."

Once at his desk, Mats read the short note from Lars' mother. Lars had instructed her to send Mats the files on the brewery. The small drive labeled "Harp and Hawk" had been an obvious choice, but she explained that she had also sent all the paperwork labeled Harp and Hawk, Brewery, and Fermentation as well.

Mats turned on the computer. The file opened without hesitation, having already been downloaded by Magee. Small whirring noises came from deep in the machine before the list screen was replaced by another. Mats looked, looked again, and scrolled down. On page after page, the screen was filled with gibberish.

"What the heck is going on here?" Mats muttered. He couldn't even open most of the files. After ten minutes, his frustration showed. He was aware of Magee, Suzanne, and Brian crowding into the room, wondering what was going on.

"Can I try?" asked Brian, nudging Mats away from the screen without taking his eyes off it.

"Are you sure?" asked Mats, a little anxious. "We don't want to lose anything on that flash drive."

"I know what I'm doing. Who do you think set up this system for Dad?"

Mats looked at Magee and got an affirmative nod.

"Now let's see," said Brian as he opened the files through the application of a program labeled INC.

"Look at that," said Mats, impressed with Brian's computer skills as well as with his ability to figure out the problem.

The screen filled with formulas and explanations of procedures. Brian scrolled down the document to its end. It was ten pages long. The last page was an explanation of cross checks and a brief personal note from Lars Bjursten, dated the day of his death. It spelled out why the process could not be challenged even though similar, less complete processes might be patented by other individuals or breweries.

"It sounds like Bjursten felt that the process might be challenged," said Mats, reading the last page. "Is that all there is in the file?"

"Yes, at least in that file. There's another folder on the drive that Cathal didn't download," replied Brian, making a printed copy of the first file.

As soon as the printer had finished, Brian clicked on the second folder. This time there were a number of files displayed. Brian selected one and opened it. It was filled with the same types of formulas and procedures as the Falconi disk, but there were more of them. Page after page of what looked to be sequential processes, each differing from the one preceding it by minor variations in the formulation, scrolled by under Brian's manipulation.

"Those are almost identical to the process that Bjursten worked out with Mr. Keohane," said Magee, looking over the boy's shoulder.

"Different enough to allow for a different patent, I'm sure," said Mats. "It looks as if he worked out all the possible variations. This is probably what he was warning us about in the note at the end of the previous file. It looks like he applied for patents for all of them."

Brian clicked off the file, translating and opening another. It was filled with research notes and references to articles on yeast fermentation. Bjursten was nothing if not thorough. The last folder was titled in Swedish.

"BREV. It means 'correspondence,'" said Suzanne, happy to be able to add to the conversation.

Brian clicked and watched the screen fill with a series of letters written in a language Mats could not read.

"Maybe we shouldn't be reading all of this," said Suzanne, resting her hand lightly on Brian's that held the mouse. "Lars Bjursten obviously wanted us to have the information in the first disk, but this looks like personal correspondence."

"Lars Bjursten is dead," said Mats. "He was probably murdered. There may be something in here that will help Schiller find his killer."

Suzanne removed her hand from Brian's. "It's in German," she said, taking over the mouse, scrolling through letter after letter.

After she had scanned all six of the letters, Suzanne returned to the one with the earliest date. "They're all written to the same man, the president of the Municher Brewery. They have to do with the development of a non-alcoholic brewing process. The first one responds to a letter from the Municher Brewery that was sent to Bjursten concerning his research. The second talks vaguely of the possibility of a parallel process not covered by previous patents. It is obvious that Bjursten is not the instigator of these questions. The third is a response to a contract that has been sent to him requiring the Municher Brewery to increase the payment at completion and adding some safeguards. The amounts are impressive, even at the present euro-to-Swedish-Krone exchange rate...about $300,000."

Suzanne looked at Mats before returning her eyes to the screen. "I guess the contract was signed, because the next two notes are progress reports. The last says that a flash drive and hard copy have all of the information, formulas, and procedures called for under the terms of the contract, and they are ready for pick-up. It's dated the day of his death."

"That does it. Make a copy for Schiller. We'll take it with us. Send the process patent formulas and information to John Powers and have him check that the patents are in place."

"You'll be wanting to hide the originals," said Magee. "I wouldn't trust the farmhouse as far as being secure if you are leaving the country."

"Got any ideas about that, Cathal?" asked Mats, knowing the answer from the smile that crinkled the old man's eyes.

"Sure, and what would an Irish house be without a loose hearthstone? How many people do you want to know of the hiding place?" Magee asked, looking directly at Mats, avoiding all the others' eyes.

Mats looked around at the group: Brian, Suzanne, Nando, and Magee. He trusted all of them. "Does Tobin know of it already?"

"No. Just me and the Keohanes," said Magee, looking at the young boy.

Brian got up and moved to the corner of the office, where a large pipe came up from the brewing vats below. Three feet from the floor there was a large gate valve at the spot before the pipe turned and entered the wall. Brian bent over the valve, turning the nuts until notches on the hex sides were all pointing up. Then he pulled on the valve handle. It slid evenly off the housing, revealing a cylindrical compartment with a tray that fit snugly inside.

"It's a dummy line, blocked off at the tank below," explained Magee. "Brian's father thought it was necessary to have a hiding place that would be fireproof as well. It's where we put the extra cash from some of the beer that failed to get inventoried."

Brian took the flash drive and placed it into the repository. Then he returned to the computer and put the hard copy into a folder, which he handed to Suzanne.

"Is there any way we can hide what we just put on the computer?" Mats asked.

"I can delete it all, as long as we still have the flash drive," said Brian. "Or I can encrypt it. Dad had me install a program that hides stuff he didn't want seen. You just need the password to convert it back to English."

"Do it, please. Give me the password later. Has that lawyer, John Powers, been able clear Brian for travel?" asked Mats.

"He has," answered Magee. "Tobin told me he didn't need a passport going to France, but as a minor he might need permission from Grady's bunch to leave the area."

"I'll phone Powers, and if he thinks it's needed, I'll talk to Grady myself," said Mats. "Suzanne, who was Bjursten writing to at the Municher Brewery?"

Suzanne opened the manila folder and thumbed through all six letters. "They are all written to the president of the brewery," she said. "Herr Dieter Rohde."

"Rohde? Rohde?" Nando stood up, his fists clenched at his sides. His expression showed barely suppressed anger.

"You know a Dieter Rohde?" Mats asked incredulously.

"Si, signore. I know a man named Rohde," said Nando with a voice Mats had never heard from him before. The name was hissed from between clenched teeth. "I told you that my Teresa was murdered by a German. His name was Rohde. Dieter Rohde. I pray that it is the same man."

CHAPTER TWELVE

When the flash drive and a hard copy had been sealed in the pipe safe, Mats sat down at the desk and began reviewing the work logs and the installation methods necessary for the first run of top-fermented non-alcoholic Harp and Hawk. The workers put the same zeal into the dry run that they had devoted to getting the brewery back into production. The long layoff, as well as the homogeneous Magee workforce, lent an air of urgency and pleasurable excitement to the running of the plant. Mats checked the overtime log again and found that the only entry was the one he had forced Cathal to place. Cathal just shrugged when asked about the extra hours for no extra pay, so Mats made a mental note to put a bonus check in with the first month that the brewery showed a profit.

"I'll need few hours to finish this," Mats told Suzanne and Brian. "Why don't you see if you can help Cathal in the brewery?"

"Let's show Nando some of Donegal instead," suggested Suzanne.

"I don't think it's safe to wander the streets, even with Liam," said Mats, looking up from his paperwork.

"I could take them sailing," piped in Brian. "My skiff is still at the dock. No one's going to mess with us on the water. We can be back in two hours, and we'll have cell coverage in the bay."

Mats saw at the enthusiasm on the boy's face and got the nod from Suzanne, standing behind him. "All right, but be back by five, and take Liam with you to the dock."

"The fishing should be good," said Brian, looking first at Nando and then at Suzanne and beaming as they arrived at the dock. They all looked down at Brian's small skiff.

"Can we be back in two hours?" asked Suzanne, not wanting to cast a damper on the boy's obvious wish to impress Nando.

"Sure. I know a place good for haddock just outside the bay," said Brian, climbing down the ladder to the floating platform and the skiff with Suzanne following just behind. They both helped Nando the last few rungs until he was safe in the boat. When they were a hundred meters from the dock, Liam turned and walked back toward the Harp and Hawk.

The weather was fair, a light mist falling on the coast, the winds light and offshore. Nando's actions answered any questions that Brian might have about his worth as a sailor. While Suzanne watched from the same thwart she had used sailing from the farmhouse two days previously, the old man rigged the sail and released the bow line. With Brian at the helm, they sailed away from the Donegal dock, heading west.

Suzanne checked her watch as Brian brought the craft to the lee of a small low-lying island less than a kilometer from shore. It had only been half an hour since they had left Donegal. She moved as Brian set the anchor and started rigging a line with a heavy bottom-feeding weight. She watched as he threw the baited hooks over the side, handing out line until the sinker hit bottom. Wrapping the line loosely once around his hand, he lay down against the side of the boat.

"You'll be in for some fun if we catch a haddock," said the boy, placing his folded sweater under his head. "That little inlet is called Malin Bay. It's not far away from where we drove this morning."

He motioned with his free hand to a rocky cleft in the cliffs behind him. "Doesn't look like much, but it was a major landing place for smugglers in the old days. Not many of them got caught using that landing."

"Smugglers?" asked Nando, his interest perking up.

"Ever since the British took our island, there have been smugglers. Maybe even before the British."

"Why was this landing so safe?" asked Suzanne.

"Two reasons. One, nobody would be crazy enough to try to land there, and second, no one wants to be on Fairies Point at night." Brian yawned. "The sea raiders, you call them Vikings, sent their advance scouts inland from this point. The first Viking settlement, or at least the first round tower in Ireland, is on Tory Island, less than eighty kilometers to the north."

"What's a round tower, Brian?" asked Suzanne. "I've seen them marked on maps, but I've never seen one in person."

The boy closed his eyes before speaking. "The first Vikings came to Ireland as traders. Da said that they even lived at peace with the Irish. It was only later, with the arrival of the Danes, that they plundered. The rape and pillage they could do at any village, but for plunder they went after the churches. After a few years of raids, some smart priest figured out that the raiders never had enough men to sustain an attack. They would strike and then fall back to their ships. The problem was that it would take hours, even days, to muster enough men to fight back. By then the raiders had sacked the church and were gone.

"Round towers were the answer to the problem. Most of the churches were built inland, so the priests had some warning of an attack. They built round stone towers only nine or ten meters in diameter at the base but some forty meters high. The priests would retreat into them with their gold crosses, goblets, and books until the Vikings left."

"Why didn't the Vikings just break down the door?" asked Suzanne, intrigued by Brian's description.

"The towers had only one door and it was over eight meters above the ground, with no landing. The priests got to the door by the use of a ladder, which they then pulled up inside after them. The top of the tower had openings where they could throw rocks down on anyone trying to gain the entrance. Even if a Viking could get to the door without being hit by a stone, he couldn't force the door because there was no way to get leverage from the top of a ladder. It must have worked because there are few accounts of round towers being breached."

Brian yawned and slid further down on his seat, the rocking of the boat adding to his comfort. "The first Vikings didn't come to raid. They came to trade." Brian's breathing was becoming slower, his voice deeper and more resonant, his eyes closed.

Suzanne sat bolt upright. Brian was speaking in the same tone and cadence that he had used in telling of his dream the previous night. She turned and looked at him. His eyes were closed, one arm across the tiller, the other holding the fishing line. She closed her own eyes as Brian continued speaking...

North Sea, 944 AD

It took less than an hour for the brothers to decide their fates. The treasure from Bloodaxe's two boats was divided, Jan taking half, while Kjell transferred the other half into Bloodaxe's great boat, along with the majority of the food, weapons, and supplies.

Kjell and Jan discussed all the options open to them. Jan had no constrictions. He could return to the land of the Franks and Goths. Redhand would not fault him for coming to the aid of his brother. Also, it was under Kjell's axe that Bloodaxe had fallen, not Jan's.

Kjell had fewer options. If he went with Jan, Redhand would surely seek him out. He had disobeyed his chief when he killed Bloodaxe. It would not matter that he had been attacked. At home he would be safe from attack, but that safety would disappear if he ventured forth a-Viking next season. A good number of his men still wanted to go home. Kjell was certain that they would be immune to Redhand's fury as long as they did not have him as their leader. Others voted to stay with him.

It was decided that Jan would tow the smallest of Bloodaxe's vessels back to the land of the Franks as his own. Kjell would give his ship, with most of the treasure it contained, to those of his men who had voted to go home. He would take Bloodaxe's great ship for his own, as its previous master would have no further use for it. His returning crew had already voted Karl, Nels' son a young giant of a man, as their captain. The third, smaller vessel, devoid of oars, sails, weapons, or treasure, was loaded with Bloodaxe's crew, along with those men left from the taking of his two treasure-laden vessels. They were held captive under the watchful eye of several bowmen.

Kjell needed more men than he had left to properly sail Bloodaxe's great ship. He knew that the captives left alive from Bloodaxe's ships expected to become slaves, chained to the oars, or worse, killed and thrown into the sea, never to reach Valhalla. He moved to the side of the great ship, looking down at those in the vessel below him.

"Who among you will sail with me?" Kjell shouted to Bloodaxe's men.

Over half the captives, some Norsemen, some Danes, answered affirmatively by beating the outside of the hull with their fists.

"Help me, brother. Pick the men you saw fight bravely. A brave man is often an honest one."

Eight men were chosen. Three others petitioned Kjell to let them come with him. He accepted two of them, rejecting the pleas of a shifty-eyed individual who was shunned even by Bloodaxe's own men.

"You will not be enslaved but will remain free and will receive a free man's share on this ship," said Kjell, as the men took their places at the oars.

Kjell looked down again on the men in the still over-crowded vessel. "This will buy you weapons and provide for you through the winter," he said as he tossed a small sack of silver and gold into the center of the boat. "My quarrel was with your leader, not with his men. You are free to go, but do not speak badly of me or my brother, nor of your shipmates who have chosen to join us."

On Kjell's order, Jan's crew returned the sail and oars to the captives.

Kjell gripped his brother's shoulder as he spoke to the captives. "We will go to our homesteads, and to the arms of our women. I give you leave to do the same."

As if disbelieving that they were really free to go, the boat full of captives hesitated. Then one of them jumped to the stern platform. "Pull! Pull!" he shouted.

The boat slowly made way under the power of the few oars, away from the threat of Falkhand's bowmen. Backward glances were few as the men in the retreating ship came to trust Kjell's words. Bloodaxe's men would know the Falkhands had treated them fairly. There would be no further recitals of the skald's saga.

Several hundred meters from the other ships, the captives raised their square sail and turned toward the Continent, already deciding that the longer trip held fewer perils than returning to confront Redhand.

When the boat was almost out of sight, Jan turned to Kjell. *"Are you sure you don't want to return with me?"*

"No, my brother, and I won't be returning home either," Gifted Kjell, slapping Jan on his back. *"My course is to the north. I have told Karl Nels' son that I will not be following him, but he will not tell his crew. Only you know that I will winter on the islands to the north."*

Jan slapped his open palm against Kjell's, then leapt to his own longboat. He placed four men in the boat to be towed and started his own crew rowing toward the east, where the vague outline of the coast lay barely visible on the horizon. As soon as the captive boat was gone, Karl, Olaf's son, gave the order to pull away. Some of his men bent their backs to their oars, while others re-stepped the mast. Kjell heard the glad shouts of weary men returning home.

Kjell's heart was heavy with a great loneliness as he watched his brother sail away. He felt alone and on the verge of a winter that might take his life and the lives of his men. There were islands to the north of the great island. He took comfort in reflecting that sufficient grain and smoked fish were stored with the treasure to last his crew through the foulest of winters. Safe harbor would be all they needed, preferably near men and women of their own kind.

Kjell's men looked at him uneasily, as if feeling his uncertainty. Kjell turned, facing their stares. Vikings were proud; none turned their eyes from the leader's as he looked at each of them in turn. They were his men, brave men. Even the new ones had already accepted him as their leader.

"If Redhand pursues me, he will think that I have taken the route across the channel here, where it is narrowest. He will not expect us to follow the coast north." Kjell grasped the steering oar of the great ship, testing the repair.

Viking war screams answered him as he looked back over his crew. "Arn Gustafson, you will be my second in command."

"Falkhand!" shouted Arn Gustafson, who stood and took his place at the bow. Arn, a man who had been with Kjell since he first went a-Viking, stood tall.

For seven days, they gained sixty miles a day against the current. The weather grew colder as they proceeded north, but when the channel widened and they entered the North Sea, the current became milder.

On the fifth day, the wind changed, shifting gradually to come from the south. It provided welcome assistance to the men at their oars, allowing the square sail to be hoisted on the mast. Kjell chafed when he first saw the dragon's head of Bloodaxe embossed on the sail stretched tight above the crew. He said nothing but noticed that Arn Gustafson also looked with contempt upon the image when there should have been only joy at the sight of a sail filled with wind.

The next night, Arn asked for the mid-watch, and in the morning, when the sail was raised, there was no dragon's head to give insult. Kjell looked up at three battle axes with three hawks sitting on their blades, cut from the cloth that once been the shape a dragon's head. Arn said nothing, but Kjell showed his satisfaction by the smile he wore.

Arn seemed to grow in stature. It was now he who occasionally took the steering oar, allowing Kjell to pass among the men, acquainting himself with the new members, looking for signs of strength or weakness. Jan had chosen the men well. Not one complaint had been heard. Instead, the newcomers had relaxed, after the first few days of attempting to outperform Kjell's men. Now they rowed in perfect harmony with the rest of the crew.

The tenth night was their first spent on the open sea. Soon after dark, the wind changed in intensity as well as direction. It blew harsh and cold from the northeast, raising waves as tall as the mast. No Viking slept that night. Morning showed them what they had felt in the darkness. Waves, capped with white, bore down on the ship, lifting it to their crests before letting it slide into troughs that hid the horizon. Kjell kept the bow pointed into the waves, which increased in size and frequency as the day grew longer.

Just before dark, at the height of the storm, a massive wave lifted the boat, turning it broadside before dropping it into the hollow that followed it. The next wave crashed against the side of the boat, washing over the gunwale, against Kjell, who was pulling hard on the steering oar. There was a crack, heard even above the howl of the wind, and Kjell was thrown back against the wall of water; the steering oar he held in his arms no longer extended past the stern rail. He shouted at his men, trying vainly to use the stroke of their oars to turn the ship again into the wind and waves. The awesome power of the waves kept the ship sideways in the trough, each wave threatening to swamp the vessel with gray water. Kjell had no choice but to try to run before the storm. Waves came up and under them, shooting them down their forward slopes before passing underneath.

All night the storm raged unabated. Not once did the skies clear long enough for Kjell to sight the stars. He knew he was far to the west of the island he had sought, and he could tell only by the glow visible beyond the darkness of the clouds that they were headed southwest. Occasionally they heard the sound of waves crashing against an unseen shore. Kjell called the man nearest him to help him set one of the oars as a replacement for the steering oar. A wave hit the stern as the man was lashing the oar in place against the rail. He was lifted high and washed overboard. Kjell reached for him but it was too late. No scream was heard, only the roar of the wind and the crash of the waves. The man had disappeared in the waves and the dark. Kjell hesitated only a moment before another wave hit. He turned to finish fastening the spare blade in place.

"I hope that it holds. If it doesn't, we will all end as that man did," thought Kjell. *"Please Njord, God of the wind and the waves, keep my ship and its men safe."*

The oar held, and Kjell was able to keep running before the storm. He had only caught snatches of sleep in the last days, trusting Arn at the helm while napping fitfully under the steering platform.

The current now added its force to the wind and the waves, pushing their craft to the south. Kjell wondered if the storm would blow them off the end of the earth, so relentless was its power and purpose. His men, fatigued by the effort of rowing and grieved by the loss of their man, lashed themselves to their seats lest they be washed overboard while they slumbered. Then, as if Njord had heard Kjell's unspoken prayer, the wind slackened and the waves changed in their rhythm, just as large but without the white stallions at their crest. Kjell thanked Njord under his breath and then, as he understood the reasons for the change, looked in panic to all sides. There, just off the port bow, was land—obscured by clouds that were the same grey-black color as the cliffs. The ship was being pressed toward them, which would surely mean the deaths of all who rode in her.

Kjell had little chance of turning the boat into the lessening wind. His men were too worn, too tired to sustain the effort. Then, barely above the caps of the waves, off the starboard bow rose an island. Low and broad, it came into view as a green line against the horizon. The ship was being driven between it and the cliffs. The change in the waves was from the bottom, rising to meet land.

As the island passed to starboard, Kjell saw several breaks in its southern coast. Instantly he made up his mind. Shouting encouragement to his crew, he gave his orders.

"Hold water!" He pointed at the men to his right. When they stilled their oars, he pointed to his left. "Pull hard!"

With held breath, Kjell sculled his own small steering oar with as much strength as he thought it could take without breaking. The ship, with its deep draft, turned reluctantly. The rocking of the ship, wallowing in the trough, left the oars either out of the water or so deep under the surface that the men lacked the strength to move them.

Pointing again to his left, Kjell shouted, "Back water! Time your pull to the crest of the wave!" Slowly the ship resumed its turn, as it were swiveling on some unknown axis directly beneath its keel.

"All ahead, pull! Pull with all your might!"

Kjell did not waste time looking at his men. He knew he would see the strain of last effort. Instead he looked at the small island drawing nearer as an indication of their exertion.

Using the steering oar gingerly, he headed the dragon ship toward a slash of white sand still half a mile away. He would not have the luxury of sounding the bottom as they approached the unknown shore. All of his men were busy at the oars, and he did not have the maneuverability to avoid any underwater rock, should there be one.

"Pull! Pull!" he urged, pressing the men for one last great effort as they neared the shore.

The first contact with land came to the crew as a hiss of keel on sand. The sudden stop threw rowers forward onto the laps of the men on the benches in front of them. As they were picking themselves up, Arn Gustafson had already leapt ashore with a line, tying it around a large boulder while the ship fishtailed in the waves.

⚜ ⚜ ⚜

Donegal Bay, Ireland, August 2003

Suzanne watched Brian as his story became more intense. She reached over and held Nando's hand. She could see tension in the way the old man was looking at the boy as well.

Brian's eyes were still closed, the knuckles of his left-hand white with his grip around the tiller of the small fishing boat, and his breathing was rapid. Suzanne suspected by the way the boy had recounted the dream that he was being supplied with information his father would have given him if he had lived. Mats' father had used bedtime stories to hide the reality of the information while still giving it to his son. Suzanne guessed that Brian's father would have been more direct. She was worried about Brian. It was unnatural how his body was moving out of sync with the rocking motion of the boat. She decided to wake him if he became more disturbed.

Brian jerked with each of his words, as if motion would supply extra meaning to the telling of the story. Then his eyes opened wide and his hand once again relaxed on the rail, awaiting a tug on the line. His voice was calm.

"Are you all right?" Suzanne asked, moving over athwart to his side at the stern.

"Yes, but I think I should tell you the rest. It was different."

"We have over an hour before Mats expects us, if you feel you can," said Suzanne, placing her hand over his that held the tiller.

Brian took a big breath, gave the line in his right hand a slow tug, and continued.

"The Vikings were exhausted. Some of the crew did not have the strength to leave the boat. They lay huddled against the central cargo. They only stayed warm because of those pressed against them. Kjell stayed awake, partly out of his sense of duty to his crew, partly because the fear of failure still gripped him.

"You can see the island is not large," Brian added, removing his hand from the tiller and pointing at the island to his left. "There was a stand of trees on the far end. They're gone now. This dream was different. It flashed from one thing to another. First Kjell was worried about the ship. It had started to leak. The rudder would have to be completely reconstructed. The trees that grew there in those days would provide with him the materials. Then, all of a sudden, it was morning, and they were standing outside a small round dwelling like the one we saw this morning at Gleann Cholm Cille, except smaller. It was made of small interwoven branches, like a basket turned upside down. A covering of sod protected the interior from wind and rain. A single opening, half the height of a man, served as the entrance.

"Arn told Kjell that there were sheep on the island as well, and fresh water. Kjell seemed half awake, struggling with the information Arn was giving him."

Brian again turned to the island. "They still keep sheep there. I think they belong to the Woolen Mill in town, but I can't see any from here.

"Suddenly they were surrounded by sheep. They were small, with short, fat tails, and they had not been sheared in months. Long ringlets of wool draped from their backs, almost to the ground. Kjell knew they would feast well their first evening on the island.

"I think I'm getting some interest," said Brian, changing the topic, lifting slightly on the line, raising and lowering it an inch at a time.

"You have our interest as well," said Suzanne. "Is there more to your dream?"

"Yes, a bit," said Brian, his eyes still riveted to the line as it passed into the water. "But it bounces back and forth.

"Now Kjell was not at the hut anymore but standing in the meadow. The sheep parted in front of him, and some of his crew were pulling two small men toward him. Kjell could see from their clothing and from the way they huddled in fear that they were not warriors. They were dressed in sheep skins. He was relieved they had not escaped and had not been harmed..."

"We found them hiding in a small cave just up the coast," said one of Kjell's men. "They speak a strange tongue, but they understand us well enough."

"Who doesn't understand the edge of a blade?" laughed a second.

"They have a boat. Nothing you would want to set foot in. It's a round craft made of bent twigs and covered with hides. It would never survive in these seas."

"Bring food and ale from the boat," ordered Kjell. He sat down on the ground, offering a place beside him to the two captives with a sweep of his hand.

As the two shepherds sat, Kjell began. "Kjell," he said, pointing to his own chest. "Kjell."

'Suddenly time shifted forward again. The ship was repaired. Kjell could speak at least a few dozen words of the new language, although his pronunciation was bad. It turned out that the sheep belonged to the holy men on the mainland. Once a month, a priest was sent to take care of their religious needs. The shepherds told him with words and gestures that the priest brought supplies, and they slaughtered five of the animals for him to take back with him.

"We will not see that priest," laughed Arn when Kjell told him what the shepherds had said. "Priests run when they see a Norseman."

"True, and that is why he must not see us," explained Kjell. He wanted to winter on the island, and he knew he wouldn't be able to do it without the blessing of the priest. The ship had been moved to a cove on the other side of the island. Kjell told his men to let the priest land, and he would talk to him before he returned to Erin, for that is what the two shepherds, Con and Fergus, called the mainland.

"The vision jumped again," said Brian. "There was a great hawk screeching, landing in a tree, his talons spread, as were his wings. It was almost as the dream wanted to finish before I woke up."

The full moon was still in the sky when a priest arrived in a larger version of the round skin boat that the shepherds used for fishing. He had four men with him. All were small in stature and appeared more suited to the slaughtering of sheep than to fighting. One drew a short knife in an attempt to protect the priest, but he was easily overpowered.

Kjell sat down in front of the priest. When he had finally convinced him that he meant no harm, he said, "Your island saved our lives. We have repairs to make on our ship before it will take us home. We will pay for the use of your island and the sheep we eat."

The priest was cringing, held by Arn, obviously in fear of being murdered, feeling forced to listen. But his confidence grew as Kjell explained, in halting speech and gestures, that his men wanted peace, and just to use the island. Kjell offered a fine goblet of silver as payment for the animals they had slaughtered and the trees they had felled. Arn let go of the priest as he was handed the goblet. Kjell suspected that the priest could see their numbers were small enough to be defeated if they landed on Erin, yet it would be difficult to dislodge them from the island. Kjell watched as the priest looked around their camp. Their staying would cost the Church nothing but a few sheep and trees. Kjell sensed the man becoming calmer and offered the promise of another fine goblet in a month's time.

The priest denied Kjell's request to trade but accepted the goblet for the use of the island. Repeating himself three times before Kjell understood him, the priest said he needed time to counsel with his superiors. But Kjell believed that to be false.

Then, before the priest could continue, Kjell said in halting words, spoken like a child, "Tell me about your God."

Brian smiled at Suzanne, shifting his back against the side of the small boat. "Now you know all of it," he said, stretching his hands above his head. "I guess being in the same waters made me remember."

Brian looked at his right hand. It moved in response to the line wound around it down an inch, then back up, then down once more. His attention was now riveted on the water as he stood to his full height, retaining tension on the line.

"There's an old fairy tale about a princess named Liban who was turned into a mermaid and forced to live forever in the waters off Fairies Point. It's said that she leads fish to the lines of good men, for it is a good man who will one day break the spell that binds her."

Brian suddenly tugged hard, a short, quick pull, bringing his hand to shoulder height. "Hang on!" he shouted. "I think Liban has brought the grandfather of all haddock to my barb!"

Suzanne and Nando did hang on, and later, when they were feasting on the fish Brian had brought to the surface, they recounted both the dream and the excitement of the catch to Mats.

CHAPTER THIRTEEN

The next morning Tobin drove Mats, Suzanne, Brian, and Nando to Ireland West Airport, where Suzanne had booked a direct flight to Frankfurt.

"I've sent for one of my nephews to meet us in Germany," said Nando, just before they boarded the plane.

"You did? Why?" Mats asked.

"We might need him if the brewery owner is the same Rohde."

"Which nephew? And why might we need him?"

"His name is Ramondo, Ramondo Guibega. You met him at Carlo's funeral. He has been working for the French government, but no longer. He will be like Liam in Ireland, offering additional protection for you and the boy."

Mats had seen Nando's reaction to the mention of Dieter Rohde, the president of the Municher Brewery, and suspected this was the reason. He also knew it would be useless to push him now. "Okay. Suzanne, would you book another room at the Richland Hotel in Frankfurt?"

"Thank you, signore," said Nando with sincerity.

Mats led the small entourage off the plane at Rhein-Main Airport in Frankfurt at eleven. Lieutenant Schiller was waiting at the entrance to the terminal, somewhat surprised to find a young boy and an old man accompanying Mats and Suzanne.

The policeman took charge, taking them through arrival with a nod to the officer. "If you give me your baggage checks, I'll have one of my men bring your things to the station," said Schiller.

"No need, Lieutenant. We have only carry-on luggage. But I would like to see Brian to the hotel before going to the station. Brian is the son of the Keohanes, the previous owners of the brewery I purchased," added Mats introducing the boy. "And this is Nando. He is an old friend. He will look after Brian while we're with you."

Schiller shook the hand of Nando, who was looking slightly confused and every year his age. Schiller felt the weakness in the old man's grip and the tremor in his fingers. "Ah yes, Nando Guibega. Inspector Medau told me about you." Schiller smiled, squeezing his fingers more tightly around the old man's hand. "He said you were more than you seemed, and a man to be trusted."

Nando looked at Schiller and then at Mats, his act of feebleness falling away as he returned the strength of the lieutenant's shake. "I thank the inspector for his kind remarks," he said, moving to Brian's side.

They left the car at the entryway of the hotel and walked as a group into the lobby. Nando tugged on Mats' arm and gave a small nod of his head toward the far end of the lobby, where a young man in an expensive suit stood: Ramondo. Mats remembered him from Corsica, but he was so changed in appearance that he would not have recognized him without Nando's prompt.

Mats continued toward the front desk, arriving just before Schiller. The clerk found the reservation and handed over three key cards to Mats, who kept one and gave the other two in sequence to Nando.

"All three rooms interconnect through the central one," said the clerk, smiling at Mats as he handed him the keys. "Front!" he shouted at a bellboy already standing next to Mats. "Room 920," he added in an officious tone as the bellboy picked up Mats and Suzanne's bags.

"Put Brian in the center room," Mats said to Nando.

"I will have you back by six PM," said Schiller.

"Let's go then." Mats nodded at Nando and winked at Brian. "Mind Nando. Do what he says."

The bellboy laid the four cases on the bed, receiving a gruff dismissal and a generous tip from Nando. After several minutes, they heard a soft knock on the door.

"Nando. It is Ramondo."

Nando motioned to the door with a jerk of his head. Brian opened it. Standing framed in the doorway was a tall man in a blue suit. Crossing the room quickly, the stranger dropped his bag and embraced Nando as Brian closed the door.

"Nando," he said in a voice filled with respect.

"Brian, this is Ramondo Guibega. He has just left the French army."

"Nando forgets it was he who enlisted me in the service of the French," said the young man, only the slightest hint of an accent to his English.

"What else was I to do with a headstrong boy of sixteen who had already grown two meters in height?" laughed Nando. It was the first time Brian had heard the old man truly laugh.

"Nando instructed me when I was younger than you are."

"He was my best student. But I have gotten older. I will train you in some things, but Ramondo will be your main teacher."

Brian gazed at Ramondo, wondering what this was all about. What was Ramondo going to teach him?

"When Nando sent me away, I could speak four languages: Italian, French, Corsican, and English. Now I speak them better and I have added German, Spanish, Farsi, and some Turkish."

Brian looked skeptical. "You didn't come here to teach me languages."

"He thinks quickly, eh?" Nando said to his nephew. "Ramondo will teach you self-defense."

"Self-defense?" echoed Brian, trying to decide if he should be excited at the prospect or pissed that Nando thought he couldn't take care of himself.

"What has you worried, Nando?" asked Ramondo, before Brian could say more.

"If the Dieter Rohde mentioned by Lars Bjursten is the man I know, there is danger to us all," replied Nando. "Brian has the Gift. He is to be treated like a Falconi."

"Well then, now that we know each other, let's go shopping," said Ramondo.

Brian and Nando waited while Ramondo changed clothes, and then the three of them left the hotel, Nando and Brian side by side, Ramondo some twenty steps in front of them. In the weak sunlight, Brian watched Ramondo. He was tall, at least six-foot two. His shoulders were mostly hidden under a leather jacket but were broad, and the neck visible above the fur collar was well muscled. His hair was brown with flashes of red, cut long in the French fashion. Back in the hotel room, it had been Ramondo's eyes that really made him stand out. They were light brown with rays of yellow sparking from the black pupil. They gave the impression that he was smiling, as if he knew some great joke that was his alone to know. Brian liked him.

"Have you found a suitable location?" asked Nando, as Ramondo stopped and they caught up.

"I think so," answered Ramondo. "I arrived just one hour before you. I phoned this one, but I have not seen it in person. There was one closer to the hotel, but this one is only three blocks away and the owner comes highly recommended. He has been the German National champion," explained Ramondo as he took the stairs by twos. Nando nodded, but Brian was mystified; what "one" was Ramondo referring to?

The stairs opened onto a small landing with three doors. Ramondo opened the first and entered, Brian and Nando following. It was a gymnasium of sorts.

"Can I help you?" asked a man who was the only occupant of the large matted room, standing in the center of the room on a rectangular canvas mat.

Brian watched as Ramondo stepped forward and bowed to the man

"I am Ray Guibega. I phoned about an hour ago. Are you Herr Wolfgang Schmidt?" Ramondo asked in German.

"Ja, but I do not open until four. I told you that on the phone." The man was massive, six feet tall, with the neck and shoulders of a weightlifter. He was dressed in loose-fitting trousers and a black T-shirt. There was a menace to the man, despite his relaxed stance.

Brian watched as Ramondo stepped forward and again bowed to the man, keeping his upper body parallel to the floor until Herr Schmidt acknowledged him with a slight bow of his own. "Please, let me explain my forwardness, Herr Schmidt," said Ramondo, the ever-present twinkle in his eye. "This boy is to become my student. We would like to rent your dojo for the week, from six in the morning until you open. Two hundred euros a day for its exclusive use, more if you have shower facilities."

"We do," said Schmidt, slowly, as if trying to find the flaw in the rental proposal. "There is liability insurance. You or the boy could get hurt. Are you qualified as a teacher?"

Schmidt was as not quite as tall as the young Corsican but looked to outweigh him by at least fifty well-muscled pounds. "With your permission?" asked Ramondo, taking off his shoes, shirt, and jacket.

Brian and Nando moved to the side, Nando taking a chair, watching as Ramondo, starting slowly, performed the ritual movements of first one kata and then another, each one gaining in complexity and violence. On and on he went, spinning, kicking, hammering an imaginary opponent into submission. Sweat began to glisten on his torso as he abruptly changed from kicking and hitting to sweeping, graceful movements that, while not as explosive or violent, gave an impression of being just as deadly. Never once did he use a technique a second time, and never did he appear tired. Then he moved to a large punching bag in the corner of the room.

Finally, after five minutes, a movement centered around a flying kick brought Ramondo near a wall with various weapons displayed on racks. He grabbed two swords. Blades flashed above and below him as he thrust and parried, sweeping the weapons in lethal cutting arcs. Suddenly he jumped in the air, bringing his feet over his head in a perfect flip and landing with the swords under his arms, standing absolutely still.

Brian, his mouth open, turned to Nando, who wore a proud smile. Then, without seeming to move, Ramondo flicked the sword in his left hand with great force. It rotated, flashing in two full revolutions before sticking point-first into the wood of a door jamb on the opposite wall. With the sword still vibrating, Ramondo's other hand sent the second sword hurtling toward the same spot. It embedded in the wood only an inch from the first.

Herr Wolfgang Schmidt moved to the center of the room and bowed to Ramondo. "You may use my dojo. The showers are free. But in return ... you used two karate techniques that I would have you teach me. I will show you what you lack with the saber."

"I would be honored," said Ramondo. "Learning is always the reward for the lessons that have preceded it."

"You are lucky, young man," Schmidt said to Brian, Ramondo translating the words from German.

"May I present Mr. Brian Keohane? He will require a gi, as will I. And this is my sensei, Nando Guibega."

Schmidt again bowed, this time to Nando, who bowed in return. Then he drew ten bills from his wallet and handed them to the German.

"When would you like to start?" asked Schmidt in heavily accented English.

"Now, if it is all right with you."

"Well, then, I had better get Herr Keohane his gi. You have only an hour before my first class arrives," said Schmidt, opening the door in which the two swords still vibrated and removing two white canvas outfits consisting of a top and pants. "Try this one on," he said, handing the smaller of the gi to Brian.

"Thank you, Herr Schmidt," said Brian taking off his shirt.

"What belt?"

"White for both of us," Ramondo answered immediately. "But I have a feeling this one will learn quickly."

⚜ ⚜ ⚜

Lieutenant Kurt Schiller spent the entire afternoon with Mats and Suzanne. He questioned them separately at first, probing for any inconsistencies in their testimony. He found none, then brought them together in his office.

"This man didn't get murdered for nothing," said Schiller. "Someone took a lot of care to make it look like an accident. A crime like that must be well planned, and a murder that is planned always has a motive."

"I had only that one piece of evidence that might prove Bjursten's death wasn't a drunken accident. Then you named the two types of wood that the man choked on, wood we didn't find in the man's apartment. How exactly did you know?"

Schiller has a lot more patience than I have. I would have asked about the mixture of oak and ash as soon as we got off the plane, thought Mats.

"I didn't know for sure. At least, I had no reason to suspect the combination of oak and ash would show up in Bjursten's apartment, but when you said what you did about the smoke, I had to wonder."

"Brian's parents were killed by automatic rifles," added Suzanne, not sure whether Mats was going to offer Schiller a full explanation. "The bullets were hollow-nosed, but they had been filled with oak and ash. Last week there was another attack, this time on a brewery delivery van. Same bullets, dummied with the same two woods. Brian's grandfather was killed years ago with a club made of the same combination."

Schiller looked at both of them. His expression gave nothing away. "You asked me not to inquire about the incident with the Irish police. Why?"

"You're part of the reason," said Mats. "You're a policeman, and a good one. Your lab went out of its way to find out what kind of smoke killed Bjursten. Well, the officer in charge of the investigation in Donegal could find nothing strange about the slugs that hit the van. Then he belittled the bomb."

"Wait!" interrupted Schiller with a wave of his arm. "What bomb?"

It took Mats almost ten minutes to explain the car bomb he had seen being placed in his rental car and Minahen's strange underreaction.

"At first it seemed like ineptitude on the part of the local police, but now I'm convinced otherwise. These were taken from the door behind the spot where Brian's parents were murdered, and these are from the brewery van that was shot up." Mats handed Schiller two plastic bags, each with a slug and a label. "They are the same as the ones police dug out and the ones we sent to Dublin for independent analysis."

"We couldn't understand why the police would hide things when it could mean our lives," added Suzanne, when Mats had finished. "At best they are very bad policemen; at worst they are involved somehow."

"Perhaps the Garda are just withholding the evidence until they have a case. We would do the same thing here." The lieutenant spoke in a measured tone. "If what you say is true, there is a connection between what happened in Ireland and Bjursten's death. And if that is so, you should be concerned that the connection is the brewery, or even you, Herr Falconi."

Mats thought of how he had changed. Almost three years ago, when he had seen his father shot in front of the Sea Hawk, he'd been consumed by the desire to retreat into his memories. His grief, and recurring thoughts of *"Why me?"* had filled him for six months. Then he had traveled to Corsica, and he had changed. He'd slowly accepted danger and even started to confront it. Now he was being pro-active in facing it. Schiller could provide him with facts about Rohde that would help him deal with the threats to Brian, to himself and Suzanne, and to the workers at the Harp and Hawk.

"Were you able to recover anything from Lars' computer? Was there any mention of a Dieter Rohde, the president of the Municher Brewing Company?" Mats asked.

"There was nothing on his computer. It might have been wiped before it burned. What is your interest in this Rohde?"

"I can only tell you that I feel the connection between these events may lie with him. Is there anything you can tell me about the man?"

"Herr Falconi, it is I who asks the questions. It is not the police's job to provide information about German citizens to outsiders. What is your interest? I am asking you again."

Mats sighed. "If Rohde is connected to Lars' death, there is a chance he is also connected to the murder of Brian's parents. I've already explained why we can't trust the Irish police to protect us."

"If you have evidence that links Rohde to Bjursten, please give it to me." Schiller's eyes hardened. "It will go hard on you if you are withholding evidence."

"I have that evidence," said Mats. "It came from Bjursten's computer and was sent to me in Ireland before his death. I will gladly give it to you if you agree to tell me what you find out about Rohde. If we can't strike a bargain, it will get messy. I came back to Germany at your request. You said you talked with Inspector Medau. He trusts me. I ask you to trust me on this as well."

In truth, Mats had forgotten to bring the file with him. It had been packed in the suitcase that the bellhop had taken to his room. Now he was glad for his lapse.

Schiller stood. "All right. If you give me the file, and what you say connects the two events, I will share what we find out about Rohde."

"Thank you. I have the information at the hotel. It contains correspondence between Bjursten and Rohde, as well as several brewing processes Bjursten was working on. He was working for Rohde at the time of his murder."

Schiller looked hard at Mats, then rose, standing straight and official. "I will look into him and his company. Would you like police protection while you're in Germany?"

"No, I don't think that will be necessary. Just the information. Dieter Rohde doesn't know me," said Mats.

"You've never met him, then?" asked Schiller.

"I didn't even know he existed until I read Lars Bjursten's letters."

"Okay. I'll drive you back to your hotel."

Mats opened the hotel room door to find Nando sitting in a chair watching TV with Brian at his side. Brian switched off the TV as Suzanne and Schiller entered behind Mats, who went to the adjoining room, opened his suitcase, and returned with a large envelope containing the printed Bjursten files. He handed the thick sheath of papers to Schiller.

"Lieutenant, there are a number of formulas and processes in there that I believe are patented in Keohane's name, but I have not yet had them checked. I would ask you to keep those to yourself until I do. I believe they might be a large part of the reason Lars was murdered."

"If they are as you say, Herr Falconi, the information will not be released," said Schiller, turning toward the door. "Please join me downstairs for breakfast tomorrow at eight. You too, Frau Falconi. I'm sure to have more questions after reading these. I should have information on Herr Rohde by then."

Mats caught the quick turn of Nando's head out of the corner of his eye and wondered if Schiller had noticed.

"Gute nacht," said Schiller. "I'll meet you in the lobby in the morning."

Nando got up, walked to the door, and double locked it behind Schiller. Then he moved to the door that connected to Room 922. "Signor Falconi, you remember Ramondo Guibega."

Ramondo entered the room, gliding rather than walking. Mats took in the man's youth, athleticism, and gentle smile.

"You should see what Ramondo can do," said Brian, jumping up and approaching Mats. "He has been teaching me jiu-jitsu!"

"Is that right?" asked Mats, amused by the boy's enthusiasm.

"It is my pleasure to teach the boy, Signor Falconi."

Mats shook Ramondo's hand. "You remember my wife, Suzanne?"

"Of course. Congratulations on your marriage." Ramondo turned to shake Suzanne's hand next.

"And he taught you jiu-jitsu?" Suzanne asked Brian.

"Just for self-defense," said Ramondo, as Brian stifled a yawn. "It's a discipline that a lighter person can use effectively against a larger foe."

"And you feel he needs this?" asked Suzanne.

"Every young boy should know how to protect himself," said Mats, eliciting a grunt of approval from Nando and a smile from Ramondo. Brian gave another long yawn.

"I think you'd better have an early dinner tonight, Brian," said Ramondo. "We will start again at six tomorrow."

"Better make it nine," said Suzanne. "Lieutenant Schiller is expecting us for breakfast. Ramondo, will you join us for dinner?"

"No, thank you," said Ramondo. "Nor for breakfast. It will be better if no one knows I'm here. Other than in these rooms, you will not see me."

Chapter Fourteen

That night, roused from a deep sleep, Mats heard the knob of the hallway door turn, the latch click, and the chain that secured the closure stretch. He sat up in bed. For some inexplicable reason, the knob was fully illuminated in a circle of bright yellow light. Gradually, Mats realized that he was dreaming, that the rough bed and crudely plastered room had no relation to the lush reality of his suite in the German hotel. Realizing that he wasn't in danger, Mats understood the signs of the Gift taking over his dream state. He had not dreamed of using the Gift for over a year before they had arrived in Ireland. This would be his third dream of his father in the last month. He lay back, giving in to the feeling of detachment from the present and the rich fabric of the dream...

⚜ ⚜ ⚜

Corsica—January 1942

From his raised position on the bed, Egel Falconi watched the knob turn. Paulo Guibega had prepared him a bed in a barn that stood some thirty meters from the main house and less from the vineyards that provided the winery's grapes. He grabbed his knife from the shelf next to the bed and swung his feet to the floor. Falconi had talked with Paulo about the German troop deployments and movements late into the night. When the need for sleep finally overcame his ability to keep a train of thought, Egel asked for a bed. One of Paulo's daughters would share her bed with Teresa.

"Signor Falconi." The soft voice of Teresa pierced the darkness. "Paulo's wife laughed when Paulo told her that I was to sleep with her daughter. Don't worry. I'll let you sleep."

She crossed the wood floor of the room, stopping to place something at the foot of the bed. The blanket lifted as she slid under it, past him, taking the little space left between Egel and the wall. Once under the covers, she rose up on an elbow and kissed him before settling back down, hugging him around the back as he settled, placing his knife on the floor. He had gone to sleep in his shirt and trousers. Now, with Teresa's form pressed against his back, he realized that the bundle left at the foot of the bed had been her clothes. He felt her firm nakedness against his shoulders and knew she had lied. She would not let him sleep, at least not right away.

The barn was dark, and neither Egel nor Teresa awoke until mid-morning. When they did, they found Paulo working in the vineyards with his daughters. They were terracing a slope on the north edge of the narrow valley that would allow them to plant two more rows of vines. With only a nod of recognition, the girls bent to the task of stacking the native rock, providing the necessary bulwark for the soil that would later be added. Paulo's wife came up behind them, carrying a load of rocks in a backpack made of bent sticks. She smiled knowingly at Teresa and curtsied in respect to Falconi before leaving for another load.

"From what you said last night, the Germans don't bother you much out here?" asked Falconi, trying to continue the previous evening's conversation despite the distraction that Teresa was providing to Paulo's daughters.

"There's a German soldier for every three Corsicans," answered Paulo, without pausing in his work. "But they stay around the ports, especially Bastia and Ajaccio. This valley has no military value. They come every few months and take the wine that has matured and been bottled. They have ordered me to plant more grapes for white wine. When the Italians were here, they wanted red. Nothing changes. They drink what I make, regardless, because it is good. They leave us alone as long as we produce enough for them to confiscate."

"If anyone, German or Corsican, should ask, I'm Teresa's uncle, Egel Guibega." Falconi was about to continue but was stopped by the giggles of Paulo's two daughters, who were speaking in whispers to Teresa and casting sidelong glances at Falconi.

"Women!" sighed Paulo. "I only hope that our next child will be a son to carry on my name."

"Both can be a source of pride," said Falconi. "Boys carry the name, but girls carry much of the burden." Egel had noticed the look of pride Paulo gave his daughters. He looked around, taking in the winery that had been given to Paulo when Falconi had left for America. The changes had been many, and they reflected the diligence of a man working for himself.

Falconi continued his thought. "Only the Guibega are to know who I am. Already Nando and Mario are marked men and must keep in hiding. I don't want to add to the list."

"It is well that you think this way," said Paulo, standing to stretch his back before grabbing another rock. "Too many plans of the Resistance have been ambushed, too many good men placed in the holding pen at Ajaccio."

"I know of one who was a traitor. He was not a Guibega. Nando made him dead."

"You will never find a Guibega who would betray you, Signor Falconi." Paulo straightened, pride and passion showing on his face like a map of defiance.

"I know, Paulo."

They had lunch on a blanket between the rows of vines. Wine, bread, cheese, and sausage were laid out by the two young girls.

"The Germans are more active than the Italians were, but they mostly operate during the day," said Paulo. "Best you sleep during the day or devote yourself to some labor. The Germans are much more likely to stop someone on the road, or question someone who is not doing chores. What will you do now?"

"I have a plan, but I need someone who is in the Resistance...someone I know I can trust to help make my idea a reality."

"Then you will want to see Antonio Guibega. He leads the Resistance in the mountains, and much of it on the coast," said Paulo. He leaned over, gathering the blanket and handing it to one of his daughters.

"Antonio Guibega? I thought he was dead."

"He is alive, but like Nando, he's a wanted man. He's in hiding in the Pentica Gorge. He is a legend. In the war, almost all of Corsica's men over seventeen fought for France. Half died, over 45,000. Antonio was shot twice. Toward the end of the war, he was shot a third time, his most serious wound yet. When he recovered, he became a guide in the Alps. When he finally returned home, you had already left for America. He is almost fifty, but he is still a force."

That evening Teresa and Falconi took the motorcycle deeper into the gray granite of the mountains that divided Corsica's east coast from the west.

"We must be careful on these roads," said Teresa, turning her head and shouting toward Falconi, who was again riding as the passenger. "The Germans don't patrol here at night for good reason. Most can tell that this is not a German engine, but there is still the risk of a wire."

"How long will it take us to get to the gorge?" Falconi shouted back.

"One hour without caution, half an hour longer if we're careful."

"Is there a place where we can meet?"

Teresa thought for a moment before answering. "Yes, the stone fountain in Bocognano." Egel could feel her take a deep breath. "The Nazis have a bounty on his head. He will be cautious."

"Let me know when we reach Bocognano," responded Falconi, resting his head against Teresa's shoulder.

When the time came, Teresa killed the headlight, rolling silently to a stop by the side of the road. She felt Egel's head rise from her shoulder. "You can see the fountain just through those trees. If I can find him, he will meet you there."

Bocognano was not a true town but rather a village with four or five shops surrounded by several small outlying farms. At the end of the main street was a colossal jumble of stone, constructed as a fountain for no reason other than civic pride.

Falconi shuffled down the village street, using the slow gait of an old mountain man. He heard the muffled sound of Teresa's motorcycle moving past the village. He walked past the few closed shops to the far side of the fountain and sat on its edge, rubbing his hands. He had been waiting for about thirty minutes when he noticed a man approaching from the opposite direction. He was dressed similarly to Falconi, but he carried a long walking stick. He wore a heavy cape that reached below his waist despite the summer heat.

"Signore?" whispered Egel as the man passed.

Antonio Guibega stopped and turned, appearing to notice the man by the fountain for the first time. Raising the hand that held the walking stick in greeting, he walked to Falconi and sat down. His face was ruddy, the skin stretched tight from the sun. There was a scar that crossed his right eyebrow and ended in a small indentation on the side of his nose. His shoulders were broad and his body exuded power.

"Antonio Guibega, welcome," whispered Falconi, offering some of the bread and cheese he was eating to the older man. "Do you know who I am?"

"Si, signore. I knew your father well."

Egel was surprised that the older man was still alive. He remembered the stories of a wild youth with a reputation for trouble outside the clan. Egel's father had been given a commission in the French navy when Egel was just a child. He had tried to get young Antonio assigned to the mine sweeper he was given, but for probably the first time in recorded history, a nation at war placed a man according to his skills. Egel's father was a skilled seaman, but Antonio had grown up in the mountains, a throwback to when the Guibegas had survived living on the slopes of the granite crags that separated the east and west coasts of Corsica.

"It is good to meet you," said Egel as they sat together— two men, one old, one pretending to be, sharing their simple dinner.

"Thank you for coming back, signore. I thought I had lost my chance to serve your family when your father died and you left. I regret that I was not able to protect him from the traitor."

Egel winced. It was suspected that Egel's father had been betrayed. Speculation centered around a man from Porto named Edmund Collette who had been transferred from Falconi's vessel just before it had blown up. Collette had been murdered shortly after the end of the war. His throat had been cut during a robbery of his home. No one had ever been charged. The French police had called it a vendetta murder, a matter resolved between Corsicans, and it was soon forgotten.

"Antonio," whispered Egel. "What are your thoughts about the Resistance, and about my father's death and that of Edmund Collette?"

"There is no need to speak of Collette. He was the traitor. He admitted it just before my knife took his life. As for the Resistance, for the first year of the war, it was as it always was. We disrupted the traffic on the coastal roads and blew up the Italians' equipment. We treated their soldiers with respect, not killing them unnecessarily, and in return they treated us as soldiers. The mountains remained ours." Antonio took another bite of cheese and tore off a piece of bread.

"When the Germans took over, it was the same. Then a special unit of troops arrived under the command of a young lieutenant and things changed. They started arresting any Corsican who they thought might be with the Resistance. They would torture them and then ship them off the island. The Germans are not content to control the ports and coast. They push deeper into the mountains each week, using motorcycle troops and fast troop carriers. During the day they patrol with their airplanes, looking for any sign of our camps. We have lost many men."

"And the Resistance?" asked Egel.

"When they started arresting people, torturing, some people turned. I am convinced that there are a number in the Resistance who report to German masters. When they're discovered, now or after the war, I will pay them a visit."

Egel looked at the man and knew that it was not a promise; it was a pledge.

For the next half hour, Egel went over his plan to form a unit separate from the Resistance but working in tandem with it. Their actions would be part of the Resistance, but they would not be compromised by any informant leaks. The operation that Egel outlined for Antonio would use few people—a maximum of three or four Guibega at any one time.

Antonio listened, every so often asking for clarification of a tactic or objective. When Egel had finished, Antonio offered suggestions as to where the Germans were most vulnerable. In less than an hour, what had been an outline for survival had turned into a battle plan. Only one thing was left to discuss, and Antonio broached it.

"Signor Falconi, what part am I to play?"

"Antonio Guibega, you will fill two roles. First, you will be my sword, my field commander. Nando will be my shield, my second in command. Teresa will be my voice. She will deliver messages and organize the troops needed to accomplish the objectives. You, Nando, and I will lead the attacks.

"Second, you will be my link to the Resistance. Our actions will be side pieces to theirs. The Nazis might learn of Resistance plans from traitors within the Resistance, but they will not learn of the collateral attacks our group will make. Can you do this without arousing suspicion? Also, I must contact the Allies if we are to be supplied with the arms we will need to be successful."

"I can do that. I told my men I was in need of a woman tonight," chuckled Antonio. "I think that I will find one and fall in love. A man in love can't be blamed for anything, since they are all crazy, old ones especially. My love affair will provide the excuse for my absences. If she were to be Nando's niece—the one who found me tonight—it would give me an excuse to see Nando and receive instructions in person."

Falconi hesitated. This would be a perfect cover for Antonio, but at the same time, it would place Teresa at greater risk. The Guibega clan would of course know the truth, but they could be trusted. Falconi looked away, indecision momentarily crossing his face.

He picked up a rock and threw it into the fountain, noticing for the first time the names chiseled into many of the stones – the names of men killed in World War I. Almost before the ripple had subsided, a shadow approached them from the dark. Antonio tensed until he saw who it was. Teresa continued forward until she was standing directly in front of the two seated men.

"Teresa," said Falconi with a smile, "what would you think of Antonio becoming your lover?"

Teresa was skilled in dealing with men, but not as a woman in love. As she took in Egel's words, her face showed rage. Falconi watched as first confusion and then chagrin replaced her anger. As the true meaning of his question became clear to her, her face lightened.

"Who would believe it, signore?" asked Teresa, a small smile of her own turning the corners of her mouth. "It is well known that no woman on Corsica will have him."

Antonio stiffened. He had remained a bachelor into his late forties not because women didn't find him attractive, but for just the opposite reason. Roaming his wide territory, it was more convenient to have several "friends" in different villages. It was not unusual for Corsican men to marry late in life. He still considered himself a good catch. He had not expected Teresa Guibega to rebuff his attentions, even if they were ones of convenience. To make it worse, the young girl, the most beautiful of all the Guibega women, was nearly laughing at the prospect.

"Antonio, don't be upset by my remark," said Teresa quickly. "Egel and I are laughing because we are lovers, a fact you would have learned the first time you met with another Guibega. I remained a virgin for almost seventeen years, and now in one week, two of the island's most desirable men offer to remove the burden from me."

Falconi was again caught unawares by Teresa's candor. *Why is it that the women of Corsica are so forward?* he wondered.

Antonio dropped his bread in the dirt. He knelt to pick it up but grasped Falconi's hand before rising, his lips pressed hard against the backs of Egel's fingers. In a voice hardly audible even to Teresa, he said, "I offer you my oath of fidelity, as I did your father. I am your weapon."

Falconi lifted him up and the three of them walked slowly out of town toward the hidden motorcycle.

"Before we meet with Nando, what would be your first objective?" asked Egel. They had stopped while Teresa uncovered the motorcycle.

"Kill the head and the body dies with it," said Antonio. "I would kill the officer who leads the reprisal unit, Lieutenant Dieter Rohde."

Frankfurt, Germany—2003

The name "Rohde" echoed like a scream inside Mats' head. His grunt woke Suzanne. Mats slowly awoke, rubbing his temples to relieve the headache that often accompanied the Gift.

"Another dream?" asked Suzanne.

"Yes," said Mats, looking at the clock radio, reading 6:42 in muted red numbers. "Another dream about my father and a Nazi named Dieter Rohde. Nando was right. I should have known the name."

Ramondo left Brian sleeping in the hotel room just before six. Dressed in black and green running sweats and carrying a backpack holding other clothes, Ramondo slipped out the front door unnoticed, just an ordinary guest trying to fit his exercise regime into a crowded day.

He ran to the dojo, unlocking the door with the key Wolfgang Schmidt had given him, and placed the backpack on the floor. The day before, he had performed classical moves, katas that demonstrated mastery of technique and discipline, proving him a capable teacher. Today, with no one watching, he concentrated on explosive, lethal moves. Had Schmidt been watching, he would have understood that these skills had no place in competition—only in events in which the loser lost more than a trophy, more than his pride.

By seven-thirty he had cooled down, showered, shaved, and dressed in the dark blue suit from the backpack. Back at the hotel, he was already seated at breakfast when Lieutenant Schiller arrived with his aide.

Schiller was waiting for Mats and the rest in the lobby at eight. He led them to a small alcove off the main dining area to a table set for six. Breakfast was conducted with the precision of a board meeting. The policeman started by asking Brian what he planned to do while Mats and Suzanne were at the station reviewing the documents Mats had provided the evening before.

"I missed a lot of school over the last three months. My teachers have given me assignments. I'm trying to make up the work this summer," said Brian. "Nando promised to take me shopping, too. There are so many stores."

"And you, Nando? What do you have planned for today?"

"I will try not to fall asleep watching TV," answered Nando. "I might get a massage. Your cold, damp climate makes my arthritis act up."

Schiller shook his head. His smile matched Mats, both of them enjoying Nando's senility act. Mats knew the policeman didn't buy a second of it.

Schiller lifted a mottled green and gray file. "Here is the information on Dieter Rohde." He made a show of opening the file and examining each document before handing it to Mats.

Mats went through the file quickly. "There is nothing about his war record in here."

"No. Germany is quite sensitive when it comes to releasing pre-reconstruction records, especially with older individuals such as Rohde," said Schiller, his palms up. "What exactly are you looking for?"

"I'm not sure," admitted Mats. "Anything that would connect him to Ireland. His war record would be a start."

"Now about the Irish police," said Schiller, changing the subject. "I agree, if what you say is true, about the bullets. I have a contact in Dublin, a good man, Desmond Fitzgerald. He is the head of the Technical Bureau of the Garda Síochána, a very thorough man. Contact him with your evidence and suspicions. He will keep your secrets."

Ramondo went to the lobby, where he waited for the group to reappear. When they did, he moved quickly out of the hotel onto the street, still busy with morning traffic.

From his vantage point in front of a store window a full block away from the hotel, Ramondo saw Mats and Suzanne get into a car with the two policemen. In less than five minutes, Nando appeared with Brian, carrying a nylon gym bag. They walked quickly down the street toward him, heading directly for the dojo. As they passed, Ramondo caught sight of two men following Nando and the boy. Unlike people who are just walking, the two men had their eyes riveted on the old man and the boy.

Ramondo looked behind the two men, making sure the tails didn't have a tail themselves. When he was certain, he walked after them, a newspaper tucked under his arm. Ramondo, Nando, and Mats had discussed the possibility of the police putting a tail on Nando and Brian. If Ramondo didn't join them outside the dojo, Nando would know what to do.

Nando and Brian paused in front of the stairwell that led to the dojo, making no move to go up the stairs. They appeared to be discussing something. When Ramondo didn't come, they moved off. Halfway down the street, they stopped in front of a cutlery store window displaying row after row of Trident Dreizack cooking knives. When Ramondo still didn't join them, they went inside.

Ramondo watched as the two men following the boy slowed, then stopped, keeping a distance between themselves and their charge. It was an amateurish tactic, one that any skilled person could easily identify. Nothing made a tail stand out more than keeping pace. Ramondo did not commit the same mistake himself. He passed the two, cutting across the street, presenting himself as a young executive with a purpose, showing only the back of his head to the men following Brian as he went into the building housing the dojo. Ramondo took the stairs three at a time. At the top of the landing, he was surprised to find the door unlocked. Cautiously, he stepped inside.

Wolfgang Schmidt, known as Wolf in the full contact competitions he entered and usually won, stood in the center of the mat in a sweat-stained tee shirt and gi pants. Ramondo bowed to the sensei and moved quickly to the window.

The two men below were looking into the window of the shop, using the reflection of the glass to keep an eye on the door of the cutlery shop across the street.

"Is something wrong?" asked Wolf, moving to the window to stand beside Ramondo.

"I'm not sure yet, but Brian and Nando are being followed by two men."

"I thought your lessons seemed urgent yesterday," said Wolf. "Is the boy in trouble?"

"The boy's mother and father were murdered less than four months ago. Since then, there has been at least one attempt on his life. I would say he's in trouble." Wolf Schmidt had trusted Ramondo with his dojo; Ramondo thought he could trust the man with part of the story in return. Besides, there was a possibility that he would need the man's assistance before long.

"IRA?" asked Wolf, studying the men on the street below.

"I don't think so. They look German."

Just then the men bent closer to the window. Nando and Brian had come out of the store, Nando with a package under his arm. As they started back toward the hotel, Ramondo turned to Wolf. "I'll be back later. Until then, please be assured that we have done nothing illegal. We are the good guys."

Ramondo followed the men, catching up with them as Nando and Brian entered the hotel. He passed through the lobby and made his way to the elevator landing, arriving just as Nando and Brian's elevator door closed. The two men came to the landing as well, standing behind Ramondo and watching as the elevator floor indicator stopped at 9. They climbed into an adjacent lift, accompanied by Ramondo, who immediately bent over and tied his shoe.

"They have gone to their rooms," whispered the smaller, mean-looking one. "If they leave, follow them. I'll go back and report."

The elevator stopped at the ninth floor. The two men got out. Ramondo stayed on, exiting on the next floor and running to the stairwell. By the time the smaller man got back down to the lobby, Ramondo was already there, wearing an overcoat and hat borrowed from the bellboy for a twenty-euro consideration. Ramondo hoped the man would be as careless in reporting to whomever had sent him as he had been in following the boy.

Thirty minutes later, Ramondo returned to the hotel, taking the elevator to the fourteenth floor to find Brian waiting for him in the stairwell. He had gotten off at the ninth floor with Nando, but he hadn't gone to his room; he'd taken the stairs and waited for Ramondo.

They took the stairs down, going by way of the kitchen to the street. Ramondo shed the overcoat and hat, returning them, to the relief of the bellboy, who pocketed another 20-euro note. Five minutes later they were in Wolfgang Schmidt's karate dojo, unwrapping Brian's purchase. Nando had chosen well. Inside a polished wood case were two chef's knives. They were not true throwing knives, which are balanced from edge to edge as well as from tip to handle, but they would do quite nicely.

"Were you able to follow them?" asked Brian as he changed into his gi.

"I followed one. The other stayed outside your room listening to Nando yell at you and watch TV. The one I followed had a fondness for beer. No more talking. Give me a horse stance." All friendliness was gone from Ramondo's voice. Brian readied himself for what he knew was about to come.

CHAPTER FIFTEEN

Herr Dieter Rohde sat behind a large polished wooden desk, listening to Bernd's report. The phone call from Ireland at four o'clock in the morning had given him little time to organize a plan, but the message had been clear. First, it was necessary to find out where the boy was staying. They had been surprised in Ireland by Falconi's sudden departure. It took them over half a day to discover that Falconi had taken the boy with him, then a little longer to discover that the American had booked a flight to Frankfurt for four. *Their intelligence was good, the information always accurate, but it wasn't efficient,* thought Rohde.

"I have Herman watching the boy. He's with an old man at the hotel," said Bernd, standing at attention in front of the desk. "The man and woman went with Schiller. I phoned Haas at the police station as soon as I saw Inspector Schiller at the hotel."

"You'd better get back and help Herman. He has his uses, but thinking on his own is hardly one of them. And Bernd, don't phone Haas again. I'll deal with the police."

"Jawohl," said Bernd, turning to leave.

"Bernd," said Rohde. Bernd stopped as if he had snapped at the end of a leash. "Look for an opportunity where the boy might have an accident."

"Jawohl. Thank you, mein herr," said Bernd, this time with a short bow. Turning again toward the door, he smiled. He liked working for Rohde.

Ramondo tried to gauge Brian's endurance. He was amazed at how quickly the boy picked up and then mastered the techniques. Still, he was only thirteen, and he needed a number of short breaks to recapture his concentration. Using what he was learning instinctively would take repetition — and that required time they didn't have.

At noon, Wolf interrupted their training session with an offer of food, which was gratefully accepted by Brian. Wolf phoned a delicatessen and ordered sandwiches and soft drinks, while Ramondo continued working Brian hard with the promise of lunch—the carrot for maximum effort.

"I have watched you for two days now," Wolf said to Ramondo, as Brian attacked the sandwich like a starving wolf cub. "You don't train him for a belt. You train him to fight."

"That's true, Wolf. As I told you, his mother and father were murdered. I am his bodyguard while he is in Germany, but I will not always be with him. He must be trained to protect himself, and quickly."

"The boy learns fast and you are a good teacher, but he needs rest," said Wolf. "Perhaps you would like to teach me the kata that you did yesterday. There was one unique arm break. It was not classic karate."

"The arm break is called 'snapping twig.' I'd be proud to show it to you."

While Brian ate, the two men exchanged techniques. Their sparring became more and more physical. Finally, they stopped, both of them dripping with sweat.

"You are the best I have ever met," said Wolf Schmidt, the intensity of competition slowly leaving his face to be replaced with a slight grin. "Where did you train?"

"Corsica to start. Nando was my teacher," said Ramondo, nodding to Nando, who sat in the corner. "The French Special Services taught me the rest. In my unit there were twenty men, all experts. You would have been number one."

"Behind you," corrected Schmidt, bowing again to the younger man.

Ramondo turned back to Brian, who still sat, holding his unfinished sandwich. "That was fantastic," the boy said. "Will I be able to do that?"

"If you keep studying," answered Ramondo. "What I am teaching you is even more valuable. No one will expect you to know how to stop a man. As a boy, you will not be seen as a threat, and that is your greatest weapon. Now finish your lunch."

Schiller went over what Mats had given him. According to the printouts that Mats had supplied, Rohde was the only person in Germany with whom Lars Bjursten had corresponded. But the interest the American had shown in the man went beyond that connection. At lunch, Schiller had excused himself and gone to his private office to review the complete file on Rohde. The American was interested in his war record. Schiller had concentrated on more recent business deals. Now, as he went back over the sketchy details of Rohde's military record, he saw the connection.

"Why do you have a file on Rohde in the first place?" was the first thing that Mats asked as Schiller returned from his office.

Damn, thought Schiller. *Falconi was perceptive, too perceptive.* It was a question he had hoped he would not have to answer.

"Rohde has been involved in several takeovers—companies that mysteriously lost their owners or top executives just before Rohde stepped in. The Municher Brewing Company is the most recent. Twice there were accusations from widows and brothers that the misfortune, although appearing accidental, was a little too convenient. The first company was a small accounting firm with some up-and-coming clients. That was in 1954."

"Does he still own it?" asked Suzanne.

"Yes, and it has grown tremendously – made him a very rich man. Later he took over one of his client's firms, a lumber company. He bought the brewery five years ago. He has made only one significant purchase since then, a hundred acres of forest in what was East Germany. The owner and his daughter died in a fire. He uses the place for retreats. Our file was started at the takeover of the lumber company. As I said, it was suspicious timing, but we found nothing illegal."

"The man was in the Nazi army, based in Corsica," said Mats, hoping to keep Schiller talking by stating a fact that the policeman was trying to hide.

"Did Nando know him?" asked Schiller.

"I don't know that for certain that they ever met," said Mats. "Nando was in the Resistance. He was still young when the war began. That was over seventy years ago. But yes, Nando knew of him. He told me there was a Lieutenant Dieter Rohde in charge of pacification. He said the man was brutal. It is the same man then?"

"Rohde was in Corsica," said Schiller. "He was injured in the German evacuation in 1943. It was reported that he had died of his wounds."

"But here he is in Frankfurt," said Suzanne, trying to take the harshness out of Mats' questioning of the policeman.

"Nothing was heard of him for a year," said Schiller, looking over the aged pages in Rohde's file. "The records listed him as dead. Then, after almost a year, he showed back up in Germany... the burns he suffered in the evacuation from Corsica were barely healed. There is a photograph showing the skin of his face stretched tight, translucent in places, bright pink in others. His loyalty is questioned in the file... whether he was to be trusted on his return, because he might have been turned in the year he wasn't heard from. But what does his Army record have to do with a possible motive for murdering Bjursten?"

"Bjursten was related to Mia Keohane, Brian's mother, but only as a second cousin," said Suzanne. "The motive is likely related to the fermentation process Bjursten had developed for Brian's dad."

"It's a new and revolutionary process for producing non-alcoholic beer. It's why I asked you not to divulge the formulas that were part of the file I gave you last night. Bjursten did the same thing for Rohde, so why kill him? Why try to kill me or the boy? It doesn't make sense to me. But I know one thing. It makes sense to someone, and that someone is very dangerous."

Schiller nodded his agreement.

Rohde's cell phone rang, identifying Karl Haas, his contact in the police department.

"Yes."

"I got a look at Bjursten's pathology report." The voice came over the telephone slightly muffled. "Schiller is good. Wood smoke in Bjursten's lungs was what set him off. That and the disparity between the alcohol in the blood stream and the stomach. Word is that he has proof that it wasn't an accident, and he's developing the case with the help of an American. The American has been going over computer files with Schiller. One of them is yours. If I hear anything else, I will contact you."

Rohde listened to the click that terminated the report. He looked around his office—thick Persian carpet on the floor, walls softened with built-in walnut bookcases, a massive desk made of dark oak inlaid with ash—all adding to the warm, efficient comfort of the work space. Bjursten's apartment had looked and felt sterile because there had been no wood, only plastic and steel. Schiller was indeed a clever and meticulous man to have picked up on that. He would have to be more careful in the future.

The killing of the boy, presented a real problem now that he was under suspicion. He had heard of Bjursten's discovery of a new fermentation process from his contacts in Ireland, but the decision to kill the Swede had been strictly his own. It had been purely an economic decision to kill the Swede. Now it added complications to the killing of the boy, which held no economic value at all for him. Still, he would do their bidding. They had saved his life, provided a focus, something to believe in, when Der Führer was proving that he had only half the answer. They had started him on a successful business career and had only asked for money when he had so much that the amount they requested didn't matter.

They had not taught him how to kill. That he already knew, but they had focused his killing, without which his business interests would never have grown so rapidly. Most important now, though, nearing the end of his years, they had given him hope for everlasting life, joining an unbroken chain that preceded him for over three thousand years. They wanted the boy, Brian, dead—so he would die.

"Have Bernd come here immediately," said Herr Dieter Rohde into the intercom on his desk, his voice as gentle as someone's favorite grandfather's. When he saw Bernd, he immediately asked, "What do you have to report?" His face moved only slightly as he spoke.

"Most of it you already know, sir," said Bernd slightly out of breath. "The old man took the boy shopping right after breakfast, then back to the hotel. Herman said the old man had to yell at the kid several times to turn the TV down. They ate lunch in the room. At five-thirty, the American and his wife were brought back by the police. They went straight to their rooms and stayed for half an hour, and then all four of them left for dinner."

"Any ideas about the boy?" asked Rohde.

"We could easily get into the rooms. The old man would present no problem."

"Bernd, don't think like Herman. This can't be traced back to me. It must be made to look like an accident. The hotel is out. Do you think they will go out again tomorrow morning?"

"I don't know," answered Bernd.

"Listen to me carefully. It is important that you do exactly as I instruct," said Rohde, lowering his voice even further. "Use the gang of toughs living across from the brewery—the ones you wanted to clear out last month."

"You mean the skinheads? What the hell for? They're scum."

"Yes, that is the point. People are afraid of them. What's more important, they look for foreign victims. Contact them without letting them know who you are or who you work for. Pay them to kill the boy. You plan the attack; you give them directions and the target. Make it look like random violence by street toughs."

"How am I to contact them and get them to do these things without letting on who I am?"

"When you wanted to run them out, I did a check on them," said Rohde after a considerable pause. He tossed a file across the desk at Bernd. "The one called Ernst has three arrests for assault, one with a deadly weapon. He has a drug habit supported by petty theft and extortion. He is your contact. Deal only with him."

"But he will see me."

Rohde smiled at Bernd like a ferret examining a mouse. "Buy two short-wave radios for cash. Send one to Ernst at the skinheads' apartment. Be careful of finger-prints and don't let the messenger see you. Put it in a box with enough cocaine to make Ernst a happy man. When you are sure he has opened it, call him. Offer him five thousand dollars and a tenfold supply of drugs if he gets his gang to do a job, one they will like, rousting a couple foreigners who can't fight back."

"Ja," exclaimed Bernd. "I can direct his gang to the boy using the same radio."

"Good thinking, Bernd," said Rohde, the taut, scarred skin of his face pulling into what sufficed for a smile. "Against the wall are some wooden clubs. They are weighted at the end and should be quite effective. Wipe all fingerprints but make sure they are sent to the skinheads and are used in the attack. Caution above all. Caution." What Rohde didn't add was that the clubs were made of laminated wood of a special kind.

"Caution," repeated Bernd, flexing his shoulder muscles to show Rohde that he was up to the task.

It was almost eight o'clock. Time to use the communicator, thought Bernd. He had watched the package delivered to the apartment by a messenger who had picked it up at a drop. The note inside, wrapped around a plastic bag of crack, said that a call would be coming at eight. It was time for that message.

Mats was restless. Twice he went into Brian's room to check on the boy. Both times he found Ramondo awake, eyes following from the couch where he lay wrapped in a spare blanket.

Mats had been aware of the Gift for over two years now. He thought of it really as three Gifts. The first part was the ability to dream of past events, even those that took place hundreds of years previously. The dreams for the most part came unbidden. They resembled time travel, placing him in the mind and body of an ancestor. They informed Mats of some special event that had transpired centuries before in or near an area he was visiting for the first time. The second part of the Gift had to do with warnings. It was almost as if an ancestor were picking the dreams, choosing the piece of history that would best warn Mats of what was occurring in the present. The third part was that the triplet Viking brothers, who were evidently the start of their line, had the ability to read each other's thoughts. Mats had not experienced this aspect and suspected that it had been lost or diluted through the centuries.

Mats could not tell for certain when the dreams were coming, but he often had a feeling of apprehension, a feeling that he was missing something. As he lay down beside Suzanne for the third time, he had such feelings. He sighed, soon falling into a fitful sleep. The dream came over him...

❧ ❧ ❧

Corsica—January 1942

It took Egel, Teresa, and Antonio Guibega two hours to ride to the coast, crowded together on the motorcycle, the back-wheel springs bottoming out at every pothole hit.

"Best to stop here," said Antonio as Teresa slowed the bike, coasting it to the side of the road.

"How far are we from the Roost?" asked Egel, who had lost his bearings more than once on the winding roads leading from the mountains.

"About five kilometers," said Teresa, and was confirmed by a nod from Antonio.

Egel looked at his watch, and then at the sky, which was still black. "Antonio is right. It is near enough to morning that the Germans could be rising. We still have plenty of time to get to Nando before daybreak. Hide the bike. Teresa can come back and get it tomorrow afternoon."

The five kilometers took less than an hour. Antonio led, staying fifty meters ahead of Teresa and Egel. At first his pace did not seem fast to Egel. It was a low-legged run, deceptively effective in chewing up large hunks of terrain over mountain trails. Falconi tried to copy the gait but found it unnatural for him. He ended up alternating between a run and a fast walk. When they reached the hill that held Falcon's Roost, Antonio stopped, allowing Falconi and Teresa to join him.

"Stay here till you hear an owl hoot three times." Without waiting for an answer, Antonio slipped into the boulders that flanked the steep trail to the stone keep that crested the hill.

Falconi and Teresa moved off the trail, waiting for Antonio's signal. Egel leaned backward against a large, smooth boulder, and Teresa immediately pressed against him, her head on his chest. His arms came around her and he bent to kiss her lips.

The three hoots of an owl came just as their lips touched. Reluctantly, Egel pulled away from Teresa. He took her hand and they moved to the trail, climbing it together.

Nando Guibega met them as they came through the outer wall of the keep. Falcon's Roost was basically the ruin of an enlarged watchtower, a place to view the road that passed below. It featured a broken stone wall around a small courtyard and living quarters. Designed more for defense than for residence, one could see five kilometers to the south and a good three to the north.

Antonio was already warming his hands around a mug of coffee as Egel and Teresa entered the room. The bottom of the tower had no windows, only a door to the courtyard and stone steps leading upward, providing breaks in the round stone wall. Nando had built a small fire in what was once the kitchen area of the keep. The flames were well shielded from the door, giving no indication of its presence until one was in the room.

"Why haven't the Germans taken this for their own? It seems to control the road in both directions," asked Egel as Nando handed him a cup of steaming coffee.

"It's too far from their base in Ajaccio. They sometimes come here during the day, but nights would mean their death."

"It's still best to keep watch. I'll be in the tower while you rest," said Nando, moving toward the stairs cut in stone to the right of the fireplace.

"I'll come with you," said Falconi.

As they reached the top floor, the first indication of dawn was starting to appear as a blue-gray line across the tops of the hills to the east.

"I spend my evenings here," said Nando as they reached the top level. "During the day I sleep in the caves on the other side of the hill. They are cool and dark, and I can rest without fear of the Germans finding me."

"Have you contacted all the Guibega?" asked Egel.

"Yes, signore. To a man, they understand and approve of an all-Guibega unit. They'll keep the secret of your identity."

"Good. You're my second in command. You'll be in charge of assigning the men we need and helping Antonio to identify our targets. Antonio will be my field commander. We three will lead the attacks at different times. I don't want to lose a single man or woman. But there's one more thing," added Egel, his voice wavering. "I left Corsica so that my children might grow up away from this island. I knew Corsica would see more violence during their lives." Egel paused, gaining courage with a deep breath. "I have been successful in America in all but one thing. I did not find the woman I love. Now, I have come back to my homeland, and I have found her. I ask you for Teresa's hand."

Falconi stopped, wishing he had thought his words out a little more, wishing he had been more eloquent. When Nando did not respond, Falconi took it as a sign that he was not in agreement with the request.

"I know she is young, but I love her. It is right."

"Signor Falconi," said Nando, slowly, as if measuring each word by how long it took to pass his lips. "I have worried about my Teresa. She is strong-willed, too strong for most men. I have also found that the best way to get her to do what I tell her is to find out exactly what she wants and then order her to do it. Does she want to marry you?"

"Yes." Falconi's answer was firm, with no hesitation.

"Signor Falconi, my grandmother was a Falconi. You and Teresa are related, but only distantly. It gives me joy that you have found each other. I only wish that it was not in the midst of war."

Teresa stepped out onto the landing, intuition telling her that she was the topic of conversation. Silence surrounded her as she walked to her uncle.

"Teresa, Egel Falconi has asked for your hand. I've told him that I would consult you before answering. What is your answer?"

"You may tell Signor Falconi that I would be proud to be his wife, uncle. Has he also told you that I'm to be the lover of Antonio Guibega?"

"No! What is this?" asked Nando, turning to Falconi, who was now plainly visible in the first rays of the morning sun.

"It is a story to give Antonio a reason to leave his regular band of Resistance fighters periodically, and Teresa a reason to go into the mountains as your messenger. Remember, we are not only fighting Germans. We also have traitors among the Corsicans."

"A good ploy," said Nando. "Congratulations. You've made me a happy man this day." He shook Egel's hand and kissed Teresa, feeling his tears of happiness wet her face as well.

"It looks like a party up here," said Antonio, still several steps below the landing.

"Come on up, Antonio. Nando has just given me permission to marry his niece."

"Ha, she that has made that choice, I think," said Antonio, shaking Falconi's outstretched hand.

"And I have," said Teresa, hugging Antonio.

Over the next hour, Nando brought food from the cave and Teresa prepared them a breakfast of eggs, scrambled with peppers, slices of cheese, and sausage. Nando took his meal to the top floor, resuming his watch.

They had just finished eating when Nando came flying down the stairs. "Germans! Take Egel to the cave," he said to Teresa, throwing a rope ladder over the back wall. "Take these with you." He thrust the breakfast plates and cups into a leather satchel, leaving a cup and one plate with the remains of the eggs by the hearth. "They have come before, trying to catch me. Antonio and I will lead them away."

Egel took a quick look out the door and saw two motorcycles, each with a sidecar speeding from the south. He turned away, holding up four fingers. Antonio did not say a word but left immediately, heading north on a faint trail that paralleled the road.

Falconi followed Teresa over the wall and down the rope ladder, bringing with him the axe he had taken from the boat and hidden at the keep. At the bottom, Teresa gave a snap to the ropes, and the ladder fell at her feet. Egel gathered it up and followed her through boulders twice as tall as a man into the hills beyond.

The cave was as Nando had described it—cool and dark.

"How long will it take for Nando and Antonio to lose them?" asked Egel, after they were settled.

"It'll depend on whether there are only four," answered Teresa. "If they have called for more, or if they have dogs, then we might be here all day and night."

They had been in the cave for just over two hours when Falconi heard a soft scrape of something hard against a boulder. Two forms stepped across the entrance, shadowed against the opening of the cave, their faces hidden, rifles held at the ready, the Lugers at their waists outlined by the contrast of the bright sunlight outside. Egel moved to the side of the cave, holding the axe, its spiked end leveled at the chest of the man on the left.

"Signore?" came the soft question.

"Nando," answered Egel, recognizing the voice and lowering the axe that was ready to strike.

Nando and Antonio entered the cave, opening their arms, putting aside the weapons that had been carried by the Germans who had pursued them.

"The Germans thought they were chasing one man. They died quietly for their mistake," said Antonio. "We'd have been here sooner, but we left the bodies on the road, two kilometers toward Ajaccio from Falcon's Roost, along with a road wire. We hid the motorcycles where you left yours and brought yours back."

They spent the rest of the daylight hours in discussion. "Other than the aircraft, which Teresa and I experienced for ourselves, what advantages do the Germans have over us?" asked Egel of the two men.

"Speed," answered Antonio. "They move their troops quickly. We've never had more than ten minutes in any attack before troops show up."

"It's not their vehicles that are their greatest advantage. It's their radios. They leapfrog us, one group telling the other exactly what to expect. It is their radios that bring the troops, not just the personnel carriers," said Teresa.

"That's an advantage we must have as well, then. Where can we obtain radios—not the Germans' but our own?"

"Getting German radios isn't a problem. As for our own," said Antonio, "there is an American submarine that brings supplies to the Resistance – the Casablanca. It runs them ashore near Bonifacio. I could arrange for you to meet it."

"Do so," agreed Egel. "I would meet the captain of this submarine."

Chapter Sixteen

Frankfurt, Germany, August 2003

"Well, then," said Schiller, turning to Mats as they finished breakfast. "We should go. I want to phone Inspector Fitzgerald this morning and introduce you. He is the head of the scientific section of the Garda and the information about the bullets is bound to be important to him."

He stood up and started toward the door as his assistant, Hans, motioned the waiter for the bill.

Outside the hotel, Mats, Suzanne, and Schiller got into the police car and waited for Hans to arrive. As they were waiting, Nando and Brian came out of the hotel and headed down the street in the direction of the dojo. The old man walked in a straight line; the boy zigzagged this way and that, covering twice as much ground in the same amount of time. They were almost at the corner, a block away, when Hans hurried out of the hotel and walked quickly toward the car.

"Sorry, I had to sign yesterday's check as well," Hans apologized as he slid behind the steering wheel.

The engine came immediately to life and Hans began a U-turn in front of the hotel. The car's turning radius was small but the street even narrower, forcing him to use reverse, backing up before being able to complete the turn. As the car again started forward, Mats caught sight of a powerfully built blond man moving out of the hotel and looking down the street in the direction that Nando and Brian had just taken. The man held a radio to his ear and was speaking with quick, jerky nods of the head.

He fits the description Ramondo gave of the man who followed Brian yesterday, thought Mats. He watched as the man started down the street after Brian and Nando.

"We have to go back," Mats said, placing a hand on Schiller's shoulder.

"Why?" asked Schiller as the driver started down the street, showing no inclination to stop or slow down.

"Please turn around," said Mats.

"What have you forgotten?"

Mats felt a sense of urgency as he saw the shape of Ramondo coming out of the hotel at a run. Hans kept a steady pace through traffic, determined to head toward the station until he received orders to the contrary from the lieutenant.

"You must turn this car around." Mats tightened his grip on Schiller's shoulder. "Now."

"Turn the car around." Schiller's order was crisp, and it was instantly obeyed.

"They're going shopping on Steffel Strasse two blocks north of the hotel," Mats told Hans.

"Please hurry," added Suzanne.

Another nod from Schiller and Hans flicked on a switch that sent a whirling pattern of light from the roof of the car.

Ramondo had stayed in back of the blond man, preferring to remain unseen, but it had caused him to lose sight of Nando. Only after the man with the phone turned the corner onto Steffel Strasse did Ramondo see the danger.

Nando had stopped on the street between the stairs to the dojo and the cutlery shop, waiting for Ramondo.

Ramondo could see past them to the other corner, where a gang of young toughs moved down the street. It was not an unusual sight in this part of Frankfurt, but even at a distance of three blocks, Ramondo could see that one of the gang was holding a radio to his ear. Then the man pointed at Brian and there was no doubt.

Ramondo had three blocks to cover, the gang of toughs less than one. They moved casually, disguising their purpose with careless, sauntering movements. Only when they had closed to twenty-five meters did they rush Nando and the boy, suddenly brandishing clubs and lengths of chain.

Ramondo was still half a block away, dodging through automobile traffic and the blaring of horns, when the toughs first made contact. There were eight of them, all wearing leather jackets and jeans. Their heads were either completely shaved or close-cropped. All were armed with weapons.

The first two to reach their prey laughed as Nando stepped in front of Brian. One lashed out with a length of chain aimed at Nando's head. The chain clinked and the old man seemed to stumble, his left hand moving up to ward off the blow. The chain, instead of finding Nando's head, wrapped around his forearm. As he stumbled, the thug at the other end of the chain was pulled against him. They touched only briefly, and then Nando straightened, the chain now in his hand as his assailant slumped to the sidewalk. The rest of the gang became cautious, more because of the chain whirling in Nando's hand than because of their fallen friend. Three of the skinheads encircled Nando, forcing the man and the boy apart.

Ramondo flew into the four men who had separated to attack Brian, his foot striking one man at an angle, just below the clavicle. The man flew backward, his head hitting the blacktop of the street with a sickening thud, his life saved only by the angle of Ramondo's blow. His forward momentum spent by the kick, Ramondo came down lightly, in a crouched position. With one swift movement, he blocked the club wielded by the second of the two, moving inside the blow and delivering a jab with the tips of his fingers. He could feel the cracking of cartilage as he pulled his hand back, the sharp exhaling of the man's breath as he fell gurgling to the sidewalk. All of Ramondo's training had been directed to this moment: to serve the Falconi in battle. Without really knowing or expecting it, and against the training of his French instructors, he let out a battle cry that the Guibegas had used for over a millennium in service of the Falconi.

Ramondo turned back to Brian, forcing himself to ignore Nando at his back. It was the boy who must be protected. Nando had been brought to Germany to safeguard him. If he was hurt, so be it. It was his duty. A skinhead had grabbed Brian around the neck. Ramondo recognized the man as the one with the radio. Now his hand held a black club high above Brian's head. He had seen what had happened to his companions and used Brian to shield himself from Ramondo. Behind him, Ramondo could hear screams in German, testimony that his uncle was holding his own.

"Behind you!"

In warning him, Nando saved Ramondo's life. A club came down hard from behind, hitting the point of his shoulder but missing his head. Ramondo felt his entire right side go numb, his right arm useless as he fell to one knee. The skinhead who had hit him raised his club for a two-handed blow; Ramondo saw the man's shadow. He rotated on his left foot, his right swinging in a wide arc, catching the side of the club wielder's knee. As the man screamed in pain, falling forward, Ramondo sprang, kicking upward, the toe of his running shoe finding the hollow beneath the man's jaw. The man's head snapped back, carrying the rest of his body with it, blood running in rivulets from his mouth and nose. As his attacker dropped to the street, Ramondo willed his injured body again toward the man holding Brian.

Brian was pulled backward by the thug with the radio while two skinheads advanced on him from the front. Brian's arms were pinned to his sides, but his legs were free. He kicked the man directly in front of him in the kneecap. Ramondo had taught him always to aim for the knee of a taller opponent, and at thirteen years of age, Brian found that almost everyone fit that description. The man grunted and stumbled backward. His partner moved to help the man attacking Nando, rather than face Ramondo.

When Ramondo was hit with the club, Brian's captor freed his club hand for a blow. Only restrained by one arm, Brian reached into his jacket pocket and brought out a knife, its fold of gray cardboard sheathing still covering the blade. The man had his club in his left hand, his right wrapped around Brian's chest from behind. Ramondo was still partially stunned, his movements sluggish, his right shoulder sloped at an unnatural angle. He could only watch as Brian took all his weight off of his legs. The man holding him tightened his grip on Brian's chest but could not prevent him from slipping down against his own groin. Then Brian straightened, twisting, not to gain release from the hold, but turning into it. The knife came around as his legs added strength to its upward thrust.

Brian had been taught to aim at the neck just below the jaw, but in their practice sessions, Ramondo had not been holding a club. As Brian thrust, the man brought the club down, deflecting the blade. The knife striking the neck would have been fatal. Instead, the blade cut through the leather jacket into the thin skin of the man's armpit. There it found a nexus rich in nerves and vessels. The cut nerve caused the butt of the club to jerk downward with a contraction of the muscles they once controlled. The club hit Brian on the forehead at the start of his hairline. Ramondo watched as Brian tried to pull the knife out for a second thrust. He never completed it, as he fell to the pavement.

Ramondo willed his body to move but the damage to his right shoulder slowed his actions at some level of the brain lower than he could control. As Brian fell to the sidewalk, Ramondo launched a kick before the man could club him again, but it lacked his usual power and snap. It landed hard enough to knock the man off balance, away from Brian's crumpled form but not hard enough to cause real damage.

"IEEE TAHHH!"

The momentum of Ramondo's kick spun him. He saw Wolf Schmidt run from the building housing the dojo toward Nando and the boy. Ramondo felt his coordination returning, his movements becoming once again smooth. Brian's assailant, holding his arm to his side, had dropped his club and taken off down the street. Ramondo looked quickly at Nando and Schmidt, standing over the boy. They needed no help.

The four remaining skinheads had broken off their attack and were running away, two to the north and one to the south, hobbling after the leader with the phone. Four lay bleeding on the sidewalk. Of these, one was dead, while another was not far from it, unable to gain air through his crushed larynx. Wolf Schmidt's opponent lay bleeding from the mouth and nose, unconscious, the copper smell of blood mixing with the scent of fear. The thug who had initiated the attack on Nando was lying on his back, still alive, whimpering, holding his broken arm, blood running from a gash from above his right eye.

Brian felt no pain as the club hit. The first sensation involved blinding flashes of red and yellow light, and then a sudden awareness that his legs didn't work. Bright lights blazed before his eyes. When they subsided, in his mind he saw the waters off the north coast of Ireland, the smell of seaweed and salt air filling his lungs. Behind closed eyelids, he recognized the small island off of Fairies Point and wondered how he had traveled so far without knowing it. Then he saw the Viking longboat beached in the small inlet directly underneath where he stood, and he knew, as he slumped to the street that he had again entered the world of his dreams ...

Fairies Point, Ireland—945 AD

"My men need women." Brian was surprised at the power in the voice, and then he realized that he was experiencing this vision through the mind and eyes of his ancestor, Kjell Falkhand.

The priest in front of him, clothed in a rough, hooded brown robe, nodded. He recognized the truth in what Falkhand said, though he did not agree with it. Father Cian had returned each month to take sheep and tend to the needs of the shepherds left to watch them. Each time, he was given something from the treasure the Vikings had taken from Bloodaxe, and each time, he instructed Kjell's crew for a period of three days in the religion of the white Christ. Odin promised never-ending women and drink in Valhalla; the priest's Christ offered peace and beauty.

"Women offer earthly pleasures but are the source of the original sin. In Heaven, God's other gifts are so great that sex is not needed."

That can't be right, Kjell thought.

Entrance to Valhalla, with its plentiful virgins and drink, was predicated on dying with a sword in one's hand. Entrance into Christ's afterlife was granted as a prize for obeying the priest's laws. It was no wonder these Christians were so easily conquered. While Kjell understood the concept of the reward of a perfect life after death, he could not understand how such a peaceful, loving God could put his religion in the hands of such strict and self-serving priests. Odin had priests to help instruct mortal men in the ways of the gods, but they were warriors first and shamans second.

Kjell knew that sooner or later the desire for women, or the lack of women to desire, would prove the unraveling of even the most hardened group of men. They could raid for women, but the winter weather made it wise to avoid the open sea, and he didn't want to raid nearby, as it would harm the trade relationship he hoped to establish.

"If you can't help us in this matter, I will ask the clans on Fairies Point," said Kjell, hoping to force Father Cian to aid him.

"The MacDonlevy, the Nulty, and the MacSwiggan live on the point," said Father Cian. "They are an unholy lot. There are parts of this land that still hold with the old beliefs. You should not deal with them nor land on the point. There are unholy things done there."

Kjell suspected that the priest wanted to keep all contact with the people of the mainland mediated through himself, or at least through the Church. His men needed women, and the priest was using them as a bargaining piece.

"Give me two days," said the priest, at last.

"Two days? Father Cian," said Kjell, hiding his true feelings behind his piercing blue eyes.

"We have many widows. Most have lost husbands to the sea," said the priest. "Our round coracles are not as stable as your craft. Perhaps I could find fifteen women who, after a suitable tithe to the Church, would be allowed to go to the island. Of course, they would have to be properly married in the eyes of the Church, and your men taking them as brides would have to convert to Christianity."

✤ ✤ ✤

Frankfurt, Germany—2003

The police car came around the corner, lights flashing, horn alarm blaring. Mats threw his door opened before the car had stopped.

"Brian!"

"He is hurt, signore," answered Nando in Corsican, kneeling next to the crumpled boy.

With a quick nod to Nando, Ramondo sprinted away, following the man whom Brian had wounded. He went past the police car as Schiller was getting out.

"Call for backup and an ambulance. Quickly!" shouted Schiller.

Schiller's backup caught the three thugs who had run, returning them to the scene of the fight. Only the leader, whom Brian had knifed, had escaped. Schiller took charge of the scene, trying to make sense of the attack and the carnage. He was methodical, establishing order in an arena that could easily have become chaotic. He went first to Brian, thankful to find that the boy was still breathing. Nando was kneeling at the boy's side.

"What is wrong with your hand?" asked Schiller as the paramedics arrived and began attending to Brian.

"Better my arm than my head," said Nando. One of the medics took his arm and gently prodded it with his fingers. About two inches up from the wrist, Nando winced.

"He has a broken arm," the medic explained to Schiller.

"Take him to the hospital after the boy." Schiller turned to the rest of the bodies that were spread across the pavement.

The first ambulance took Brian, unconscious, to the hospital with Suzanne.

"And who are you?" asked Schiller of the large man standing protectively next to Nando.

"I am Wolfgang Schmidt. I own the karate school." Schmidt pointed to the sign under the windows of the dojo two doors down from where they stood.

"How are you mixed up in this?" asked Schiller, remembering what he had read about Germany's answer to Jean-Claude Van Damme.

"I was upstairs when I heard a disturbance. I saw these scumbags, eight of them, attacking an old man and a boy. What would you have done?"

Schiller looked at the array of clubs, chains, and knives scattered about the pavement and wondered that exactly.

"You're dead, man. We know where you live, you bastard," hissed a skinhead who had tried to run away and been brought back for Schiller to question.

"I think your driver wants you," said Schmidt, pointing over Schiller's shoulder. As Schiller turned toward Hans, Schmidt sent a kick into the face of the skinhead who had threatened him. Schiller turned back to see Schmidt still standing casually at Nando's side and the skinhead keeled over backward on the pavement, blood pouring from his nose and mouth.

"What is happening to Germany that we produce such scum?" asked Schmidt.

Schiller had no answer.

"Where was the jogger when you arrived? Did you know him?" asked Schiller, ignoring the unconscious man bleeding at his feet.

"I didn't see any jogger. I saw the old man and the boy being attacked. Maybe there was someone else, I just didn't notice."

Nando was even less help. He thought the man who had attacked him had hit himself with his own chain. He seemed confused and only vaguely remembered a jogger. As for Mats, he had said he was concerned when he saw a man with a radio to his ear follow Brian and Nando from the hotel. That was why he had asked Schiller to turn the car around. He knew nothing about the jogger and had only seen what Schiller had seen upon arriving in the car.

Schiller could not help but feel he was not getting the full story from Falconi. It seemed inconceivable that a stranger would join a fight, then run off without anyone learning a thing about him. The three skinheads that his men had captured all told the same story. They were to attack the old man and the boy for a payoff in drugs. Their leader, Ernst, who had brokered the deal might know more than that, but they didn't. Ernst was well known to the police and would not be hard to find, especially if he was injured.

Mats approached Schiller as he finished questioning the skinheads. "I'm worried about Brian. If you are finished with me for now, could I go to the hospital?"

"I don't need to tell you not to leave Germany without my permission," said Schiller. "Is there anything else you would like to tell me before you go?"

Mats hesitated, only slightly, but it was enough to tell Schiller that he was right in thinking there was more that Falconi was not telling.

"If I think of anything else, I'll let you know. Can I please go to see Brian?" Mats' concern for the boy was obvious. Schiller noticed that he had not asked about Nando, who had also been taken to the hospital.

Schiller knew on some level that he was being played. There were so many unanswered questions. Where was the leader of the skinheads? Who was the jogger and why had he joined a fight that was so unequal? Also, there was no sign of a large blond man with a radio, the one Mats said he had seen. Either he was fictional, or he had fled. Mats had told him he was worried about Brian's safety on the first day, and he had all but accused Rohde of Lars Bjursten's death. Schiller had just caught a glimpse of the man in the running suit as he went after the last skinhead, yet no one seemed to know who he was. The injured thugs, and those who had been caught by his backup, said the jogger had caused the most damage.

The attack had been witnessed by two shop owners. One ran a bakery directly across the street from where the fight had occurred. He had been placing fresh loaves of pumpernickel in his display window when the skinheads attacked Nando. Not only had he watched the fight—from behind a door he had quickly locked—but he was more than interested in telling Schiller about it.

"I knew the skinheads were trouble when I first saw them," he said into Schiller's tape recorder.

"Where were they, then?" asked Schiller.

The baker pointed to a spot two shops down from where the bloodstains marked the point of the attack.

"I was worried about being robbed. I locked my door. Then, all of a sudden, they run toward the old man and the boy. One of them was swinging a chain. I couldn't see what happened next, exactly, because they had their backs to me, but I think the old man was struck, because he stumbled. But instead of the old man going down, the thug with the chain ended up on the sidewalk. He must have hit himself with his own chain!"

Ja, Shiller thought to himself. *Old helpless Nando Guibega.*

"And what happened next?" asked Schiller, concealing his thoughts.

"Well, the old man started grappling with another one, and by that time all of the thugs had arrived." The baker stopped for effect, getting a rolling of Schiller's hand in encouragement. "That is when the jogger joined in the fight."

"The jogger?"

"Yes, a jogger, a German, I think. I have seen him before, running on this street. He came running from that direction." The man pointed toward the hotel.

"You say he was German?"

"He was tall, blond, but not as blond as you, Lieutenant. And thin. He wore a black and green running suit, Adidas I think."

"And then?" asked Schiller, not wanting the man to start debating the merits of different manufacturers' running suits.

"The jogger was hit by a club. The boy also was clubbed and went down to the ground and that was when Herr Schmidt rushed to the rescue. If he had not helped, I fear the others would be dead."

"Herr Schmidt? That is Wolfgang Schmidt, the owner of the karate studio?"

"Yes. By this time, there was quite a lot of shouting. I'll tell you one thing; I wouldn't want to be those skinheads with Herr Schmidt in the fight."

"And then?"

"Then your car came around the corner and everyone started running."

"Why would the jogger flee?" asked Schiller, more to himself than to the baker.

"He went after the thug that struck the boy," answered the baker, making sure he was speaking directly into the small microphone.

"Then why hasn't he returned?"

"Perhaps he hasn't caught him yet."

From the corner, Bernd had watched the attack. The street was almost deserted. It should only have taken a few seconds. Then a man had run past him and joined the fight. At first it seemed the odds were overwhelming, but the young man in the jogging suit was very skilled. Bernd watched with fascination as two skinheads went down quickly from his kicks. Still, he had done little more than disrupt what seemed the inevitable conclusion. Surprisingly, the old man and the boy were not the easy victims he had thought they would be. Bernd had thought of joining the action, but while he would have helped, he would also have been seen, and this was to be strictly another skinhead attack on foreigners. While Rohde would applaud the boy's death, it would not please him if it was viewed as anything other than random violence. When the jogger had been struck from behind, it had seemed their plan would still work, but then another man had joined the fight. Why two Germans would pick this incident to butt into was beyond him. Most of his countrymen thought they'd had enough of foreigners, especially Muslims and Jews. When there was a skinhead attack, there was usually no interference.

Then the police car had come around the corner. At least Ernst had escaped after clubbing the boy. Bernd had watched carefully; the boy had fallen to the ground and had not moved. He would have preferred to have seen five or six more blows to his head, but it appeared that one had been enough.

Moving to the Mercedes, he used the radio to call Ernst.

"Ja," came the answer.

"Where are you now?"

"The boy stabbed me. I have to get to a hospital."

"Where are you now?" Bernd repeated. "I'll help you."

"I'm on Schomberg Strasse."

"Listen carefully. Go to the corner of Schomberg and Steffel. I'll be there in less than a minute. I know a doctor."

"Hurry. I'm bleeding."

Bernd put the communicator back in his pocket and took out his car keys. If the boy was as dead as he appeared to be, the plan had not gone that badly after all. The skinheads knew nothing.

Yes, he said to himself as the motor roared to life. *Things have worked out quite well.*

Frankfurt, Universitätsklinikum Hospital—2003

Brian hovered on the cusp of consciousness. His arms and legs would not move, nor his eyes open, but he could smell the stringent odor of antiseptic and feel the sharp prick of something on his arm. He tried to open his eyes, but a heaviness overwhelmed him, and he felt himself returning to his dream. Slowly the smell of antiseptic was replaced by that of unwashed bodies and the tang of salt air. In his mind he opened his eyes and saw men in the longboat looking toward him, a short expanse of grey water before them.

Fairies Point, Ireland—944 AD

Kjell had agreed to the priest's plan with the stipulation that his men had the right to pick their brides. He had left five men on the mainland to pick the women and marry them according to the priest's ritual. Their safety was assured by Father Cian, and Kjell would return in three days, picking them up and leaving five more. The priest seemed surprised that Kjell would not take a woman himself until all his men had satisfied their needs.

As they rowed on their outward course, Kjell looked up the steep cliffs to what was known as Fairies Point. The priest had warned him that the peninsula was enchanted and the old magic of the island still held there. There were some places that the word of Christ had not yet reached, and this point of land was one of them. Father Cian had seemed anxious as he warned him about the area. Banshee, little people, and dwarfs, he said, roamed there at dusk, casting spells that even he could not counter. They were not the same shadow creatures, trolls, goblins, and giants that were feared in the north lands, but Kjell felt the same uneasiness in the telling.

As they rowed to the north, Kjell saw a shadow in the cliff. From sea it looked as if the cliff was unbroken, but now, with the sun quartering, there was a deep shadow that helped with depth perception. Kjell ordered his men to row nearer while he made sure that his eyes were not betraying him. Along the south-facing border of the bay there were many landings, but each one they passed had smoke from fires rising above it. Kjell suspected that one day he might need a place to land without being under the eyes of Father Cian, or the MacDonlevies, Nulties, and MacSwiggans, for that matter.

As they swayed up and down in the swell, Kjell became sure that what he was seeing was a narrow cleft in the cliff barely wider than the longboat with oars out. With caution, he moved his ship closer. As he did, a miniature fjord opened to him. Just inside its exit to the sea was a steep, sandy beach.

"Watch for rocks," he shouted to his bowman as he carefully guided the strokes of his men to set him on the tiny strand. "Wait here. I will be back before the sun is an hour from setting."

Kjell jumped ashore. He started up a path leading to the plateau above. It was a zigzag route that looked rarely traveled. For five minutes he climbed back and forth up the high cliff before finally reaching the top. The trail opened on nearly flat land, running slightly downhill away from the cliff. In the distance, Kjell saw a stand of trees.

He was halfway to the woods when he stopped, afraid to move. A lull in the wind brought a sound to him that was at once sweet and foreboding. It came in snatches from the woods in front of him, the wind breaking the pattern before it reached his ears. Kjell moved forward cautiously, taking care to set his feet in places that would not betray his advance. The sound became clearer as he moved forward, and at last he was able to identify it as music. It was a harp, an instrument he had heard played before but not with the skill of the musician in the woods. It was as if the gods were striking the strings, creating a melody meant for their enjoyment alone.

Kjell remembered the priest's warning about the land on which he now stood: enchanted magic, he had said. What if the harp was indeed being played by the fairies who were supposed to live here? His need to find the source of the music overcame his fear, and he moved again, slowly, so as not to startle the musician.

He had reached the woods when a voice joined the music of the harp. It was a woman's voice, and it fell like small silver bells on his ears. It ranged up when the harp went down, providing a harmony at once beautiful and enchanting. The words were in the Irish tongue, making Kjell grateful for the time he had spent with the shepherds and the priest learning the language.

The song was about the beauty of the stream and how it was like the love of a young woman, giving life to all things it touched before finally falling to the sea, its usefulness spent on the journey. They were sad lyrics, set to music so sweet that it made Kjell sink into the melancholy feeling that washed over him. He waited until the song had stopped before he moved through the last of the dense brush to the stream just beyond.

Next to the stream was a small hill, and on top of it was a bench of carved stone. Sitting on the bench was a young girl. In her lap was a harp, called a clairseach by the natives, the sound box held between her knees. Tears cascaded down her cheeks, wetting her full white gown. She was both the singer and the musician.

Kjell moved into the small clearing and sat quietly on the edge of a log below the hill. His eyes filled with tears that matched the girl's, so tender and touching was the song. He watched as she pressed her eyelids together, causing another gush of tears. As he reached up to wipe them away, he made a rustling sound.

Surprise, not alarm, showed on the girl's face as she looked at him. For several minutes they remained still, neither saying a word, the sound of the water moving in the stream providing a background for their thoughts. Then, as if she had come to a decision, the girl strummed the harp once more, this time in a lively rhythm, reminding Kjell of the dancing flight of fireflies. He sat listening as the girl joined her voice to the harp for just one chorus before again allowing the instrument alone to tell the story. When she finished, Kjell could only smile and nod.

The girl was perhaps fifteen, already entering womanhood, but having not quite arrived. She was thin with long arms and fingers that were delicate to behold as they coaxed the harp to do her bidding. Her skin was fair, like that of most of the natives, almost as fair as Kjell's, but unlike his, her hair was black. Her eyes mirrored the water of the stream, a deep blue, reflecting the shadows the trees cast upon her.

She played a third ballad, one about the sea and a mermaid who had once been a princess, forever banned from the land by the spell of a sorcerer.

Kjell thought again about the priest's warning and wondered if he was falling under a magic spell, so enchanting were the setting, the music, and the girl. Then, as she strummed the harp for the final chord, the base chords of the instrument echoing from the sound box, she spoke to him.

"You must go." Her voice was as musical in speech as it had been in song.

"I am Kjell. I am sorry if I have disturbed you."

"You've not disturbed me. You have done me honor by giving my songs your tears." She stood, holding the harp in front of her. "You must go before you are harmed, for then I will be to blame for not making you heed my warning."

"I fear nothing but leaving your presence," said Kjell.

"But leave is what you must do, and now. My keepers will be here at any moment, and it will not bode well for either of us. How did you come to be here?"

"I came by boat." Kjell pointed to where the creek emptied into the gorge. "There's a path."

"It's best that you retrace your steps, and quickly."

"I would know your name. To which family do you belong?"

"My name is Ecca and I belong to no family."

Placing the harp down, she moved quickly to his side, taking his hand and guiding him toward the edge of the forest.

"I am a chief in my own land," Kjell told her.

"That will avail you not if my masters find you here. Where is the path by which you climbed the cliff?"

Kjell was hastened by her sense of urgency. He pointed at the high grass that still showed the steps he had taken earlier. She took him by the hand and led him quickly to the cliff's edge. She stopped and looked over it. Kjell heard sounds behind him and turned. Four men were just exiting the woods at a full run. Kjell weighed the odds of combat. He had spent the last five months avoiding trouble with the natives. This was not the time to change his strategy.

"Will they harm you?" he asked.

"No. They protect me, at least until mid-summer."

"Will I see you again?"

"I'll come to the pool again on the morning ten days hence. If you are already there, in hiding, I'll sing for you again."

"I'll be there, fair Ecca."

"Please be safe, Kjell." She smiled at him, turning away, running toward the men, who were now less than forty paces away.

Kjell watched her move away for several steps before leaping down the trail at a full run. He stopped on a rocky shelf just twenty feet above the beach and looked back up at the top of the cliff. A man stood outlined against the sky, holding the girl by the arm. There was tension in his posture, as if Ecca was straining away from his grip. The man was dressed in a full robe of the same white material as Ecca's dress. He had a staff in his hand but no weapons. The man was almost as tall as Kjell and did nothing but stare, standing still, as if evaluating Kjell as an enemy. Without looking away, Kjell ran down the last part of the trail and was pulled onto his longboat by his men.

CHAPTER SEVENTEEN

Frankfurt, Germany—2003

Bernd moved the Mercedes through traffic, slowing as he looked for Ernst. There was light traffic on the street and almost no one at the intersection. He was just about to use the radio when he saw the skinhead moving toward his car from the alley across the street. The man still had on his leather jacket with an American Confederate flag stitched across the shoulders. Bernd could see the blood stain that had soaked most of its left side. As the Ernst neared, Bernd got out and went to the trunk, taking out a dark blue woolen blanket. He opened the door, placing the blanket over the seat and headrest before moving aside for the wounded man.

"The god-damned kid had a knife. I'm bleeding like hell."

"I'll get you to a doctor," said Bernd, reaching over and helping the man into the car. "Is the boy dead?"

"I think so. I clubbed him pretty good," said the Ernst, his bravado returning in the safety of the car. "Some guy helped the kid. He stopped me from cracking the kid's head a few more times to make sure. Then another guy jumped in as well. I thought since I had done what you wanted, I'd better cut out."

Bernd pulled the Mercedes away from the curb, back into the flow of traffic.

"You did well. You've earned your reward, but first let's get you to a doctor." Bernd turned the car into a parking garage under a large office building. Inside he drove down two floors, backing into a stall partially hidden by the elevator column.

"This doctor is good. I've used him myself," said Bernd as he opened the door for his passenger.

Ernst got out, slamming the door shut with his knee. He had made two steps toward the elevator when Bernd grabbed him from behind, raising his chin expertly with his left hand as he severed the man's carotid artery and trachea with the knife he held in his right. Bernd continued to hold Ernst upright until his blood stopped spurting. He did not want blood on the car. He was amazed at how much blood the heart of a dying man could pump through a severed artery, as well as how far it spurted. He could feel the hot moistness on his hand and fingers. As the man stopped struggling, he continued the cut down across his chest toward the blood-soaked armpit. Bernd took the radio, wrapping it in the blanket, which he threw into the trunk of the Mercedes.

Mats and Suzanne sat at Lieutenant Schiller's desk. It had taken over three hours for Brian to regain consciousness, and Suzanne had been with him every minute. Mats had remained with Schiller for over an hour at the scene of the attack while the shop owners related their accounts of the assault into his tape recorder. In most cases, eyewitness accounts vary greatly, but in this instance, they were remarkably consistent. Only the role of the mystery jogger varied from witness to witness. The shopkeepers both gave the same account of the man's arrival and his part in the fight. Nando Guibega had not seen him at all, or so he said. Wolfgang Schmidt had testified that no one but the old man and the boy had been fighting the skinheads when he had looked out of his window. Brian, when he had awoken in the hospital, could not remember anything of the fight, neither the skinheads nor the jogger who had been his savior. His last recollection was that he and Nando were on their way to return a knife they had purchased. He couldn't remember stabbing his assailant, an event that all the non-combatant witnesses agreed had occurred just before the man had clubbed Brian into unconsciousness.

Of the four skinheads who had run, three had been picked up by the police only minutes after they had fled the scene. The other came across Schiller's desk as a homicide report. A skinhead wearing a leather jacket had been found dead in a parking garage two miles from where the attack had taken place. The other skinheads confirmed that it was indeed Ernst Graf, the man who had organized the attack.

"We seem to solve one mystery, only to have it lead to another," commented Schiller, picking up papers and tapping them on the edge before laying them back down on his desk. "Now we have accounted for all eight of the men who attacked your friends, including the one that the boy stabbed. The blood on the paring knife matches his blood type, and the wound under his arm matches as well."

"What is the problem, then?" asked Mats.

"The problem is how he got dead. It was made to look like the boy's knife thrust had killed the man. A cut was made from the puncture wound under the arm diagonally up across his pectoral region and through his throat."

"You're not blaming Brian for his death, are you?" asked Suzanne.

"Someone wants us to," said Schiller, "but they didn't think it out too well. The suspect died in a parking garage two miles from where Brian stabbed him. He couldn't have gotten that far without a car."

Mats sighed his relief that Brian wouldn't have to live with the man's death.

"If he drove there and died, you would expect his car still to be there," said Schiller, looking intently at Mats. "Then there is the matter of the wound under his arm. It had already started to clot when the man died. Either the man had the fastest-clotting blood in the world, or the wound across his throat was done later. From the looks of the amount of blood in the garage, it was done there. Then, to top it off, there is the matter of the radio."

"Radio?" asked Mats, although somehow, he already knew the answer.

"One of the other skinheads said that Graf, that was his name, Ernst Graf, had gotten a package with a radio in it, along with some money and drugs. He talked to someone at least three times. There was no radio on the corpse, yet he didn't appear to have been robbed. I suspect when we find the man in the running suit, we'll find the radio and our murderer. Witnesses say the jogger went off after the dead man. It looks like he found him and killed him. I've put out an all points arrest alert for the man."

"A man with a radio came out of the hotel just as we were driving off," said Mats. "He was peering down the street in the direction Nando and Brian had taken. It worried me. It's why I had you turn the car around."

"Yes, you said that before. What did he look like?"

"He was no skinhead. He had on a suit. He was about six foot, thick through the shoulders and neck, short blond hair. His back was to me. I could recognize the body but not his face."

"What worried you about him?"

"The other night," said Mats, choosing his words carefully, "there was a man watching us. At first, we thought he was one of yours. He was muscular, blond with short hair. When he left, Nando followed him to the Municher Brewery. There's your connection. The connection is Rohde."

"Why didn't you tell me someone was watching you?"

"I didn't want to alarm Brian at breakfast, and there wasn't time in the car. When I saw the man with the radio come out while we were turning, it made me nervous."

"Three men dead, four if you count Bjursten. Death sort of follows you around, doesn't it?" asked Schiller in an accusing tone.

"May I remind you, Inspector, that we wouldn't even be in Germany if you hadn't requested that we come? Eight German thugs attack an old man and a boy, and you act as if we are to blame."

"Easy, Herr Falconi," soothed Schiller. "I am aware of all that. It's just that men are dead, and you are involved, even if you don't know how."

"I know how it looks," said Mats. "I'd help you if I could."

"Something you should know," said Schiller softly. "There were three clubs and a chain dropped at the scene. One of them had the prints of the dead man in the garage. All three were the same—well made, hollowed out at the end, and filled with lead. They were made of wood, oak barrels with ash handles. It kind of ties them all together with Bjursten's death and your bullets, doesn't it?"

"Damn!" exclaimed Mats.

"We can be fairly certain they were after the old man or the boy, with a man guiding them by phone," said Schiller. "With his second cousin and his parents already murdered, it's most likely the boy."

"I'm sure Rohde is connected to this," said Mats.

"Rohde might very well be involved, but I don't have anything on him, no motive. The work he contracted from

Bjursten was paid for. None of your letters say anything about him, other than that he commissioned a brewing process. And why would he want to kill an Irish junge? It just doesn't make sense."

"Rohde was a hardcore Nazi," said Mats, "despite what you don't tell me about what's in his war file. He was in charge of crushing the Resistance on Corsica. He was brutal. Rohde sent a lot of good men and women to German concentration camps. He tried to kill Nando."

"Are you saying it was Nando they were after?"

"No, Nando had never been to Ireland until after Bjursten's murder and the attack on the delivery van. It's been sixty years since Rohde tried to kill him. I don't think that Rohde would even recognize him."

"What about the man in the running suit? The way he came to Brian's rescue, I suspect that you know who he is."

"I hired him to act as Brian's bodyguard, only the attack was so sudden that he was caught a block away. He didn't kill the skinhead in the garage. He followed him but lost him when the man was picked up at the corner of Schomberg and Steffel, at least that is where the trail of blood ended at the curb."

"What's his name? Where is he now?"

"I will tell you only if your promise me that you will not charge him for the deaths of the skinheads who attacked Brian."

"That was strictly self-defense. There were enough eyewitnesses that he has nothing to worry about."

"His name is Ramondo Guibega. Until recently he was with the French National Security agency. I will have him phone you."

"He must come in."

"He has already left Germany to repair a broken shoulder caused by one of the skinhead's clubs. If you still need him, when he can travel again, he'll come back."

"I could put out a warrant for him."

"You could. I told you about him because I don't want you barking up the wrong tree, wasting time looking for him for the murder in the garage. Phone Inspector Medau. Give him Ramondo's name. Medau will give you his background and assure you, as do I, that he is not your murderer. As for us, I think you can see why it's to both your and our advantage to have people think that Ramondo was just some passing German, a good Samaritan. It would be best that whoever is after Brian shouldn't know that he is being protected. It would just make a bodyguard like Ramondo less effective. It was he who followed the German who was watching us to the Municher Brewing company's offices."

Now things make more sense, thought Schiller, tapping his pencil on his desk. "You're right. I would have spent a lot of effort finding your bodyguard."

"One thing that might add to your worries instead of reducing them," said Mats. "During the War when Rohde was on Corsica, he was effective because he had men inside the Resistance. It's how he operates. I would bet that he has contacts inside your police force."

"It's not likely but thank you for the information. I will check to see if anyone has shown an interest lately," said Schiller. "I see no reason not to tell you more about Dieter Rohde. You know he was in Corsica in charge of an SS squad ordered to stop the Resistance. He was being flown to Britain when his plane crashed in northern Spain. He was presumed dead, but a year later he turned up in Berlin. From his file, it appears that his account was never really believed by the Reich. He was scarred from burns and never trusted again with command. Somehow, he evaded trial for war crimes. He is now quite wealthy."

"Thank you for trusting me with the information," said Mats with sincerity, shaking Schiller's hand firmly.

"There is still your Irish police problem. I'm sure that Des Fitzgerald will be able to help you. He's somewhat of a maverick, even within his own division, but if there has been any impropriety in the Donegal force, he will uncover it."

"We'll see him first thing back in Ireland, which will be as soon as Brian is able to travel. We'll book into Dublin. That's as long as you have no problem with us leaving."

"Your leaving will make my life easier. You're free to leave Germany with the same stipulation – that you return for the trial of the skinheads, or if something breaks with Bjursten's murder," said Schiller, wondering if Dieter Rohde indeed had a mole inside the department.

Nando took the elevator to the ninth floor, accompanied by a plainclothes police officer. The man had been assigned to him when he was discharged from the hospital.

"I'm too old to be breaking bones," said Nando to the young man as the elevator reached the ninth floor.

The policeman nodded; he had been warned by Lt. Schiller not to be taken in by Nando's frail old man act. Nando Guibega was old, but he was dangerous—still strong, still alert.

The elevator door opened, and the young policeman stepped out into the hallway, holding the door open with his right hand as he scanned the passageway left and right. He opened the door to Nando's room, entering first, checking the closets and the bathroom, trying the doors to the adjoining rooms and finding them locked.

"Okay," he said, motioning Nando inside, closing the door, then taking his station outside in the hall.

Inside, Nando turned on the TV and sat down on the chair next to the sofa. A minute later, Ramondo slipped from the connecting door from Mats' room, locking the door behind him before doing the same to the hallway door.

"You're so important that they need to protect you?" whispered Ramondo, as he settled down on the couch next to Nando.

"Ach, I had to allow it. They're doing the same for Brian."

"He's all right, then?" asked Ramondo, relief evident in his voice.

"He's still in the hospital. He's awake, probably with a concussion, but he'll be fine."

"I lost the trail of the one who struck Brian. I've told Signor Falconi."

"He's no longer a concern. He's dead. Signor Falconi told the police who you are but that you're out of the country."

"Why? No one got a good look at me."

"They thought you murdered the one that got away. Someone slit his throat. Signor Falconi wants the police looking for him, not you. How is your shoulder?"

"I've already seen a doctor. I told him I fell off a bike. It's my collarbone. I won't be able to use my right arm for six weeks."

Nando saw for the first time that his nephew's right arm was immobilized, strapped tightly to his side. "Three months for me," said Nando, raising his cast.

"What will Signor Falconi do?"

"He's going back to Ireland as soon as Brian is able to travel. I have to stay here. They want to replace the cast in a week. They are concerned because of my age that the healing of the bone could be difficult."

"Does he want me to go with him?"

"No. He wants you to leave Germany, then phone this Lieutenant Schiller. He wants you to go to Corsica and heal. He's very happy with the job you did."

"I'm not. I almost allowed Brian to be killed."

"I should have seen the danger," said Nando. "Recognized it earlier. It's my fault."

"What does Signor Falconi want me to tell the police?"

"The truth. He trusts this Lieutenant Schiller."

"Do you, Uncle?"

"Yes," said Nando. "You must do as Signor Falconi says. He wants you away from any investigation here in Germany. Go to Corsica and call Lt. Schiller. But Signor Falconi did not say how long you have to stay in Corsica. I need you to be back here in two days. Use one of your other identifications. Understand?"

"Yes."

"Good. I have unfinished business here in Germany."

Nando turned back to the TV. He seldom worried about getting old, closer to the wood. He was proud of his memory and conscious of not using it to live in the past, the trap that many old people fell into. Now, though, with the memories of Dieter Rohde overwhelming him, he allowed himself to remember the war. Before Falconi left for Ireland, he would tell him what his dreams as yet had not—things about his father, Egel.

Ramondo sat down on the couch. Nando paid him no attention, still staring at the screen, remembering...

Corsica—December 1942

The distance from Ajaccio to the southern tip of Corsica measured only seventy miles. Their small group—Egel, Teresa, Nando, and Antonio—covered it in two days. They were forced to leave the road only once to avoid a German patrol, who seemed wary of traveling at dusk.

Nando contacted Marcello Pieri, the local leader of the Resistance, just before dark. It was unusual for Nando to come to Bonifacio, but his stature was such that Pieri agreed to his request to arrange a meeting with the captain of the submarine that supplied the Resistance on the southern part of Corsica.

They spent the night separated, Nando staying with Pieri while Falconi and Teresa lay under the stars of the moonless night. Antonio knew when three in a sleeping camp would be a crowd and left after dinner, explaining that he had a friend he had neglected for months who lived on the outskirts of Bonifacio.

Two days later Nando, Teresa and Falconi rowed a mile offshore from a small inlet five miles to the west of Bonifacio and climbed out of the fishing boat onto the deck of the submarine Casablanca. They secured their boat to the sub before making their way to the sail hatch, where Captain L'Herminier waited for them. Teresa stayed in the small boat, lashed by a single line to the deck.

The captain was used to dealing with the Resistance, not only on Corsica but in Sicily. He understood the nature of the meeting and the standing of the two men who were joining him. Still, he had to be cautious of putting his vessel at risk.

Falconi and Nando followed the captain to his cabin, where the door was closed after them by a guard with a gun.

"So. What is it?" asked the captain. Nando was known to him, as he had met with him once before almost a year earlier. The other man he did not know.

"The Resistance has a traitor, probably more than one," explained Nando. "This is the leader of a secure group, an elite fighting force allied with the Resistance but separate from it. He is called Maquis."

"And your real name?" Captain L'Herminier looked at Falconi. Nando could see him evaluating Egel as he stood, his arm outstretched to shake hands.

"Maquis will do for now," said Falconi, reaching out with his right hand.

"Very well. Maquis it is," said L'Herminier, taking Egel's hand.

"He can be trusted," said Nando. "He can give you Ajaccio."

As they talked for the next half hour, Nando could see the trust building between the two men. Egel Falconi's excellent though accented English helped, but it was his manner and forthright answers to L'Herminier's questions that fostered the captain's confidence.

Falconi promised to disrupt the German efforts in the area where they were strongest, the port of Ajaccio. When he and Nando left the ship, he took with him a quarter of the supplies that had been due to be given to men of much less character in Sicily. Explosives, guns, ammunition, and most importantly a radio were loaded into the small skiff and stored expertly by Teresa.

Nando flashed a light toward shore: two short, then long.

Ashore, Antonio, with a flashlight hidden in his coat, flashed back the agreed upon signal—two longs and a short.

Even with the safe signal, they were cautious as they pulled up on the small gravel beach to the right side of the inlet. Nando and Falconi jumped out with their rifles at the ready when Antonio did not greet them. Minutes passed, and then Antonio came down the trail.

"A vehicle went by on the road. It didn't sound German, but I wanted to make sure the road was clear."

Teresa had already divided the supplies into four backpacks. Shouldering one, she passed the others to the men, and without a word, they started north.

CHAPTER EIGHTEEN

Dublin, Ireland – 2003

Inspector Desmond Fitzgerald met Mats, Suzanne, and Brian at the Dublin Airport, which for some reason reminded Mats of the one in Oakland, California. Fitzgerald reminded him of no one he'd met before. The man was slight of build—not short, but slight, like he might have been one of the great Irish milers in his youth. Mats estimated that he was in his late forties, but it was hard to tell. Fitzgerald's head might have been balding, but maybe it just looked that way because of the great bulge of his high forehead. Beneath the forehead was a face full of small features; the little eyes, nose, and mouth fit together quite nicely.

"Mr. Falconi?" he asked, as Mats presented his passport to Customs. "Des Fitzgerald." He extended his hand. "Herr Schiller, our German friend, suggested I should meet you privately before having you come to the office."

"Glad to meet you, Inspector," said Mats as the Customs officer returned his passport.

Fitzgerald's presence—his badge displayed, linked with the title of Inspector—was not lost on the official, who passed both Brian and Suzanne with a cursory look and stamp while still trying to look efficient.

"Have you visited Dublin before?" asked Fitzgerald as he led them to his car, carrying Suzanne's bag.

"No. We've only been in Ireland twice before and both times we flew into Shannon. I'm afraid that we've only seen the western counties and not very much of them. Brian, of course, is Irish and lives in Donegal."

"That's all right, then. They say that civilization starts west of Shannon. I'm from Lahinch myself." Fitzgerald placed the overnight cases in the back of the small Ford and held the door for Suzanne. "Trinity College is one of the sights one must see when in Dublin. I've taken a conference room. We can talk out what's troublin' you."

Fitzgerald wove his way south through the heavy traffic. Mats liked the man and could see why Schiller held him in high esteem.

Fitzgerald parked in a restricted space, placing a placard on his dash. He led them into an imposing building, passing through the space occupied by the Book of Kells, giving the group a chance to view the famous bible. Then he led them through the massive library and up a staircase to a private room. Everyone took seats except for Mats, who remained standing.

"Before we begin, Inspector," said Mats. "You should know why Lt. Schiller asked that you see us privately. We don't trust the Garda in Donegal, and by extension, at least one person in your department. Lt. Schiller trusts *you*, however, which is why he suggested we bring our concerns to you." Mats placed a large manila envelope containing the German tests and findings on the table in front of Fitzgerald.

"Lieutenant Schiller was reluctant to say much on the phone, but I trust his judgment. Why don't you start by telling me about your problem from the beginning?"

"I own a restaurant in California. Two years ago, I started importing French wines from Provence. It grew into a business, a good business. I was looking to add a beer to the line, preferably a non-alcoholic beer. That's why I came to Ireland. It turned out that a small brewery in Donegal, the Harp and Hawk, was for sale, and better yet, just before Brian's dad died, he had developed a new unique process for brewing non-alcoholic beer. We bought the brewery a few months ago, and that's when we met Brian, who is the son of the couple who had owned the brewery. They were murdered."

"It is a serious thing to accuse someone in the Garda of misconduct," said Fitzgerald, his eyes narrowing. "How is it you are involved with Lieutenant Schiller?"

"Well, at first we couldn't find the formulas for the non-alcoholic brewing process," said Mats. "Lars Bjursten was a Swedish biochemist who was Brian's mother's cousin. He developed the process with Brian's dad. We flew to Frankfurt, where Bjursten was working, to meet him. When we arrived, there were police and firemen all over his apartment building. Bjursten was dead...his apartment had caught fire. That's when we met Lieutenant Schiller."

"Bjursten was murdered, then?" asked Fitzgerald, suspecting the answer by the mere fact of Schiller's involvement.

"Yes, Bjursten was murdered, as well as Brian's parents, and we would be dead as well," said Suzanne. "Lt. Schiller saw the attempt on Brian's life in Frankfurt. I think it's time the police took this seriously. We are tired of being targets. Tell him about the car bomb, Mats,"

"Bjursten's death was made to look like an accident," said Mats, putting a hand on Suzanne's arm, "but Lt. Schiller was suspicious and demanded a thorough autopsy. It turned out that Bjursten died of smoke asphyxiation, but the smoke came from wood, and there was no wood in the apartment. The wood smoke came from the same types of wood as the bullets that killed the Keohanes were tipped with."

"Good work," muttered Fitzgerald under his breath. "So, what is this about wood-tipped bullets?"

"The brew master, Cathal Magee, dug a few slugs out of the brewery door at the site where the Keohanes were killed. He also got some from the headliner on our van that was shot up a couple months later. He sent them down here and I brought a few to Schiller. Both sets were hollow-nosed and filled with splinters of oak and ash. That's the same wood combination that killed Bjursten."

Mats watched as Fitzgerald's brow furrowed, as if he was trying to recall the case. "The Keohane case is still open, but it's thought to be a political killing. I don't remember anything about the bullets, or about any car bomb."

"That's the reason Lieutenant Schiller didn't want to talk to you in your office or fax you these reports." Mats tapped the envelope, sliding it closer to Fitzgerald. "Magee, he's the brew master, sent his slugs to a friend in your department. The friend told Magee that the slugs came from similar guns and the bullets were modified in the same way, both sets tipped with wood. Yet the policeman in Donegal, Constable Minahen, told us there was nothing strange about the bullets and the attacks were probably unrelated because the bullets were from completely different weapons."

"It'd be normal for the Garda to withhold specifics of a case. Even from a victim. I know the chief in Donegal. He's a good man."

"He's a man who endangered our lives by lying about the bomb," said Suzanne, her tone sharp and accusing. "Mats said that the explosives in our car were bound with sticks of wood as well."

"This bomb," asked Fitzgerald, "tell me about it."

"It was placed in our rental car while we were staying overnight with Brian," said Mats. "I was awake and saw it being placed. Minahen told me they found it to be a small charge that might have been in the car for weeks. He didn't know I had watched two men at the car and seen it up close when I raised the hood in the morning. It was not a small charge, Inspector, and it wasn't in the car for weeks."

The inspector picked up the reports from Schiller, reading through them quickly. There was a cover letter that corroborated Mats' story about the murder of Lars Bjursten. It also told of the attack on Brian and Nando Guibega and the makeup of the clubs.

"Whew," whistled Fitzgerald, his face grim as he considered the prospect of a dirty cop. "If what you say is true, this is serious. Let me get the file on the Keohane murders and compare them to Lt. Schiller's lab reports."

"Inspector Fitzgerald." It was the first time Brian had spoken since the introductions. Fitzgerald looked at the boy, noticing the green discoloration extending from his hairline down to his left eye.

"Yes, son."

"There's my grandfather as well."

"What about your grandfather?"

"He was beaten to death in Ballinrobe. The Garda found the weapon, a hurling stick also made out of oak and ash. Would you still have the file on him?"

"If it happened in Ireland, we'll have a file," said Fitzgerald sharply, all semblance of ease gone from his voice.

Fitzgerald drove them to the Ariel House southeast of Trinity. It was a nice accommodation across from several embassies. He wished them a good evening, knowing that no such luck would follow him this night. He would start by phoning Schiller from a public phone, then spend the rest of the night digging through the files on the Keohane murders. It would not be fun, especially if he found some dirty Garda at the bottom of his dig.

Mats spent the evening with Brian watching an Irish hurling match on TV. The rules seemed simple enough. One team took their clubs and tried to dismember the other team. The only mystery was that sometimes an official called a foul.

Mats was reluctant to let Brian sleep alone because of his concussion, so he had a rollaway placed in their room. It was no sooner made up than Brian was in it. Shortly afterwards, with the lights still on, he was on his way to sleep.

Suzanne and Mats smiled at each other. They acknowledged the bond of love that had grown between them and the boy. They knew without discussing it that they would adopt Brian if Irish laws allowed.

Brian turned contentedly away. With a warm feeling of love surrounding him, he dreamed.

The Island off Donegal, Ireland – 945 AD

Two hours before dawn, Kjell, with a crew of sixteen, pushed the dragon ship into the sea. Phosphorus flashed alongside the boat in the moonlight as they rowed slowly toward the mainland. There was an occasional glimpse the cliff, which helped Kjell hold his course until the narrow cleft in the shore became clear. The tide was high, all but covering the small sandy beach below the cliff.

At the tiller, Kjell thought about Ecca, his excitement to see her again and hear her songs distracting him from holding course. Kjell had described her to the priest, asking to which family she belonged. The priest knew of no such girl, certainly no such girl on the point, which was frequented only by villagers drunk past reason.

As a seafarer, Kjell was at once superstitious and suspicious of superstition. Most tales, he had found, had some basis in truth, but he had never found anything supernatural in this fact. The way some had attributed to black magic the ability he and his brothers shared to read each other's thoughts was a case in point. Most people were afraid of what they couldn't understand, and they made up frightening tales to validate their fear.

Kjell stepped ashore, climbing the path to the top of the cliff. It was still dark, and he relied on touch, memory, and the fading moonlight to guide his feet up the narrow trail. As soon as he reached the top, he made for the forest at the head of the fjord. No fires glowed on the peninsula, no signs of life, save an occasional ground bird frightened by his passage.

When he reached the banks of the creek, dawn was just breaking but not yet penetrating the forest's grim darkness. He selected a large oak and climbed its massive trunk. Twenty feet above the ground, obscured by leaves, he settled back against a crook in a branch and waited.

As the sun rose over the eastern mountains, Kjell worried that he had climbed too high. The branch on which he rested gave him a clear view of not only the creek and clearing below but the approach to the forest. He started to move to a lower branch, for he reasoned that if he could see the surrounding countryside, those moving toward the glade could also see him. He had just started his descent when movement inland stopped him. Slowly he inched down, making sure he made no quick movement that would catch the eye of the small party approaching. He counted six figures, all clad in white robes. Kjell caught the glint of light on the metal tips of spears. His first thought was that the maiden,

Ecca, had betrayed him. As he remained hidden high in the tree, the group came close enough for Kjell to identify Ecca, holding her harp, flanked forward and aft by five men. They were clad in robes of the same white cloth as she, but they carried spears rather than musical instruments.

As Kjell watched from above, the men spread out. Two went to the cliff's edge, one to the north and one to the south of the small creek that flowed through the forest. The other three, including the bearded leader, entered the woods with the young girl. They stopped almost directly below Kjell, the girl taking a seat on the stone bench while the three men moved about, searching the underbrush with their spears. After some time, their leader came back to the girl, who was holding her harp in her lap.

"Play," the bearded leader commanded, as if he were addressing a subordinate.

"I will play when you are beyond the sound of my voice. My songs are for the gods of the forest, not for their servants," replied Ecca, haughtily.

The bearded one snapped his head toward her as if to reprimand the headstrong girl, but he stopped short, his shoulders rounding in submission.

"Yes, my princess," he muttered. "I'll come for you two hours before dark."

Then he turned, and with the two men following, he left the clearing, leaving the girl alone.

Kjell remained motionless, almost afraid to breathe, until he saw the men join the two who had returned from the cliff. Together they moved back along the path until they were again out of sight.

Kjell felt uncomfortable, looking down at the girl from his hiding place. He had led his life being honest with his brothers and with all others as well. Now he felt like a thief, stealing something by trickery instead of earning it with the strength of his sword arm.

The girl began to hum, her voice vibrating in perfect harmony with the sounds emanating from the soundbox of the harp. Kjell was so captivated by the melody and her voice that he almost failed to translate the words:

> "You who hide in the branches above,
> Sitting like a snow-white dove,
> Better to have your feet on earth
> To hear my song of love and worth."

The maid's voice was soft, barely audible above the gentle strumming of the harp. When she finished the verse, she looked up and smiled.

"They're gone and won't return till well after mid-day," she said.

Kjell climbed slowly to the ground, trying not to make a sound, as if any noise would break the enchantment he felt at seeing the girl again.

"How did you know I was hiding in the tree?" he asked as he approached her.

"I was disappointed when I did not find you in the clearing, but happy because my keepers would have slain you. Then I realized that a strong man who weeps at a sad song would be here. You were not on the ground, so you must be in the air."

"Who are those men?" asked Kjell, taking her small white hand in both of his.

"They are my keepers."

"The bearded one called you 'princess.'"

"It is my title, at least until the summer solstice."

"Who are you?" asked Kjell, almost pleading for an answer that would tell him how to proceed with this girl who was a woman in all but years.

"I am Ecca, princess of the northern Druids."

"I thought Druids were the stuff of tales, invented to frighten children. Mothers tell their young to behave or the Druids will come at night and take them away."

"They are right to frighten their children," said Ecca. "I am one whom they took fifteen years ago. I do not know where my village was or who my parents were. All my life I have been with my keepers, moving from place to place."

"Are you a slave, then?" asked Kjell, still holding the girl's hand.

"A slave, a captive, a princess, a sacrifice," said the girl, tears now streaming down her face.

Kjell could contain himself no longer. He rose from his haunches, pulling the girl up and to him. His arms went around her, encircling her with his strength. She raised her face to his, looking at him through tear-filled eyes, then accepted his kiss.

They stood holding each other for long minutes, kissing with more tenderness than passion. Finally, Kjell held her at arm's length. "Tell me about your keepers."

"They are holy men, wise men, sorcerers who deal in magic. Before the Christian monks came, there were Druids in the court of every chief. They've been forced into hiding, but they still hold sway over many people."

"Are they all on this point of land?"

"Oh no. They move freely among the families and the villagers. It is only during ceremonies that they don the robes of Druids."

"And you, Ecca? Where do you live when you are not here?"

"There is a small gathering of huts two miles from here. I am not allowed to leave. You are only the second person I have ever met who was not one of my keepers."

"How can that be?" asked Kjell, perplexed at the calm with which Ecca described her almost complete isolation.

"My earliest memory is from when I was four. I was already with my keepers, although for the first few years, there were women as well as men."

"Why are you singled out?"

"The gods gave the Druids a sign. But perhaps it is not as terrible as you imagine. In the Druid society, I am treated as a princess. I have been educated in the arts as well as in music."

"To what purpose, if you are never allowed to see anyone but your Druid wardens?"

"We worship the old gods: the god of the forest, the god of water, and the god of the sky and land. Once a year, they are offered a blood sacrifice. This spring at the equinox, it will be my blood that is spilled on this altar rock."

"What! We Norsemen also have gods, of the sea and sky and land, but they only require that we die bravely in battle to be admitted to Valhalla. The only blood they demand is that of our enemies. What your gods demand is not proper."

"The gods require a maiden such as I, although sometimes a prince of particular virtue is selected. Not every year is the sacrifice human. Animals that benefit man are also used as appeasement."

"Do you truly believe in these gods?" asked Kjell, trembling with fury at the waste of life in offering this girl as a sacrifice.

"It is what I have been taught. I have known of my fate since childhood, but I have watched the offerings of goats and deer and I have seen no appeasement—no change in the weather, no improvement in the crops except what could be explained by nature's usual course."

"There is a reason the Druids hide you. Good men of any religion would search them out and destroy them if their ways became known. How long do we have before they return?"

"We have the whole day, unless they become suspicious."

The girl returned to the stone bench, beginning to strum her harp again. "Tell me about your gods, but also tell me about yourself and your people."

For the next few hours, they spoke of their lives. Kjell recounted sagas of Odin, Thor, the Valkyries, and Freyja, the goddess of fertility, love, and desire. Ecca seemed impressed that a female figure was a Norse god. He told of growing up at the sted of his father. He told of his banishment by Redhand and the storm that had blown him off course to the island, and he told her that he loved her.

Throughout their talk, Ecca strummed her harp, letting the melody follow the mood of Kjell's tales. When he finally ended his stories and told her of his love, she stopped playing. She looked at this man, so foreign to any she had ever known, with his leather-wrapped leggings and his short sword. In his eyes she saw truth, not the craftiness or need to dominate in those of her keepers.

"Come with me. Leave the Druids. Be my wife," whispered Kjell, looking at Ecca with eyes that pleaded for an answer.

All of her life, Ecca had been told what to believe, what to do, how to worship. Now this man asked her to choose. Her emotions told her to take his offered love and deny the teachings and lifelong commitment forced on her by her keepers. In the time since they had first met, when she slept, she dreamed of caressing his brow and kissing his lips. She had known in her heart what she would do if the man came again to the pool in the forest. If he took her, she would go with him. If he left her, she would accept her fate. She had not envisioned, even in her dreams, that he would give her a choice.

"I will go with you, Kjell Falkhand. Not because of your gods. Not because of your strength. I go with you because you cry at my songs when they are sad and smile when they are happy. I believe that you will value me for myself and not for what I represent to the gods. I will go with you because you tell me of your love and I believe that it is true."

"Let us go then. My ship will return to the inlet at my signal."

"It is not that easy. My keepers watch this place, even though you do not see them, and they will reach us long before we get to the trail."

"I will call my men," said Kjell, reaching for a horn at his hip.

"No. The warriors will hear the signal as well. They will kill your men as they come up the trail."

What Ecca said was true, Kjell realized. One archer at the head of the cliff would be able to hold off his entire crew.

"I will not have blood spilled on my account," Ecca continued. "I would rather give my own life than have others bleed for me. There has to be another way, and you must find it, Kjell. We must act today, for there is talk of moving me to a new warren."

As Kjell contemplated the disturbing thought of losing Ecca, she played her harp more loudly. "The wind is strong today. My notes will carry to my keepers, even if the melody does not. As long as I am playing, they will not approach."

"If you hide with me in the tree, they might not find us. They might think that you had escaped. We could wait till night and then climb down the cliff."

"They will find us. I used to hide in trees when I was a girl. They remember; they may not look for you, but they will look for me."

Kjell stood, bending to kiss the girl on the lips. "Keep playing. I will be back." He looked at the pool, then at the stream running from it. The water would find a way to the ocean, and so must he. He followed the stream as it flowed through the forest, which grew to the edge of the cliff. Carefully he moved out of its shadow, keeping low as he edged to the point where the stream cascaded over the cliff to join the surf below.

Kjell did not like what he saw—a waterfall, the exposed rock worn smooth as it fell to the sea. The first drop was over fifty feet. Below there was a rocky ledge with water hitting off the shelf before falling for another forty feet. Kjell pressed his body as far over the ledge as he dared but could see no handholds or means of climbing down. He could understand why the narrow trail he had climbed was used even though it was far from the glade to the south; it was the only access to the shore below.

Staying low, Kjell returned to the glade. Ecca was still playing her harp—still on top of the steep mound, sitting on the stone bench—but the melody turned sad when she saw defeat written on Kjell's face.

"If I'd thought to bring a rope," he said, shaking his head. "There are two forty-foot cascades."

Tears flowed down the young girl's cheeks as she listened to the words that spelled her doom. Then a sudden sharp sound in the distance, the sound of metal against metal, broke both of them from their melancholy.

Kjell leapt to the oak, climbing quickly to a point where he could see the fields that led to the glade. He had climbed only two-thirds of the way to his earlier perch when he saw the first of the white-clad warriors running toward them. Their speed and disregard for concealment told him that he must have been observed leaving the forest on his way to scout the falls. Quickly he started down, jumping from one branch to another in order to gain in the ground. With ten feet still to go, he reached for a branch, grasping it in haste. It bent under his weight, and unable to support its load, it broke.

Fortunately, the fall was nothing. Kjell rolled as he hit the leaf-covered floor of the forest, the broken branch still clutched in his hand. Ecca ran to him as he stood.

"Your keepers are running this way with weapons in hand." Kjell looked away from the girl's tears, studying the oak branch in his hand. He threw it down, bouncing it off the ground, hitting a tall, thin ash sapling that was struggling to rise above the leafy canopy. Kjell watched the tall young tree tremble with the impact. Then he leapt toward it, taking his axe from his belt in the same motion.

"Perhaps the gods of the trees and forests will protect us after all," said Kjell, swinging his axe the base of the sapling. Such was his strength and the sharpness of his axe that the ash fell at the second blow.

The tree had a small branch off its main trunk that separated just above the ground. Kjell's blow severed it an axe handle's length from its crotch, leaving a hook at one end and the leafy branches on either end of the pole. The main trunk had no branches, the sapling using most of its energy to grow high enough to share the sunlight with the older, higher trees.

"Come. We must hurry." Carrying the sapling in one hand and holding Ecca's arm in the other, he ran toward the waterfall. "I hope you remember how to climb trees." Kjell took his helmet from his belt, placing it on his head as they reached the precipice. Without waiting for an answer, he slid the leafy end of the tree over the side of the cliff, holding onto the notched end, which he fitted into a small depression in the stream bed only inches from the edge.

Seeing Kjell holding the tree in place and hearing the yells of her keepers, Ecca slid over the side, grasping the tree as she shimmied down it to the rocky ledge below. The tree was long and thin, but still she had a five-foot drop. As soon as she landed, Kjell tested the purchase of the top end and followed her. Upon landing, he raised the sapling, then lowered it, hand over hand, over the second waterfall. As he held the tree steady for Ecca, he heard the keepers arrive at the ledge above him.

A shout to their fellows announced that the princess was escaping. Kjell was fortunate that the first of the keepers to arrive at the falls was armed with only a sword. He was halfway down the second falls when the first archer arrived. The initial arrow was well aimed. It hit his helmet, glancing off it and nicking his shoulder. The wound was not deep, but the next shaft could prove fatal. He let the wood of sapling slip through his callused hands, only gripping tightly when he felt the first of the leafy branches.

Ecca had already moved off the second shelf and was climbing down a rough path beside the water course. Below the second landing, the creek cut away to the north, following a fault in the cliff. The change in direction, as slight as it was, shielded Ecca from the archer above. Kjell hit the landing hard, turning his ankle on the uneven stone surface. He ignored the pain, raising the pole as he brought it down, using it as a thin, ineffective shield against further arrows from above. Just in time, he moved the tree in front of him, as an arrow struck its thin trunk. The archer did not get another chance as Kjell, following Ecca down the face of the cliff, moved out of sight. Protected from above, he paused; taking his horn from his belt, he gave three sharp blasts.

Ecca surprised Kjell with her agility. He was unable to make up distance on her as they flew away from the danger above. They were almost to the beach when they met the first of Kjell's crew. His men used shields to protect Ecca from the arrows being shot blindly from above and the rocks being dislodged and thrown over the cliff. One of the men was injured when his leg was pierced by an arrow.

Ecca's eyes showed a mixture of wonder and fear as Kjell lifted her with one arm into the longboat. She had told him she'd seen boats before on the bay that led inland, but she had never been in one. He grabbed the steering oar, placing her at his feet. Her eyes were wide, as the rocking motion of the men pushing away from shore unnerved her. Kjell looked up and saw movement on the cliffs above. The white-robed Druids were running along either side of the cliff, taking up positions that the vessel would have to pass beneath.

"Watch out! Above you!" shouted at Kjell. "Every other man, ship oars. Protect the ship and your mates with shields. The rest, pull for two."

They had taken only two full strokes before the first of the boulders fell toward them. It landed short, close to the cliff, its splash hitting the men on the forward oars. The second also came from the right side, this time tossed with more vigor toward the center of the fjord below. It would have struck the boat but for the Viking shield held at an angle. The rock seemed to compress the man underneath. His shield, held at arm's length, folded with the contact, followed by his back and finally his legs. Then the man recoiled from the impact, returning to full height and looking up for further danger.

When they were finally clear of the land, Kjell left the stern and examined his crew. Three had deflected stones, and only one had hit the boat, and that on the steeply angled bow strakes. The man who had parried the first stone could not flex his wrist, but still he rowed with one arm, unwilling to play less of a role in the eyes of his chief. He was one of the men who had joined Kjell from Bloodaxe's crew. He would be accepted fully among the others for his show of courage this day.

After he had checked his crew, Kjell knelt beside Ecca. "My keepers will come for me," she said softly.

"That is good," responded Kjell, stroking her cheek with the back of his fingers. "They will find Kjell Falkhand more than ready."

Ecca frowned at the thought of bloodshed. Then, as the knowledge that she was free to choose her own life filled her mind, her frown began to fade. She stood and kissed Kjell full on the lips.

The stroke of the oars did not vary in the least, but the men could not hide their smiles as their leader turned red like a youngster not yet bloodied in battle.

CHAPTER NINETEEN

The Ariel House—Dublin, Ireland – 2003

Suzanne looked over and saw Brian moving in his rollaway bed. As she watched him thrash about under the sheets and blankets, she knew he was dreaming. Tomorrow, like Mats, he would remember the dream. It would not be lost, as dreams often are upon awakening.

Mats did not awaken as Suzanne pulled the covers back up under her chin and settled back on her pillow. She was glad Brian was in a different bed. Anyone sharing it with Brian would be black and blue tomorrow. She lay back down on her own pillow and closed her eyes. Roughly half an hour later, Mats' own kick convinced Suzanne to abandon the thought of sleeping in either bed. She got up, wrapping herself in a spare blanket, sat in a chair, and watched Mats in his own fitful dream, listening to his muffled words in the Corsican dialect of the Guibega...

Ajaccio, Corsica—1943

Summer had almost passed. It had been a hard season for the Germans. Only the longer daylight hours had prevented the Resistance from wreaking more havoc on the Occupation forces. The night belonged to the Resistance.

With the success of the Maquis and his small band of Guibegas, the established Resistance became bolder and more effective as well. They even took the name "Maquis" for their own organization, a development that made Falconi happy. It confused the enemy, helping to hide the existence of the Guibega as a separate, elite fighting force.

Egel had been able to radio Captain L'Herminier the routes of German forces, and he had seen Allied fighter planes taking advantage of the information. The German perimeter was shrinking ever closer to the port of Ajaccio.

Through the haze of his dream, Mats felt the morning sun warm the back of Egel as he and Teressa watched Rohde's command post a mile in the distance from the tile roof of the Alta Mira.

"They're going on another demolition run," said Egel as Teresa scanned the scene below them with the glasses, hooded with a towel to prevent any reflection.

"They will leave us nothing," she spat.

"They're covering their own retreat," said Falconi. "Bombing things that would be useful to the Allies. But you're right; if we don't stop them, they'll destroy everything, including the port."

A month before, Falconi had discovered where Rohde was billeted. The German no longer led troops against the Resistance, although he still arrested civilians, some of them women and children. Now, Rohde led his crack troops against the very elements the Resistance used against him. He was blowing up mountain passes, rural roads, bridges, and tunnels.

Egel watched as Rohde came out of the building and climbed into the staff car.

"That bastard," Teresa swore under her breath.

"I'll radio Captain L'Herminier and the lookouts to the north," said Egel, noting the vehicle's route.

As they lay next to each other in the attic of the Alta Mira, Falconi could sense Teresa's fury. She was becoming increasingly angry about their inability to capture or kill Rohde. Only after making love did she seem content.

Teresa's rage, which mirrored the general feeling among the Guibega, convinced Falconi it was time to plan a direct action against the Germans. The Resistance had become strong enough to consider launching a frontal attack. Daily, Allied fighter planes were seen over their coast, guided by Resistance spotters. If the Allies could provide air cover, the Resistance could attack Ajaccio. It would be dangerous, more dangerous than any strike so far, but it would shorten the Occupation, perhaps ending the war on Corsica.

Antonio Guibega was still a commander in the regular Resistance. Most Corsicans now suspected that an elite band of guerrillas existed, led by a legend called Maquis, but no one as yet suspected that Antonio was his general.

Falconi planned the raid to take place on the seventh or eighth of September, whichever day the Allies could provide air support. The day before the Resistance attacked, he would send the Guibega unit through German lines to safe houses inside the city. When the attack started, they would encircle Rohde's command post.

Rohde had shown no inclination to use his SS men to fight alongside the regular German troops. Falconi counted on him keeping them in reserve around his headquarters, as he did during air raids.

For almost a year, Falconi had maintained his pledge not to lose another Guibega. Having the Guibega inside the German perimeter during the assault on Ajaccio would be more dangerous than any previous operation, however. This time they would be surrounded by German forces who could trap them inside their lines. This might be the last time Rohde would be vulnerable. If he left the island, the chances of the Guibega ever completing their vendetta would be small.

Falconi radioed Captain L'Herminier, apprising him of the German's pattern of demolition.

"When do you think they will evacuate Ajaccio?"

"Soon. The last bridge they blew up was only ten kilometers to the north. One of my men tells me they have rigged the port to blow as well, but I have only one man on the waterfront. Still, I trust him." It was one thing to have his band of Guibega relying on his leadership—they had for centuries—but making a prediction that might affect thousands of Allied troops was more responsibility than Falconi wanted to shoulder. "I think it must be within a week."

"Humph," said L'Herminier, coughing out the sound. "Monsieur Maquis, would it be possible to mount a diversion as soon as September 8?"

"Captain, I radioed today to ask if you could provide air cover for an attack on Ajaccio by the main force of the Resistance on that same date. It will be more than a diversion."

"Interesting! You said the main force. Will your unit fight with the Resistance?"

"No, sir. We have our own objective."

"And what is it?"

"We will attack the troops that are responsible for the destruction. They are also the ones that have been targeting the Resistance."

"I see. Where will you be? Can you tell me that? I don't want our bombers inadvertently harming your men."

"Ajaccio. Four blocks inland from the docks," said Falconi, his voice as cold and sharp as steel. "We will mark the roof of their headquarters with a white X for your bombers. My men will chance your bombs, but there is something you can help us with."

Falconi went over his plan in detail, while L'Herminier wrote down the list of the supplies he needed to air drop to the Maquis.

❧ ❧ ❧

For two days, the Guibega infiltrated Ajaccio. They brought with them the supplies that had air dropped in the hills north of Ajaccio. Of the Guibega, only Antonio would return to outside the German perimeter, necessary because he was to lead the regular Resistance forces and coordinate the external operations with those of the Guibega. By the evening of September 7th, all forces were in place, hiding, awaiting only the morning to provide light enough for the attack.

"French soldiers will land on the beaches just south of Ajaccio on September 8th," said L'Herminier over the radio on the evening of September sixth. Falconi expected them to neutralize the German troupes at the port.

On the evening of September 7th, the radio buzzed softly. Falconi picked up the receiver.

"Monsieur Maquis, the Battalion de Choc hasn't been released and no other troops are available," said Captain L'Herminier, his disappointment apparent even through the oversized earphones.

"Keeping everyone in place is impossible," said Falconi. "I will have to move my men back out through the lines of Germans, or proceed with the attack."

Antonio helped him make the decision. Leaning over Falconi's shoulder, he said, "The Resistance felt strong enough to attack before they knew of the Allied troops; if we still have air cover, we will be successful."

"Sir, if we proceed, will your falcons still fly?"

"Yes!"

"Then you will have your attack. The Resistance will take Ajaccio."

"Godspeed and good luck!" came the reply.

Falconi sent his men in squads of three to the houses surrounding Rohde's command post. One man in each squad carried a dozen-meter-long section of hose jammed with sticks of dynamite. Of the other men, one was skilled in silent killing, carrying both bow and knife. The third was armed with the American-made M-1 carbine, carrying two additional rifles and enough ammunition for the other men.

The German day started precisely at 0600. Revelry was sounded, and the night watch went from barrack to barrack, rousting those who would relieve them.

With the concentration of troops in Rohde's command post, both Falconi and Teressa felt it would be folly to try to force an entry. The Guibega would keep the Germans pinned inside while the squad on top of the nearest building would take the roof. Once in place, they would lay the explosives and two long strips of white cloth in the shape of an X, the target for the Allied fighter-bombers. Egel and Teresa and a small reserve of six men would co-ordinate the attack from the roof of the Alta Mira.

"I hope the target won't be necessary," said Teresa, at Falconi's side. "I want the pleasure of seeing him killed. Before you came, he arrested thirteen of us. Five were young women. Three were my cousins. Now we hear the men were sent to concentration camps and the women were used for the pleasure of the German officers. Rohde will be punished. It is my pledge."

Falconi looked at this woman he loved. The hatred in her eyes gave weight to her words, and for a second he was afraid for her.

⚜ ⚜ ⚜

Antonio's voice came over the walkie-talkie. "We are in position. Are your men ready?"

Falconi answered. "Yes! Start the attack."

"Now?"

"Now!"

The first shot was the only one identifiable as a single sound. At the two German outposts guarding the outskirts of Ajaccio, mortar rounds and rifle fire poured from the houses and boulders lining the roads. One roadblock managed to contact the main garrison in town; the other was not quick enough, an explosion taking out the phone wire and the communication center radio together.

At the first sound of gunfire, the normal activity around Rohde's headquarters was thrown into disarray. Men rushed from the barracks to the headquarters and then back out onto the street, forming a perimeter around the building. It was what Falconi had hoped for.

"How's it going, Antonio?" asked Falconi over the walkie-talkie.

"Good, Signor Maquis. Half the Germans are down. The others are dug deep, awaiting their armor to save them."

"The mines have been set, then?"

"Yes, signore. Last night under the noses of their sentries."

"I count nine or ten who came out," said Teresa to Egel as he disconnected from Antonio. Her glasses were riveted on the activity around Rohde's command center.

"I wish there were more," said Egel, knowing he was risking the lives of the Guibega as he flipped the channel and lifted the walkie-talkie again to his lips.

"This is Maquis. Ten men are outside the building. Begin the attack."

Falconi watched the square as rifle shots echoed up the slopes below him. Germans fell to the pavement, collapsing in odd positions against stacks of sandbags. Three of the soldiers tried to make it back into the building, but none got as far as the door. Gunfire was returned from the second-story windows of the three-story building.

Egel watched as three of his men gained the roof using planks from the adjacent roof. Two started to unroll the long strips of white material, one crossing the other at mid-point to form an X, while the third stood to the side of the entrance door to the roof. As the first two laid loose roof tiles on the material, the door opened. A soldier, only partially visible to Falconi even with the use of the field glasses, barely saw the morning light before he was killed by a Guibega knife. A German behind the first pushed the man's legs out with the butt of his rifle, slamming the door shut from inside. The two Guibegas, having completed the marker, joined their colleague at the door. They jammed the German's rifle through the door handle, running a rope around the small enclosure that housed the door. Satisfied that it was jammed, they moved to the side of the building, the rifleman peering over the side as one of his fellows rigged a grappling hook, throwing a rope over the edge so that it hung to the side of the windows below. The third man grabbed the rope, climbing over the side, going down hand over hand to the level of the third story windows. Wrapping his foot around the rope for purchase, he took an axe from his belt, swinging it against the glass of the window.

Falconi could not hear the breakage, but he could see the man look up. On the roof, the man with the rifle lit the fuse sticking from the end of the hose and threw it to the man on the rope. With one movement, the man hanging with one hand caught the bomb with the other and threw it through the broken window. The man on the roof worked the rope, lowering it down the side of the building until the other man, still dangling, was next to a second-story window. Before the suspended man could repeat his actions, there was a loud explosion and the window above him blew a fiery billow of smoke and glass onto the street below. The task was repeated on the second window. As the Guibega reached the third window on the ground floor, he again the broke the glass. A gun, followed by a head, appeared through the jagged panes. For the Guibega above, it was like shooting fish in a bowl. A single shot and the German's body hung dead over the sill as the third explosion obliterating the contents of the room behind him.

Teresa was first to see them: airplanes approaching from the southwest. She did not speak, just touched Falconi on the shoulder and pointed.

"Leave the roof immediately. The bombers are coming!" Falconi shouted into the receiver. He watched as the man on the rope was pulled up and over the edge. Two men of the unit ran over the plank to the adjacent building; the third stayed on the roof, planting the remaining hose bombs along the jammed roof enclosure before following the others in their escape.

The first of the planes hit targets at the port. German Messerschmitts had already made their way into the air by the time the Allied bombers arrived over the city, but they were unable to penetrate the web of protection provided by the British fighters. At first Falconi thought that Rohde's building had sustained a hit. A large explosion blew smoke and flames high into the air. When the air cleared, he saw that the enclosure containing the door on the roof had been completely blown away by the hose bombs.

"Look," said Teresa, pointing at the flaming rooftop. The marker had been destroyed. The two cloth banners were no longer in position; one was shredded, while the other hung over the side of the building like bunting for a parade. Only with luck would the pilots identify the target.

All the hose bombs were to be used on the windows. Falconi looked at the destruction on the roof. *It would have been better if they had taken the unused hoses with them,* he reflected. *Not only is the marker ruined, but the explosion makes it look like the building has already been bombed. The planes won't bomb it now. It'll be harder to force them out.*

From the port, German tanks and armored personnel carriers were moving out to aid the perimeter checkpoints. They drove close to the sides of the buildings, keeping their exposure to the aircraft above as minimal as possible. Falconi watched them as they headed north toward the fighting at the outskirts of the city. *At least that part is going as planned,* he thought as he watched the column through his field glasses.

As the German relief columns reached the halfway point, they stopped. The officer in command could be seen with his hand to his ear, holding a radio. He lowered his arm, issuing orders punctuated by sharp movements of his hand. Immediately, one of the personnel carriers and twenty men, about a quarter of the column's total strength, turned around and started back toward Rohde's headquarters.

"Germans headed toward Rohde from the east," said Falconi into the walkie-talkie, a new devise provided by the last shipment. "A personnel carrier and twenty men on foot."

As Falconi transmitted his warning, Teresa shimmied backward and off the roof. Falconi did not know she had gone until he saw her small, lithe body running down the hill from the Alta Mira, leading the six men he had left in reserve. In front of him, the main German column had again started toward the point where the Resistance was still firing on the Germans at the checkpoint. The sounds of the Allied planes obscured the engines of the German relief column.

"Antonio, they come. One tank, three armored cars, and about a hundred soldiers. About two minutes away now."

"We are ready for them," came the cracked, static reply.

Falconi watched Teresa's small band quickly catch up with the German relief column. Falconi wanted to be with her, to be near her and protect her, but he realized he could do much more to help her if he stayed where he was, using his position to direct his men. He took a deep breath and closed his eyes. The Germans were getting close to where Antonio's squads had deployed.

The morning sun at his back threw sharp shadows on the town, accentuating the angles and doorways of the buildings on either side of the Rue Frasseto. The dun-colored walls of Rohde's headquarters contrasted with the blue and yellow hues of the surrounding buildings. Falconi looked through his glasses but could see no sign of any of his men as the Germans approached the intersection bordering Rohde's headquarters. Without warning, from the windows on the second story of the building across the street from Rohde, six quick shots were heard. The Germans were well trained and immediately moved to the side of the building, hitting the doors that opened onto the street with the butts of their rifles. The personnel carrier swung its turrets in the direction of the shots, spraying the side of the building. Falconi saw that six German bodies lay in the center of the road. One was moving in spasm, clawing its way to the protection of the armored vehicle. Then from the bright yellow building to the north, more shots were fired. This time the Germans were pressed against the building across the street, as if on the receiving end of a firing squad. Three more Germans fell, and then two more as they tried to respond.

Movement on the roof of the northern building caught Falconi's attention. Three men were crouched below the low tile façade. Then Falconi saw a long, thin object tossed over the edge into the swarm of soldiers below. The timing of the fuse was perfect. The hose took one bounce and exploded with a red flash of light and sound. It took only one enemy with it, but the confusion caused panic among the remaining troops. Half bolted back up the street they had just come down and directly into the withering fire of Teresa's rear guard. A second explosion flashed red, taking the front wheel of the personnel carrier, which spun with a screech of metal before coming to a stop in the middle of the street. The wind blowing off the shore brought the smoke and smell of gunpowder and explosives to Falconi on the roof of the Alta Mira, causing his eyes to water as he divided his attention between the battle raging below him and the German relief column making its way toward Antonio.

With over twelve men dead and his vehicle disabled, the German commander on the streets below Falconi shouted an order and the rest of his men took off down the street at a run toward Rohde's headquarters. The

Guibega marksmen had no qualms about shooting at the backs of the Germans. Five more were downed before they could reach the small square, their gray uniforms mingling with the black ones of Rohde's squad. In all, fewer than five members of the original relief column reached Rohde.

At the roadblock, the anti-tank mines that had been laid according to Antonio's direction worked perfectly. Resistance fighters who had stayed hidden along the route from the city to the guard station for over thirty hours fired on the Germans with relentless precision. Falconi had not lost a single man; Antonio was not as fortunate. The exposed position of the German post meant that his men would also be exposed as soon as they fired. Still, the devastation to the German column was frightening. A detail of Resistance fighters ran across the road at Antonio's order, cutting off the German's retreat. Falconi watched through his glasses as the Allied planes strafed the column that was pinned from either side of the road. Great fiery flashes erupted among the German troop carriers, followed seconds later by the sound of loud concussions. Less than two hours after the attack had begun, Antonio radioed Maquis.

"Signore, the Germans here have surrendered."

Falconi, still lying on the roof of the restaurant, looked toward the perimeter and saw groups of uniformed Germans surrounded by Resistance fighter in clothing more suited to farming than war. He forced himself to answer. "Good, my friend. Come to me now. We have Rohde trapped in his headquarters." *Two goals—one accomplished, the more dangerous one left undone.* He raised the walkie-talkie to his lips. "Teresa, hold your position. The Germans have surrendered to Antonio. I'll join you in a few minutes."

Dublin, Ireland– 2003

Desmond Fitzgerald tapped his fingers on the computer keyboard. If you counted the Swede as part of the extended Keohane family, the elaborately staged murder Lieutenant Schiller had uncovered connected four murders. As to Brian's grandfather, the Garda did have a file, and the murder had been committed with a wooden hurling stick. The unusual combination of oak and ash had been mentioned but only in passing, as no fingerprints other than the murdered man's had been found on its bloody handle.

As for the bullets, an investigation would produce the proof one way or another. But if the slugs had been doctored, why didn't the ballistics report mention it? Why had the report on the explosives placed in the rental car been filed as a separate incident and not cross-referenced with the Keohane file? Also, the file's description of the explosive package differed from Falconi's.

Fitzgerald rubbed his eyes and looked at the clock. It was after three in the morning. He knew he'd better get some sleep before he finished tickling the files tomorrow to see who might giggle. There was just too much information that had been swept under the rug or at least not given its proper due. He would phone Kurt Schiller in the morning and thank him for the warning. Slowly, he shuffled the files into a neat stack. Tomorrow would be busy.

Mats awoke, still enclosed in his dream. He was drenched with sweat, the sheets clinging to his body. He tried to jump off the bed. He found the floor much closer than the eight-foot drop onto the courtyard of the Alta Mira that he had expected. His toe stubbed the hardwood less than two feet below the surface of the mattress and brought him completely back to the present with a start to find both Brian and Suzanne watching him from across the room.

"Are you all right?" asked Suzanne, coming to his side.

"Yeah," replied Mats, his orientation to the present returning to him in waves.

"Did I look like that last night?" asked Brian. "Suzanne told me she could tell that I had a dream as well."

"You didn't hit the floor," said Mats with an embarrassed smile on his face. "Have you two had breakfast?"

"No, and neither will you if we don't hurry. They only serve until ten," said Suzanne, kissing him on the forehead.

The Ariel House Bed and Breakfast resembled a small hotel in its breakfast spread: three types of fresh fruit, two kinds of juice, coffee, porridge, pancakes, bacon, eggs, sausage, and of course, potatoes, shredded and fried to a golden brown. They completed breakfast and the accounts of their dreams at the same time. Suzanne said not a word during the entire meal, but both Mats and Brian had questions concerning the other's visions.

"This is the second time you have dreamed about the Druids. What do you know of them?" asked Suzanne of the boy, speaking for the first time since they had sat down to eat.

"Not much," answered Brian. "They were sort of priests for the Celts in the old days before St. Patrick, I think. I have a book with a chapter on them, but our teacher told us to pass over it, that they were just charlatans, made insignificant by St. Patrick and the true faith."

"We'd better get ready to go," said Suzanne, folding her napkin and placing it beside her plate. "Inspector Fitzgerald will be here in less than fifteen minutes. Perhaps he can fill us in on the Druids."

CHAPTER TWENTY

Dublin, Ireland – Garda Headquarters

"What can you tell us about the Druids?" Mats asked Fitzgerald as they sat down in the conference room.

"Druids? You mean the old-time sorcerers?" Fitzgerald studied Falconi's face. It was dead serious, the color under his eyes telling the inspector that Falconi was as worn out as he was himself.

"Yes, Druids," repeated Mats.

"Well, now, I can't say I remember much about them myself that wasn't just children's tales. But Trinity is the right place to find someone to tell us about them. Why do you want to know about them?"

"Brian remembered something about wood being sacred to them. The ritual aspect of the murders and the attempts on Brian's life made me wonder," said Mats, not wanting to mention Brian's dreams.

"Wait here," said Fitzgerald. He got up and left the room. In fifteen minutes, he returned with a tall dark-haired man with deep-set eyes and a permanent slouch to his posture. Fitzgerald introduced the man as Father Cleary. The priest shook each of their hands in succession, demonstrating a strong grip through the almost feminine softness of his skin.

"You're wanting to know about the Druids, now, are ya?" he asked in a soft County Cork accent. "The truth is that we don't know all that much. There are secondhand oral accounts by priests that are almost of no use, and only two written histories. Our only close look at them is through a text by a Roman scribe who encountered them in northern France."

"Why don't you tell us what you know, and we'll stop you if we want to know anything more specific?"

"It would help if I knew what you were looking for," said Father Cleary.

"There have been several murders with ritualistic features concerning the use of certain woods. We're gathering information," said Fitzgerald. His officious tone suggested they should get on with it.

"All right then," began the resigned priest. "The Celts came to Ireland in several waves between 450 BC and 250 BC. With them came the Druids. They were part shaman, part priest, part medicine man. In Europe, the Celts were overrun. Their religion was supplanted first by the Romans and then by the true faith. Here in Ireland, we were spared the legions of Rome. In fact, the Celts enjoyed an almost unbroken reign as a people from the time they conquered the Fir Bolg until they were in turn invaded by the Vikings in the late 800s AD. The Celts were by nature a superstitious people, and the Druids preyed upon this trait. They promoted magic and mysticism, but they also became intellectual leaders. They formed schools. The most learned of them became famous and occupied important positions in the courts of kings."

"Did they perform blood sacrifices?" asked Mats.

"Blood sacrifices? The sun was their major deity, but they also had gods of the forest, sea, and earth. There is one account of human sacrifice; it is given in third person by a young scribe who did not write of further accounts supporting the claim. But scientific investigation has shown that their altars were at some point bathed with the blood of both animals and humans. Why do you ask?"

"And their use of particular kinds of wood?" said Mats, evading the question.

"The places where we find their stone altars have curious arrangements of ash trees. Clusters that might be generations-old plantings. It has also been noted that the dolmens are often shaded by old oaks," answered Father Cleary, trying to remember specifics from readings he had long ago put out of his mind.

"Is the religion still active?" asked Mats.

"The Druids were more of a cult than a religion. Their power fell with the arrival of St. Patrick. The first major confrontation came on Good Friday at Tara. There on a hill, St. Patrick lit a fire to commemorate the resurrection. The fire was lit two days before the Druids lit their own great fire. Patrick's burned far brighter, with an unearthly light. Granted, the affairs of that time were recorded by priests, and even I read some of the accounts with skepticism. It is enough to say that Patrick won the hearts and minds of the people.

"Patrick met with King Laoghaire of that region, who had two beautiful daughters, Ethne the fair and Fedelm the ruddy. The princesses were under the instruction of Mael and Caplit, the two master Druids at Laoghaire's court. The Druids conspired against St. Patrick, and using their magic, they brought down a terrible darkness on him, his companions, the castle, and the Plain of Magh. The darkness lasted three days and three nights. Then, on Easter, Patrick blessed the entire plain and light came again, leaving only the two Druids in darkness. The Druids converted shortly afterward, along with Ethne and Fedelm, effectively ending the Druid influence in Ireland. But this is getting to be more of a lecture on

Patrick than on the Druids. Is there anything specific you would like to know?"

"I asked if the religion was still active," Mats reminded him.

"Well, there's a small splinter group in England that claims to be the spiritual descendants of the ancient Druids. They dress in white robes and strut around a bit at the summer solstice, bother people at Stonehenge, that sort of thing. They are colorful but more an oddity than a religion."

"How about here in Ireland?" asked Mats. "Any Druid activity?"

"None that I know of," said Father Cleary. "There has been a resurgence of the Celtic language taught in schools, but after St. Patrick, there was a rapid decline the Druid cult. There has been no mention of them for centuries. I would say the Druids are nonexistent now."

"Any chance of a secret society?" suggested Suzanne.

"Ah, sure, in that we as a people love our secret societies. This kind of thing, however, could hardly escape the notice of the Church now, could it? No, if someone here had heard something, then I would have heard."

"Thank you, Father Cleary. I hope we can call on you again if we have more questions," said Fitzgerald.

"Would you be answering a question of mine?" Father Cleary asked, looking at Inspector Fitzgerald and then at Mats.

Fitzgerald nodded.

"Do *you* believe there's a secret society of Druids?" asked Father Cleary.

"Can't say," said Mats before Fitzgerald could stop him. "There have been four deaths and an attempt on Brian's life that all involved some use of ash and oak. We feel Brian's life is still in danger and the only clue, as weak as it is, is the Druids' use of those woods. Do you know whether oak and ash have any particular significance in the Druid religion, other than growing near their altars?"

"The Druids had as their most holy place the well-springs of rivers. To this day there are fine groves of oak and straight lines of ash, extending down the path of the sun from their places of worship. I would say yes, they held those woods sacred."

"Well, thank you for your time, Father. You have been most helpful." Inspector Fitzgerald got up, signaling the end of the lecture, to the disappointment of the priest. Anything concerning religions other than his own in Ireland interested him. A scholar he was, but also a staunch supporter of the Republic, and at times he had even provided his secular absolution to the IRA.

"Interesting," said Fitzgerald, as Father Cleary closed the door. "Lt. Schiller's description of the clubs used in Frankfurt was the same as the hurley that killed your grandfather, Brian. Very unusual. This morning I phoned several of the hurling supply companies I could find, and none of them had heard of such a stick ever being manufactured. I also took a look at the report on the slugs that were sent to us for ballistics. As damaged as they were, they were not dummied, and they were a different caliber from the ones that were checked in the German lab."

"Do you think they were switched in Donegal or in Dublin?" asked Mats.

"Mr. Falconi," said Fitzgerald, hissing his words through tightly drawn lips. "You're not Irish, so I will give you the benefit of the doubt about that remark. It is just as likely that the slugs you provided Lt. Schiller had been switched. Lots of people would like nothing better than for the Garda to make fools of themselves. There is no better way than to try to play on regional differences, play one Garda against another. So, with that said, we'll just tread a little lightly as to whose mistake it was until we find out if there are any other spent bullets to substantiate your samples."

"That's all well and good, Inspector, but we are the ones who were almost blown up, and some of us almost clubbed to death," said Mats, his voice rising.

"I understand," said Fitzgerald. "I have a couple thoughts about how to substantiate your statements. Please bear with me for a day or two. Another thing you should know about: the man in charge of Donegal County, Constable Robert Minahen, is top notch. We bring in people from the districts to train with us, learn our techniques. Minahen has been down at least three times, and each time, he impressed his instructors. Top grades in everything from ballistics to handling a crime scene. Less likely that a mistake was made in his office than in lots of other counties."

"He still lied to me about the explosives in the car," said Mats.

"Again, I'm having only your word on that one."

Suzanne reached across the table and put her hand on Mats' forearm. "That's true, Inspector, but two things are fact. One, except for Brian, who has lost his parents in this mess, we are newcomers to Ireland. We have no vested interest in anything but Brian's safety. The second is that this conversation could be avoided completely with just a little police work from you. It is clear that you are either testing us, or mad at some inconsistencies you have discovered on your own."

Fitzgerald smiled for the first time since he had picked them up at Ariel House. *"She's right that a little investigation would make things clearer*, he thought." "Let's go downstairs. I want you to look at a couple bomb packages I had our man make up and see if you can find one that looks like the bundle that was under your bonnet. Then I'll drive you to Donegal."

Compared to the German police station, the headquarters of the Technical Division of the Garda Síochána looked like a poorly maintained clerk's office. Where the Germans had crispness and electronics, the Irish had clutter and in-out baskets.

"This is Sergeant Sean Mulcahey," said Fitzgerald. "If a bomb is found anywhere in Ireland, he or his staff go out and disarm the thing. He's laid out some of the more common devices used by the IRA. Take a look and tell me if any of them look like what you saw under the bonnet."

Mats walked to the table and pointed to the fourth bundle from the end. "This one. It has the same types of explosives as the one in the car. The one in the car was bigger, though. Twice as many sticks, and they were bound every third one with a piece of wood of the same length. Everything was wrapped in a wire that ran toward the firewall."

"Were the explosives sticks a different color?" asked Mulcahey.

"No. Everything is the same except for the size of the bundle and the wood. That's why I was surprised when Minahen told me—"

"That will be enough, Mr. Falconi," interrupted Inspector Fitzgerald. "Do you think you three could find your way back to my office now? I have some business with the sergeant."

Mats led Suzanne and Brian up the stairs. "It was obvious by the look on that sergeant's face that he was concerned about the bomb I pointed out," whispered Mats as they reached the next floor. "And Inspector Fitzgerald is concerned about the integrity of his department. He still isn't convinced that what we say is true."

As soon as the door closed behind the American, Fitzgerald lost his easy grin and turned to the explosives expert. "What is that stuff?" he asked, pointing to the device Mats had identified.

"It's a powerful compound that has been showing up for the last six months. It is manufactured in Russia, Georgia, be specific, from a petroleum base and shipped to Libya. It's very stable in both wet and dry climates. A definite advantage here in Ireland, especially in Dundalk, where this batch was recovered. It's very easy to detonate if properly primed. A watch battery could do it."

"And could a batch the size the American described do a right job on a car?" asked Fitzgerald.

"Could it now! This one on the table could take out this building. One stick would take a car on a merry ride," said Mulcahey, patting the bundle of explosives.

"If this was the type Falconi found, why would such a large load be placed in a car?" asked Fitzgerald.

"Either the bomber didn't know the strength of the explosives, or he wanted them really, really dead," said Mulcahey.

There is a third possibility, thought Fitzgerald. *Whoever planted the bomb wanted to make a statement.*

"Refresh my memory, Sean. How were you notified about the bomb from Donegal?"

"Donegal has two officers who are trained in explosives. If either had found something he was unfamiliar with, he would have called us in. We got the call from Donegal after the rental car agency mechanic had found it. They had already been dispatched to the scene. Three hours later, we got a second report saying that it had been removed and defused."

"You saw the device then?"

"Oh yes. They sent it down by car a day later with the normal packet. It had two small sticks of dynamite that I couldn't have set off if I'd wanted to. The primer had no juice and it was covered with road dust, the kind you would find under the bonnet of a car. We picked up no prints at all from it. Just a few areas where the technician's gloves had smudged the dirt in removing it."

"Minahen told Falconi that the bomb might have scared them but would not have caused serious injury. He said it might even have been in the car for a while," said Fitzgerald.

"I agreed with him. I wrote so in my report."

"Is there any way the American could mistake the device he described for the one you examined?"

"Take a look for yourself. This is the very same bomb that came in from Donegal." Mulcahey pointed to a small dirty device at the end of the table. "What do you think?" He hefted the small dirty bomb and placed it next to the one Falconi had pointed out.

"Did you personally receive the device from Donegal?" Fitzgerald brushed the back of his hand toward the small device.

"No. It was already unpacked when I came to work in the morning."

"How about on the other end? Who sent it from Donegal?"

"What's up, Des? How did you know about that?" asked Mulcahey

"About what?" asked Fitzgerald, his instincts now fully attuned.

"I asked the same question when I saw the bomb. No one signed it in here. It was just labeled 'Donegal Station.'

There was a description of the car and the disarming procedure. The American and his wife were mentioned and the repairman who found the thing, but not the Keohane boy. It was on the proper form and stationery, but there was no signature."

"Neat. Just neat," said Fitzgerald. "If Falconi is right and the bomb was switched, we have no way of knowing if the damned thing was substituted before it left Donegal or here. If it was in Donegal, we will have to go clomping around the whole mucking station to establish the chain of custody the bomb went through before it got in the dispatch. Are these things safe to carry?"

"Now would I be having them around if they weren't?" said Mulcahey.

"Let me take these two with me then."

"You'll have to sign an evidence custody release," said Mulcahey, handing Fitzgerald a form. "Good luck to you on this one, Des."

"Thanks. I have a feeling I'll be needing it."

Fitzgerald walked into his office with a brown canvas sack under his arm. Mats was talking to Suzanne and Brian in the small area in front of his desk.

"Well now," said Fitzgerald, relieved that he was at least beginning to formulate a plan of action. "Give me just a few minutes to clear my desk and I'll be getting you back to Donegal." *Just one piece of hard evidence is all I need to bring this to the chief,* thought Fitzgerald. Davey Costello, like the heads of most divisions, was more a politician than a policeman. He wouldn't be happy to have a report on his desk implying an internal problem, especially without absolute proof.

Fitzgerald took out his cell and pressed his messages. He was just getting used to the electronic intrusion of the damned thing—constant access to instant information, and people having constant access to him as the price he had to pay for it. If he'd had his own way, he would have kept the five secretaries that the damned phone system had replaced. The last message stood him straight up at his desk. It was from Lieutenant Schiller.

Fitzgerald turned to Mats, Suzanne, and Brian. "I hate to be shunting you around like this, but I wonder if you could wait outside for a minute. I have to return a phone call."

He walked them into the common area, where he caught a secretary's eye. "Maureen, would you be a love and get these fine people a cup of your famous tea? See if you can find a soda for the lad. My treat."

As Maureen stood, tossing her auburn hair as she rose, Fitzgerald walked back to his office and closed the door, his cell phone in his hand.

"Inspector Fitzgerald."

Schiller's voice came clear over the phone. "Thanks for getting back to me so quickly. I take it you have met my little troupe? What do you think of their story?"

"Very interesting. I'm going to Donegal with them this afternoon."

"We've had a development here."

"Go on. They're in the next room."

"My report mentioned the skinhead who was killed in the garage after attacking the boy and the old Corsican."

"Yes."

"The jogger who interfered in the fight with the skinheads turned out to be the old man's nephew. At first I thought he might have killed the skinhead who got away. But he phoned me after Falconi left...his name is Ramondo Guibega. He says he chased after the skinhead but lost him. He thought the man must have been picked up by a car. He saw bloodstains that stopped at the curb with a little puddle, like the man had to wait for a while. We checked it out; the stains were fresh and the blood was the same type as the murdered man. Guibega checked out as well. He was a member of the GIGN, the anti-terrorist squad in France, highly decorated with security clearance. His account rings true. Then we got lucky.

"The building where the killing took place has a lot of doctors. Yesterday morning a patient saw our tape sealing off the area where we found the body. She had been to the dentist on the day of the killing for an impression of her tooth. Evidently the dentist had ruined her makeup during the appointment and she was sitting in her car, putting it back on, when she saw a black Mercedes pull up and two men get out. One was the victim and the other was a muscular, blond-haired man. They disappeared from her view behind the elevator column, but seconds later the blond man went back to the car and drove off in a hurry. She didn't think anything about it at the time, but one of our investigators was going over some notes at the site when she came back for her crown cementation appointment yesterday. She asked our officer what the tape was for, and the day and time clicked. She positively identified the skinhead victim, both by his clothes and facial photographs. She was also able to identify the killer. His name is Bernd Lepold. He works, or used to work, for a man named Dieter Rohde. Rohde owns the Municher Brewery. Falconi knows about Rohde. He had me check him out earlier in connection with the murder of the Swede, Lars Bjursten."

"This was the man killed by smoke inhalation?"

"Yes."

"Have you picked up Rohde yet?"

"No. That's why I wanted to get in touch with you. You might have a problem."

"I'm checking out Falconi's story. I'm not sure that we've a problem here. At least not in the central office, but something is funny," answered Fitzgerald, finding himself becoming defensive.

"Don't be too sure," said Schiller. "That's what I told Falconi when he mentioned that Rohde's modus operandi was to get someone inside the controlling organizations. I had our switchboard watched while I obtained the warrant for Rohde. Sure enough, we have a rotten apple. When we got to the brewery, Rohde was gone. A phone call had tipped him off. His secretary thought he might have headed for a farm he owns in the eastern sector. I had a helicopter pick me up and fly me there. That was last night."

"I take it you didn't find him."

"Not exactly. When I arrived, there were fire engines all over the place. The flames were still consuming the house and they were trying to contain the fire from getting into the nearby forests. When things cooled down, we were able to uncover one body. It was burned beyond recognition. Almost to the bone. The dental work was intact. We got Rohde's file from his dentist. Our dental forensic expert made a positive identification of the skull with X-rays. I went over the findings with her this morning before she started practice. Root canals, crowns, and a porcelain bridge. The X-rays were identical to the ones she had taken of the skull.

"Then I got more than lucky. I mentioned that a man in his eighties as rich as Rohde could afford to have such nice dental work. Our dental expert was surprised. She estimated the skull that she had received was from a man in his thirties. I asked her if there was any way the X-rays could be forged. She said not the films themselves, but certainly they could be remounted with the wrong name and date. She went back to the dentist's handwritten chart and sure enough, the description of the work he had done for Rohde didn't match the X-rays. Rohde had laid a very clever trap and we almost fell into it. He had substituted another person's X-rays in his file. Right now we are going on the assumption that the body is that of the murderer, Bernd Lepold, and that Rohde has fled."

"And Rohde is now linked to the attack on the boy."

"Ja. Now you know why I wanted to get in touch with you immediately. Rohde might be coming your way."

"Thank you, Kurt. The next time you're in Ireland, I owe you a Jameson's."

Mats had barely gotten used to driving on the left side of the road as the driver. Now as he rode in the front left passenger's seat with Fitzgerald driving, he was drowsy from his fitful sleep the night before. His eyes closed, and he rested his head against the passenger's window, braced against the gentle turns of the car. As the soft drone of the motor and the gentle motion soothed him, he closed his eyes and dreamed.

Ajaccio, Corsica – 9 September 1943

It had been twenty-four hours since the Resistance had attacked Ajaccio. Near the port, the German forces were too concentrated, their artillery too strong, for the Resistance to attack. All other areas of Ajaccio were under Resistance control. Throughout the previous day, the Corsicans had to watch as the Nazis loaded two ships with men and supplies, taking them off the island.

Rohde and his men were cut off from the docks, unable to re-establish contact with the departing Germans. The Guibegas who surrounded the building effectively sealed off any hope of escape. The Allied troops had landed a day late, after most of the regular German troops had escaped.

Teresa Guibega looked devotedly at the man she had come to love. The evening before, with the sounds of battle echoing through the dark, they had been relieved of their watch and had used the time not for sleep but for making love. Hours later, the softness and tenderness that were so much a part of their lovemaking were gone and again Teresa wore the stern countenance of the Guibega.

"I'm going to check on Rohde," she stated, starting for the door, showing the impatience that made it impossible for her to sit still.

They were at a stand-off. Without artillery, they could not force Rohde and his men out of the building, and they could not attack it without suffering losses of their own. Antonio had promised them the use of a field piece captured by the Resistance as soon as they could find any ammunition, but so far none had been found. To make matters worse, Rohde seemed to recognize his predicament. The arrogance of his black-shirted troops made them unpopular among the regular soldiers and made it unlikely that any serious attempt would be made to cut an escape route for him. Teresa and Falconi had discussed it and suspected that Rohde was holding out to surrender to the Allies rather than the Resistance, who would give him much worse treatment. So while Rohde seemed content to wait, the Guibegas were not.

"Paulo! It is Teresa." She had approached the building next to Rohde's headquarters from the alley behind the building.

"Ciao, Teresa," came Paulo's reply.

"Where are your men?" asked Teresa as she moved from room to room from the back of the building to the front door, where Paulo lay behind a table, watching Rohde's southern wall.

"They're on the roof. One can watch the alley better from there. I'm glad you came. You must have been reading my mind. I think I ate something bad last night. I have stomach cramps. Could you watch my post while I relieve myself?"

"Of course. I need something to do. This waiting... It's no good."

"I know what you mean. I'll be back in fifteen minutes," said Paulo as he shimmied backward into the building and stood, arching his back. "I'm going to try to find some goat's milk and cheese."

"You better hurry. I would rather be gassed by the Germans than by my own side," said Teresa, laughing at Paulo's obvious discomfort.

Paulo laughed too as he hurried from the building, using the same route that Teresa had used to enter. Holding her rifle in front of her, Teresa crawled into the spot behind the table. She shifted her body into a more comfortable position, settling in for what she expected would be closer to a half-hour wait, rather than the fifteen minutes Paulo had promised.

Twenty minutes later, Teresa checked her watch. She thought she'd heard a noise. She moved back into the room, standing by the window while keeping her vigil of the street.

"Well, well, well. Girls fight the Third Reich, too."

Teresa spun, her rifle coming three quarters around before it stopped. In the rear doorway of the room stood three Germans, their guns trained on her.

"Rohde," hissed Teresa. "How did you get here?"

"Ah, I see you know me. Unfortunately, I do not know you. Or do I?" Rohde gestured to the two soldiers, who moved quickly into the room, disarming Teresa. "A young woman fighting with the Maquis. I had plans for how you might entertain the German officers when I captured you. Now it seems you will serve a different purpose. Bring her!"

The soldiers pushed Teresa back through the opening into the back rooms. In the second room there was a pile of dirt to one side of a small hole in the floor where the Germans had tunneled beneath the street. A fourth German stood guarding the hole.

"In five minutes, bring the rest of the men through," commanded Rohde. He had hoped they would capture a Corsican so that he could use his clothes to escape, but the woman was so small that it would have been ridiculous even to try. Besides, she would be a better shield than a man.

Rohde positioned one of his men ahead and one behind. He kept hold of Teresa with his Luger held against her back. As they left the alley, cutting diagonally across the street and down the Rue Campi, Rohde kept looking up at the windows for signs of the snipers—those Resistance fighters who had made his escape impossible for the past two days. He knew they were there, marking his retreat.

Teresa saw the men moving on the rooftops and in the windows and cursed herself for having been captured. Without her as a hostage, Rohde would be dead already. Behind them, the sound of rifle fire announced that the remaining Germans in Rohde's stronghold would not be following them.

They were nearing the Rue Napoleon when three men appeared from a doorway. Walking directly toward her were Egel Falconi, Nando, and a short bald man with a large nose and piercing eyes dressed in an English officer's uniform.

"Stop," commanded Rohde, bringing the pistol up to Teresa's temple. "I do not want to harm the girl, but I will if you do not step aside."

"You and your men have been abandoned. Your last transport has sailed. You are alone," said Falconi. "Corsica is now free. This is Sir Alfred Hamerton. He commands the British forces."

Rohde tried to look past Falconi. He couldn't see the pier where the last evacuation vessel had been docked, so he couldn't confirm the truth of Falconi's words.

"If what you say is true, I will surrender my troops to the British."

"It is true. Release the girl," said Hamerton.

"I will when I see the dock."

Sir Alfred nodded and the three stepped aside, allowing the Germans and the girl to pass. Falconi followed Rohde, leaving twenty meters between them for comfort. Teresa's safety was his only thought.

Rohde turned the corner and saw the truth in what Falconi had said. Teresa felt an increased pressure of his gun against her temple as he kept her between himself and Falconi. She knew his only hope now lay with the British, but Falconi spoke for the group.

"Who are you?" shouted Rohde, still holding the gun to Teresa's temple.

"I am a man of honor, and I add my pledge to Sir Hamerton's that you will be allowed to surrender if you let the girl go," said Falconi.

Rohde pulled Teresa to the cover of some oil drums, still flanked by his two remaining riflemen. "You, man of honor, bring the Englishman here. You will get the girl."

Teresa could see what was going to happen. Rohde, a monster who had caused the deaths of so many men, women, and children of the Guibega, would be sent to some British prison for officers, and after the war he would go free. With a strength that surprised the German, she turned, knocking his gun hand away, and punched straight up, hitting his throat. As he staggered back, she passed between the oil drums and ran at full speed toward the safety of the nearest building.

Rohde recovered to see his men standing frozen in indecision. He tried to order them to shoot, but his voice would not come, an effect of Teresa's blow. In rage, he brought his gun up and fired three quick shots. Two of them found Teresa's back, one piercing her lung and the other her heart.

Teresa had not even fallen to the pavement when the first of the rifle shots echoed between the buildings. From the windows above the intersection, men were shooting. The man to the right of Rohde went down first, then the soldier on his left. Rohde knelt behind the drums, trying to pull his handkerchief from his pocket to wave as a banner of surrender.

The tracer bullet did not hit Rohde. Instead it hit the oil drum behind which he was cowering. The container erupted in a great fireball, the remnants of the fuel inside it exploding in a flash of flame. Rohde was engulfed. He spun around and ran, the flames fanned into even more fury by his frantic motion. Whether by design or luck he ran, still burning, over the timber curb that marked the edge of the pier and fell into the water.

Nando and Sir Hamerton were the first to reach the pier. Falconi had run to Teresa. He reached her as the last of her blood was pumping from her pierced heart.

"I would have made you a wonderful wife," she mouthed, her words softer than a whisper.

"You're already my wife," he cried as she died in his arms.

They fished Rohde from the salt water, more dead than alive. His face and hands were burned to a state of grotesqueness. He was not expected to last many hours.

"I understand the pain and grief this man has caused you," said Sir Alfred Hamerton. "He is a foul murderer and should be treated as such. But I don't think you fully realize what is at stake here. There are reports coming to us about Nazi death camps that go against the convictions of all civilized people. They are said to be used as the Nazis' final solution for Jews and other undesirables. This is the first officer we have captured who actually sent people to those camps. He has knowledge that could not only help the Allies but turn world opinion against Hitler and the Nazis for good."

"He must die," said Nando, who had taken over as spokesman for the Resistance. Falconi had come to stand by his side but was silent, tears running down his cheeks.

"At least let me try to preserve him long enough to question him," said Hamerton. "Then, if he dies of his burns, it was his lot."

"The man is dying. Let Nando question him. He'll get your answers," said Falconi, knowing that one way or another, the man would die at the hands of the Guibega.

"No!" said Hamerton.

"All right," said Nando. "But two of my men guard him at all times."

Hamerton agreed. "We have a corpsman. He isn't a physician, but he has proven to be a magician with burns. Damned if he hasn't saved at least three of our lads already in this war. I believe he'll get a ribbon or two for his work even if he is a paddy."

"A paddy?" asked Nando.

"Yes. He's Irish, you know."

Chapter Twenty-one

Ireland, September 2003

Mats awoke with a start as Fitzgerald came to a stop at a hard left turn in the town of Collooney.

"Sorry," said Fitzgerald, intent on the road ahead, missing that Mats' reaction had had nothing to do with his driving.

Mats looked over his shoulder at Suzanne and Brian in the back seat. "How long have I been asleep?" he asked.

"About fifteen minutes," answered Suzanne.

Now I know Rohde's connection to Ireland, he thought. He would have to wait to tell Brian and Suzanne when they were out of the car. *I also know that my family has as much reason for a vendetta against Rhode as the Guibega do. Nando was right. If I was meant to know, I would know.* But now all was clear. There would be no need for secrecy.

The rest of the journey through the lush green landscape of central Ireland was made in relative silence. *How like Corsica Ireland is, despite the differences in weather,* thought Mats: small towns and villages populated by families that are fiercely loyal to their own; the natives resilient, survivors of both invasion and oppression; island people.

"Were you present when the repairman found the bomb?" asked Fitzgerald abruptly.

"No," answered Mats. "The last look I had at it was when I pulled the battery cable ... I just closed the hood and phoned the rental agency, saying the car wouldn't start."

"So, the local Garda think you knew nothing about the bomb until they told you? Why didn't you tell them the truth?"

"I told Lieutenant Schiller. I thought I told you as well," said Mats, patiently.

"Maybe you did now, but refresh my memory, anyway, if you please." They had already passed through Sligo and some of the landmarks were becoming familiar to Mats. They were less than an hour from Donegal, and Fitzgerald was slipping into what Mats was beginning to recognize as his official personality.

"I thought it would be better if whoever tried to kill us thought we were just dumb lucky rather than on to them."

"Ah yes. I would have done the same myself, had I thought about it."

Inspector Fitzgerald turned off the highway before reaching Donegal. A hundred yards down a narrow potholed road, they came to a cottage with a detached garage, separate but obviously part of the property. A recent model Ford was visible inside the structure, its boot lid up.

"Mr. Falconi, come along if you'd like," said Fitzgerald as he pulled the key from the ignition.

The two men walked up the short stone path. It was like many of the houses outlying Donegal town—thick white stucco walls on top of a foundation of stone.

Fitzgerald knocked loudly on the door. "Tohey! John Tohey. Open the door, please."

They heard shuffling behind the door; then it opened, a smallish, dark-haired man holding the inside knob as a barrier to their entering.

"John Tohey?" Fitzgerald said again.

"That's me."

"I'm Inspector Desmond Fitzgerald. I'm trying to tie down some loose ends on the car bomb you discovered. You're the man who found the bomb in the rental car, were you not?"

"Bomb?" said Tohey, a look of pure innocence on his face.

"It would be better for you if you gave me straight answers," said Fitzgerald pointing a finger at the small man's chest.

"Ah," said Tohey stepping back. "That would be about two weeks ago. Yes, that was me. I got a call from the agency I work for that a car wouldn't start."

"You got a good look at the device, did you?"

"And how could I not get a good look at it, the bundle of sticks as big as my toolbox and all? Scared the shite out of me, it did."

"Good. Then you could tell me which of these looks most like the one you saw under the hood of the car." Fitzgerald took the two bombs out of his case and laid them on a chair just to the left of the door.

"Am I in some sort of trouble here?" asked Tohey, looking at the two bombs. "I swear I never saw the bomb before that day, or after it for that matter. I only put the car back running after Minahen's bunch got through ripping it apart."

"You're not in any trouble as long as I get straight talk from you now," answered Fitzgerald, looking behind the man and seeing a packed suitcase just inside the door. "Answer my question."

"It was like this one, but bigger." Tohey pointed to the device that Mats had identified earlier.

The trail of the bomb switch had just gotten much shorter.

"You look to be leaving in rather a hurry, Mr. Tohey. Where might you be going?"

"I'm off to visit relatives in Lahinch," said Tohey, nervously.

"Would you like to tell me why you're leaving just now?"

"Can I ask, Inspector, if you were active in the movement in the old days, like most of the Garda?" asked Tohey.

"I was," answered Fitzgerald, with a candor that surprised Mats.

"Then you'd understand the phone call I got not an hour ago. I was told to leave Donegal for a month. From your questions, I'm an eejit for not leaving sooner."

"The IRA told you to leave?"

"They don't identify themselves, now, do they? And here you come asking about the bomb."

"Did you watch the bomb defused?"

"No. They sent me away, and grateful I was."

"Who sent you? Constable Minahen?"

"No, it was a sergeant. I didn't get his name. I don't remember him offering it."

"Okay. Go visit your relatives, Mr. Tohey. Phone this number when you reach there. It's my cell. If I don't answer, leave a message as to where you are." Fitzgerald gave the frightened man his card with his number scribbled on the back. "Don't let anyone else know where you are. If someone already knows, then go elsewhere, but keep in touch with me. 'Twill be trouble for you if you don't."

Fitzgerald drove the remaining four miles to Donegal. As he pulled up in front of the large brewery doors, Mats reached over and honked the horn. The gate opened and Magee came out to meet them.

"Inspector Des Fitzgerald, this is my foreman, Cathal Magee." Mats made the introductions casually, but there was nothing casual about the look he saw Magee give Fitzgerald. Mats realized that Magee had recognized the man as a Garda as soon as the car pulled in and was treating him coolly.

"Inspector," said Magee, without offering his hand, as the group got out of the car.

"Magee," acknowledged Fitzgerald. Mats saw that the evaluation going both ways. "Mr. Falconi tells me you were the first to get to Brian's parents after the shooting. Could you show me their positions?"

Magee looked quickly at Mats, receiving a nod before answering. "I was in the office at the top of the stairs. The first I heard was a round of fifteen or twenty shots, then another blast, perhaps as many as three. I ran down the stairs, but before I could open the door, that small one there, I heard a screech of tires. By the time I got to the street, both Mr. and Mrs. Keohane were dead."

"Where did you find them?" asked Fitzgerald.

Mats moved to Brian's side and put an arm around the boy's shoulders, but Suzanne reached in and gently pulled the boy toward the stairs to the upstairs office.

Magee answered by moving through the door, stopping in front of the large delivery gates. "The mister was here. The stains of his blood are still to be seen, even if the chalk marks have washed away."

"And the boy's mother?"

"She was about here."

"Now, where do you think the gunmen stood?"

"I think they were fairly close together. At least, at first," answered Magee.

The inspector's questions are good, thought Mats. *He is trying to reconstruct the murder scene, and he isn't going to rely on the reports.*

"Give him the whole of it, Cathal," said Mats.

"The bodies were there. The majority of the bullet holes, here and here. That would put the gunmen … about here." Magee walked into the street to a point that intersected the two lines drawn mentally from the still apparent scars in the building and door.

"Mr. Falconi said you recovered some slugs?"

"That's right. Minahen went over it pretty good but there were a few they missed—here and here." Magee pointed to a space between the timbers where he had retrieved the bullets.

"They must have been wanting to be real sure of the job. There were also shots fired almost straight down into the bodies," finished Magee with disgust.

"Let's see if we can find another slug or two," said Fitzgerald.

"The other day I noticed a mark that might be just that." Magee led Fitzgerald to a spot at the wooden gates, pointing up to a small scar under the top of the doorjamb.

"Have you a ladder and a knife?" asked Fitzgerald as he moved his practiced eyes over the gate and the front of the building. "Looks like there might be another here as well." Kneeling down, he ran his fingers over a crack between the street and the foundation of the building. There was a small chip on the right side of the crack.

By the time Magee had the stepladder in place, Fitzgerald had widened the crack with his own pen knife and had worked the flattened slug of lead from its resting place. He let Magee climb the ladder, cautioning him not to scar the slug if he found one. He was no longer concerned that Magee had switched the bullets. The one he had found on his own told him all he needed to know. The slug was hardly damaged, as the sides of the crack had stopped the bullet before its tip came into contact. The ballistics expert might have had trouble identifying its caliber, but no one would miss the fact that the hollow nose was filled with what looked like the broken end of a toothpick. Mats' description of the slugs was correct—not the official Garda report. Perhaps the use of the wood was evidence of a cult, as Falconi and the boy had suggested.

"Who was in charge of removing the bullets?"

"Minahen was all over the place like a coat of paint. But Sergeant O'Deaver worked on the bullets pretty much by himself. He had some sort of metal detector," said Magee. "Were there any bullets recovered from the bodies?"

Inspector Desmond Fitzgerald, born in County Clare, knew Magee's type. They pretend to be slow but in truth are among the cleverest men on earth. Magee had asked the question that he himself had missed. The bullets that had ended up in the bodies of Brian's parents would have been collected by the coroner. They would have been placed in a separate container and subject to a separate analysis from the ones sent by the Donegal Garda. Fitzgerald had not considered the absence of a report in the file until just now when Magee had mentioned it.

"You're a clever man, Cathal Magee. Are you clever enough to tell me who committed this murder?"

"I can tell you who didn't. They made it look like it was IRA, but it wasn't. The boys didn't have anything to do with it. They'd like to find out who means to lay the blame on them, though."

"You've been in touch, then."

"You might say I've heard things," replied Magee.

"Who, then?"

"Well, it isn't the IRA, and it isn't someone who wanted the Harp and Hawk. No one exactly rushed forward to buy it until Tobin brought Mr. Falconi."

"What about Tobin?" asked Fitzgerald. "He profited by the sale in commissions."

"Tobin?" echoed Magee, almost laughing at the thought. "I don't think Tobin's been in Donegal more than twice in his life. He couldn't harm anything but a bottle of Jameson's."

"So who then?" Fitzgerald asked again.

"Someone with a real hatred inside them, Inspector. I've thought hard about it and I can't figure out who would have such a hate. The Keohanes were good people. You can tell that by Brian. I don't know of anyone who disliked them."

"And Falconi?" asked Fitzgerald, sure of Magee's answer but wanting to gauge the old man's reaction.

"He's a surprise. I didn't know what to think of him at first. Now I trust him completely. It was the way he treated the boy, treated him with respect, he did, gave him a third of the brewery. Treated me grand, and the men as well. He knows what he's about business-wise. Even Tobin, who I thought didn't have a clue when I first met him, turned out to be a clever one at the distributing end. Doesn't look like Falconi's going for a fast punt, either. He really pushed to get the non-alcoholic piss bottled so that he could export it to California. You asked me what I think of him? I think he's got some Irish in him."

"That's the feeling I get as well," said Fitzgerald. "Thank you for the information, Cathal. Oh, don't be saying anything about the slugs we found, will you? In fact, it would be better if we had never talked."

A call to the Donegal Garda office was enough to locate Minahen. He was having lunch at a pub called McDaid's.

Fitzgerald had wanted to talk with Minahen alone, and the pub gave him an opportunity that was better than he had hoped for. Minahen was sitting in a small booth across from the bar, a bottle of Harp and Hawk in front of him. He stood as the inspector entered.

"Des, nice to see you. My office said you had called. Sit down, the stew and the beer are both good."

"Thank you, Robert. The ride up took longer than I had expected."

"So, you're just up for a holiday, you say?"

"That, and I'm trying to fill in a few holes in Dublin's file on the Keohane murders." Fitzgerald watched Minahen as he shifted slightly in his seat but showed no other sign of discomfort.

"I've made no secret that I feel the counties should have jurisdiction over local problems," said Minahen.

"Is that what it is, a local problem?"

"The Keohanes' murder? Tell you the truth, I don't know what it is. But if you were up here digging around on any other case, I'd be on the phone to Costello before you finished your stew."

Both men stopped talking as the publican, complete with a red nose and white apron, placed a large plate of bread and two bowls of stew in front of them. "Another for you there?" he asked Minahen, pointing at the beer in front of him.

"Might as well. One for my friend here as well, Peter, seeing as he's on holiday and not on duty," Minahen added, seeing Fitzgerald nod. "Now, just what holes are you trying to fill?" he asked as the bartender walked away.

Fitzgerald waited until the beers were on the table and the publican far enough away not to overhear their conversation before he answered. "Have you seen either of these before?" he asked, hefting his case onto the table and opening it so the top hid the contents from the bar.

Minahen looked inside the case. Then with his left hand, he slammed it shut.

"What the devil are you trying to do? Those have nothing to do with the Keohane case."

"Then you've seen them?"

"Of course I've seen them. One is from the American's rental car. The other is one of Mulcahey's mockups. I've taken the detonating device apart a dozen times."

"Which one came from the car?" Fitzgerald asked softly. He lifted the lid of the case again.

"This one, for sure. What are you up to, Fitzgerald? Don't be playing games with me." Minahen reached out and touched the small explosive device before using the same meaty finger to point at Fitzgerald.

"Lay off, man," said Fitzgerald. "Something stinks in this case. Two people saw the big one in the car, not the firecracker that you say was there."

"Who?"

"Tohey, the mechanic who discovered the thing, for one."

"Tohey, Tohey," spluttered Minahen, loudly enough that the bartender turned his head toward their table. "Tohey was plastered. God knows what he saw. He was lucky we didn't pinch him for drunk driving."

"Someone else saw the bomb before it was removed and corroborates Tohey's description."

"Impossible."

"Did you see the thing while it was still in the car?"

"I saw it after it was removed by my squad."

"That's not what I asked."

"No, then. I didn't see it in the vehicle. I was up near Letterkenny. Someone had poached two red deer in Glenveagh Park. I didn't get back until the bomb had already been removed. Look, Des, we get a lot of bomb threats up here. You wouldn't have time to breathe if we called you up for every single one. O'Deaver took the call. He took the bomb equipment to the Keohane farm. By the time I got there, he had already disarmed the thing."

"And that's the device he removed?"

"Yes. It was already in the explosive container. We sent it down to Mulcahey."

"Did you write the report?"

"Yes, but the bomb was hardly worth the effort. It was crusted with road grime. It was probably in the car for some time. We're running the history of the rental now."

"Robert, I've always thought you ran a good office up here in Donegal. What would you think if this report came to you?" Fitzgerald took a folded paper from his coat and handed it to Minahen.

Minahen looked at the report before tossing the two stapled pages back to Fitzgerald. "This didn't come from me. There's no signature."

"No mention of Brian Keohane, who would have been in the car too, or the fact that the car was at the Keohanes' farm. Nothing to tie it to the Keohane murders." The fact that Minahen didn't look again at the report told Fitzgerald that he hadn't missed the deletions on his first reading. "Now, if you had two eyewitnesses report that there was a large lethal bomb in that car, one completely different from the one you sent, and then this letter came across your desk, what would you think?"

"Tread lightly, Fitzgerald. I can't explain the report. I have a copy of the one I signed in my file and I'm sure it's different, but the small bomb is the one that came from the car. Are you accusing me of covering this thing up?" said Minahen.

"Right now, I'm just trying to figure things out. Then there is the question of the bullets that killed the Keohanes and the ones that struck the van. They were doctored, but the slugs sent down from Donegal station weren't."

"What the devil are you talking about?"

"I retrieved a slug not an hour ago from the brewery gate. It had been dummied; a splinter of wood stuck in its tip. Some others were sent down independent of yours and they were dummied as well. I'm willing to bet that when I get those from the coroner, they will be hollow-nosed as well," said Fitzgerald, watching for Minahen's reaction. He saw a flash of anger, then a hard expression set like stone on the other man's face.

"O'Deaver recovered the slugs at both shootings. He's a local man. I've been grooming him. Just made him sergeant. If he's covering something up, it's my fault for not watching him."

Fitzgerald kept his eyes on the Donegal chief. There was anger followed by resolution. It was an honest set of emotions. Fitzgerald believed that Minahen was telling the truth.

"Right now, it looks like things are bent on your end. I don't think central station is all clear either, but bent things are, and I want to know by whom. If O'Deaver is to blame, he had to have others involved. Work with me on this, Minnie." Fitzgerald couldn't read Minahen, whose large, flat face had all the expression of a tombstone. If he was straight, it would come out soon enough. The important thing was that the trail of the bomb and bullets had now narrowed to the Donegal station and to Sargent O'Deaver.

On his own end, Fitzgerald had some questions as well. It had taken almost four hours to drive to Tohey's place from Dublin. He hadn't phoned the Donegal station until after he'd left Tohey. But someone had warned Tohey, and that someone was well informed as to his movements. The only people in that category were in the Dublin central office. Fitzgerald knew how Minahen felt—what it was like to be betrayed by one of your own.

❧ ❧ ❧

The morning after spending the night at the farm, Mats took the van to the Harp and Hawk to tend to the business piled on his desk, leaving Liam Magee to guard Suzanne and Brian.

Cathal Magee had carried out all of his orders, stopping only at a point where Mats' input was absolutely necessary. The old man had a genius for organization. The non-alcoholic beer was being cold warehoused, awaiting the last vouchers for grain spirits on the import license. The output of the regular Harp and Hawk was staying at peak production, even with the runs of "piss," as Magee insisted on calling the non-alcoholic batches. They needed to buy another delivery truck and hire drivers. Tobin had found deals on several used vehicles and had already interviewed two of his relatives as potential drivers. Magee had even extrapolated the amount of overtime the plant would need if the demand kept going up under Tobin's relentless wholesaling.

Even the new label for the NA product had come off the printers looking better than Mats could have hoped. It had the same emotional impact as the regular Harp and Hawk label, as if it was a statement of Irish independence. Hawk's Brew—NA—a good name for the best non-alcoholic product he had ever tasted.

Mats, his eyes tired from the paperwork, finished signing the last of the instructions and started to rise from his desk to call Magee into the office. The stress of the last few days had caught up with him. His legs seemed leaden, slow and tired, as he started to stand. He sat back down in the chair with resignation, closing his eyes and allowing dreams of Corsica to blot out the reality of the present...

❧ ❧ ❧

Ajaccio, Corsica – 14 September 1943

The Mediterranean sun beat down on Egel Falconi. In the days after Teresa's death, he had stayed at the Alta Mira, receiving Guibega after Guibega on the balcony overlooking Ajaccio. All of them seemed to know of the loving relationship between the Maquis and Teresa. The women cried tears when giving their thanks for his leadership and condolences for his loss. The men were stoical, but pride and pain were evident in their faces as well as in their strained words of gratitude and regret.

The day before Teresa's funeral, Nando requested a meeting with the English Lord, along with Antonio. Falconi joined them.

"Sir Alfred, give Rohde to the Corsican Resistance for judgment. Many Resistance members and civilians, even children, were killed because of this man. It is we who should judge him," said Nando.

"I understand your feelings and those of your people," replied Hamerton. "But you must also understand our position. First, the man is cooperating. We are getting our first good look at the scope of the German concentration camp operation. Second, what he did was done while a soldier at war. He was under orders to fight the Resistance movement, and casualties are to be expected in war."

"The man took young women and children," hissed Nando.

"I understand your grief. I saw him shoot your niece, but again, she was a fighter in the Resistance."

"She was unarmed. He shot her in the back," said Falconi, the menace in his voice causing Hamerton to straighten.

"Look," said Hamerton, trying to sound authoritative but knowing that the men in front of him had stature as leaders that might be equal to his own. "Rohde might still die from his burns. My medic has him well enough to interrogate for a few minutes a day, but I'm told he could get an infection at any time. He won't be out of danger for another ten days."

Falconi stepped in front of Nando. "Get your information fast. I have a feeling he won't last that long," he snapped at Hamerton, then turned abruptly and left the room, followed by Antonio and Nando.

"I suspect Hamerton will try and fly Rohde off Corsica, perhaps to England, as soon as he can travel," said Falconi as they exited the English compound. "We must take our revenge before that happens."

"It will be done," said Nando through clenched teeth.

Falconi was known as the Maquis to the Guibega alone. To the Allies who arrived in Ajaccio, he was only a Corsican—Nando's brother, Carlo. Many people asked about the Maquis, who had become a legend in the retaking of Corsica, but Falconi was pleased his secret remained within the clan.

Falconi knew that Sir Alfred Hamerton suspected he was Maquis, but he didn't know him as Egel Falconi. He too thought he was simply Carlo, Nando's brother. But Hamerton had been in communication with Captain L'Herminier and undoubtedly had his description. It would only be after Falconi left the island that Hamerton would discover that Nando Guibega had no brother, and his only sister, older by twelve years, had died when Teresa was not quite three years old.

On the fifth day after Teresa's death, she was given the ultimate honor. She was buried with the full ceremony given to a Guibega killed in the service of the Falconi.

She was placed in a boat-shaped trench, lined with rocks and filled with hardwood kindling and logs. The funeral pyre was lit, and the Guibega approached the flames one by one, each placing a fagot into the flames. Her remains were cremated to the chants of the entire Guibega clan. In the end, they celebrated in her honor with songs of happiness and bravery, dancing, and much wine, repatriated from recaptured German stores.

❧ ❧ ❧

Harp and Hawk Brewery—Donegal, Ireland 2003

Mats' cell phone vibrated in his pocket. He had been in a deep sleep and was unsure of how long it had been ringing, still inside his vision of Teresa's funeral. He fumbled, trying to get the phone out of his pocket, and it dropped onto the thick area rug at his feet. Luckily, it didn't break. The screen showed Nando was calling him.

"Nando, are you all right? How is your arm?" Mats was still muddled from being awakened from his dream.

"I'm fine. There is no swelling under the cast. I'm phoning to warn you. Dieter Rohde has faked his own death and left Germany. Ramondo traced him to Ireland. He might already be there."

"Lt. Schiller phoned yesterday and said the same thing. We are with Lt. Fitzgerald of the Dublin Garda and we're being very cautious."

"Perhaps you should leave Ireland. It would be safer if Ramondo and I were there."

"Suzanne thinks the same thing, but only if we could protect Brian by bringing him with us permanently. Nando, I must speak to you about something. I know about the death of your niece, Teresa, and the love between her and my father." There was a silence on the other end. "What I don't know is why Rohde didn't die of his burns or how he escaped from Corsica, back to Germany."

Nando did not answer immediately. The silence had become uncomfortable before he finally sighed, speaking softly in response to Mats' question.

"The corpsman who was taking care of his burns was friendly with our guards. He explained how beneath the gauze he stretched a thin cambium layer of the yew tree over Rohde's burns. The porous film acted like a second skin. It allowed the raw dermal layers beneath the bandages to breathe while being protected from infection. He said his ancestors had been using the cure for a thousand years. After three days, Rohde stabilized. On the fourth day, with the bandages still covering all but the man's mouth, Lord Hamerton started questioning him.

"On Friday, September 25th, sixteen days after Teresa was killed, there was a weekly air transport departing for England. We learned that Hamerton planned to evacuate Rohde on that plane to England. We made plans so that he would evacuate a corpse.

"The corpsman outsmarted us. On the morning of September 18th, a week early, after changing his patient's bandages, he gave the British soldiers guarding the prisoner written orders to transfer the German prisoner, Lieutenant Dieter Rohde, to the scheduled airplane. Rohde was to be under the guard and care of medic third class Grady. The orders carrying Lord Hamerton's signature were forged.

"Things were hectic at the newly repaired airstrip. No one questioned orders signed by Lord Hamerton. Rohde and Grady with his medical kit were put on board the transport plane. The plane was over Spain before it was discovered that both Grady and his charge were missing. By that time, it was too late."

"What did my father do?" asked Mats.

"At Teresa's funeral, four days before the flight, he told me he would be leaving Corsica. He made me promise that if a son or daughter of his ever came back, I would not tell them of the love he had for my Teresa. The next day he was gone. That was three days before Rohde disappeared. That was the last I heard of Egel until you met Carlo in Ajaccio, except for two rather large transfers of money to the Guibega accounts in 1950 and 1975."

"And Rohde and the corpsman?" asked Mats.

"The plane crashed and burned near the village of Jaca, in the foothills of the Pyrenees, some hundred and twenty-five miles west of Barcelona. There were four bodies aboard, all burned. One was partially covered in bandages. It was reported that they were the bodies of the flight crew, Rohde, and the medic."

"But Schiller told us that after a year, Rohde made it back to Germany, alive!" said Mats, his voice rising.

"Yes, almost a year after the crash, the corpsman made it back to England. We assumed that Rohde made it to Germany as well, but we were unable to trace him."

"You say the corpsman's name was Grady?"

"Yes," answered Nando, a slight quiver in his voice.

"I have had dealings with a Grady here in Ireland. He is too young to have been your Grady, though."

"Would you like me to come to Ireland?" asked Nando.

"No, you and Ramondo stay there and heal. I'll take care of things here." Mats disconnected, thinking hard about what it all meant.

❧ ❧ ❧

The Harp and Hawk Brewery—
Donegal, Ireland 2003

A knock brought Mats completely back to the present. Cathal Magee entered without waiting for a response.

"Are you all right?" Magee asked, seeing Mats standing, drawn and confused, at the desk.

"Yes. I just took a nap. Tell me, Cathal, do you know Grady's father?"

"Of course. Kenny Grady. He was a smart one, like his sons, only more helpful," said Magee, staring past Mats as if trying to conjure up a proper image of the man. "He was a medical man. Came back from the war and helped a lot of people with his cures, until the proper doctors shut him down, of course."

"Is he still alive?"

"Nah. He died twenty years ago, lost at sea in a great storm. The young Grady lives at his farm now, the place you took a look at with Liam."

"Can you describe him for me?" asked Mats.

"I can do better than that. I have a picture of him at home. We were on the same hurling team. Did right well too. He was small, but he was the fastest man in Donegal. Got to the all-Ireland finals in 1948."

CHAPTER TWENTY-TWO

Brian awakened with the need to get away from the house, to be alone. Fishing was an excuse. The long tacks toward Inishmurray in his skiff promised not only good fishing but also solitude. He had to do a bit of talking to convince Suzanne and Liam Magee, who had been sent down from Donegal to protect them while Mats was away, that his skiff would be as safe as the farmhouse, but he wore them down. The sail across the bay had given him three salmon off his troll line. He knew that Suzanne had understood that he wanted to be alone.

Without trying to replace his mother and father, Mats and Suzanne had become like family. He felt a bond with Mats because of their dreams, both of them seeing the same Viking confrontation between the Falkhands and Redhand, but through the eyes of different ancestors. Sometimes Brian wished that his own father had instructed him more fully in how to interpret the dreams. But that had not taken place. He was thankful that his father had at least left him with more knowledge of the Knack than Mats' father had with what Mats called the Gift.

It was clear that everything that had happened was directed toward his family. Mats and Suzanne were only in danger because of him. As Brian fished the bank, he went over the problem again and again in his mind. Mechanically, he tended the sail and pulled fish after fish into the boat, hardly aware of his own actions. At last he came to a decision. He would leave Donegal. Others had done it who were a lot younger than he. He was sure that the violence would stop when he was no longer present. He loved Mats and Suzanne too much to see them end up as his parents had, shot and bleeding in the street.

As he returned across the bay, the wind turned southerly, allowing Brian to leave the sail unattended. By the time he could make out the jetty, he had all of the fish cleaned.

As Brian entered the inlet over which his house was perched, his senses sharpened. The house seemed as he had left it five hours before. There was no sign of activity, nothing to warn him of danger, except a strong intuitive feeling that something was wrong. Brian knew Suzanne would be watching, that she would be worried about him and would greet him at the jetty. Sailing as close to the shore as he dared, he dropped sail and shouted, "Suzanne!"

Suzanne did not come out, but for a brief instant, Brian saw a head in a black ski mask fill the kitchen window.

Brian wasted no time, quickly raising the sail and tacking back out toward the center of the bay. As he moved away, two men with rifles ran toward the shore. Brian ducked under the boom, putting the sail between himself and the men on shore, as shots were fired. The skiff moved quickly out of the small inlet and into the shipping channel.

To the west, motoring toward Donegal, was the thirty-foot fishing trawler *Kathleen*. Owned and captained by Johnny Meehan, the *Kathleen* fished commercially from the Donegal docks. Brian had occasionally crewed for Meehan in summers past and knew it would not be easy to catch his attention. Meehan was known for paying more attention to his bottle of Murphy's than to his course as he came in after a good catch.

Brian's luck held. He was off the *Kathleen*'s stern when Meehan caught sight of the small sailboat and the boy hailing him. He slowed the *Kathleen*, allowing the smaller vessel to catch up and come alongside.

"What's up, Brian my boy?" Meehan shouted from the cabin as Brian made fast.

"Permission to come aboard and use your radio, Captain!" shouted Brian over the low throb of the *Kathleen*'s twin diesels.

"Permission granted."

Brian could tell before he set foot in the cabin that the catch had been good. There was a redness in Meehan's face that exceeded the effects of the sun and wind. Today only Meehan and his mate, crew, and drinking partner, Paddy James, had taken her out. Both watched Brian climb the five-step ladder to the bridge with half-full tumblers clutched firmly in their calloused hands.

Brian ran to the radio, flicked the switch to SEND, and gave the *Kathleen*'s call letters, which were taped across the top of the radio. Moments later the harbor master's reply blared out of the small speaker on the console.

"Chief, this is Brian Keohane on board the *Kathleen*. Would you please patch this to the Harp and Hawk? The number is 255-3541."

"Just a second, lad," came the voice over the receiver as Brian turned his back on the two interested men on the bridge.

Brian waited for what seemed an eternity before Mats picked up the line.

"Mats, something happened at the house. I went fishing in the skiff. When I came back into the cove, I saw a masked man at the window. Two men with guns ran to the shore, but I got away." His last words were almost a whisper into the mouthpiece.

"Did you see Suzanne or Liam?"

"No, only the two gunmen."

"Where are you now?"

"I'm on a fishing boat, the *Kathleen*, heading for the dock. We'll be berthed in twenty minutes or so." Brian didn't know who might be listening to the ship-to-shore, even if he could keep Meehan and James from hearing. Mats would be warned and that was all that mattered.

"Cathal and some of the men will be waiting for you. I'm going to Suzanne."

Brian turned to Captain Meehan as the connection was broken. Surprised at his own sense of calm, he said, "I'd appreciate it if you squeezed the throttles for the rest of the trip, Captain."

The captain, having heard most of the transmission, swallowed the last of his drink, put the glass aside, and pressed the throttle to full ahead. Cathal Magee and four of his nephews were waiting for the *Kathleen* as she docked.

As Magee whisked Brian away to the brewery, Mats was approaching the Keohane farmhouse. The Magees with him were all young, fit, and very serious. Four of them had stuffed themselves into the rear seat of the car, leaving the front for Mats and Dermot Magee, who took the driver's seat.

They made one stop, taking less than a minute, but it was time that felt interminable to Mats. As they pulled to a stop, the rear doors opened and two men, brothers, went to a work shed standing against the protected side of a small barn. They expertly lifted off a board that attached the shed to the side of a stone wall and, out of a narrow opening, removed three automatic rifles and a wooden toolbox heavy with handguns and ammunition.

They threw the cloth coverings back into the hiding place and replaced the board before running to the car.

Dermot was already flooring the accelerator when Mats yelled, "Stop!"

The car slid to a halt on the gravel road, throwing the men in the back seat together. They came up alert, looking out the window for the reason Mats had stopped the car.

"Is the shed open?" Mats asked, turning toward the men who had just gotten in.

"Yes," came the quick reply.

Mats ran from the car to the shed, opening it, the doors hiding his head and torso. Seconds later he ran back to the car, jumping in as Dermot again jammed the car into first gear. As they moved back onto the coastal road, Dermot looked over at Mats. Cradled in his hands, as if he were measuring its weight, was an axe.

As they approached the curve that would bring them in sight of the Keohane farmhouse, Mats had Dermot stop the car. He got out and walked carefully over the crest of the hill, staying low. In front of him, the house stood serene and solitary against the gray western sky. There were no signs of Suzanne or the masked man. Mats returned to the car.

"Dermot, make your way around the house. Secure the jetty, but leave someone here to guard the road."

Taking the driver's seat, Mats took the car around the curve, turning off the road and up the four-hundred-meter drive to the house. He parked to the side of the garage, out of sight of the house. He went to the front door, feeling the weight of the axe in his hand, holding his panic in check that he might be too late to save Suzanne.

The front door was unlocked; the main room empty. Mats stepped in, calling Suzanne's name. He ran to the staircase, taking the steps two at a time. Their bedroom was empty, as was the bathroom. He scanned the rooms, seeing no sign of a struggle. Running back down the stairs, he saw through the kitchen window that Dermot was at the back door, gun at shoulder level. Mats checked Brian's bedroom and found it unoccupied. With no sign of Suzanne, he ran to the kitchen to find Dermot kneeling next to Liam, who was tied up and bloodied on the floor.

"Is he alive?"

"Yes, he's been bashed in the head, but he'll be all right. He's taken worse in family squabbles. Any sign of Suzanne?"

"Nothing. Her suitcase is gone and some personal things. Her cell phone was on the floor next to the bed," said Mats.

"Why would they want Mrs. Falconi?" asked Dermot.

"I don't know, but if she's hurt, whoever they are will pay. Leave two men here. Have them phone Cathal. Tell him to keep Brian at the Harp and Hawk. We'll be there in twenty minutes."

⚜ ⚜ ⚜

The Harp and Hawk Brewery—Donegal, Ireland

"Tell me about what you saw, Brian," said Mats, watching for signs of panic on the face of the boy.

As Brian told what had happened, Mats nodded his approval. The boy had not panicked. He had reacted coolly and correctly at the house, and he was thinking clearly now as well.

"Liam," said Mats to Cathal's nephew, who was getting the cut on his head cleaned. "What happened at the house?"

"I heard a noise outside. As I went through the kitchen door to check it out, I was hit from behind. I don't know how long I was out, but when I woke up, I was tied up and blindfolded. I heard someone yell and the back-door slam, and then I heard shots. A minute later they were taking Suzanne away. I heard her yell at them, but I couldn't make out her words. I think they were in French. Then I heard a car drive off."

"Dermot, find Inspector Fitzgerald and bring him here. Speak only to the inspector." Mats turned back to Brian, clasping his shoulder. "You did well, Brian, used good reason. You might have saved Suzanne's life as well as your own."

"Why did they take her, Mats, and why did they want to kill me?"

"I don't know, Brian, but I suspect we can find the answer in our dreams. Almost three years ago, when my father was shot, I started to have the dreams that eventually led me to the killer. The dreams told me the 'why' behind what was happening to me. This time, except for the one dream that explained our relationship, my dreams have been of my father during World War II. Yours have been about Vikings in ancient Ireland. I think mine are directing us to the person we are dealing with, and yours are giving us the 'why.' Someone is trying to kill you; that's for certain."

In less than half an hour, Dermot arrived back at the brewery with Desmond Fitzgerald. The inspector sat quietly as Brian related his story again. Mats added what he knew, from finding the house empty to not seeing anyone coming toward Donegal on the coastal road as they had driven to the house.

"Brian, do you know for sure that Suzanne was still in the house when you were shot at?" asked Fitzgerald.

"No, sir," answered Brian.

"Liam heard them leave with Suzanne after the shots," said Mats. "He was tied up but awake."

"And you haven't received any ransom demands?" Fitzgerald tapped his pencil on the pad on which he had been taking notes. "You're going to have to report this to Chief Minahen. There is definitely something going on in the Donegal station, but I trust Minahen."

Fitzgerald paused. "We rarely have abductions here in Ireland, Mr. Falconi. Too small a place, really. Everyone here minds each other's business. Rarely, the IRA will take a hostage, but not a foreign woman. Can you help me think of any reason anyone would take her?"

"It's Brian they're after. He was supposed to be with Suzanne. I have no idea why they would take her. They took her personal things, her suitcase, her brush and comb. There would be no reason to take those things unless they wanted to keep her alive."

Inspector Fitzgerald tapped his pencil again. *The bomb in the car, the bullets in the van—all seemed aimed at taking the boy's life, but why? Why Brian?*

"I think we must bring Minahen in as soon as possible," said Fitzgerald. "Would you send Dermot to bring him here?"

While they waited for Chief Minahen, Fitzgerald questioned Mats about Suzanne, searching for clues as to why she would be abducted.

"Suzanne knew nothing of the murders or the brewery operations. Her only connection is that she feels deeply for Brian. Inspector, she's been gone over six hours now," said Mats. "If it was a kidnapping, wouldn't we have heard a ransom demand by now?"

"Ordinarily I would say yes, but the fact that they took her personal effects must give us hope that she hasn't been hurt," said Fitzgerald. "Is there anything else you can think of?"

Before anything else was said, they heard the downstairs door open, and seconds later, they heard the bulk of Minahen climbing the stairs. He came in, looking at the group before taking the hard-backed chair beside the desk where Fitzgerald sat. He listened to Brian's story, asking a few questions to make sure he understood exactly what had happened.

"Understand, I've hired most of the men in my crew. Almost all are local lads. Now this—an abduction, a kidnapping of a French woman. Two murders, a bombing, a van shot to pieces, attempts on a boy's life, and now a kidnapping. Desmond, you might be right about things being not quite right in my department."

Mats paced the floor of the small upstairs office in front of the desk Fitzgerald was using.

"Dieter Rohde and Grady," he said, stopping in front of the desk.

"Grady, the solicitor? And Rohde? How are they connected? Do you think they might have something to do with the kidnapping?" asked Minahen.

"I don't know, but Nando told me that Grady's father knew Rohde on Corsica. They went down in a plane crash while Rohde was being transferred to prison in England. They were thought to be dead, but Rohde escaped to Germany before the end of the war. Grady's father made it to Portugal, to England, and then to Ireland. It was over a year between the plane crash and the time they both finally showed up. That's the connection. We know Rohde was involved in the attempt on Brian's life in Germany and that he is probably now in Ireland."

"After Dad died," said Brian, "Mr. Magee told me that Mr. Grady, as probate officer, was selling off everything in the brewery, devaluing the worth of the Harp and Hawk.

I went to Mr. Grady's office and asked why he was handling things that way. He didn't answer, but he made a phone call, and a few minutes later a Garda took me in a squad car to the Widow O'Dwyer out on the coast."

"My wife has been kidnapped and the boy is in danger. I don't think it's safe in town. I'm taking Brian back to the farmhouse to see if we can find a clue as to where they have taken Suzanne. If there is going to be a demand, it will probably come to that phone."

"Perhaps you'd be safer in town?" Minahen prompted Mats before looking at Brian, including him in the suggestion. "I can assign some men for protection."

"I'll take several of the Harp and Hawk's workers with us. I'm sure we'll be safe," replied Mats.

"I'll have no gun play," said Minahen as he lifted his massive upper body with a thrust of his hands on his knees. "There's no chance that Mrs. Falconi was just called back to France? No note that you might have overlooked?"

"No," Mats said with certainty. "Liam heard them leave with Suzanne."

"All right, then. I'll be getting back to the station. I'll send officers out to start knocking on doors. I'm not one to give guarantees, Mr. Falconi, but we'll find her."

An hour after Minahen and Fitzgerald left the Harp and Hawk, Mats, Brian and four well-armed Magee men acting as their bodyguards were back at the farmhouse. The sun was setting below the hard line of the Atlantic, coloring the clouds between the farmhouse and the horizon red with reflected fire.

"Minahen seems genuinely upset about his department's failure to solve the crimes against you and your family," Mats said, glancing at Brian. "I trust him to search for Suzanne, and Fitzgerald is covering Solicitor

Grady, probably better than we could. Still, I think our best chance to find Suzanne lies with ourselves."

The four Magees used the downstairs bedroom, the back seat of the car, and the couch, while Brian slept with Mats in the upper room. Even with the guards downstairs, Mats wedged the blade of the axe under the door, kicking it into place with the heel of his shoe. He knew in his heart that Suzanne was still alive. She was in danger, but for now at least, she had to be safe.

Mats envied the boy's slumber, knowing that he would spend the better part of the night waiting for a ransom demand and worrying about Suzanne.

Just before midnight, Brian began twitching, making shuffling movements with his feet. Mats kept still, afraid to disturb the dream being given to Brian. Mats' heart went out to the boy as he watched him dream. They were so alike. They had both lost their parents to violence, both were last in the lineage that had begun with the Viking triplets, and both had the power of the Gift—a power each had had to discover on his own.

Brian had become accustomed to seeing events through the eyes of his ancestor, Kjell Falkhand, but sharing the emotions of an adult was confusing. When he awoke and began to tell Mats of his dream, his vision sharpened. As he described what his ancestor Kjell Falkhand had seen—an exquisite sunset, with a beautiful woman at his side—a feeling Brian could not identify passed through his body...

The Island off Donegal, Ireland—946 AD

Kjell ducked under the lintel of the entrance to his dwelling. Taking Ecca's hand, she followed him out into the late afternoon sun. She still had the flush of lovemaking on her cheeks and brow.

"It is truly beautiful," said Ecca, her arm tightly around Kjell's waist. "It's as if Bal set the clouds on fire for us to enjoy."

The late afternoon sun was setting in the west, filling the clouds with shades of red and gold.

Kjell's love had deepened during the forty days since he had rescued Ecca from the Druids on the mainland. They had spent their time sharing their lives and their love. Ecca had greatly added to Kjell's knowledge of the Irish language, and he in turn had taught her his own. When they were not together, he watched as she helped the other women with the words and customs of their new men.

The men fished every day and twice a week bartered for beer and grains on the mainland. A miniature Viking village was nearing completion on the southern end of their small island. The dwellings were a mixture of rectangular and round houses, depending on how strongly the women felt about domestic matters: round in the Irish tradition, rectangular if the man felt strongly about domestic affairs. Both structures had their entrances facing west. The single men had placed their hall five hundred paces to the north, building a rectangular-shaped structure that mimicked those found in their own land.

"At sea, the sunsets put this one to shame," said Kjell. "Soon I'll see them again. I must leave the island for several weeks."

"Take me with you," pleaded Ecca, pressing her slight frame against his arm.

"We've spoken of this before," said Kjell, with a little irritation. "We need to trade. If we cannot trade, then we must raid the Angles and their villages. Both are dangerous."

"I'm not afraid of danger. I am only afraid of being without you," Ecca said firmly.

"On a longboat gone a-Viking, a woman is considered bad luck. If any of the men were injured, or even if the plunder was small, it is you they would blame."

"Then send them, but stay with me."

Kjell could feel her shudder even through the skins he wore. "You'll be safe here on the island. We'll stock enough meat and fish for you."

"That is not what I am afraid of," said Ecca in a small voice. "We have shared much in these past weeks. There is only one thing I have kept from you, my love, and that is the day of my death."

"The day of your death?"

"Yes. Every decade or so, a human sacrifice is required," said Ecca, looking out to sea rather than at Kjell. "The better the sacrifice, the more pleased Bal will be. The most satisfactory offering is a virgin, one who has been raised as nobility, educated, and talented in song and verse. This winter the head Druid decreed that this was such a year. This year I was to be sacrificed on the longest day of summer. That day is only two days away."

"I know you were to die as a sacrifice to Bal, but I've saved you from that fate. And you are no longer a virgin."

"That will not stop the priests. They know where I am. It will make little difference to them that I'm now your woman. Bal will receive me even more readily if they wrest me from the arms of a Viking."

"And if they don't have you?"

"They will find another maiden, and any misfortune for the next ten years will be blamed on my selfishness. They will still seek my death."

"Then I will put an end to these evil men and their human sacrifices. Where do they perform their blood rituals?"

"At their most sacred altar. The flat rock I sat upon as I sang to you in the forest is where they would spread me and cut my throat, then collect my blood. You cannot stop them."

"Why do you say this?"

"Many of the chiefs still adhere to the old arts. Even those who don't are frightened of the consequences of the Druids' spells and poisons."

"My men can stop them."

"There are more than you can imagine, trained warriors among them and sorcerers who can weave magic spells to confuse you. Your men would be defeated."

"You have not seen Vikings in battle. We would not lose."

Kjell gently turned Ecca toward him and saw the absolute certainty of her belief. Ecca was not a woman who lacked courage. She was intelligent, and she knew the Druids. Kjell looked down on her by his side and reluctantly accepted her words as truth.

Brian stopped relating his dream. His mouth was dry. He didn't know how long he had been talking to Mats. He got up, went to the bathroom, and drank two glasses of water. Mats remained seated on the side of the bed.

"Is that all of your dream?" he asked.

"No. That is only the good part. You must hear the rest."

Slowly, Brian's voice became lower, his eyes unfocused, as he continued relating his dream.

The Island off Donegal, Ireland—945 AD

That evening, the new moon left the island dark, only the light of the stars intermittently visible through the clouds to aid the men on watch. Two Vikings guarded the longship. Another patrolled the small cluster of dwellings. Halfway through the moonless night they would be relieved by three others, who would watch until the small village roused itself at dawn.

Shortly after sunset, Kjell had been led back inside their dwelling by Ecca. His concern over her belief in the day of her death, and their argument about his leaving to go a-Viking, was soon forgotten with her touch and kisses. He awoke near midnight, leaving the hut to relieve himself in the pit the men had dug just outside the perimeter.

Neither Kjell nor those on watch heard the soft splash of waves against leather as six round coastal fishing vessels, each carrying six men, landed on the north end of the island. The sentries still had half their watch to stand when the first, on the outskirts of the village, had his throat cut from behind. Soundlessly, a group of six men stepped over his fallen body and slipped from shadow to shadow down the incline to the beach where the longboat was beached on the gravel shore. If the darkness provided the Druid warriors cover for their movements, it also made it difficult to locate their prey.

The first guard at the boat was dispatched as quietly as the man in the village had been. In the hold of the ship, Lars, the blacksmith, was hunched over at the base of the single mast when his partner was killed. He heard nothing to alert him to the danger. As the five assassins joined their leader next to the mooring line, one of them stumbled on the loose gravel. Lars, greasing the ring that helped to raise the single yard arm of the square sail, stopped and listened. There was almost no light, but the sun-bleached interior of the lapstrake longboat stood in sharp contrast to the ink-black night beyond. Lars, who had converted to Christianity a month prior, reverted to the cry of his ancestors.

"Odin!" he shouted at the top of his lungs as he saw three dark shapes climb over the starboard rail and move swiftly toward him. His battle axe, already in his hand, caught one of the shadows squarely in the chest. He was not quick enough to repel the other attackers. Two knives entered him simultaneously but failed to silence his call.

"Odin! To arms!" he yelled before the men stabbed him for a third time, this time in the chest. In a final dying effort, Lars raised his axe in both hands and brought it down on the head of one of his all but invisible attackers.

Kjell, already awake, was the first to act. He echoed Lars' cry, which reverberated through the still of the night. In all but one of the sleeping huts, men sprang to their weapons and ran to the skin-covered entrances. One man had spent the first three hours of darkness making love to the Irish woman who had given the Druid scout the information about the camp. He slept the deep slumber of one fully sated and overcome with the weariness of pleasure. His woman, who would be responsible for many Viking deaths, had inadvertently saved the life of her own man.

Kjell had no weapon. His first responsibility was the protection of the Viking longboat. Most of the Druids had taken positions on either side of the hut openings. As Kjell's Vikings left their dwellings, they were attacked from both sides. But the element of surprise lasted only seconds as the Vikings heard the clash of weapons and cries of their fellows who had preceded them into the night.

Kjell saw a small flame lighting the bowels of the ship. Two men were climbing over the railing. He grabbed a rock from the beach and leapt at the nearest man. The rock hit the man's unprotected head. As the man fell to the ground, Kjell lost his balance and fell on top of him. In the dark, the second man misjudged his target. His sword hit the top of Kjell's metal helmet at an angle, deflecting off it and twisting in its downward course. The flat of the blade hit Kjell's shoulder at an angle, sending paralyzing pain through his body. Kjell grabbed the fallen man with his good hand and rolled him over on top of him. The second Druid saw only one shadow below him. He stabbed downward into the form, forcing the point of his sword deep into the flesh of his fellow Druid.

Kjell felt the impact of the sword enter his human shield. It entered the man's back just below the ribcage and passed through stomach and muscle. So great was the force behind the blow that the tip of the sword exited the body and started into Kjell's own. At the first feeling of steel, Kjell rolled over, still holding tight to the dead Druid. The sword was twisted from his assailant's hand. Before the man could react, Kjell kicked out, his foot hitting the standing Druid squarely in the knee. Kjell, son of Falkhand, had been in battles since he was twelve. Where he could have felt uncertainty or fear, he felt only rage at having been surprised. He still could not feel his left arm, but his legs had regained enough control to support him. As the man fell, his knee crushed and useless, Kjell struggled to his feet and, more by instinct than design, picked up the fallen sword and killed his attacker.

He was no longer in immediate danger. He stood above the two dead Druids and fought off a wave of nausea, steadying himself on the sword. Around him he heard sounds of battle. Instinctively he moved toward the water, toward the longboat. Above all else, the safety of their vessel meant survival.

Kjell joined two of his men on his way to the beach. Without the element of surprise, the Druids were no match for the battle-hardened Vikings. In the longship they found two Druids fanning a fire in the bowels of the ship. They died quickly. Two men lay dead beside Lars, proof that he had died as a Viking.

With the help of one of his men, Kjell covered the roaring blaze with the heavy square mainsail. The heat could be felt through its thickness, but there was no bed of coals to sustain the flames once the oxygen had been removed. The ship had been damaged but perhaps not past the point of being seaworthy.

Leaving his men to guard the ship and water the embers, Kjell jumped to the beach and ran back toward the fighting that could still be heard on shore. His left arm still hung useless at his side, the pain of running adding to his awareness of it. The bachelors, sleeping together in the community longhouse, had fared the best. They had immediately taken up battle formation, locking shields, protecting each other's flank, as they had done against numbers far more threatening than the Druids imposed. They had moved from house to house, yelling for the men inside to stay until they had secured the entrance from the assassins who lay in wait. As the number of torches grew, the Vikings became the masters of the battleground. The Druids now panicked. Turning away from the light of the torches and the flashing blades of the now organized Vikings, they fled to the north.

Kjell met the group in the center of the cluster of dwellings. He entered his own; finding Ecca gone, he grabbed his axe and rushed outside. Leaving half his forces to flush out any remaining attackers, Kjell led the rest of his men after the retreating Druids.

Kjell's men moved swiftly through the darkness, their torches casting shadows that danced as if they had a life of their own. A small hill bordered the stream as it flowed from the inland forest. As the Vikings ran over the crest, they saw two round boats being filled with men, ready to join two already loaded, sitting outside the small line of breakers.

The Vikings screamed war cries as they hurtled down the slope. One of the round boats pushed into the water, its passengers frantically rowing against the shore break. The second was not as fortunate. Kjell, hampered by his injury, was still coming down the embankment when his men reached the sides of the strange still-beached craft. The Druids screamed in terror, some jumping into the surf in a vain attempt to reach safety. In seconds the carnage was complete.

Kjell watched as the second boat gained deeper water beyond the breakers some ten meters from shore. Seeing only Druids in the craft, ignoring the pain that shot through his left side, he drew his right hand back and threw his axe end over end at the retreating boat. His weapon was balanced, as much as an axe could be. It flew in a high arc straight at the craft, looping in elliptical rotations as it descended. The axe came down in the exact center of the boat. It sliced through the wrist of one of the Druids, severing it before continuing downward through the hides that formed the skin of the boat. As water poured into the interior, the men called frantically to the two crafts some fifty meters further out to sea, but they had seen the flash of the axe and put more effort into their oars.

After the last of the Druids from the sinking coracle who had reached the shore was dead, Kjell slashed the sides and bottoms of the two remaining beached round crafts. Then he and his men ran back to their camp. Upon arriving, Kjell ordered that two wounded Druids were to be left alive for questioning.

"Five of our men are dead," reported Arn Gustafson as Kjell led his men back into the clearing. "Bo has a wound in his stomach that should take him to Valhalla before the first light." Arn hesitated, wondering whether to continue, allowing Kjell to digest the information he had already offered.

"What else?" asked Kjell. "The ship?"

He recognized the hesitation as an obvious departure from the normally blunt and sparse speech of his second-in-command.

"The ship is fine, but they have killed three of the women."

"Ecca? What of Ecca?" demanded Kjell, grabbing Arn's tunic with his good hand.

"Two of the women saw her dragged away soon after the attack started. They carried her to the north while you were protecting the longboat."

Panic flowed through Kjell as he closed his eyes and envisioned his axe slicing through the coracle. He stopped, focused on each of the shapes in the boat, each face as if it were turned toward him. She had not been in either of the two groups they had stopped from leaving the island.

"Where are the wounded Druids?" he asked, already knowing the answer he would receive from them. The timing of their attack had told him all he needed to know. Ecca was still their intended sacrifice for the summer solstice. Her blood would be spilled on the flat altar stone on which her music had first captured his heart. Grief swept over Kjell, and he saw the concern of his men as they noticed the drooping angle of his shoulder.

"Kjell, let me see to your wound," said Arn, stepping in front of his leader. "The Druids will last for your questions."

"We must go after them. We must save Ecca." Kjell started to push through, but Arn Gustafson's firm hand stopped him.

"We can do nothing until daylight. The ship seems only slightly damaged, but we don't know for certain if it is seaworthy. By the time we find out, it will be impossible to find their small boats in this black night."

Kjell nodded, his blood lust fading, recognizing the wisdom in Arn's words. "Bring the healer. I don't think the blow has broken a bone. My shoulder can be snapped back into place. I will need its strength to take my revenge."

Chapter Twenty-three

After the telling of his dream, Brian went downstairs while Mats showered. After breakfast and several cups of coffee, Liam headed outside to guard the house and to relieve his cousin, Edward. When Liam was gone, Brian turned to Mats.

"We may not know where Suzanne is now, but they will keep her safe until tomorrow."

"I know they took her things, but why do you say she will she be safe until tomorrow?" asked Mats, distress sounding in his voice.

"Because if our dreams are right, she will be at the dolmen at Fairies Point tomorrow at noon."

"How do you know?" asked Mats.

"Tomorrow is the twenty-first of June, the summer solstice. The longest day of the year. They will bring Suzanne there, the same as Ecca."

"Is that the place you described in your dream? Where your ancestor first saw Ecca playing her harp?" asked Mats, already suspecting the truth from the look on Brian's face.

"Yes, and also where he captured her from her Druid masters. There's a stone bench on top of a mound next to a stream. At least there was eleven hundred years ago. Ecca was taken from Kjell Falkhand to be sacrificed there at summer solstice."

The tension showing on Brian's face made him look older, as if he had aged in the space of the evening. Mats had not treated Brian as a child since Germany, and now, looking at him, Mats knew he never would again.

"And you think Suzanne is to be sacrificed?" Mats asked incredulously.

"I think that is the message of my dream."

Just before noon, a car pulled into the driveway and parked next to the brewery van. Out came four Magees, including Cathal. Inspector Desmond Fitzgerald was behind the wheel. One of Cathal's nephews was sailing Brian's skiff back to the farm.

Once inside the house, Fitzgerald lost no time in assuming command. "I phoned Dublin last night. Troops are on their way here. We'll find her."

"We know where she is, Inspector," said Mats slowly, his voice calm but firm, belying the panic he was suppressing.

"You do? Where?"

"She's safe. They haven't hurt her."

"You didn't answer my question, Mr. Falconi. Where is she?"

"You remember what we asked Father Cleary– about the possibility of a secret society professing to be Druids?"

"Yes. The ritualistic use of wood that the Druids held sacred. I also remember Father Cleary saying it was unlikely there was such a sect in Ireland."

"Likely or not, she is being held by a secret society of Druids, and they are armed."

"Where?"

"I don't know right where she is now, but I know where she will be tomorrow. She will be moved to Fairies Point around noon."

"And how do you know this, Mr. Falconi?"

"One of Cathal's nephews overheard four men talking at breakfast." Mats knew he couldn't disclose Brian's Knack as the source of the information; he would never be believed, for one thing.

"Four men just let him overhear their conversation? Don't you think that was a bit convenient?"

"They didn't know they were being overheard," Mats lied. "But with your help, I'm willing to risk the life of my wife on the information being true."

"Twelve noon on Fairies Point," said Fitzgerald. "Have they contacted you with ransom demands?"

"No, but I'm sure she will be there."

"Mr. Falconi, I want you to hear this. I know all about the incident two years ago in France. Inspector Medau told me all about how you took matters into your own hands. There will be no independent action by you in Ireland. I have thirty men arriving inside of three hours. Minahen has been alerted as well. We will take care of it."

"That's all I can ask for," said Mats. "Just let Brian and me help you with your plan. We know the area better than anyone else. Please don't go charging in with guns blazing, because they'll kill my wife."

"We won't put her in jeopardy. Now then, let's take a look at the area," said Fitzgerald, pulling a map of County Donegal from his jacket pocket.

An hour later, Fitzgerald had his map penciled with troop placements suggested by Brian. The boy had placed the Garda off the roads, a mile from the center of the grove where the altar stood. If the Druids repeated what they had done with Ecca, the Garda would take care of the bulk of Druid followers while leaving the center of the forest alone. Everyone was to be in position by morning the following day.

"I trust Minahen," said Fitzgerald. "He recognizes that his own station is compromised, probably by Sergeant

O'Deaver. He knows we can't use his men because there may be more than one loyal to O'Deaver among them."

"Then why tell him at all?" asked Mats.

"A couple reasons. He can be of great help in forming our plans and deploying our men. It is, after all, his county. He can also keep an eye on O'Deaver and warn us of his movements. If this is, as you suggest, a sect, O'Deaver stands to be at Fairies Point or covering for them."

Mats looked out the window at the sea. Fitzgerald had brought back memories of his showdown with Colletti, the drug lord who had almost taken his life. It was true that two years ago he had acted independently of the law, but things were different now. Then, the authorities had known nothing of the situation prior to his meeting with Colletti, because there had been no hard evidence of his drug ring until just before the confrontation. Even Inspector Medau would have passed off Mats' allegations as unfounded concoctions. There were also the Guibega, who had provided Mats with a hardened group of soldiers.

This situation was different. He was still being warned by his dreams, augmented by those of Brian, but this time the police already believed him. The Garda was giving its cooperation, which was necessary considering the size and organization of the group they were facing. Most important, here in Ireland he did not have the Guibega. The Magees were loyal and capable, but they lacked the hardness of the Guibega that had enabled Mats' ancestors to survive the centuries surrounded by enemies. Still, Mats was not going to let Suzanne's life rest with the Garda. He would find a way to save her, and then Fitzgerald could take over.

When Fitzgerald left to organize plans with Minahen and meet his men coming from Dublin, Mats and Brian went to the second-story bedroom alone.

"Tell me all you can about the forest," said Mats.

"I've told you everything that happened in the dream," said Brian.

"You told me what happened. Now I want you to give me descriptions. I want to feel like I was in the dream. Describe the trees, the paths through them, the stone bench, everything that Kjell Falkhand saw, felt, said, and did. Have you ever gone there yourself, Bri?"

"No, but my dreams make me feel like I have," answered Brian. "One thing, though, Mats. I know our first responsibility is to the living, but after Suzanne is safe, I want the men who killed my parents. I don't want Mr. Fitzgerald to take them to trial. I want to see them dead."

Mats looked at the thirteen-year-old, who had grown into manhood in the space of a few months. He could feel the blood of Viking warriors in his own veins, and he knew that the same blood flowed in Brian's. The cold blue eyes in a face that had yet to see a razor were unnerving. Until that moment, he had not thought of Brian joining him as he tried to save Suzanne. Now he knew that it would not only be wrong but also impossible not to include him.

Brian took almost an hour to relate his knowledge of the forest to Mats. Unlike in the first recounting, Mats interrupted often, asking for some details that he could not yet visualize. They alternated closing their eyes, one to recount the dream and the other to set it in his own memory. In the end, Mats felt that he could pass through the small forest with the familiarity of one who had been there before.

"Remember, my dream was of the forest as it was eleven hundred years ago. Who knows how it has changed?"

"For some reason, Brian, I think we will find it has changed very little," said Mats, placing his hand on the boy's shoulder. "Now let me tell you my plan."

After almost an hour of discussion, with the sun still high in the sky, Mats called down to Dermot Magee.

"Wake us at ten this evening!" he said, and then he closed the door and fell heavily into bed.

"Mr. Falconi. Mr. Falconi." The words followed a soft knock on the door. Mats looked at his watch. It was exactly ten PM.

"Brian, wake up."

Brian didn't move at first, but then he slowly turned, looking groggily at Mats as if drugged. Dark shadows like bruises showed below his eyes, and his gaze seemed focused on some object in the distance, beyond the walls of the room.

"Brian, what is it? What's wrong?"

"There are things you should know," said the boy.

"Tell me while we take the skiff. We don't have much time to spare."

Brian swung his feet over the side of the bed and rubbed his eyes with the heels of his hands. He dressed quickly and followed Mats to the jetty, sending the small craft down into the water on the stone ways. Once the sail was full with wind, with Liam in the bow, he began telling Mats of his dream.

⚜ ⚜ ⚜

Fairies Point, Ireland—945 AD

The night before the solstice, Kjell took those men who were still fit to fight in the longboat to the beach below the point. Quietly, all but five men debarked, leaving the skeleton crew to take the longship and wait offshore. The raid on the island, coming just two days before the summer solstice, had been no coincidence. Now that the Druids had recaptured Ecca, he was sure they would sacrifice her life, as planned, when the sun reached its zenith. He had no choice but to hope they would also use the same place, the sacred altar in the sacred grove of trees.

Kjell led the small band of Vikings up the cleft to the steep, slippery cliffs that bordered the stream. Using ladders they had hastily constructed before leaving the island, they scaled the moss-covered falls. Some twenty feet below the top of the cliff, Kjell positioned his men so they could not be seen from above. He ordered them to stay out of sight until he called to them using the screech of a diving falcon. Then and only then, they were to come with all the speed they could muster.

Kjell went up and over the cliff. Once on top, he hurried into the forest, watching for an ambush. He was safe. There were as yet no Druids in the sacred grove. He quickly found the stone bench that, come daylight, would serve as a sacrificial altar. The stream that ran less than five paces away was four feet lower than the bench that rested on top of a wide mound, raising it above the surrounding forest floor.

Kjell looked for a hiding place, knowing from his previous visit that there would be none save the tree branches that grew overhead. Resigned to climbing the tree, Kjell was fully aware that while the leaves would hide him and give him a perfect observation point, they would also make it difficult to gain the forest floor with either speed or stealth. It was during his descent that he would be vulnerable. He had no idea of the number of Druids who would take part in the sacrifice. The dozen men he had hidden just below the cliff's edge could hold their own against double their number, but as with Kjell, they would be at risk as they gained the top of the cliff.

In his belt, Kjell had secured two additional battle axes. Across his shoulder he'd slung a bow with a quiver of eight arrows. He climbed the tree, finding a crotch that both supported his weight and allowed him a full view of the stone altar below. Breaking a small branch with his hand, he hung the bow and quiver on the remaining notch.

If Kjell had to use the bow, it would be a difficult shot. He was not used to launching an arrow straight down at his target. Some among his Vikings were good bowmen; his brother Jarl was one of them, but Kjell did not rank himself in their class. Sea-raiding Vikings were much more adept at the hand-to-hand fighting that followed a swift raid ashore from their longboats than with the bow and arrow. Finding no answer to the problem of descending from his hiding place, Kjell wedged himself in the branches of the great oak and with the understanding of a warrior that he would need all his energy the next day, went to sleep.

He was awakened by the sunlight hitting his perch long before it impacted the darkness of the forest floor. There was no one in the forest, but across the grasslands to the east, he saw a procession of men dressed in white robes moving slowly toward the glade. Kjell strained, trying to identify individual features, trying to see if Ecca was among them, but he could not.

It took almost an hour for the procession to reach the woods. They were two hundred yards away when he finally recognized Ecca, surrounded by bearded priests. She wore a white robe like the others, but her head was bare, her long black hair falling well past her shoulders. As she approached, he saw that her hands were bound in front, her every movement watched by the priests on either side.

The procession followed in double file, more than a hundred men making up the group that approached Kjell. There were too many for the dozen men he had brought with him. No matter: he would give his life to save Ecca from the fate the Druids had planned for her.

If he died, he would stain many of the white robes with blood before he entered Valhalla. His men would follow him to their deaths as well, but Kjell was not happy about the odds he was asking them to face. Ecca was his prize, not to be shared with his men as other booty was shared equally.

As the Druids moved to the edge of the woods, they separated into two ranks. The greater of their numbers consisted of the younger men with only white hoods and no robes. These would be those who didn't have the status to enter the sacred ground. Kjell was amazed at their number. They fanned out, positioning themselves in a semi-circle some half-mile from the woods. Three of them left the group and went to the top of the falls that Kjell had used hours before in the dark, taking defensive positions there, while the others turned toward the woods and chanted in low tones.

Ecca had told him about the forest, and about the spring that fed the stream: how it was the most sacred of all the Druid holy places. She had told him how the shade of the trees was offered only to those men who had attained an exalted position through study or valor, and that the Druids had allowed no tree to be felled there for over six hundred years.

Kjell watched the remaining Druids—older, bearded men in white gowns and hoods—make their way into the forest on barely discernible paths to the stone altar. Even the five approaching the altar were segregated by rank. Two had white beards and moved as if slowed by age. The other three, younger, acted with deference to the two older men. Ecca was led to the stone bench by two of the younger guards.

It would be possible to kill one, even two, before the others realized they were under attack. Even if alerted, the warriors ringing the forest would take time to get to the altar, but the three men he had seen going to the head of the falls worried Kjell. He started to climb down slowly, to be nearer to Ecca should an opportunity arise to save her.

One of Ecca's guards removed her harp from a sack. Another untied her hands. Kjell watched as she accepted the instrument and began to strum it. Her voice was soft, blending with the wind in the leaves, as much a part of the forest as the birds and the stream that flowed through it. It was nearing mid-day, the sun climbing toward its highest point in the heavens. The tall priest, his white beard showing beneath his cowl, stood nearest to the altar, obviously in charge of the others in the elite group.

Ecca finished one song, continuing smoothly into another without missing a note in the transition. She was as calm as on the first day Kjell had seen her, the day he had fallen in love. She sang in harmony with the soft notes from her harp, raising her voice only to accentuate a note or a lyric. Some of the words Kjell could understand, while others were old words or ones modified for the verses, words he had not yet learned in his studies.

The old Druid looked up into the sky. The sun was just starting to penetrate through the leafy vault over the clearing. Kjell froze in his descent, knowing he would be seen if the man turned around. Most of Kjell's body was shielded by the thickening trunk of the oak as he moved toward the forest floor, but he was still high enough that its girth did not hide him completely.

The high priest looked back toward the altar and gave a soft, quick command to the other men. Without comment, they all moved to the spring that gave its water to the pond and the stream beyond. Kneeling, the smaller priest took a gold bowl from the folds in his robe and filled it with clear spring water. Kjell could see the effort on the old Druid's face as he rose from the ground, holding the bowl in two hands. He almost stumbled before catching his balance with effort, straightening. He moved to the stone bench and recited incantations as he poured water over the bench top. He repeated this act twice more, while his attendants repeated a verse with each ritual washing of the stone. When this was done, the high priest took the bowl and fit it into a depression in the surface of the bench that Kjell had not noticed previously. There was a ridge that was visible on the outside of the bowl, and it fit exactly into a slot in the depression, holding the bowl in a fixed position below the surface of the altar.

All the time Ecca kept singing as if in a trance, her fingers touching the harp lightly, producing notes of absolute clarity.

The priests all had their attention focused on the bowl and the wet stone of the altar. This was the opportunity Kjell needed to gain the forest floor. There were five of them, but two were old and all were completely absorbed with the altar and the movements and incantations of the high priest. The tree trunk was wider now but offered fewer hand and foot holds, slowing his descent.

Kjell felt his foot lightly touch dirt, seconds later followed by his other foot. The men were still unaware of his presence. He took one axe, then the other, from his belt, and placed the bow and quiver against the trunk of the tree. Ecca was still singing softly, her words somewhat softer than before.

Kjell thought to launch two arrows before throwing an axe, followed by his own rush attack. With luck he would not miss and would be on them before the head priest or his companion sounded an alarm. Moving back behind the tree, he wet his lips and began the call of the falcon that would bring his men over the cliff. He took a deep breath, his senses heightened, but before the screech passed his lips, he stopped.

Ecca, without changing either the pitch or cadence of her singing, was now singing in Norse, the language Kjell had taught her on the island. "Do nothing now. Wait until I call you, my love," she sang, then immediately reverted to old Irish.

If the Druids noticed the foreign words, they didn't show it. They stared, as if under a trance, toward the altar, unaware of Ecca's warning.

Kjell sucked in his breath, trusting Ecca, heeding the warning. He inched his head around the trunk of the tree some thirty feet from the cluster of Druids. The two older priests moved to positions on either side of Ecca. Kjell would strike to kill the younger guards. The older priests would be slower to react. He hoped to silence them before they called for those ringing the forest, at least giving him time to reach the falls.

Ecca increased the volume of her song, accentuating the lyrics with a voice so sweet it seemed otherworldly, making Kjell's heart ache with love for her.

Sunlight was filtering down into the forest, unobstructed by the morning clouds that had by now moved across the land. The high priest looked up through the leaves, then down at the shiny metal disc at his side. The sun was reflecting off a portion of the concave surface, moving slowly to fill the bowl as the sun reached its zenith.

"Not yet," sang Ecca, as if sensing that Kjell was about to attack the six priests.

For the second time, Kjell forced himself to relax, to repress the rush of adrenaline that was coursing through his veins.

There must be drainage grooves in the altar stone that flow into the bowl, thought Kjell, as the high priest scraped the top of the altar on either side of Ecca's head and chest with the tip of his knife. He straightened, relieving the tension in his back. All the men who were crowded around the altar looked at him expectantly, anticipation and rever-ence vying for equal space. He looked at each of them and then at Ecca before he spoke again.

"Tie her," he commanded two of the younger priests.

The two young men moved quickly to where Ecca lay, still singing her soulful melody as the men grabbed her arms and took her harp from her hands.

"You do not need to restrain me," she said calmly.

"Tie her!" the high priest ordered again. "Continue to sing to Bal. Your voice will be praise enough."

He motioned toward the altar with a nod of his head.

Firmly, Ecca's guards bent her backward over the stone. One of the guards placed a loop of pure white rope, braided from the same material as her robe, around her wrist. He passed it under the stone to the man on the other side, who tied it to Ecca's other wrist, cinching it tightly enough to prohibit movement but not tight enough to cause discomfort. Spread as she was across the stone altar, with her neck above the grooves that would drain her blood to the gold bowl, Ecca kept singing.

"Now, my love. They will be watching the sun fill the bowl. Save me now," Ecca sang in Norse.

Kjell needed no further command. Stepping from behind the tree, he threw one axe as he took his first step toward the altar. He had decided to use his axes before his bow, as the twang of the bow string would alert those at the altar. Before his first axe had struck, he launched the second. His first target was struck from behind at the base of the neck and crumpled immediately in a heap. The second of Ecca's guards saw him fall and bent slightly to help. Kjell had anticipated his movement toward the fallen companion. The man moved into the flight of the second axe, which tumbled through the air, over the outstretched Ecca, embedding deep in the man's chest.

Reaching for his bow, Kjell let two arrows fly in rapid succession, each finding its mark.

Kjell covered the remaining ground before the fourth priest fell. The second guard remained standing, looking down at the axe embedded in his chest. As Kjell scrambled up the mound to the altar, the head priest stood where he was, his eyes still fixed on the gold bowl; the sun's reflection now burnished the back of Ecca's head like a halo. The high priest raised his head, his knife at Ecca's throat. It was not to be. Kjell grabbed the aged Druid from behind, covering his mouth with his hand as he used his knife to silence the man and forever remove him as a threat to Ecca's life.

Turning toward the sea, Kjell now let out the screech of the hunting peregrine falcon, then cut through the rope that bound Ecca to the stone altar. He grabbed her arm, attempting to pull her toward the safety of the cliff.

"No," she whispered, moving away and grabbing the bowl that had been meant to catch her life's blood.

"My men are at the cliff where the water falls over," said Kjell, looking down at the bowl. The sun was being concentrated by its convex golden surface and reflected down the length of the altar where Ecca had just been bound. One of the dead priests had fallen over her harp, and she tried to tug the instrument out from under him with one hand.

Kjell, seeing that she would not leave without the instrument, pushed the man off, roughly. Ecca grasped the harp and without further words, they moved quickly off the mound and down the stream bed toward the safety of his men. As they came near the cleft, they met Arn Gustafson, who moved past them, taking a position to guard their retreat. A few steps later they came upon the rest of the Vikings fanned out in a tight semicircle around the stream as it fell toward the sea. Three white hooded Druids lay crumpled at the head of the falls. The defensive line opened for them as they passed through and started down the crude ladder to the two men Arn had left below on the first ledge.

In two minutes, Kjell and Ecca were safely on the longship. In less than a minute more, the rest of the Vikings had joined them, taking up the oars without command.

CHAPTER TWENTY-FOUR

Donegal, Ireland—The Skiff 2003

Mats trusted Brian's dream. He now knew what to expect and the exact time to expect it, not just the location where it would all occur. He would still have to rely on intuition to translate the dream to modern times, but his intuition would be better than guessing without Brian's input. The Gift—the giving of dreams of ancestors' deeds—had never failed Mats in the three years he had been experiencing it, and he was sure that Brian's account would also prove as faithful. Twice already they had saved the boy's life. Now Mats must trust them to save Suzanne's.

Captain Johnny Meehan and his boat, the *Kathleen*, were waiting for them a mile offshore. Mats had not wanted to chance that the vessel would be heard coming into Inver Bay. It was easy enough for Brian's skiff to sail out undetected and meet the larger craft.

Mats had asked the captain to come alone. He would not need Paddy James as a mate. Brian would help him run the boat and Liam, who had come with them in the skiff, would add an extra hand. If Meehan had been a Druid, he would likely have killed Brian at sea when he had boarded the *Kathleen* after escaping the trap at the farmhouse. Mats had to trust others as well: Fitzgerald, the Magees, even Minahen, if he was to save Suzanne's life. To add Meehan to his list of accomplices was of small concern.

Only the faint light of the stars aided Brian as he approached the *Kathleen*. So dark was the night that the skiff touched the port side before Captain Meehan was aware they had arrived. At once, Mats and Brian scrambled over the side and passed the line down to Liam, who attached it to the bow before hoisting himself aboard as well. Once in the cabin, Brian asked the captain's permission, then took the helm, turning off all lights, both cabin and running, and started the trawler inching ahead, the diesels humming a low throb below the deck plates. As they moved farther from shore and around the point of land on which the Keohane farm was perched, Brian increased the throttle to full power. In less than twenty-five minutes, he anchored the boat safely a half-mile off Fairies Point.

"How far are we from land?" asked Mats, looking toward the sounds of breakers.

"Less than a mile," answered Brian.

"Captain Meehan," said Mats, addressing the man as he would a trusted lieutenant. "Stay here until Brian returns. Do not run any lights. Don't use the radio, either to send or receive. Be a hole in the water. When Brian returns, sail back to the farm and let him off in the skiff. Then go back to Donegal. Say nothing of this night."

"What if the lad doesn't return?" Meehan asked, knowing there was danger in what his passengers were doing.

"He will be back on board by three AM. You just get him back to the farm before dawn," said Mats. "If he doesn't return, stay here and wait for my call, until three in the afternoon. Then return to port."

Mats turned to join Liam and Brian in the skiff. Throwing off the line, Mats sat beside Liam at the oars, Brian handling the tiller. They moved away from the fishing trawler, losing it in the starlight after only ten strokes.

Behind him Mats could hear the breakers drawing closer as Brian steered toward the unseen cleft. There was trust between the man and boy, trust forged in past generations, a bond between men of the sea.

"Pull hard. Six hard strokes," said Brian, as Mats felt the lift of the waves and the increased momentum of the boat beneath him. The sides of the cliffs opened as the breakers moved them into the narrow cliff-lined channel.

They were just finishing the sixth stroke when Brian swung the tiller hard to port, using the speed of Mats' and Liam's efforts to turn the skiff against the surge of the incoming tide and onto a small beach.

Mats was first to jump to shore, pulling the bow of the boat up the steep incline as Liam and Brian came after him.

"Follow me," instructed Mats as they tied the skiff to a rock high on the shore, leaving the boat near enough the water to allow Brian to re-float it by himself.

"Will you be able to get back to the *Kathleen* by yourself?" asked Mats

"Of course," the boy answered. "What wind there is, is with me."

Upward along the narrow path cut into the stone, Brian led Mats and Liam. Back and forth up the cliff they made their way, backing down only once when the boy missed the switchback and came to a dead end. In fifteen minutes, they had gained the top of the cliff. Without waiting, they moved directly to the forest some four hundred meters away.

"Does it all still look as it did in your dream?" asked Mats.

"Yes," Brian replied softly, as they moved through the forest to the clearing where the stone altar still stood.

Brian led Mats and Liam to the point where the stream flowed over the rocky cleft on its way to the ocean.

The centuries since the age of Kjell Falkhand had seen erosion of the cliff face. The stream now started its fall a good twenty meters closer to the small forest. Carefully they climbed down the stream bed until they reached a shallow depression under a narrow, rocky overhang. It wasn't a cave, but it would shield Liam from view from the cliff above.

"Liam, I want you to stay in this spot and hide until I call you."

"How long will that be?" asked Liam, hefting the automatic rifle and the pack stuffed with ammunition and food and placing them under the ledge.

"If all goes well, sometime just before high noon. Make sure you are ready, but be careful. There will likely be Druids, as many as three, stationed at the top of the cliff. Be aware; Suzanne may be dressed like her kidnappers." Mats was concerned that Brian's dream had told him of three guards. Had he known before; he would have brought help for Liam.

Carefully taking handholds, Mats and Brian made their way back up to the edge of the cliff. It would be easier for Liam in the daylight but more dangerous, since he would be exposed to view at the top of his ascent.

"Well, let's see how accurate your dream was," said Mats, as Brian led him back to the altar.

Brian climbed the mound, followed by Mats. Crouching on the other side of the raised stone, Mats felt for the concavity that had held the bowl in Brian's dream. It was there, and radiating from it, Mats could feel with his fingers faint grooves through which the blood of the sacrifice would flow. Some of the grooves were filled with moss, but others nearer the bowl were clear of debris.

"I suspect our friends have performed many sacrifices here over the years. Hidden on private land, away from prying eyes, I imagine they felt quite safe. That will change tomorrow."

Mats turned. "Brian, thank you for your help. Now it is important that you get back to the farm and phone Fitzgerald. Warn him of the numbers he will face. Do you understand?"

"Yes."

"Stay with him; guide his men. The Druids who ring the forest should be his priority. Should Fitzgerald ask where I am, tell him I got a message from Suzanne's captors. You don't know where I've gone. Now get going."

Mats had struggled with Kjell Falkhand's decision to hide in the tree. With modern weapons, Mats would not be as limited as the Viking chief had been, but after his first shot, he would be just as exposed. He would also be liable to Irish law. The tree was not a perfect hiding place, but Mats couldn't see any other place that would allow him concealment when Grady and his group approached. Then he remembered something. He could not place whether it had been a bedtime story of his father's, a dream, or an account from Mateo's journal, but it came to him now as a clear recollection. Moving some ten meters to the north, away from both the altar and the pond, he began cutting a large rectangle with his knife in the turf, leaving one long side attached. After he had loosened the surface, he scooped the dirt out, hiding it in the hollow under the roots of a tree. Then, lying down, he covered himself with the turf like a blanket. The soil gradually took on his body's warmth, and he dozed off.

Voices awoke Mats. He raised his arm and examined the illuminated dial of his watch. It was just before seven, too early for the ceremony. The sun would not reach its zenith for another five hours. Mats forced himself to remain calm, reassessing the situation as he did so. There were sounds of men around the altar. Slowly lifting the front edge of the turf blanket, he could see men in the clearing. They disappeared from his vision, but he could hear their voices moving away, then returning to the altar, one distinct voice giving commands.

Mats caught a brief glimpse of two men as they moved off toward the waterfall where the stream fell to the sea. Then there was silence, a sign that Liam had not been discovered in his hiding place under the cliff. Brian had been right about the sacrifice and the altar they would use.

The six hours of sleep that Mats had forced upon himself had been needed. There would be no reason to move until Suzanne was brought to the forest, but accepting that fact, in the pitch-black confines of his lair, he worried that he wouldn't be as successful as Kjell had been in saving his love. Lowering the turf except for a small breathing hole, he lay and waited.

Almost three hours passed before he again heard voices. The first was the same commanding accent of the leader. Other voices responded to the commands, short half-answers in Gaelic that Mats guessed were acknowledgments of their leader's wishes.

Another fifteen minutes went by and he heard other sounds: a guitar, and voices sounding far away, chanting in Irish to its strummed chords. The music came closer and closer to the altar. The ground, which had provided warmth the evening before, now felt cold. Despite the chill, Mats found himself sweating in anticipation. He flexed his muscles, pumping them with blood, reducing the cramping caused by hours of inactivity. It was only minutes before noon. He was sure that Suzanne had arrived.

Mats shifted his right hand slightly and felt the reassuring presence of the axe along his side and the pistol at his back, tucked under his belt. Several minutes passed. In the distance, the guitarist moved easily from one song to the next. Far away, voices could be heard singing with the music in a soft chant, the words foreign to Mats' ears.

Mats raised the edge of the turf slightly and risked turning his head to look at the mound and the altar stone on top of it. As if taking a cue from the music, men began moving toward the altar. Four of them gathered around a tall priest who stood with his hip resting against the stone.

"You don't need to tie me," Mats heard Suzanne say as two guards brought her to the altar, her French accent heavy with anger and strain.

Mats heard the mumbled responses of Suzanne's captors but could not tell if they had taken her at her word or lashed her to the stone, as had been done to the Druid princess over eleven hundred years before. Again, he flexed his muscles, then raised the turf higher. He could make out the man who stood next to the altar. The Druid was stooped with age but still taller than the slight priest who hovered at his side. Three other men, guards in unmarked robes stood nearby.

All attention was focused on Suzanne. *If Suzanne was to be saved, he must act now.*

Mats rose silently, the turf sliding to the side, small pieces of dirt dropping to the ground as he stood. He reached for the revolver. He had jammed the weapon beneath his belt at the small of his back, but it was not there. It lay in the ditch, half covered by lose dirt. There was no time to retrieve it. He ran quietly toward the altar, bringing the axe to shoulder height. There were five Druids ringing the altar, holding hands, making an unbroken circle around Suzanne, who was tied face up, her back to the stone. The flat end of Mats' axe hit the nearest man just above the neck, pitching him forward onto the altar and across Suzanne's legs. The second man crouched, still holding his fellow's hand. Mats threw the axe and saw the man's face collapse as the axe hit the Druid just above the bridge of his nose. The man's hands went to his face as if to hold in his broken sockets and push his eyes back into place.

Mats felt the instincts of his ancestor's training take over his motions. He grabbed the axe from the ground and knocked the knife from the smaller priest's hand with a flick of his wrist, then shoved the head of the axe straight forward into the man's chest. Through the white robe, Mats could feel it strike just below the ribcage. The man bellowed, bending forward in pain before slumping to the ground, where he lay gasping next to his two companions, but the warning had been given. Three Druids would be no more trouble this day, but the remaining had been alerted.

The Druid leader and a guard were still standing. They stepped apart, spreading the distance between them, wielding daggers in their hands. Mats started to back up, trying to draw them away from Suzanne and the altar. The guard moved with him, but the man who had been giving the commands stayed at Suzanne's side. Mats could now see that she was tied by her wrists by a line that went under the altar.

The Druid moved after Mats, sidestepping as he passed the altar. As he did so, Mats dropped the head of the axe on the man's wrist. There was no power behind the blow, but it was enough to dislodge the knife, which fell point first into the dirt. Mats brought the axe up in a sweeping strike as the man bent to retrieve his knife. The sharp corner of the blade caught him under the point of his jaw, splitting his mandible in two and progressing up through the base of his brain.

"Liam! Liam!" shouted Mats.

He was about to throw the axe at the head priest, but hesitated as his target raised his hand, saying in a loud voice, "Move and I will kill the woman!"

Mats looked to the altar. Suzanne was still held by the rope. He had failed. The high priest stood with his knife at her throat. Mats' back was exposed to the other men, who would be coming from the falls to the aid of those in the glade. He turned back to the high priest, who still stood, his knife at Suzanne's throat.

"Cover him," the priest commanded the small priest who rose wheezing with difficulty. While the high priest watched he replaced his knife with a pistol from his robes.

From behind him, Mats heard a gunshot. A scream penetrated the woods from the direction of the cliff. Agony filled the howl, which lasted several seconds. When it ended, so did Mats' hope. It was Liam's voice.

"The solstice has passed. You have ruined our ritual," said the high priest, pointing his hand high toward the sun. "Your wife's life is no longer important to us, but I suspect it is to you. Put down the axe."

Mats could see no alternative. There might still be a chance to save Suzanne, but not in the present situation. The guitar and chanting had stopped. Mats hoped that Fitzgerald had captured those outside the forest. *Fitzgerald is both a blessing and a danger,* thought Mats. *He could help, but if he charges in, the priest will kill Suzanne.* Her life was in his hands.

"You say her life is not important to you. How do I know that you won't kill her?"

"The solstice is already past. She's of no use."

Mats tried to place the voice coming from under the hood. It was speaking English but in harsh, measured tones, with the slightest trace of an Irish lilt covering another accent. He was sure that he had not heard it before.

"And if I put down my axe, what then?"

"You will accompany us to the forest's edge. When we are safe, I will release her. You get your wife, and we wait for the next summer solstice."

Mats could not think of a way out of the trap. He dropped the axe next to the man lying on the ground at his feet.

"Good. Now move to the side." The leader pointed to a spot some ten feet away.

As Mats moved, the Druid bent stiffly, cutting Suzanne free of the altar and then retying her hands behind her. Thrusting her in front of him, he moved to the priest Mats had hit in the chest. The man was still, gasping. As the small priest caught his breath, he knelt unsteadily by the men on the ground, checking for a pulse at their necks.

"Pat is dead. Daniel is alive but unconscious," he said in a heavy Irish accent. "Without attention, he will die."

"And Kevin?" asked the leader, motioning to the last man Mats had felled.

"Dead," said the small priest, without even looking at the man with the split jaw.

"You are quite resourceful, Mr. Falconi, and very good at killing," said the leader. "How did you discover our temple?"

"You have an informer," Mats lied.

"In that case, the Garda who have been arriving must also know our whereabouts."

"They are surrounding the forest," said Mats. "It will go easier for you if you give up."

The Druid leader threw back his head and laughed. The small priest, carefully watching Mats, moved to the axe and picked it up, holding it uncomfortably in his hand.

The two men who had gone to the head of the cliff returned, bowing to the tall Druid.

"Bring the woman," ordered the high priest. "You, Falconi, walk across the creek and follow that trail. We will follow you. If you turn, if you run, if you shout, we will slit your wife's throat, and my men will shoot you. Do you understand?"

"I understand. When will you set her free?"

"When we are safely on our way. Now walk."

Mats waded across the stream and started down the trail, looking back for Suzanne. The tall Druid was directly behind him, covering him with a pistol. Then came Suzanne with the two guards, both with handguns covering her front and back. Last in line came the small priest who had checked the men Mats had killed, a knife in one hand, Mats' axe in the other.

Damn, thought Mats, as he continued down the foot-path. He and Brian had each been given a dream. Brian had seen Ecca saved by his ancestor, Kjell Falkhand. But in his dream, Mats had seen his father's love, Teresa, killed right in front of him. *Please God*, thought Mats, as he started back down the path. *Allow me to save Suzanne.*

CHAPTER TWENTY-FIVE

Two men hid in a shallow ditch, their clothing of ruddy Irish tweed rendering them almost invisible against the earth. They watched as one unit of Garda, then another, made its way toward the outline of the forest on the coast a half-mile to the south. The taller of the two men moved his hand slowly until it lightly touched the hand of the other, pointing to the north. No sound was made, only eye contact conveying the warning. To the north, two young men wearing white hoods were crouched low, creeping toward the woods.

"This is our chance to get to the forest. Our people will need help."

As the taller man stood, he unsheathed a large knife, cutting four lengths of cord from a coil attached to the side of a brown knapsack. Looking back at the smaller man, he nodded. Then both moved silently after the two hooded men.

They walked quickly, making no noise. In less than a minute they had caught up with the two youths, who after a brief struggle were blindfolded, gagged, stripped of their hoods, and tied up. Without comment, two men, now wearing white hoods, moved toward the edge of the forest.

The poorly defined forest path was already threatening to break through the dense growth at the wood's edge.

As he made his way, Mats tried searching his memories of his ancestors for a solution that might save Suzanne's life. Even though Mats was unarmed—except for the knife he had hidden under his pant leg at his ankle—the Druids were wary of him. They had not come close, not even to bind him as they had done to Suzanne. The high priest's warning kept repeating in his mind: *"If he turns, kill the woman!"*

Mats did not trust the Druid's word that he would leave Suzanne unharmed. *He must have some plan for escape. She will be his hostage, and then he will kill her,* he thought.

"I understand your religion's use of blood sacrifices," said Mats, without turning around. "But why try to kill the boy? Why kill his parents, the Keohanes?"

He hoped that if he could get the head Druid talking, it would offer him a chance to save Suzanne. Mats heard a quick intake of breath behind him.

"There is good reason," came the guttural reply.

If he is still planning to kill Brian, Suzanne is surely still in danger, thought Mats as they neared the forest edge.

At a bend in the trail, he turned his head just enough to see the tall priest following him by three steps, pistol in hand, pointing at his back.

"Stop!"

Mats heard the command as he reached the last trees.

"Step to the side of the trail. Remember, your wife dies if you do anything stupid." The leader walked past the group, watching Mats as he moved to the very edge of the forest. There was no gradual diminishing of the number of trees; they seemed to just stop in a line, like the mushrooms in a Fairy Ring.

"Bring them out," ordered the leader, from five steps into the lush grassland that bordered the forest.

Mats heard the beat of a motor. As he passed through the shade of the last tree, the sound became more distinct, identifiable now as a helicopter. He watched as it appeared over the forest and hovered some fifty meters away. To the south, several hundred meters off, he saw a large group of people being held at gunpoint by a ring of Garda – not a hundred as in Brian's dream, but certainly more than fifty.

"I'm going to take great pleasure in killing you, Mr. Falconi," said the tall Druid as he stopped the group with a raising of his hand. "You have cost me a number of good men and a respected identity. I fear that I've not exactly been truthful about your wife. I'm sure that Ler, god of the sea, will be more than happy to receive her now that Bal has been denied."

Mats looked past the Druid leader and saw two hooded Druids lying bound with ropes in the tall grass between him and the place where the helicopter was hovering. The Druid followed his gaze, also taking note of the two disabled men. Mats looked for the Garda who must have captured them, but he saw no one. The tall Druid was obviously concerned about the two bound figures. Moving to the closest one, he kicked the man, getting no response except a soft moan.

The Druid priest nodded to his smaller companion. "Bring me the woman!"

"Take me. Not my wife. I've killed your men and ruined your ceremony, not her!" shouted Mats over the clatter of the helicopter.

"No! It's me you want," screamed Suzanne, as she was prodded forward by the smaller Druid.

Mats looked at her, a desperate glance at this woman he loved.

"What you say is true," the tall priest answered Mats. "But I'll kill her just the same, if only for the pleasure it will give me."

Turning toward the hovering helicopter, the leader reached up and removed his hood. The pilot, recognizing him, began descending.

Mats edged toward the leader, still kept at a distance by the knife at Suzanne's throat, and the knife of the Druid guard in front of him. Wind from the rotors whipped the robes of the two priests, who had separated themselves and Suzanne from the two Druid guards. Broken twigs and small clumps of grass thrashed in dizzying patterns as the helicopter touched down.

"Load her first," said the leader to the smaller priest now holding Suzanne. "We'll drop her in the ocean." He turned to Mats. "You I will kill."

The wind from the helicopter blades blew, whipping the head priest's hair back and forth as he took his handgun from the folds of his white robe. Mats had not recognized the voice, but he recognized the face from Schiller's file. The skin pulled tight against the bones of the face still framed the cold blue eyes of the young Nazi from his dreams: Lieutenant Dieter Rohde.

The blades on the aircraft circulated with less intensity, but the noise was still deafening. Rohde slowly raised his hand, pointing the pistol at Mats.

Suddenly the scene in front of Mats erupted in motion. First, the bound Druid near where the small priest was holding Suzanne was lying still, his hands tied behind his back. Then he was standing, Suzanne was free, and the small priest's arm was bent behind him, the knife that had threatened Suzanne on the ground. Rohde started to swing the barrel of the pistol in Suzanne's direction, but stopped, pointing it again at Mats.

Mats fought the instinct to dive back into the woods. As Rohde swung his gun, Mats lunged toward the Druid leader, only to be stopped by the knife of his guard. The blade entered his chest only a fraction of an inch before stopping against the flat of his rib. Mats leaped back, pulling away from the knife. His attacker whipped off his hood and Mats recognized him as Minahen's man, the one he had seen in the Donegal station on his first visit. His hooked nose was prominent even before the hood was removed: Sergeant Ed O'Deaver. The man smiled, his lip curling over a row of uneven teeth.

"Get out of the way! You're blocking my shot!" shouted the tall Druid.

"He's mine," snarled O'Deaver.

As O'Deaver advanced, the second guard moved toward Mats from the side.

A shot rang out. Mats heard the sound of a bullet hitting soft flesh, followed by a gurgling moan. The second guard went down. From the woods staggered Liam Magee, holding a pistol, his chest and right arm a mosaic of blood as he fell to his knees. There was movement to Mats' left where the small priest was still held fast. It was Ramondo. Suzanne was safe.

"Mats!" the warning was screamed by Suzanne, drawing Mats' attention back to O'Deaver. The sergeant lunged at him, using his knife like a fencer. Mats side-stepped the thrust, hitting the man's wrist with his hand and forcing it upward. As it had two years ago in France, the training of his Corsican ancestors took over. Mats took his own blade from the sheath strapped to his right ankle and stepped around his opponent's thrust, bringing his double-edged knife up under the man's armpit, between his ribs and into the heart. The attack ended as quickly as it had begun. Red stained the man's robe before Mats even withdrew the blade. As O'Deaver slumped over, what had been a stain became a sopping mass of red-soaked cloth as blood spurted from the open puncture wound.

Mats stepped away, spinning toward Rohde, seeing the weapon coming to bear, when a length of rope flicked up from the grass at the German's feet. The second bound Druid stood, whipping the rope around Rohde's extended arm and pulling it down, the gun with it. A sudden jerk caused Rohde to lose his grip on the weapon as the man, still holding the end of the rope that had appeared to bind him, placed himself between the Druid leader and Mats. The man was much shorter than the German. He removed his cowl, exposing a shock of unkempt white hair and the lined face of Nando Guibega.

"So, you are still murdering women," hissed Nando.

The German looked at the man standing before him, awareness slowly transforming into recognition.

"Ah, the Corsican traitor. The one with the niece who fought against the Reich," said Rohde, taking a knife from his robe.

"Yes, and one who has looked forward to this moment," said Nando Guibega, holding his knife in his right hand. "Ramondo, make sure Suzanne is safe."

"I'll take care of her," said Mats, moving toward Suzanne.

The Druid priest who had held her removed his hood, revealing thinning gray hair. He stood with his hands at his sides, seemingly bewildered by the sudden turn of violence. Ramondo ran his hand over the Druid's robe, removing the man's handgun, and placed a strong hand on the Druid's thin shoulder from behind. The man showed no sign of resistance. As Ramondo directed him, he moved toward Mats with a bent, shuffling gait. He stooped by the two Druid guards who lay bleeding at Mats' feet.

Mats did not recognize the old man. He was small, and without the hood, a good eight inches shorter than Ramondo, who kept his grip. The Druid's white hair and beard were unkempt, his hands small and delicate. As the man bent over O'Deaver, Mats suddenly understood. The man was a doctor, more concerned with saving others' lives than with protecting his own. Ian Grady's father had not died at sea, as Magee had believed. He was one of the Druid elite. Mats could not help but feel sorry for Grady as he tried to aid the sergeant. O'Deaver would die regardless of the healer's ministrations.

Mats turned back toward Nando and Rohde. The two ancient rivals were circling each other, each with a knife in his hand. Mats felt a surge of fear for his friend. The two men were of a similar age, but Nando was smaller in stature. His left hand was contained in a cast that extended to just below his elbow. Mats stepped toward Nando, trying to position himself to help his old friend, but was stopped by the outstretched hand of Ramondo.

"This is my fight," shouted Nando. "One that I have prayed would come for the last fifty years."

The two men circled, feinting, testing each other's reflexes, neither committing to an attack. The German stood more upright, making the most of his height and reach advantage. Nando fought in a crouch, his head and shoulders forward of his hips, his legs bent.

Mats held Suzanne, O'Deaver's blood soaking into her white robe. Ramondo stood with one arm still bound to his chest, the other hand holding the shoulder of the kneeling old healer. After the life passed out of Sergeant O'Deaver, Grady attempted to help the man whom Liam had shot. Mats looked again at the helicopter, but the pilot, still sitting in the cockpit strapped in his belts, was watching the two old men fight with as much interest as Mats.

Rohde was the first to commit. His knife was larger and heavier than Nando's thin, almost elegant blade. Rohde feigned a straight-ahead thrust, apparently anticipating that Nando would sidestep it to the right, away from his injured arm. As the knife moved past Nando, Rohde quickly changed direction, pulling it back and slashing waist high at Nando. It was a well – planned maneuver, one not designed to kill but certainly to wound an opponent whose reflexes were dulled with age. Mats began to cry a warning, but he knew it would be too late. It was also unnecessary. Nando had anticipated the slash, even if Mats had not. As Rohde's knife came back and across at him, Nando countered, bringing his free hand down on the blade of the knife.

Rohde looked amazed as his weapon flipped from his hand. The blow should have severely cut Nando's arm, but the hard plastic cast was a weapon in itself. There was no chance for Rohde to evade Nando's blade. It came up at him from the Corsican's crouched position, catching him in the throat just below his Adam's apple, the power of Nando's legs forcing the blade up and through the spinal cord at the base of the German's skull.

"I can die now with a clear heart. You are avenged, my Teresa," cried Nando in Corsican, as Rohde convulsed at his feet.

Mats knew his father would also rest easier with Teresa's killer dead. It was right that Nando had settled the debt.

He turned as the helicopter's engine started to race. Great clouds of dirt buffeted those on the ground as it rose into the air, then banked, heading east toward Donegal.

"Stop him," shouted Nando, pointing his bloody knife at the fast-moving helicopter.

"Don't worry," Mats said to his old friend. "Fitzgerald's men will track it." He turned his attention back to the Druid healer who knelt near him.

"Why? So much death. Why?" asked Mats, almost pleading for an answer that would make sense of what had happened.

"Nonbelievers have never understood us," said the healer in a resigned voice. "They think we should be happy in bondage. The Vikings, the Danes, and now the Catholic Church, have held us in contempt, causing our people to suffer their dogma. As a teen, I was brought into the faith and shown the ancient ways of healing. During the war I was able to save many wounded, including Herr Rohde. When I returned after the war, the government stopped me from helping people. I was not a real doctor, they said, so I became lost at sea—presumed dead, living in solitude with my family, helping people of our faith."

"If you are a healer, tend to Liam here," said Mats, letting go of Suzanne and kneeling at the side of Cathal's nephew.

"This one will live," said Grady, quickly checking Liam's wound before returning to the man Liam had shot.

Mats watched the Druid as he ministered to the Druid guard.

"This is my son, Ian," said the healer. "He will also live, no thanks to Rohde."

"Healing people is one thing; violence against women and children is another. Why did you turn to violence?" asked Mats.

"The violence was never mine," said Grady as he bandaged his son. "In ancient times, those trained in healing also knew poisons, knew how to kill, but they were always healers first. Before the war, I was ordered by the elders to find men who could provide a strong arm for our sect. I recruited Rohde. Our Grand Elder at the time thought him perfect for his vision of our future. After the war, in Herr Rohde the two skills became separated. There were no checks on the violence. Rohde quickly rose in our ranks, becoming more powerful. The violence around him became more commonplace. This is the result. It was Rohde's obsession to kill the boy, not mine. Look what it has brought us! I am a healer, not a killer."

Grady rose to his feet. "Your arrival was our downfall. You did the one thing Rohde could not tolerate. You drew attention to seemingly unrelated deaths, and in doing so, to our society. How did you discover us?"

"It was your use of particular woods that allowed us to make the connection," said Mats.

"Ah yes, the sacred woods. Herr Rohde insisted on their use."

"The authorities will see every member of your murderous sect exposed and prosecuted," said Mats.

"You will never accomplish that. We're too well hidden amongst our people. Let it be enough that you have killed Rohde. I promise, there will be no more attempts on the boy's life."

"That's more than I can say about yours," said Mats. "I suspect the Garda will have a field day getting you hanged."

"Ah yes. Well, you should know that there is no capital punishment in Ireland," said Grady, putting his blood-stained hands in the folds of his robe. "On the other hand, I know things that no other man knows, methods I must pass on to my fellows."

Without warning, two balls of red yarn appeared in Grady's hands. Before Mats or Ramondo could react, the old man threw them to the ground, where they exploded in vast billows of foul red smoke.

"Stop him!" yelled Mats, as a thick red haze misted up from the meadow's grass. The smoke billowed, obscuring Grady and stinging the eyes of those still in the meadow. Beneath its cover, Grady ran with a spry shuffling gait into the woods. Neither Mats nor Ramondo could reach him before he was lost to sight among the large trees. Several minutes of searching only proved what Mats had expected as they entered the forest: Kenny Grady was gone. He knew the woods. It would be futile to search further. Now that his identity was known, the Garda would try to apprehend him. The society of Druids had been seriously breached. If Mats took Fitzgerald at his word, the inspector would put an end to their sect.

"Mats, Mats!" came a cry from the edge of the woods. Running along the periphery of the trees, followed by Fitzgerald, Minahen, and a half dozen Garda, was Brian. "We saw a helicopter." Brian stopped in front of Mats before looking at the rest of the group. "Nando! Ramondo!" he cried, and then ran to Suzanne.

"Are you all right?" Brian asked, noticing the blood on Suzanne's robe before reaching up to touch her cheek.

"Yes. I'm just fine." She pulled Brian to her, hugging him as much for her own comfort as for his, Mats suspected. He joined in the hug.

"Only one of the men who held Suzanne in the forest escaped," said Mats to Fitzgerald, as the inspector came up behind Brian. "Grady, the father of the solicitor. He ran back into the forest."

Fitzgerald jerked a thumb toward the woods and nodded at two to his Garda. "We'll find him."

"Not likely," Mats muttered under his breath.

"Wasn't he supposed to be dead? A fishing accident?" asked Fitzgerald.

"He's old, maybe older than Nando, but he's still very much alive," said Mats.

"I take it this is Nando?" Fitzgerald turned to the old man.

"I'm sorry, Inspector," said Mats. "I'm still in a bit of shock myself. This is Nando and his nephew, Ramondo Guibega."

"Why am I not surprised? I've been told about your background, Ramondo. Do you want to tell me what happened here?"

"I suspected they would bring Suzanne to the altar in the forest," began Mats, before Fitzgerald could protest. "I came last night and hid. Around eleven, they brought Suzanne. I disabled a couple of them who threatened her at knifepoint. You'll find them back at the altar in the woods. But before I could reach the others, the leader threatened to slit Suzanne's throat."

Fitzgerald looked at Suzanne. Mats knew Fitzgerald could see what he saw, the lingering terror in her eyes. But Suzanne was already gathering her strength, and her nod in response to his questioning glance was firm.

"The leader," Mats said, pointing at Rohde's body, "directed us under gunpoint to this spot, where the helicopter was waiting. He was going to kill me here and throw Suzanne into the ocean to appease his God, Ler."

"Nando and Ramondo saved us," added Suzanne.

"I saw much of what happened. It was self-defense, but how did you two get here?" asked Fitzgerald of Ramondo and Nando.

"We came across two young Druids. We tied them up back by the farm. We took their hoods and pretended to be tied up. It was the only way we could get close enough to Rohde." Nando stared at the inspector, who waited for more of an explanation.

"Tell Inspector Fitzgerald the whole story," prompted Mats with a nod to Nando.

"Yes, signore. We were attacked by this man's thugs in Germany," said Nando in his old man voice. "They tried to kill the boy, but they ended up only breaking Ramondo's shoulder and my arm. The German police want him for murder." Nando pointed at the body at his feet.

"This is Dieter Rohde?" asked Fitzgerald. His tone told Mats that he was trying to fit the pieces together, remembering Schiller's report.

"Yes," replied Nando in a cracked voice. "We found that he had flown to Ireland, so we followed him. Sixty years ago, he killed my niece, Teresa. He tried to kill Brian and Mrs. Falconi, and he tried to kill me. Now he is dead."

"You killed him with a knife?" asked Fitzgerald. Mats could see the inspector assessing the case against him and Nando. Both dead men had knives near their hands, knives exactly like the ones held by the Druids captured by Fitzgerald's men outside the forest. Mats' shirt was bloodied from his stab wound . He might have been looking for a fight, but it was clear the Druids had provoked it. Eyewitnesses would corroborate his account, and he would be acquitted.

"We were about to enter the forest," said Ramondo, seeing that Nando was too emotional to continue, "when we heard Rohde order Signor Falconi into the meadow. We lay down and pretended we were tied up."

Ramondo looked down as Grady's son moaned, moving for the first time since Fitzgerald's arrival. "This man is Grady's son. His farm was the place where Suzanne was held captive. He's been shot. As for the rest, it is as Nando said. We were lucky to be in the right place at the right time and lucky that our injuries did not prevent us from helping."

Mats had not moved; he, Brian, and Suzanne remained in their embrace. They were a family.

CHAPTER TWENTY-SIX

The door to the upstairs office at the Harp and Hawk opened and Inspector Minahen joined the group inside.

"Thank you for seeing me here. There's still work to be done at my office to repair the damage O'Deaver has caused. I'm not sure I've yet uncovered all the men he and Grady corrupted."

"Have you found the old man?" asked Mats.

"No, but we will. The texts we found at the farmhouse that Mrs. Falconi helped decipher included a list of the local Druids and much information about their sect."

"I was glad to help, but I only identified the language and gave an idea of what they contained before they were taken away," said Suzanne, clearly unhappy.

"It's not that I didn't trust you," said Fitzgerald. He had disagreed with Minahen over allowing an outsider, particularly one who was involved with the case, translate what they had found. "If I didn't have Father Cleary and his group of experts from Trinity College do the translation and preservation of the volumes, there would be hell to pay. They have confirmed your first perception. One text was about medicaments and cures; another was about rituals and sacred rites. It was in that one that the use of sacred woods in assassinations was detailed. The one you translated gave us a list of Druid followers. It's the third one that provokes the questions. It recounts the kidnapping of a Druid princess who was groomed to be sacrificed, her rescue by a Viking named Kjell Falkhand, and the decades of famine and loss that followed. If they are translating correctly, for over three hundred years, one of the objectives of the Druids has been to eliminate all of Falkhand's blood line. I can't help suspecting there might be a connection to the murder of the Keohanes."

Mats watched as Brian took in the information, but the boy remained silent.

"How was it that you were able to translate the books so quickly?" Fitzgerald asked, looking directly at Suzanne.

"That was my job, my position of expertise, at the Bibliothèque in Paris," said Suzanne. "The texts were written in an ancient form of Celtic, one that was used primarily in what is now southern France and northern Spain. If you know the ancient roots, it is easy to translate the modern, but it's more difficult if you know the modern to understand the original. The translation of an old text was what brought us together three years ago," she added, smiling at Mats.

"That's essentially what Ian Grady has told us," said Minahen. "He's been cooperative in most things, other than where to find his father. It was his task to translate the texts and bring them up to date. He swears that neither he, his brother, nor his father had anything to do with the murders – that it was just Rohde and the group under him, which was headed by O'Deaver in Ireland."

"And you trust him?" asked Mats.

"We have not caught either of the Gradys in a lie. There are questions they just won't answer, however. Ian says that two hundred and thirty years ago, their leading scholar was killed along with three men he was training to take his place. With their deaths, there was no one who could read the records. Knowing that the ancient texts held information about cures, Ian's father tasked him with translating them, which he did. As he gained power, Rohde became more interested in the rituals, including sacrifices and assassinations. It was he who insisted on the use of sacred woods."

"One of the last things old Grady said was that there would be no more attempts on Brian's life," said Mats. "Oddly enough, I believe him. I truly believe he was first and foremost a healer."

"Then why try to kill Brian? Why murder his parents?" asked Suzanne, hugging Brian around the shoulders.

"That is something the Gradys won't talk about, other than to say it was O'Deaver's doing under the orders of Rohde," said Minahen. "They both claim they didn't know anything about the murders and the attempt on Brian's life until after the fact.

"The main reason I wanted to see you all was to tell you that the preliminary hearing on the deaths of the men in the forest and Rohde has been completed. Nando, you and Mats will have to stand before a judge for the final ruling, but it will be ruled self-defense. Lieutenant Schiller's report on Rohde's actions in Germany, as well as my testimony about what I observed, will make that clear. The same for Liam. I'm told he is recovering nicely."

"He's fine," said Cathal, speaking for the first time. "Except that when he drinks beer, it comes out the bullet hole."

Both Minahen and Fitzgerald rose, smiling, and shook hands with the group. Nando closed the door behind them. After they heard the outer door close and the Garda car pull away, Brian addressed Nando and Cathal Magee.

"My father told me that three hundred years ago, the only Falkhand left was a woman. She married a Keohane. When Grady translated the text of our family tree, Rohde would have learned our family history."

Mats looked at Nando. It was the way of the Falconi. Brian would grow up to be a leader in the Falconi tradition. Ramondo would become the war chief of the Guibega when Nando was no longer capable. With Teresa's vendetta satisfied, Mats' father would smile down on them from either Heaven or Valhalla, whichever place he reposed, and wait for the children that he and Suzanne would bear, and to whom they in turn would pass on the Gift.

THE END

ACKNOWLEDGEMENTS

Any writer draws help and inspiration from many sources. I am no different, and probably more dependent than most.

The Mill Valley Library Writer's Group, which has managed to survive as a group despite the closure of the Library due to the pandemic deserves my first thanks. Our twice a week online meetings are not only a source of inspiration for me, but a wonderful preview of their own works. They are a diverse group of extremely talented individuals of published authors, who are brutally honest in their criticism and joyous in their help and recommendations. John Byrne Barry reminds me on almost every reading that scenes are better for the reader than narration. Kate Moore, whose encyclopedic knowledge of English literature, as well as her ability to offer improvements in both plot and the technical aspects of my words cannot be overstated. Barb Elwell never fails to comment on my readings, regardless of how busy she is, offering critical advice on how to end a scene. Asma Aschen who reminds me that there are whole worlds out there that I know nothing about. John Geoghegan, who writes wonderful non-fiction, but encourages me in writing tales about knights, Vikings, battles and vendettas. These people have become more friends, than associates.

Thanks to Anne Lamott, who set me on the path of a writer years ago when I suddenly became president of the

Alumni Association of a major university and dreaded the writing it would entail. "Just start writing a book. By the time you re-write the first chapter twenty times you will have all the skills you need," was her advice.

Matthew Nelson, my oldest son and severest critic, who can read a draft and quickly point out what isn't working and why.

To Sarah Goss, self-confessed word junkie and English professor at the University of San Francisco. She never tires of reading and re-reading my drafts, correcting my mistakes in typing and punctuation. She is great and I love occasionally sitting in on her classes and see how she keeps her students enthralled in the usage of the English language.

Pat Lyle reads my drafts and offers help. I would think her master's degree from Oxford would put her above reading tales of Vikings, and Druids. It's not the first time I've been wrong, but it still surprises me.

Brian Van Camerik designs my covers, and I've asked in this volume to provide me with the maps that the readers requested in *FALCONI'S GIFT*. Artists of his caliber are said to be temperamental, and even if Brian wasn't, I would think that dealing with me would make him so. He still remains a joy to work with.

Thanks to Josh Freel at Waterside Publications who shepherds my manuscripts through the final process.

Bill Gladstone, is my agent at Waterside, who has put up with me, on and off the golf course for thirty-five years. He is simply the best.

Finally, thanks to my wife Kellie, who endures the tippy-tap of the keys, and the closed door to my study when the creative juices flow. She is my love and inspiration.

If you have enjoyed *HAWKS BREW*, the second book in the Viking Saga Series, please consider writing a review on Amazon Books. It not only guides the author in writing the rest of the series, but alerts other readers to tales about Vikings, murder, and historical fiction.

Other books by Gary Doc Nelson:

HAMER by Doc Nelson, available on Kindle and Amazon Books. A modern-day political murder mystery connected to a historical drama centering around the signing of the Magna Carta.

FALCONI'S GIFT by Gary Doc Nelson, the first of the Viking Series. Available on Kindle and Amazon Books.

A MORAL STANCE by Gary Nelson, a true story of the 1951 University of San Francisco Football team that gave up a chance to play for the National Title because they would have to leave their two African American players at home as seen through the eyes of Pete Rozelle the team's publicity manager. Available on Kindle and Amazon Books.

SOON TO BE RELEASED:

THE BLACK SPOT. The third book in the Viking Series

A GOOD IDEA AT THE TIME. A murder mystery and love story revolving around Speed Dating and college Basketball.

www.ingramcontent.com/pod-product-compliance
Lightning Source LLC
Chambersburg PA
CBHW070800030726
47504CB00003B/639